romance after getting laid off from her job as a technical writer—and quickly decided happily-ever-afters trumped software manuals. She lives in Northern California with her family and six cats.

If you liked *Off Limits* and *Ruled*, why not try

A Week to be Wild by JC Harroway
Legal Seduction by Lisa Childs

Discover more at millsandboon.co.uk

OFF LIMITS

CLARE CONNELLY

RULED

ANNE MARSH

MILLS & BOON

First Published in Great Britain 2018
by Mills & Boon, an imprint of HarperCollins*Publishers*
1 London Bridge Street, London, SE1 9GF

Off Limits © 2018 Clare Connelly

Ruled © 2018 Anne Marsh

ISBN: 978-0-263-26638-2

MIX
Paper from
responsible sources
FSC™ C007454

Printed and bound in Spain
by CPI, Barcelona

C016427985
01|19

OFF LIMITS

CLARE CONNELLY

MILLS & BOON

This book is for romance readers everywhere,
who fall in love again and again with the characters
of our creation.

You give our stories life just by reading them.

Thank you.

PROLOGUE

The stars are not wanted now: put out every one;
Pack up the moon and dismantle the sun;
Pour away the ocean and sweep up the wood.
For nothing now can ever come to any good.
                                        —WH Auden

'You've got the Prime Minister calling in ten minutes.'

Jack nods, showing not a flicker of response at the prospect of this. Then again, nothing about Jack Grant is what you'd expect. For a self-made billionaire-investor-cum-philanthropist-cum-sex-god, he is wild, disrespectful of authority and the establishment, and rough around the edges. Deliciously so.

Take this situation: Jack, in his bed, naked as the day he was born, uncaring that he should have been at his desk an hour ago. That I can see most of his beautiful back and backside. That my insides are clenching with hot, steamy lust.

'About…?'

It's a lazy drawl as he flips over and pierces me with those intelligent green eyes. His accent is pure Irish brogue. Like Colin Farrell after a night of cigarettes and booze: deep, hoarse and throaty.

'The latest episode of *The Great British Bake Off*.'

I roll my eyes. We've been negotiating to buy a huge swathe of Crown land for the last six months; it's at the highest level of negotiation and, given the media interest, the Prime Minister has become involved.

'What do you *think*?'

His laugh is a rumble that barrels out of his chest. 'Well, every man needs a good scone recipe.'

'And you've got one?'

'Sure.'

He grins. It's a grin that is at once devilish and charming, and I know how easy it must be for him to get women into bed. And that's before you factor in the body, the money, the power.

'Nine minutes,' I snap.

His grin unfurls like a ribbon on his face. My heart *kerthunks*. I ignore it. Stupid heart.

'Did you book Sydney?'

'Yes.'

He arches a brow at my impatient tone and, as if to contradict it, stretches in the bed, his arms high over his head, his body gloriously on display for me.

'And, Amber?'

I don't mean to sigh but when the Prime Minister's office is calling I feel there should be some air of responsiveness. Jack, apparently, doesn't agree.

'All arranged.'

Lucy's sister is taking a year's sabbatical from her job as an executive at a bank to manage the foundation's start-up year. She's insanely qualified and personally motivated.

'Salary agreed; she'll be based out of Edinburgh, as we discussed.'

He nods, but makes no effort to move.

'Seriously, Jack. Eight minutes. Get the hell up, already.'

'Ouch. Did you get out of the wrong side of bed this morning?'

He runs his fingers down his chest, drawing my attention to the ridges of his abdomen, the flesh so perfectly smooth and sculpted. My mouth is bone-dry.

'No.'

'You're even crosser than usual,' he teases, and my lips tighten impatiently.

As it happens, he's right. I got The Invitation this morning. The one that arrives every year, beckoning me to come and pay homage to my parents' marriage.

Ugh.

It's my least favourite social event—and the one time I'm forced to remember who I really am. The one time a year my parents recall me to the mother ship, reminding me that no matter what I do, professionally or personally, I'll always be Gemma Picton. *Lady* Gemma Picton.

Ugh.

'Sit down. Tell me all about it.'

He pats the bed beside him and I roll my eyes again, hoping he won't know how sorely I'm tempted. Just once I imagine giving in to *this*—the electrical current that is arcing between us. I never would...never could. He is as off-limits as hell is hot—the stuff of fantasies and nightmares.

'No, thanks.'

'What is it?'

'Nothing. Personal stuff,' I say, and he shrugs.

But there's curiosity in his eyes. A curiosity I have to ignore. Along with desire. Lust. Want. Need.

We have our boundaries and we definitely know better than to cross them.

Jack pushes the sheet off, exposing the tattoo that curls across his lower back and snakes around his hips to the tops of his legs. It must have hurt like hell to get it done—especially on the skin of his thighs, right near his cock.

I asked him once why he'd got it. His answer? *'Seemed like a good idea at the time.'*

He doesn't care that I see him naked. It's not the first time and undoubtedly won't be the last. Sometimes I wonder if he's goading me, waiting for me to react. After all, it's classic workplace sexual harassment.

Except it isn't. Because I'm not harassed.

I'm amused. And more than a little turned on.

In the two years since I started working for Jack I've probably seen him naked on average once per week. That's over a hundred stare-fests and he is *totally* worth staring at. I don't think he used to be like this. Before *this* there was *her*.

Lucy.

His wife.

But she got sick and died, and two months later I came to work for him and he was like this. Dark and brooding and desirable and sexy and messed up and mourning and fascinating.

This sleeping with anything in a skirt is post-Lucy. Same as the copious Scotch-drinking afterwards. It's sensual self-flagellation but he won't see it that way.

So, no matter how much I want to stare at his naked arse, I know he's for looking at—not touching. Like when Grandma used to take me shopping at her favourite Portmeirion boutique and I was allowed to stare at the intricate floral and botanical artwork for hours on end, but never, ever to touch.

Because touching might lead to breaking—and, yes, touching Jack would, I fear, break me.

'See something you like?'

Another drawl—he's so good at that. He lets words slide out of his mouth like liquid chocolate.

'Nope.' My smile is saccharine. 'Seven minutes.'

I spin on my heel and leave, a smile playing around my lips as desire pools between my legs.

Gemma is staring at me, and the mood I'm in I feel about two steps away from going all 'Me Tarzan, You Jane' on her. I want to grab her round the waist and pull her down on my length. No foreplay. No teasing. Just her…taking me deep.

In my fantasy she's not wearing panties and she's left her brain at the door—because real-life Gemma would quote me a thousand reasons not to have sex even as she was moaning in my arms.

Last night was fun. At least, it started off as fun.

But the woman I brought here...Rebecca? Rowena?...
talked too much.

She'd wanted to be romanced.

I wanted to screw.

So I gave her cab fare and showed her the door.

And now I have a raging hard-on and an assistant—
she hates it when I call her that, so I do it often, even
though she's technically my in-house counsel—who
seems to have moved into my sexual fantasies permanently. When did *that* happen?

I rack my brain, trying to pinpoint the moment I
went from observing her to obsessing over her. From
looking dispassionately at her in those suits she wears
one day, and the next imagining how long it would take
me to strip her out of one.

I don't think it was one *day*, though, because that
implies some switch was flicked. No, I think it was a
look as she got into my helicopter in Spain. A laugh
over dinner. Hearing her hum as she stared out of a
window, her mind obviously running at a million miles
an hour.

Then there was that blackout we were once caught in
at the City office. The fire alarm shut the place down,
closing us inside an elevator for close on an hour, with
just the dim flicker of emergency lights that made her
legs look so long and smooth. By the time they cranked
the doors I was about ready to pin her to the carpeted
floor and screw her senseless.

Yeah, that was probably the moment I realised how
much trouble I was in.

I'm not interested in a relationship. But I do want

to fuck her. And I think she wants it, too. I've seen the way her caramel eyes drop to my arse when she thinks I'm not looking.

But I'm always looking lately.

CHAPTER ONE

SHE MIGHT AS well be naked. The dress is skin-tight, bright red and low-cut. Tiny straps slip over her shoulders. The dress is short, too. Not indecently short but, *Jesus*, her legs are long and smooth, and while she's wearing that dress I find it impossible to look away.

She's hotter than any woman here—and that's saying something, given that this launch event has brought together most of London's elite. There are models, actresses, singers, athletes, and lots of those women who've married for money and now make it their life's work to live up to their husbands' expectations.

And then there's Gemma.

Her blond hair is pulled into a ballerina bun, her face is serious and her body is like pale silk that I want to wrap around me.

She's said something funny, going by the way the guy with her leans forward and laughs. Is he her date? A frown pulls at my brow. I stare harder. Did she bring a date? Isn't she technically here as my plus-one?

Seeing her with another guy does something dangerous to my equilibrium. A possessive impulse threads through me, knotting at my chest.

I pull a couple of champagne flutes from a passing waiter and cut through the room. I'm aware of people trying to get my attention but I have no time for them. Gemma is in my sights.

'Jack…'

Her lips purse as I approach; her eyes flick to me in that way she has. How is it possible for one person to imbue a simple gesture with a measure of cold disdain even when there's the hint of a smile somewhere in that symmetrical face of hers?

I hand her a glass of champagne and she takes it, her fingers briefly wrapping over mine. Immediately my mind puts them elsewhere on my body.

'You remember Wolf DuChamp?' she says. 'He manages our accounts in New York.'

I remember his stupid name, but not the man himself. Nothing memorable about blond, pretty-boy looks and that air of Ivy League he seems to wear like a coat.

'Sure.' I extend my hand, knowing I have to meet the convention even when my body is singularly focussed on Gemma.

'Good to see you again, sir.'

Gemma's lips quiver. I hate being called 'sir' and she knows it. Out of nowhere I have an image of her saying it to me, bent at the knees, her eyes moving up my body to meet mine as her lips clamp down on my length. Okay, maybe in some circumstances I could make an exception…

What the hell am I thinking? These fantasies are one thing, but screwing Gemma cannot happen.

Cannot happen. Might as well get that tattoo added to my collection.

'I was just explaining the software overhaul we're looking at to Gem.'

Is he trying to piss me off? First of all by removing the very nice image I was enjoying by talking about software. And then by referring to Gemma as 'Gem'—as though they're best buddies who paint their nails together.

'I'll summarise it for you later,' she says, sensing my impatience though I suspect not the reason for it.

'It'll make a huge difference to our operations,' Wolf pushes.

'Gem' angles her body a bit, turning away from me, giving me a chance to escape.

'I'll look into the feasibility. The problem is going to be short-term. We'll need to make sure the systems are protected during the transfer of data. You handle some of our most sensitive work—a data breach would be unacceptable.'

'I've thought of that, too,' Wolf carries on—and I am dismissed, it would appear.

Across the room a platinum blonde with a sensational rack and legs that go on forever is trying to catch my eye.

I want Gemma, but I can't have her. And I'm not one to wallow in self-pity. There's plenty of fish in the sea.

I have two rules when it comes to the women I fuck.

No commitment.

No redheads.

Commitment was for Lucy.

And Lucy was a redhead.

I freeze. A vision of Lucy is in front of me, a scowl of disapproval on her face. I messed around a fair bit before we met, but nothing like this. I've taken it to a whole new level and I don't care. Except for that scowl. Even in death I don't want to upset Lucy.

What did you expect, Luce? You left me a pretty big void to fill.

Don't blame me, I hear her snap back. *Your life. Your choice.*

Yeah, right.

My eyes wander of their own accord back to Gemma. She's got her head bent now, and Wolf's fingers are typing something into his cell phone. She nods and smiles, then presses a hand to his forearm. My stomach rolls on a surge of emotion I don't much care for.

I stalk towards the blonde as though she is the only woman in the room.

'I'm Jack Grant.'

Her lips are painted a bright red. She purrs. 'I know who you are.'

'Then you have the advantage.'

Her lips part. 'From what I hear, telling you my name wouldn't serve much purpose. You won't remember it tomorrow, right?'

I laugh, appreciating her honesty. 'No...' I lean forward so that my lips are only a whisper from her ear. My breath flutters her hair and I see a fine trail of goose bumps run across her skin. 'But you'll remember *me* for the rest of your life.'

Her laugh is husky. She's everything I would usually find sexy, but in that moment she's just passably acceptable. If I'm honest, I'm bored. It's a phone-it-in flirt. A *What the heck?* situation.

'We'll see...'

'Can I get you a drink?'

'I can share yours,' she murmurs, her eyes dropping to my champagne flute.

I didn't even realise I was still holding it. I extend it to her on autopilot, watching as her lips shape over the glass and she tilts it back. The liquid is honey-gold. She passes the glass to me and I take a sip.

'Let's get out of here,' she says, with a throaty laugh in the rushed words.

I nod, reaching down and putting a hand in the small of her back. Gemma and Lucy are both in my head now—a fascinating occurrence. A *new* occurrence. Are they ganging up on me? Would they even *like* each other?

Lucy was so soft and sweet. She looked at me like I was her saviour and I suppose I was. I ripped her out of her old life, away from a boyfriend who used her as a punching bag, and I made all her dreams come true.

But fate is a bastard of a thing, and it only had bad news in store for Lucy. For a while she managed to jump tracks and sit on a different train, and then— *bam*. It took her. You can't outrun destiny, can you?

Gemma is nothing like her. Her personality isn't so much hard edges as a single hard face. She is smart— smarter than me by a mile—and focussed in a way that is completely familiar to me. She is also sexy. I don't know how I know that, but I do. She acts so damned cold around me—as though she's never so much as *heard* of an orgasm, much less experienced one. It makes me want her more. Want to show her for the liar she is. To make her orgasm again and again until 'cold' is a very distant memory.

'Jack.'

She catches me as I'm about to leave the room. Her eyes briefly meet the blonde's. There is nothing beyond a polite acknowledgement of her existence. That iciness is there. I want to push Gemma backwards against the wall and kiss the hell out of her. Right here.

'You're scheduled to speak in twenty minutes.'

Whoops. Even for me that's a bit of a slip. I don't usually let anything get in the way of business—even my sex life.

'We'll be back by then.'

Blondie surprises us both. Her meaning is unmistakable.

Shit. I can't remember the last time I had a quickie in the car. Is she seriously suggesting it?

Gemma shifts her attention to her phone. She runs that iPhone as though she designed the thing. Her fingers fly over the screen like it's a part of her. Her complacency pisses me off.

'Okay. The talk can be brief. Just an outline of what the foundation is hoping to achieve, thanking the commercial partners, yada-yada-yada.'

'Yada-yada-yada?' I grin slowly, my eyes linking with hers, daring her to forget the coldness and complacency.

She looks at Blondie and her smile is perfunctory. 'Have fun.'

* * *

Of course Jack nails the speech. Not so much as a hair on his head looks out of place. The tuxedo is immaculate. The white shirt crisp. The bow tie in place as though glued. He speaks eloquently about the foundation and he also speaks with humour, so the crowd laughs.

I don't.

I am wondering about the blonde.

No. I'm thinking about Jack—but they're thoughts that I need to run a mile from. This *can't* control me. I've worked my arse off in this job, twisting myself in mental knots to stay on top of my workload without breaking a sweat, and I am *not* going to let the fact that my boss is impossibly hot get in the way.

Instead I let my attention drift to Wolf.

He's talking to someone else now—no doubt about that bloody software. His face is serious, and that makes me smile. Because Wolf is pretty much always serious.

Warning! Warning! Warning! It flashes inside my mind. Because I don't *do* serious, and if I let the flirtation with Wolf keep going I think he's going to see roses and candy and wedding bells.

God help me, I can't think of anything worse.

I am suffocating at the very *idea* of being a bride in white, having Wolf waiting for me at the end of an aisle. He would definitely want children, too. Three of them. And he'd expect me to be the obliging baby-maker and carer. He'd look at me with those puppy-dog eyes, sadness and disappointment on his features, if I so much as dared suggest we get a nanny.

Maybe I could be like Marissa Mayer and have a nursery built into my office? The nanny could be based there, so I could still be one of those hands-on Pinterest-type mummies. Wolf would never even need to know I'd hired someone to help.

But Jack would. He'd *hate* that. A baby crying when I'm trying to talk to him about tariffs on our Chinese imports? No, he'd probably seduce the nanny and then I'd have to either fire her or kill her.

Okay, *now* who's getting ahead of themselves?

But Wolf has caught me watching him and his heart is so on his sleeve he might as well be a cartoon character, with one of those thought bubbles popping out of his head. I *have* to let this opportunity pass me by. He's not right, and when he realises that I'm not going to leave Jack and move to Manhattan, working with him will become a nightmare.

I look away.

Right at Jack.

He's standing in front of me.

The band has started to play and I've been so lost in imagining the hell of my future with Wolf DuChamp that I haven't realised.

'Did you like the speech?'

'Looking for compliments?' I sip my champagne, pleased at how quickly I'm able to recover. 'What's the matter? Wasn't she suitably impressed?'

His eyes clash with mine. He's angry. *Ooooh.* Why? Have I hit the nail on the head somehow?

'Are you wondering if I can please a woman in fifteen minutes?'

He shifts his body infinitesimally, but enough to spark something low in my abdomen. Anger. Resentment. Heat. Warmth. Need.

Fuck.

'Believe it or not, I haven't given any thought to your bedroom prowess,' I lie, shifting my attention back to the room of people. London's elite swirl around us, and I am wanting to swirl away with them.

'Liar,' he says, so softly I think I've misheard.

Because we can't go there! He knows that—I know that. Every bone in my body wants him, but my brain is still in charge. I don't want to screw up my career, but it's more than that. I *love* Jack. Not in *that* way. I mean I love working with him. Even when he's at his assholiest, he's become one of the biggest constants in my life. How stupid would it be to rock the boat?

I imagine, briefly, that we indulge in an affair and it ends—because Jack doesn't do permanent—and then I imagine not seeing him again.

It makes me ill.

I don't want to think about it.

I don't want to risk it.

'The speech was good.' I bring the conversation back onto far safer ground, trying to fold my desperate realisations away neatly into a box I won't open again.

'Tell me something, Gemma,' he says, and the tone of his voice is still dangerous to me.

He hasn't got my silent memo, obviously, because

his words prick the blood in my veins until it gushes and gurgles through me—he's flirting with me.

I use my most businesslike tone. 'Oh, I don't know if you really want me to do that. You might not like what I say...'

His eyes lance mine. It's like being sliced through.

'What's the deal with you and that guy from New York?'

Who's he talking about? Oh. Right. 'You mean Wolf?'

His lips curl derisively—that's one of my favourite of his expressions. I don't know if he realises how dev-ilishly sexy he looks.

'Who calls their kid after an *animal*? Especially when he's the least wolf-like person you can imagine.'

'I don't suppose they knew that when he was born,' I say, but a smile is pushing at my lips. He's right. Wolf is handsome, but in a very neat and tidy kind of way.

'Is he a wolf in the bedroom?'

The question catches me completely off guard. It's wholly new territory for us. Invasive in a way I don't know if I like but am worried that I might.

Still, challenging Jack is what I do. That's who we are.

I tilt my head to one side, assessing him for a mo-ment, before volleying back, 'How was the blonde?'

'She was dull,' he says with a shrug and no hesita-tion, apparently having no qualms discussing his sex-life with me.

'Where is she?'

'At her house. Waiting.'

'For you?'

He shrugs. 'I said I might stop by. It seemed like the only way to get rid of her.'

Wait. He *hasn't* slept with her? No, not slept with. Fucked. The thought is oddly elating, though I can't help but feel sympathy for the woman he flirted with and then sent packing.

'You really are a bastard,' I mutter. 'Are you going to go to her?'

His eyes are probing mine now, and I feel like every single one of my fantasies, my dirtiest, hottest dreams, are playing out between us like a kinky Pensieve for his pleasure.

Yes, I'm a Harry Potter diehard. Hermione was one of my first role models.

'Maybe.'

My stomach turns. I am used to this feeling with Jack. In the first six months we worked together I wasn't so adept at dealing with his vivid love-life. I blushed whenever I found evidence of his nocturnal activities, and I couldn't always meet his eye. But now? Well, now I've had two years to practise acceptance.

I smile blandly. 'Well...' I shrug as though my heart's not racing and my nipples aren't throbbing. 'Have a good night.'

'Wait.' His words are commanding, and so too is the hand he clamps around my wrist.

I jerk my face towards his, the breath exploding out of me. We *don't* touch. No more than an accidental brush of fingers from time to time. That's impossible to avoid when you're together as often as we are.

Definitely not like this.

His thumb pads across my inner wrist, and when I don't say anything he pulls me, hard and fast, so that my body rams into his. We are surrounded and yet we are alone. There is a void that engulfs us. Like a sensual electric fence.

This is all new and all wrong. And so right.

His body is tight. Hard. Hot. Just as it is in all my fantasies. It takes every single ounce of my willpower to close my mouth and let my breath return to normal. To look at him as though he's lost his mind, not made me lose mine.

'Yes, sir?'

His eyes flare. I meant it to put him back on his guard, to remind him of the boundaries of our relationship, but I might as well have struck a match over gasoline. He doesn't let me go.

'Dance with me.'

The air around us is charged with expectation and I just know he's asking for more than a dance. Does he expect me to say no? I don't like living up to expectations, and I'm not going to give him a reason to think I'm afraid of what's going on between us.

'Fine.' My smile is tight. It stretches over my face like sunburn.

He expels a breath, long and slow, and places a hand in the small of my back. No…just at the very top of my arse. His fingers are splayed wide and they press into me firmly, so that I'm propelled towards him. His other hand links with my fingers, wrapping through them.

I focus on the band, my eyes taking in the details of their appearance while I concentrate on looking completely calm. I'm not, though. I'm weak when I want to be strong, and I need something that I shouldn't.

'This dress is sensational,' he says, immediately shattering my attempts to find calm.

'Is that your informed fashion opinion?'

Too tart. I soften the snap with a smile. It's a mistake. His eyes are mocking, his own smile sardonic.

I look away again immediately.

'It's my informed opinion as a red-blooded male.'

'What do you like about it?'

Warning lights are flashing in my mind, clamouring for attention. They are bright and angry. What am I *doing*?

'Let me see,' he murmurs. 'The colour. The way it's literally glued to your skin.'

He drops his head closer and heat spirals inside me; my blood is a vapour of steam in my veins.

This isn't right. It's not us. He sleeps with other women and, sure, he flirts the heck out of me, but that's harmless.

This doesn't feel harmless.

The music slows and I slow with it, putting some space between us with what I tell myself is relief.

'Get me up to speed on the New York situation,' he says.

'I intend to.'

I'm snappy because I'm uncertain. I'm completely wrong-footed by his nearness, his touch, and my own desire for him is swamping me. I need a minute to regroup, but his fingers are giving me no time. They're throbbing across my spine, my arse, and I am heating up by the second.

'Tonight. Now.'

I angle my head towards Wolf unconsciously. He's still locked in conversation. I have no intention of going home with him, and yet I resent Jack's implication that I don't have a life of my own.

'It's not urgent.' My words are stiff. 'It'll keep till tomorrow.' And I force myself to pull completely free of Jack's grip.

It's the equivalent of grabbing a lifeline from the side of a sinking boat. It's slippery, and I'm pretty sure I'm not strong enough to hold on to it for long enough to save myself. Drowning is inevitable.

'I want to hear about it tonight.'

It's a challenge. A gauntlet. He gives me a lot of latitude in my job because he knows how much I do. And I do it well. But at the end of the day he's my boss, and I don't know if anything is to be served by refusing him this request.

'Fine,' I say with a shrug of my shoulders. But I'm not going to let him think he's won. 'I just need… twenty minutes.'

I disconnect myself from him and try not to register how my body screams in frustration.

I saunter off towards Wolf before I can see if Jack's reacting in the same way.

Wolf is deep in conversation when I approach. 'May I have a moment?' I look with a hint of apology towards the men he's with.

'Sure.' He grins at me. A nice grin. He really is

good to look at. Not groundbreaking, earth-shattering, but *nice*.

He puts a hand on my elbow but I am leading *him*, walking quickly out of the ballroom, seeking privacy for no reason other than to give Jack a taste of his own damned medicine. That and to send a loud and clear message. He doesn't control every part of me.

'All good for later?' Wolf asks.

I smile. 'No, it's not. I have to work tonight, actually. I'm going to brief Jack on the software situation.'

'Tonight?' He arches a brow, his voice rich with disbelief.

'He micromanages *everything*,' I explain. It's true. 'And he's impatient as hell. I just want to make sure I have all the information.'

He nods, not quite hiding his disappointment. 'Let's recap.'

And that's how I spend the nineteen minutes I have. Well, eighteen… I allow myself one minute to pull a bit of my hair loose from its bun and to pinch my cheeks, making them appear flushed with pleasure.

Jack is waiting for me in the limousine twenty-five minutes after I left him. I imitate breathlessness as I step inside, and enjoy the way his eyes sweep over me with undisguised speculation.

'Ready?'

It's not what I expected. I nod, but as I do so I feel like maybe I'm agreeing to something I don't understand. Like there's a hidden meaning I don't yet know.

'Yeah. Let's go.'

CHAPTER TWO

I'LL SAY THIS for Jack. He knows how to do *this*. Late-night entertaining is clearly his forte.

His office is dimly lit and he's switched on some kind of acoustic guitar album that's humming low in my abdomen. The vocalist has a husky rasp and it's doing very strange things to my equilibrium. He mixes two martinis with a maraschino cherry in each.

I arch a brow as he hands me mine. 'I hate cherries.'

'Interesting,' he murmurs, his eyes hooked to mine. 'Why?'

I stare at it and swirl the glass, sipping the alcohol and wincing as the slightly medicinal flavour assaults my back palette. 'They're weird. Plasticky.'

'Not the real ones.'

'No.'

I swallow, wondering at the way my gut is churning and my pulse is racing. I need to bring it back to business. It's the reason I'm here with him.

'The server in Canada can pick up the slack, but it's going to slow things down.'

'By how much?'

'Just a few seconds' lag. It's unavoidable, given the distance.'

'A few seconds?' He shakes his head. 'There's nowhere closer?'

'Not that can handle this amount of data.'

He throws his drink back in one motion. 'And *Wolf* thinks that's acceptable?'

He says his name with obvious derision.

'You think he'd go to the effort of flying out here to propose it if he did?'

'Well, he's banging you, right?'

I can't hide the angry intake of breath. Sure, he's always rude. And demanding. And I've learned not to give a shit. I don't expect the same courtesy from Jack Grant that most people pepper into life. But this is too far even for him...even when we've been flirting all night.

'His suggestion is professional,' I return softly. A warning lurks in my words. Does he hear it?

Apparently not. Jack is like a cat with a mouse.

'But you are fucking him?'

'God, Jack,' I snap, standing up.

His eyes follow the fluidity of my movement. They're narrowed. Assessing. He's reading me like a book. But I'm too angry to care. Too worked up, as well. He's halfway to being drunk, and he's obnoxious, and since he pulled me hard against his body I'm a bit mushy.

I hide my mushiness, though. I hide it behind a veil of anger. 'That's none of your damned business.'

His eyes flick to mine. There's a lazy arrogance in his features but anger palpitates off him.

'He works for me. You work for me. If you're fucking him I want to know.'

'What I do in my own time, and with whom, is up to me. Until the day it starts affecting my job performance you should just butt out.' I jut my chin, my eyes sparking with his. 'Got it?'

He looks calm, controlled, but I know there's an undercurrent of emotion just beneath the handsome surface. Because I know Jack. Probably better than anyone else on earth.

'You don't strike me as coy,' he says.

'Because I'm not.'

I step backwards. The wall is behind me. I brush against it, feeling cornered and unbelievably confused and turned on by this strange turn of events.

'So answer the question.'

'Am I fucking Wolf?' My question emerges as a husk in the night.

'Yeah.' He moves forward. An infinitesimal step. 'You know everything there is to know about me, don't you? So why keep your secrets?'

I open my mouth to say something snappy, but shut it again. He's right. I know a lot about him. Not the 'everything' he claims, but a lot.

'You could always lock your door if you want to be more private about your love-life.'

'*Sex*-life,' he interjects swiftly, on autopilot, and I know it's because of Lucy that he's so emphatic on this point.

I don't know anything about his wife. I presume she was a nice enough person—although agreeing to marry Jack does make me question both her sanity and her judgement. But maybe he was different before she died. Maybe his bastard impulses weren't so apparent?

'So you're going to live out the rest of your life like this? Moving from one woman to another, never getting to know a thing about them beyond their cup size and their sexual proclivities.'

His eyes drop to my breasts and I can tell he is assessing *my* cup size. *Crap.* My nipples strain hard against the flimsy fabric of my dress—it's too tight for a bra, and sadly I don't really need one.

His smile is self-satisfied and I want to slap it off his face. I fight the urge to cross my arms and cover my involuntary reaction.

'I'm trying to get to know more about you right now,' he says.

My pulse is hammering hard in my veins. His revolving-door bedroom flashes before me in an instant. The number of mornings I've arrived to find him asleep after a busy night of… Best I don't imagine that right now.

'Are you afraid I'll judge you?'

I open my eyes to find him right in front of me, his head bent, his body just a hair's breadth from me. A soft moan escapes me before I can catch it.

'You? You think you'd have any right to judge me after parading half of England through here?'

'Not half of *England*,' he murmurs, a smile shifting over his face. 'Half of London, maybe.'

'How do you justify it?' I ask, feeling a dangerous pull towards a line of questioning my brain is shouting at me to back away from. 'You think Lucy would be happy that you're fucking your way through a smorgasbord of women just because you won't have an actual relationship? Is there a sliding scale of monogamy that the dead expect?'

A muscle jerks in his cheek. I recognise that I'm stirring him up and still I don't stop. I'm angry, too! He doesn't have a monopoly on thwarted desire and pent-up frustration.

It feels good to goad him! *So* good!

'You think what you do is fair to these women?'

His smile spreads slowly, but it is cold, angry. 'I don't hear any complaints.'

Boom! It's the proverbial match to the fuel of my anger. I explode.

'You boot them out before you even know their names half the time! Where, exactly, would they lodge their complaint? My God, Jack. Of all the chauvinistic, selfish, careless—'

He lifts a finger to my lips, silencing me with the touch. His eyes on mine are intent. Heat builds inside my blood, at fever pitch now.

'You know…' His fingers dip into my drink, fishing out the bright red orb at its base. 'You have a tendency to be judgemental.'

My sharp intake of breath is dangerous, given his finger's closeness to my mouth. He runs it across my lower lip and I don't pull away. He holds up the cherry with his other hand. My eyes slip to it of their own accord.

'Haven't you ever discovered that you like something you thought you hated? Haven't you ever been wrong?'

I shake my head, not really sure of the question he's asking. He surprises me by lifting the cherry to his own lips and sucking it into his mouth. I watch for a moment, and as his finger drops from my mouth I try to say something. I'm not sure what, and I'll never have a chance to find out. He brings his lips to mine, pressing the cherry into my mouth, rolling it around before sucking it back into his and crushing it.

The flavour is all around me and I no longer care. Because it is dwarfed by something else: the taste of *him*. Cherry flavour is on his tongue, evaporating in the flame of our kiss.

His lips crush mine, silencing any words, sucking them out of me, and a new heat spreads in my body. His kiss is punishment and it is possession. I cannot explain it better than that. It is a moment of clarity in which my anger seems to evaporate temporarily before it is back and I am kissing him—just as hard, with just as much fury.

My tongue lashes his and my hands are in his hair, rough, pulling at him, and I am kissing him as though I am still shouting at him with my touch.

He groans angrily and his body weight holds me to the wall, his strong legs straddling me, pinning me where I am. I think my brain is trying to tell me something, but I can hear nothing above the pounding of my heart and the rushing of my blood.

Desire is a whip, and it is lashing at my spine.

He drags his lips lower, nipping the skin of my shoulder with his teeth and teasing the racing pulse-point in my neck with his tongue. I groan, tilting my head back, knowing I need to stop this madness but accepting we are past that.

A line has been crossed. Not just crossed! Obliterated! There is newness to this. But I want to shape it, not be shaped *by* it. I need to be in charge—at least to some extent.

'Why do you care?' he asks, bringing his mouth back to mine and kissing me with enough force to hold my head hard against the wall. His hand drops to my dress, lifting the hem, and his fingers slide between my weak, shaking legs.

'Care...?' I mumble. What is he talking about?

He breaks the kiss but I have no space to think—not when his fingers are sliding inside me, his hand easily pushing aside the barrier of my flimsy underpants.

Oh, my God. I'm about to come. I swear, I'm this close. He swirls his finger around my wet muscles, teasing me, feeling me, and I am his. Completely.

'Why do you care who I fuck?'

The question is a gruff, deep demand.

I blink my eyes, trying to think straight. But he moves his thumb over my clit and I shiver, trembling in every bone of my body as I feel the wave building around me.

'I don't,' I snap through gritted teeth, sweat sheening my brow.

My eyes are shut, so I don't see him dip his head forward. It is a surprise when his mouth clamps over my breast, his teeth biting down on my nipple through the silky fabric of my dress.

My stomach lurches as he drags his teeth along my nipple, pulling, making me throb with pleasure. And his finger pushes deeper, then draws out. My own wetness glides across my clit as he thumbs my nerves, and I am lost. Exploded. Gone.

Heat shoots through me, bursting me apart, and I am panting loud and hard as he moves his head to the other breast.

Shit. It's too much. My muscles are clenching and my legs are hardly able to hold me up. I have had amazing sex, but something about this has blown all my experiences out of the water. Is it the illicitness of being with my boss?

My boss.

Jack Grant.

I groan in awareness of a moment I will undoubtedly regret, and then I groan at my weakness because I can't stop. There is a compulsion—no. An awakening. It is an acceptance of a truth I have fought too hard and for too long.

Two years of looks, laughs, infuriating arguments and differences of opinion have been leading to this. Two years of finding him in bed and fantasising about climbing in with him. I have resisted because he is my boss and I love my job—and because he's Jack-bloody-Grant. I have resisted acting on my deepest desires, but now I find it is impossible not to welcome his.

His hand drops to my side. His fingers dig into my flesh just enough to make me arch my back forward, but his hips rock me against the wall, crushing me with strength and passion. Hell, he's good at this. So, *so* good. So much better than I imagined.

And I've imagined a lot.

I whimper—a sound I don't think I've ever made in my life—as he brings his mouth back to mine, but the ghost of his kiss lingers on my breasts, making them painfully sensitised.

'Now do you think women complain after they leave me?' he asks, and he is stepping away, backwards, his eyes glinting in his handsome face as he stares at me with a confusing lack of passion.

There is colour in his cheeks and his chest is shifting hard, as is mine, with the pain of laboured breath. But his voice is steady and his eyes are cold.

His question doesn't make sense. I lift a finger to my breasts. They're tingling and swollen. I stare at him, unusually slow on the uptake.

'I give them what they want. What *you* want.'

And he turns sharply, stalking across the room and grabbing another drink. His back is to me as he throws back the glass and swallows, but I hardly register the movement. Shock is seeping into me. Shock at what we've just done.

Holy hell!

Was he proving a point? I am trembling, moistness slicks my underwear, my dress bears the marks of his kiss, my mind is tumbled—and he is *nothing*?

Feminine pique stirs in my gut. I fantasise about slipping the dress from my body and storming across

the room. About pushing him to the floor and straddling him, making him admit he wants me.

I know he does. I felt the proof of his desire hard
against my stomach. But sanity is returning, and with
it the realisation that we have done something very,
very stupid. There is no turning back. No unwinding
time. I need to salvage my pride and get the hell out
of his office before I do something really stupid. Like
ask him to finish the job he started.

'I'll email you a full report on the server's feasibility tomorrow.' My words are pleasingly stiff.

He grunts. 'There she is. My cold-as-ice assistant.'

I straighten my back. I have *never* been his assistant and he knows it. He's goading me. Spoiling for
another fight?

I narrow my eyes. 'Oh, I'm not cold,' I hear myself
say. 'I'm very, *very* turned on.'

Perhaps my honesty surprises him. He turns his
face, angling it towards me without actually looking
in my direction.

'If you'll excuse me, I'm going to go and…blow off
some steam.'

I walk out of there calmly, even though I am awash
with doubt. Let him make of that what he will. If he
imagines me going to Wolf… So what? If he imagines
me going home to masturbate, looking at a picture of
him, then let him.

I don't know if I give a shit.

It is cold when I emerge from The Mansion, and
drizzling with rain.

One of the decisions I made within six months of

coming to work for Jack was to move to Hampstead, where he lives. The hours I work, I don't want to lose any more to a lengthy commute.

The Mansion is at the end of a long lane that comes out near the Heath, and just around the corner from a happy little school is my townhouse. A Dickensian brick with a shining red door and window boxes that have been sorely neglected over the summer. I should have planted them with pansies and strawberries, as they were when I first moved in, but I've never got around to it.

I shoulder the door inwards and slam it closed behind me with true relief.

But then I make the mistake of shutting my eyes and there he is. Jack Grant…head bent forward…mouth moving over my breast. I curse darkly—a string of angry words that would have knocked my mother sideways if she thought I even knew such language—and stride to the mirror in my entrance way.

My breasts are covered by two dark, wet marks. I lift my fingers to them and trace their outline, shuddering at remembered sensations, desperate for more. More of him. More of this.

I groan loudly and stomp through to the kitchen.

What the hell just happened? He's my boss. My *boss*! And I know what he's like. I know how messed up he is. For two years I have kept all this swirling desire at bay. Why couldn't I control it tonight?

I pour myself a glass of wine in the hope that it will somehow reach back through time and wipe the experience not only from my memory but also from existence. It doesn't. Each sip reminds me of him, and the faint overtone of alcohol hits the back of my throat, making me crave him.

This is *not* good.

I walk more slowly through the house, up the narrow stairs—two flights. The house is tall and skinny, with one or two rooms on each of its five storeys. My office is on the first floor; my bedroom and bathroom are on the next. There are three bedrooms on the next few levels, and a roof terrace right at the top. I love it, but I am not here nearly enough.

I kick my shoes off, then flick the light on with the base of my wineglass, narrowly avoiding spilling Pinot Noir on the beige carpet. I pad over the carpet and strip off the dress as I go. I'll give it to charity as soon as I can.

In just my still-damp underpants, I climb into bed and pull the duvet up to my chin. Wineglass in hand, I stare at the wall.

It's not *that* bad, is it?

People must do this kind of thing all the time. We work together. Hell, we practically live together. Something like this was kind of inevitable.

I cringe.

It's so *not* okay. Wasn't I just congratulating myself a few days ago on the Very Important Lessons I've learned from watching female bosses get derided and demoted over the years? Surely the cardinal sin for any woman in the workplace is to get involved with a colleague? And definitely not a senior, super-rich, super-yummy, fuck-around kind of colleague.

Ugh!

There are only a handful of us that work at The Mansion. Jack's two assistants, his driver, a bodyguard and me. We are all bound by a strict notion of confidentiality, and I think most of his staff are too afraid of me to get on my bad side anyway. So it's not gossip I fear.

It's Jack. And it's me. It's the respect I suspect I have sacrificed by letting this happen.

Letting it happen? My brain is outraged. My brain, after all, *did* try to stop it.

Sorry, I wasn't listening. I won't make that mistake again.

I pour the wine into my mouth, wincing at the astringent taste I really don't enjoy. I'm tired. It's been a long day and a weird night.

The last thing on my mind as I fall into a tortured, sensual sleep is a question about what tomorrow will bring.

He's at his desk when I arrive the next morning, coffee steaming in front of him, dark head bent. I move past, telling myself I would never do anything as cowardly as tiptoeing even as I hold my breath until I'm past his doorframe.

'Gemma? Get in here.'

Shit.

I squeeze my eyes shut, suck in a deep breath. I can do this. We just kissed.

You didn't 'just kiss'. He stuck his finger deep inside you and made you come.

Shut up, brain.

He sucked on your breasts and you fell apart at the seams.

Seriously, I'm going to lobotomise myself.

'Gemma?'

With a silent oath, I spin on my you-can-handle-anything Jimmy Choo heel and stride into his office with my very best appearance of calm.

'Oh, hi, Jack.'

Crap. He's wearing the pale blue shirt that makes his eyes look like bloody gemstones. It's unbuttoned at the neck and I can see a hint of dark hair curling above the top button.

'I didn't realise you were here.'

His smirk shows my lie for what it is.

'Sit.'

I arch my brow, staying exactly where I am, ignoring the wall to my left. The wall he pressed me against while he explored me intimately. My eyes stray to the bar instead. To the cocktail he was drinking last night.

'Sit,' he says again, and there is something in his voice that makes my nerves twitch.

There is promise in that command. Promise and heat.

'How are you?' The question, softly asked, makes everything inside me tremble.

'I'm fine,' I snap, to counteract that response. 'And busy. What do you need?'

His smile spreads slowly across his face. It is fire and it is flame and my brain is beginning to get very, very anxious.

'How did you sleep?'

Does he know I dreamed of him? That in my dreams he did very, very bad things to me?

I swallow, crossing my arms over my chest as the memories nip at my heels. They are in the room with us, swirling around him, me and the things we did. I can't give them more air.

'Did you want something?'

He stands up, and I am frozen to the spot as he moves confidently across the room, shutting the door and clicking the lock in place.

'I slept badly,' he says, ignoring my question, his voice sunshine on my cool flesh.

'Mmm…?' I murmur, making sure no warmth conveys itself to him. 'Maybe you should have tried a sedative?'

He strides to the chair across from his and holds it out. Shooting him a look laced with my fiercest resentment, I sit down, careful not to so much as brush against his fingertips. Fingers that have now been inside me—that have not just touched me, but have breached my barriers and found my throbbing heart.

Fingers that have undone me.

I am holding my breath again. Is that how I'm going to get over this little hurdle? Suffocate myself? Is that even possible? I'm pretty sure we have some breathing trigger in our brains, but my brain is a bit pissy with me so maybe it would conveniently forget about the button.

I push air out consciously, quietly, and he takes his seat.

'Anyway…' I prompt impatiently.

His smile is a flicker. Is he *laughing* at me? Arrogant arsehole! That'd be just like him. See? That's the problem! I *know* him. I'm not one of his other women. I know that he is as bastardy as he is sexy.

'How did you sleep?'

I blink at him, my eyes wide. 'You've already asked me that.'

'You didn't answer.'

I expel a sigh that speaks of anger. 'Like I always do. Seriously, Jack. My desk is covered in paper. I have to get to work.'

'*I'm* your work,' he says with a shrug.

Insolent bastard.

He leans forward, and while his face is casual there is an urgency in the flecks of gold that fill his eyes. 'Did you see him last night?'

I want to remind him of the salient fact I pointed out the night before. It's not his damned business. But I'm not sure I can say that with such conviction now that I've tasted his mouth; now that I've been stunned by his desire.

Can I skirt around his question?

'*You're* my work? Okay, the thing is I have the New York guys waiting on contracts, you have a meeting in a week that I have to prepare for and Athens wants your input—which means *my* input—on a lease agreement. And I need to—'

'Quiet.'

God! Don't hate me, but when he's bossy I *love* it. And he's almost always bossy.

I glare at him across his desk; it's best if he doesn't know that this is just about my favourite version of him.

'You're fucking telling *me* to be quiet?' I lean forward, and we're close now: almost touching. 'Seriously?'

'You're pissed off.'

'Damn right, I am.'

His laugh is soft. Throaty. Hot. 'Because we didn't finish?'

I flick my eyes shut. My cheeks are hot. 'What do you need?'

'Are you in a relationship with him?'

'Who?'

'Wolf DuChamp?'

I hide a smile. 'So you *do* know his name?'

'*Now* I do.'

His expression is unreadable. But deep inside me something stirs. *Hope.* Because isn't there an implication there that he knows about Wolf because of *me*? Because he wants to know about *my* life?

'So? What's the deal?' he asks.

'Are you jealous?' The words are a challenge; they escape unbidden.

His response is razor-sharp. 'Why would I be jealous?'

Crap. A stupid challenge, apparently.

'Forget it.' I scrape the chair back and stand, my eyes not inviting argument. 'Is that all?'

'You haven't answered me. How can it be *all*?'

I expel a breath angrily. 'I like him.' I shrug.

It's true. Not romantically, necessarily. But he's a nice guy. Good-looking. It doesn't matter that I've already ruled out a relationship.

'Are you fucking him?'

My expression is ice—even I can feel the chill that spreads through the office.

'Isn't this the question that got us into trouble last night?'

He stands up, slamming his palms against the desk, his eyes lashing me. 'Are you *fucking* him?'

It's loud. Not quite a roar, but close to it. I'm startled. This is outside the bounds of anything that's happened between us and we both know it. Then again, I guess we've obliterated boundaries now. They—like me—are in a state of flux. Changeability that is unpredictable and not good.

'Go to hell.'

I turn around and walk out of his office, but my knees are shaking and I feel really weird, as if I could cry—which, for your information, I haven't done in years. I *literally* don't cry. Not at sad movies. Not when my cat died.

But I'm shaking, and if he follows me I'll be really lost.

He doesn't.

I storm over to my desk. I wasn't lying or exaggerating. Piles of paper clutter every available inch of the thing. I turn my back on them and stare over the Heath, my eyes brooding.

This is a damned nightmare, isn't it?

My brain nods along smugly. *Told you so.*

CHAPTER THREE

It has been a week and I'm still here. What's more, my brain and I are almost friends again. I have been behaving. Working hard, speaking politely, keeping my sexy, kinky 'if only' thoughts hidden behind a mask of disinterest.

Of course it helps that I've hardly seen Jack.

He's been in Tokyo for four days, on a trip I would usually do with him.

Here's how it would go: Private jet. Limousine. Luxurious hotel accommodation—his apartment there is being remodelled. Meetings. Late-night debriefing.

You get the picture, and you no doubt see the risk.

'I have too much on,' I said when he'd decided he needed to go personally. 'Seriously, there's no way I can leave the office now.'

He ground his teeth together, looked at me as though I were pulling some soppy, emotional crap and then he nodded. 'Fine.'

He's due back today and my desk is no clearer—it's just a different heap of papers that covers it now. My phone bleats and I grab it up, my nerves not welcoming the intrusion.

Perhaps my impatience conveys itself in my brusque greeting.

'You sound like shit.'

The cackling voice brings an instant smile to my face. 'Hi, Grandma.'

'Where've you *been*, lovey?'

'Oh, you know…' I eye the paperwork dubiously. 'Living it up.'

'If only. Let me guess. You're at work?'

'You called my work number, so I suspect you know the answer to that.'

Another cackle. 'Are you coming to see me any time soon? I have something for you.'

'Another lecture on my priorities?'

'You're a smart girl. You know your priorities are out of order.' She sighs. 'Take it from a woman at the end of her journey. There's a big, beautiful world out there, and even if you devote your life entirely to travelling you'll still never get to see everywhere and everything.'

'God, that makes me feel both nauseated and claustrophobic. It's saccharine and overly sentimental even for *you*, Grandma.'

She laughs. I love her laugh. My grandma shines a light with her smile alone.

'Everyone's allowed a bit of sentimentalism at some point, aren't they? Especially at *my* age.'

'I travel *everywhere*,' I point out, flicking my calendar onto my screen and scanning it. 'In fact I'm off to Australia next week.'

Crap. With Jack.

'Oh, yes? That wouldn't be a work trip, would it?'

I grin. 'No. And by no, I mean yes—but I imagine I'll still get time to pet a koala.'

'You know they're not just crawling around the streets? You actually need to go bush to find one.'

I burst out laughing. '*"Go bush"?* Grandma, you're a Duchess. I think it's in the manual that you're not allowed to "go bush"—or go anywhere, really.'

I'm not joking. Grandma really *is* a Duchess. She married my grandpa, who was a decade her senior and had come back from the Second World War with what we'd now know as post-traumatic stress disorder. She was a nurse, and his family hired her to care for him—to "fix" him. She quit on the first day. There wasn't anything wrong with him, she declared. He was just different.

They got engaged that afternoon.

It's the only fairytale I believe in—and only because it has a macabre degree of reality to it. Grandma *did* fix him. He made her a princess—of the social variety—and she made him whole in a different way, just like she said.

We lost him years ago, and now *she's* the one who's a little bit broken. But still amazing. The most beautiful person in my life. My other constant.

Jack and Grandma. *Great.* An emotionally closed-off sexy widower that I should definitely know better than to want, and a champagne-swilling octogenarian, relic of the aristocracy. These two are the anchors in my life...

I shake my head, my smile rueful.

'Pish! I'll have you know I went bush and did a great many other things in my time.' She sighs heavily. 'And now it's *your* time—and you're spending it in some ghoulish house on the edge of the moors.'

'It's a mansion, actually, with state-of-the-art offices. And it's Hampstead Heath—not a moor.'

'Still...' A huff of impatience. 'You'll come this weekend?'

'I promise.'

I click in my calendar and make a note. Without entering my plans straight into my calendar I'm running blind. My eyes are dragged of their own accord to the entry for my parents' anniversary. *Ugh.*

'I suppose you got your invitation?'

'Mmm...' It's a noise of agreement that could mean a thousand things. 'Very elegant paper.'

I stifle a laugh. 'Stiff and unyielding.'

My implication hangs in the air, unspoken.

'Ah, well. At least there'll be booze.'

'And lots of it.'

I run a finger over my desk. Grandma and I got rather unceremoniously sloshed at the previous year's anniversary affair. If we hadn't been related by blood to the bride *du jour* we definitely wouldn't have been invited back.

'We'll do a rehearsal at the weekend,' she says, and I hear the wink in her words.

'Perfect. See you then.'

'Good, darling. Ta-ta.'

My phone rings again almost as soon as I hang up, and the smile is still playing on my lips as I lift the receiver and hook it beneath my ear. 'Yeah?'

'Gemma.'

His voice gushes through me like a tidal wave crashes over the shore. We've been in constant contact while he's been travelling—but only via email or text, and only in the most businesslike sense.

At no point has he reminded me of the way his mouth pushed me back, tasting me, robbing me of comprehension and hammering every last one of my senses. At no point have we discussed how he made me come against the wall of his office.

Hearing his voice now is as intimate and personal as if he strode into the room and straddled me, reached down and kissed me...

'I'm meeting some clients in the City. I need that presentation on the Tokyo project, as well as an up-to-date cost analysis and the report I had done. Meet me in an hour.'

It almost sounds like a question, but we both know it isn't. My body hums with vibrations. *I'm going to see him again.* It's the most alive I've felt in a week. My abdomen clenches in anticipation. Of what?

My body is getting carried away, but thankfully my brain is still lucid-ish. 'Fine,' I hear my brain say, cool and unconcerned. *Liar.*

There's a pause and I wonder what's coming next. 'Good.'

The little tick of approval sends a thrill along my spine. I hate that. I repress my pleasure.

'And, Gemma? Rose has something for you.'

I gather the documents he needs and quickly run through the project presentation, then step out of my office, laden with files and my MacBook Air.

Sophia and Rose are in the office they share, heads bent, and I smile crisply at them. 'I'm meeting Jack in the City. He says you have something for me?'

I address the question to Rose, who reaches into her desk and pulls out an envelope. It has his dark, confident writing across the front. My name, scrawled in his handwriting. I resist the urge to run my fingertip over the letters.

'Thanks.' I nod crisply and Sophia reaches for her phone before I've said another word.

'Hughes—Miss Picton is travelling to the City.'

'Thanks.' I nod, pleased that things are working efficiently.

I hired Sophia to replace the last of Jack's assistants to quit. He's run through about six since losing Lucy; my own job has been filled a dozen times at least. I think it kind of bonds Sophia and me—a similar determination not to fail runs through us both.

'Will you be long? Shall I move your two o'clock?' asks Rose.

I can't reach my phone and can't remember off the top of my head what I have at two. I guess my blank stare conveys that, because Rose smiles at me kindly. How she's managed to work for Jack for three years is beyond me. She's a butter-wouldn't-melt kind of woman, and yet there's a quality to her that makes her oblivious to Jack's demanding requests and lack of charm.

'Carrie Johnson.'

'Right.' I nod distractedly, thinking only of the mysterious envelope. It's small and there's something inside.

Carrie is my friend who's looking for a new job—I have her in mind for something with the foundation, though I don't know exactly what yet. She was made redundant in the last round of restructuring at her company, and she's brilliant and incisive—far too clever to let go.

'Yeah, shift it to tomorrow. Thanks. Please apologise for me.'

'Here.' Sophia scrapes her chair back and walks towards me with outstretched arms. 'I'll help you to the car.'

I hand over some of the papers gratefully. The offices are in a separate wing of The Mansion, and we step out onto the short path that winds through a manicured garden before opening out into a gravelled courtyard. It's really well designed to keep business away from personal life—not that Jack has much of a personal life outside his fuck-fests.

At least, not that I know of.

I slide into the back of the limo, distracted; I don't think I even acknowledge Hughes, which is unusual because I like him and we usually have a nice banter going.

You know everything there is to know about me.

I'm startled. The words come from nowhere and

I look over my shoulder, half expecting to see Jack's cynical smile. Is that even true? Do I *really* know him that well?

We've spent a heap of time together, that's true. But I don't know if I would say I consider us well acquainted. Out of nowhere the memory of his lips on mine sears me, pressing me back into the leather seat with a groan.

I reach for the envelope, and now I give in to temptation, running my finger over his scrawled writing before tearing the top off.

My emotions are mixed as the object inside falls into my palm.

The distinctive dark red foil denoting a Cherry Ripe confectionery bar is instantly recognisable. I check the envelope for a note; there isn't one. But his meaning is clear.

I can't help it. I tear the paper off the bar and inhale.

Cherries will remind me of Jack forever. I don't think I can say I hate them anymore.

My gut clenches as I recall the intimate way his finger circled me, teasing every nerve ending, finding where to press to make me moan.

Fuck.

A shiver dances along my spine and it is still pulsing even as the car pulls into the underground car park of the City high-rise that houses Jack's offices. I gather he used to be based here a lot more. It was only after Lucy died that he set up shop, so to speak, at his home.

I make a point of smiling brightly at Hughes as I step out of the limo, laden with documents.

'Need a hand, ma'am?'

'I'm fine,' I demur.

I can't help but wonder if my cheeks are burning after the delicious thoughts that have travelled along with me.

Why did he stop? What happened to push him away from me?

I wanted everything. I wanted *him*. That technically makes me a complete idiot, right? Because I know he's a total man-whore, and I know it would make my job pretty untenable to be fucking Jack, but in that moment none of it had mattered.

Which only goes to show that I need to be even more on my guard with him.

I am *not* going to let this get out of hand. There are plenty of hot guys out there. Plenty of men who can kiss you like you're their dying breath.

Except I don't think that's necessarily true...

I've dated a fair few guys—most of them smart, handsome, powerful. I have a thing for that sort of man, I suppose. But none of them has done *this* to me. My mind is still mushy. I only have to close my eyes and remember the way it felt to have his body pressed hard to mine, almost holding me up with the weight of his strength, and I'm having palpitations and flushing to the roots of my hair.

The lift whooshes up and reminds me of the glass elevator in *Charlie and the Chocolate Factory*. It seems to be building up speed as we get nearer the top, and my tummy lurches as I imagine it bursting through the ceiling and flying into outer space.

It doesn't.

Is it wrong that I'm just a teeny bit disappointed? I always thought that looked to be so much fun—the way that elevator flew all over London's skyline.

The offices are buzzing, and it's so strange to be back in this kind of environment that I freeze for a moment, simply soaking in the noises. Anywhere else I've worked, it's been like this. I was like a headless chicken most days, surrounded by people who were every bit as harried and exhausted as I was. Exhaustion used to bleed into energy, so that I fed off a state of perpetual tiredness.

Someone rushes past, arms full of papers, and that reminds me that I need to do something with the files I'm carrying. I begin moving quickly down the carpeted corridor, eyes straight ahead lest I be called upon to answer a query. The problem with being Jack's right-hand woman is that people see me as a substitute for him. I cannot visit this office without being waylaid with a dozen queries at least. Only I don't feel like talking to anyone at this point in time.

The conference room is at the end of the corridor. Two enormous timber doors provide entry to it. I shoulder my way in, making straight for the table, and I've just dropped the files down onto its glass top when I realise I'm not alone.

There's a movement to my right. No, a shadow more than a movement. But it captures my eye and I turn around slowly, careful to keep my expression neutral, because deep down I know who it is.

'You're here already,' I murmur, pleased with how unaffected I sound.

Especially when he's wearing his charcoal Armani suit with a crisp white shirt. And a dark grey tie. *Oh, God, help me.* I turn around, on the pretext of straightening the documents, but I feel the moment he starts to walk towards me and sweep my eyes shut.

My heart is pounding and my blood is gushing. What happened to pretending not to be affected by him? To keeping him at a distance?

'I'd say it's quicker to get here from City Airport than it is from my place.'

His voice is barely above a growl. It's primal and animalistic and a slick of heat runs through me.

'How was Tokyo?' I skirt around the table, laying information packs down as I go, checking each space has a glass of water.

He shrugs. 'Fine. And here?'

But his eyes are dropping. He's looking at my breasts as though he wants to take them into his mouth. As though he's remembering the way it felt to suck my nipple through the fabric of my shirt.

I moan, low and soft, so soft I don't think he catches it, but his lips flicker and I am in serious trouble. They are beautiful lips. Not full, but rather sculpted as if from stone. His face is peppered with stubble, as though he hasn't shaved the whole time he's been away.

I turn away, my breath uneven. I don't know what to do.

'As usual,' I say, no longer dispassionate, no longer smooth. My voice is jerky and unnatural.

I want to kiss him.

I *need* to kiss him.

I realise it in an instant and I turn around, back towards him. Our eyes meet and I feel a pulse of heat that I know I'm not imagining. It's a need so deep, so desperate, that I instantly imagine us fucking on the glass-topped conference table.

Is he thinking the same thing?

He takes a step towards me, his eyes latched to mine, his expression almost haunted. I part my lips on a breath and he stops just in front of me, catching that breath with his chest, and I can almost feel his lips on mine. It's a phantom kiss, but no less mesmerising than a real kiss because he's so close I can smell him…I can feel the warmth emanating from him.

'Did you get the chocolate bar?' he asks, and I feel my skin heat with memories.

I nod.

'Did you miss me?'

His voice is low and hoarse. I should laugh at him. That's what I would usually do. So why does his question fill me with a dawning despair? I can't ignore it. I'm suffocating under the realisation that I *have* missed him.

'Yeah, right,' I mutter, hoping it sounds more convincing to him than it does to me. 'I've been sitting in my office pining for you every day. One kiss and I've been writing your name in my notebook with little love hearts around it.'

I roll my eyes for good measure and so miss the moment he narrows his.

Jack isn't a man to be mocked. I know that, but honestly I wasn't intending to goad him. And yet I'm in no way surprised when his mouth crashes down on mine—for real this time, nothing phantom about it.

His hands pull through my hair, letting it out of the bun I looped it into earlier this morning. His fingers fist around it, holding my head under his so that his mouth has full access to me. And he *plunders* me. There's no other way to describe it. His mouth is a weight on mine and his tongue is angry.

Fierce heat pools between my legs.

He pulls on my hair as his mouth pushes mine, bending me backwards until my spine is on the conference table.

'Did you miss me?' It's a demand now, as he separates my legs and stands between them.

His cock is hard. I can feel it and unconsciously I writhe lower, trying to press myself against him, to connect myself to him.

His laugh is a dark imitation of the sound. 'Not now.'

It's a gruff warning, but insanity is cutting across me. I need him. If I don't have him I am going to scream. Sense is gone. Rational thought impossible. Even my brain seems to have momentarily forgotten itself.

I'm wearing a grey woollen dress and he rubs his hand over my breast, cupping it, holding me tight as his fingers graze my nipple. The fabric of the dress is coarse and the friction is unbearable.

His kiss is an insufficient prelude. I need so much more.

'More?' he murmurs, and I realise I must have spoken aloud.

He pushes my dress up my legs, and groans when he connects with the lace tops of my stockings. He digs a finger under one of my suspenders and then snaps it, hard, so that I make a sound of complaint. It's quickly muffled by a groan of pleasure as his fingers find my panties, pulling them roughly down my legs.

He stares at me and I wonder if I look as wanton as I feel. Hair tumbling around me like a golden halo, face pink, dress hitched up around my waist, legs spread around him.

His eyes are mocking as they meet mine. 'Haven't missed me, huh?'

I know I should say something sassy, pithy. Put him in his place. If his hard-on is anything to go by he's missed me, too. Or fantasised about me, at least.

'Like a hole in the head,' I murmur, but it's lacking spark.

He laughs, his hands firm around my calves as he spreads my legs wider, and before I can anticipate what he's going to do he brings his mouth down on me, running his tongue across my opening, lashing me with that same intensity he's just kissed me with. He pummels me, his tongue flicks my clit, and I am crumbling. I arch my back and stretch my arms over my head, my whole body trembling as wave after wave of need builds inside me. I'm so close to coming that I have to bite down on my lip to stop myself crying out.

'Have you missed me?'

He brings his mouth higher, dragging his tongue over my belly button, and his fingers push my dress up my body. His fingers find one of my nipples through the fabric of my lace bra and I jerk, because I am too sensitive already. I am only seconds from falling apart.

'Please…' I groan, moving my hips nearer to him, needing him to release me from this sensual torture.

'Please what?' he asks with a quiet anger I don't understand.

'Please,' I insist.

'Say it.'

Our eyes clash; it's a battle of the wills. I don't care enough to try to win it. At one time I would have fought tooth and nail, but not now. Now only one thing matters to me.

'Fuck me, Jack.'

'Here? In the boardroom at my office?'

I am going to hell. I don't even want to think about what my brain's going to have to say.

'Yes. Now. Please. Fuck me,' I whimper, so hot that I need him to *do* something. To fix this.

I drop my hand to my clit, but when I touch myself he grabs my wrist and pulls it away.

'No, that's cheating,' he whispers, his eyes on me as he loosens his belt and pushes his pants down just enough to release his gorgeous, glorious cock for me to see. I've seen it so many times, but now…? It's for *me*.

'Please…'

His eyes hold mine as he layers protection over his length, quickly, easily.

I push forward on the table, seeking him, and then he thrusts inside me, slamming me hard, and I feel the coiling of a pleasure that I cannot control. It is hot and fierce, and I cry out at the invasion that is so much better than my wildest fantasies.

His hands on my shoulders pull me up; he's so strong and I am lost in the moment. He pulls me against him and lifts me off the table so I can take him deeper, and I have a fleeting moment of gratitude for the heavy tint on the windows that surround the boardroom. His cock is spearing me, and I am wrapped around him, and he kisses me again—a kiss of such ownership and possession that I don't think I'll ever be able to lie to him again.

I *did* miss him.

'You want this?' he asks me, lifting my hips easily, gliding me up his length before pushing me down and making me cry out, my back arched, my nipples hard.

I nod.

'I didn't hear that.'

'I want this,' I groan, my fingers tearing through his hair, my mind completely scattered.

His laugh is throaty as he lifts me once more, but this time he eases me down to the floor, stroking up my dress as he goes.

I know outrage must show in my face, and I know he appreciates that.

'You want me.'

Mortification, anger and impatience are firing bullets across my desire.

I reach down and cup his hard-on, my eyes issuing him with a challenge. 'And you want me.'

He nods slowly, his eyes locked to mine. There is

no mockery there now; instead I see something darker. Resentment.

'I want you.'

He turns away from me, pulling his pants up, buckling his belt, his shoulders set square.

He turns to face me, his expression suddenly businesslike. 'We'll talk after the meeting.'

I blink. The meeting. *Shit.* It's the reason I'm here but how quickly I've forgotten its existence.

My eyes fly to the clocks on the wall, each showing a different time zone. There are minutes to go before the others are expected, which means they could literally arrive *now.* I run my hands down my dress, then neaten my hair. No time to pin it back into a bun so I just smooth it with the palms of my hands until it sits neatly around my face.

I turn to face him, intending to ask for my underpants back. But the look he gives me is so fulminating that I lose my voice.

'You look like you've just been fucked,' he says darkly, and I sweep my eyes shut, shame spiralling through me.

What the hell has come over me?

I stalk towards him, my hand extended, waiting for the scrap of lace he must have somewhere, but he grabs my hand and jerks me against him once more.

'I like the way you taste.'

And he pushes me against the glass, and his hand pushes between my legs, and he pads a thumb over my clit. I'm already at breaking point. His body traps mine, but he doesn't kiss me. He watches me from a distance as he torments me with his thumb, moving faster until my breath is ragged and my eyes are huge.

'I want to taste you tonight. I want to spread your legs and dip my tongue inside you. Then I want to flip you over and take you from behind. You are so fucking hot when you're turned on.'

I whimper—a sound of pure confusion—because the pleasure of his words combined with the torment of his touch is almost more than I can bear.

I swear—a low, throbbing whisper—as my pleasure bursts like a waterfall. I come. I come hard. And as I do he slips a finger deep inside me, swirling it against my walls as my muscles contract. He stays there as I fall apart and then he glides his finger out and lifts it to his mouth, sucking on it while his eyes watch me.

The door is pushed inwards. It happens so quickly. I am still breathless, and I'm sure my orgasm is written all over my face. It's not like it was my first time, but this was *Jack*. He's Jack Grant—seriously sexy.

He should come with a health warning.

I hear my colleagues move into the room and I turn away on the pretext of getting myself a coffee from the back of the room.

He still has my underwear, and the tops of my legs are wet with the evidence of my own satisfaction. My breath is uneven.

God, this is going to be the longest hour of my life.

'Gem.'

Is that what everyone in the universe except me calls her? Her back has been towards me for at least three minutes and I've gone through the greetings and I'm waiting for her to turn around. I want to see her full red lips, her messy hair, her passion-soaked expression, and I want to know that I did that to her.

She angles her head sideways to greet Barry Moore, one of the transition team consultants on the Tokyo deal. 'Hey...'

Her smile is cool, her expression calm. The only sign that she was ravaged by me only minutes ago is that her nipples are straining against the fabric of her dress—something that might be explained by the ice-cold air conditioning.

'You did a great job on the summaries—thanks.'

'You got my email, then?' Her voice is calm and clipped, as always, those haughty, aristocratic syllables like plums in her mouth.

'On the flight over.' He nods, his eyes briefly dipping to her breasts so that I am flooded by an urgent need to bodily shove him aside.

'Jack? Shall we begin?'

I draw my attention away reluctantly, turning to the manager of the takeover team. 'Yes. Take a seat.'

I nod towards the table and find myself drawn to one seat in particular. I press my hands to the tabletop, right where Gemma's legs were spread, and my eyes seek hers.

She meets them with fierce resentment.

She's pissed at me.

I just made her come in what I gather to have been a spectacular fashion and she's angry with me. Mind you, I guess I didn't really choose my time or place well. Leaving her breathless and wet right as some of the company's most senior staff filed into the room might explain her anger with me.

I sit down, my eyes not shying away from hers.

She chooses a seat at the other end of the table, on the opposite side. I cross an ankle over my knee and something catches my eye. Something dark and small. With a smile, I reach down and lift her underpants off the floor, palming them thoughtfully.

Her eyes are watching me and I see embarrassment creep along her cheeks, creating a hole in the armour of her professional composure. Her beautiful neck moves visibly as she swallows. And while I have her attention I lift my finger to my mouth and run it over my lower lip thoughtfully, tasting her openly.

Even from this distance I hear her sharp intake of breath and I smile.

I'm going to make her do that a *lot*.

CHAPTER FOUR

'I BELIEVE YOU have something of mine.'

Like my dignity. My self-control.

The meeting took almost two hours, and I managed to concentrate for the most part. But every now and again my insides would clench, reminding me that Jack had driven himself inside me—that he'd made me come against the glass windows of his boardroom and he hadn't experienced the same pleasure. I should have felt satisfied by that, but instead I was annoyed. Like he had proved how easily he could tear me apart and I hadn't done the same to him.

'Yeah…'

His smile makes my heart pound. Desire is slick in my blood, heavy and needy.

'So?' I put my hand out, then retract it, remembering belatedly that he has a habit of yanking me towards him when I give him the chance.

'So…' He reaches into his pocket and retrieves the underpants. 'I like the idea of you not wearing them.'

I roll my eyes. 'What a cliché. Do you expect me to dress a certain way for you from now on?'

His smile is a flicker at the corner of his lips. 'No…'

He wraps an arm around me easily, pulling me to him. Of course he doesn't need my hand as an invitation. He has arms and hands of his own, and if he wants to touch me Jack Grant isn't going to wait for a bloody invitation.

'But if you did I'd enjoy doing what we just did over and over.'

I'm wet again. I can feel it building and I know that only fucking him—properly—is going to release this beast of need inside me. But I'm still fuming with Jack. How dare he do that to me right before an important meeting?

'No way,' I snap. 'Never again.'

He raises a brow, his smile genuinely amused. 'Really?'

And he reaches around for my hand, dragging it to his cock. I stare at him, challenging him, showing him I'm not afraid, as he curls my fingers around his length, rock hard inside his suit pants. My heart begins to bang into my ribs so hard that I absent-mindedly wonder if anyone has ever broken a bone that way.

'You *don't* want me to sprawl you out on the table and fuck you so hard you forget your own name?'

I want that so badly—but I have enough self-respect to know that he's playing with me. That the way he can knock me sideways is insulting.

And so I shrug. 'I think you've got a pretty fucking exaggerated idea of your abilities in bed.'

His laugh sends sparks of warnings through me. 'Really?'

'I'm not telling you anything you don't already know.'

I jerk away from him but my hand forms a fist; it wants to go back. To grab his cock and hold it tight.

'You want a demonstration of how wrong you are?'

'Arrogant son of a bitch...' I mutter, my eyes scanning the room until they land on my vintage Balenciaga bag.

I scoop it up, sending him a fulminating look. 'Keep them.'

I want him to chase me. To follow me and slam the door shut. To press me against it and moan into my mouth. To beg me to get on the floor and let him take me. Because at the smallest sign of conciliatory, normal behaviour I would do anything Jack asked of me.

But he doesn't.

I leave and I don't even know if he watches me go—I am too proud to turn around and check. My knees are shaking as I make my way through the corridor. It's only early afternoon, and I have a mountain of work to do, but suddenly I'm not in the mood.

I don't want to be near Jack.

Oh, really? my brain prompts sarcastically, rolling its eyes with such force that my head starts to throb. *Really?*

Really.

I jab my finger onto the lift's 'down' button and wait. As I step in I see Jack emerge from the boardroom, looking every bit the confident billionaire bachelor.

Ugh.

I press the button for the car park impatiently, and slam my palm against the 'door shut' button, holding my breath and praying I can avoid a shared lift ride with Jack to the basement. I'm not sure if I'd shout at him or jump him but neither is advisable.

I tell myself I'm glad when he doesn't arrive, jam his hand in the closing doors, out of breath from racing to catch me like men do in movies. The lift cruises downwards, taking my plummeting stomach with it.

Hughes is waiting in the limousine. I smile at him tersely as he steps out and opens the door for me, grateful to slide into the luxurious leather interior. I stare at the screen of my phone and that ridiculous sense that I might cry is back.

What the hell is happening to me?

I tap out a quick email to Sophia, asking her to clear the rest of my afternoon—from memory I had a phone conference scheduled and I'm really not in the mood. Nothing won't wait until tomorrow.

I double-check the itinerary I've been sent for the Australia trip—it's jam-packed, but that makes sense. Jack's too busy—and so am I, come to think of it—to go halfway around the world on holiday.

He's setting up an office in Sydney, which will start with a staff of almost four hundred to oversee two of the companies he's recently acquired there, as well as a winery in New Zealand that he's bidding on, should he be successful. It's a huge venture, and it's the first time I've been involved in anything like it.

Challenges like this are another reason I love working for Jack. Really, I was hardly qualified for this kind of job when I started working for him—my background in law and then banking give me excellent corporate insights, and yet this just works. He's always challenged me. Trusted me. Thrown down gauntlets and stood back to watch me pick them up.

He's doing it now, isn't he? Pushing me in ways I could never have imagined. But instead of meeting his challenge I'm acting like a terrified child.

A frown tugs at my lips. Why have I just run away from him? He wants to fuck me and I want that, too.

The car door opens abruptly and I tilt my head upwards, expecting to see Hughes's face. It's Jack instead, and he's visibly pissed off.

Ignoring the way my pulse immediately starts to fire in my veins, I send him a look of barbed curiosity. 'Yes? Can I help you?'

He doesn't answer. Instead he leans forward and taps on the glass that separates Hughes from us, then settles back into the seat beside me. The car glides out of its parking space, moving through the underground car park with finesse.

'Jack?' I snap, angling in my seat to face him fully.

'Not now.'

My eyebrows shoot upwards. Even for the dictatorial side of Jack, this is a tad too much. *'"Not now"?'*

'No.' He turns to face me, and there's such a searing...*something* in his expression that I blink several times, trying to understand him. This—us.

But I get *nada*.

'Okay, but I think we need to talk,' I respond after a moment.

He glares at me and my temper bubbles. 'I don't want to talk. I want to fuck.'

My jaw drops. 'You don't just get to *say* that!'

A muscle jerks in his cheek. He turns away from me, sits back in the seat, his body rigid, his face tight.

'Not another word.'

I'm not afraid of Jack. Not even a bit. Many times I've gone up against him, arguing my case until he either sees it my way or at least understands my perspective. I won't do that now. I'm too fond of Hughes, and the idea of subjecting him to the tirade I'm about to unleash doesn't appeal to me, so I bite my tongue—literally—curling my fingernails into my palms as I stare out at the City.

It takes me a moment to realise we're not going towards Hampstead.

'I want to go home,' I say coldly.

His look is one of silent impatience, but before he can say anything the car pulls into yet another underground car park and comes to a stop right near the lift.

I can't describe how lost and confused I feel. I'm a swirling tempest of rage and insecurity, uncertainty and doubt. It's as though I'm in the middle of a swamp, reeds tangled around my ankles, water rising.

I want to fight with him. I'm angry. But I don't know what about! Putting into words what I feel seems impossible.

And then he speaks.

'Come with me.'

Three simple words, but they are enough because there is a plea in their depths.

I nod slowly, and there's a plea in that, too. *Please don't hurt me. Please don't use me.* I haven't even realised I feel it until this moment, but the idea of becoming to Jack what all those other women are is unpalatable. I weigh that against my need for him, and desire wins. I can only hope I won't regret it.

He pushes the button for the lift and then swipes a keycard. Soon the elevator is soaring towards the heavens—I'm in another lift, only this time with Jack Grant by my side.

'Am I allowed to talk now?'

He glares at me, then stares ahead until the lift doors open.

I guess not.

I stand with my hands on my hips, angrily admonishing him with my look. 'Nuh-uh. I'm not getting out until you tell me what's going on.'

'What's *going on*?' His tone shows incredulity.

He turns back into the elevator and lifts me easily, throwing me over his shoulder in a way I have only ever fantasised about. He carries me into an apartment—a palatial space. I gain a brief impression of glass, steel, white leather furniture and a state-of-the-art kitchen before he's storming down a tiled hallway and turning into a room.

A bedroom.

With an enormous bed in the centre and floor-to-ceiling windows that show a glinting view of London below.

'You are driving me crazy—that's what's going on. And I don't want to want you like this. I'm sick of waking up about to fucking explode because I've been dreaming about you. I'm sick of looking at you and imagining you naked every time we're in the same damned room.'

He drops me onto the bed but I'm too shocked by his angry confession to care. So he *does* feel it, too— this burning, all-consuming, unwanted, unwelcome, unasked-for need.

'So, if it's all the same to you, I want to fuck you properly—right out of my head—so we can go back to working together like damned adults instead of horny teenagers.'

My breath is burning my lungs, exploding out of me in fierce bursts. 'You think you can *fuck me out of your head*?'

'Yes.' He stares down at me, flicking his shirt open button by button.

My eyes follow his movement and though I've seen him naked before it was never like this. He's never been naked *for me*.

'Why? Why now?'

'Because I need you *now*.'

Still, my brain is shouting at me and, having ignored it in the past and had it lead me into disastrous temptation, I push up on my elbows and roll off the other side of the bed.

His eyes stay trained on me even as he continues to undress, and my throat is dry, parched. I feel like I've been dropped from a great height; I'm in free fall with nothing to grab. Gravity no longer exists.

'How *dare* you? You drag me here, to your…your… lair…' I spit angrily, only to have Jack burst out laughing.

'My *lair*?' He throws his head back.

He's so sexy. God, this isn't fair. I know what I should do. I know what I *need* to do. But he is laughing at me, and my pride is being thumped with each sound he makes.

I jump back onto the bed, storm across it quickly and step off the other side, surprising him with the force of my body against his, knocking him partway to the floor. He catches his balance, his hands steadying me even as I keep on pushing until we are at the wall.

'I'm not some nuisance you can get rid of. An itch you can scratch and lose.' I push a fingernail into his chest and glare up at him, my eyes firing at his.

'So what *are* you?' he demands roughly, his chest moving with each strained breath. 'Why are you all I can think of lately? Why do you consume my every damned waking thought? What sort of magic is this?'

I have needed to hear these words and they fill me with something I don't understand. There is awe and confusion, and anger, too—because he is just like Mr Darcy, telling me he loves me against his will.

Only Jack's not promising love so much as sex, and Mr Darcy would *never* have made Elizabeth Bennet come pressed hard against a glass window on the forty-second floor of a high-rise in the City of London.

You know what else Lizzy wouldn't have done…?

I drop to my knees in front of him, and before he can guess what I want, or say anything to stop me, I move my mouth over his length, taking him deep—so deep that I feel him connect with the back of my throat.

'Holy hell, Gemma,' he groans, but he doesn't pull away.

His hands drop to my hair, tangling in its blond lengths. It is still wild around my face from when he almost fucked me in his office. His fingers pull at it and I glide my mouth over his shaft, rolling my tongue across its tip and tasting just enough of him to make my insides clench with fevered desire. I squeeze my fingers around his length and then take him deep inside my mouth again, my eyes travelling up his honed body to meet his. I see the swirling depths of emotion in them…I see that he is as lost as I am…and it is all that keeps me going.

If I'm going to feel like I have no clue who I am anymore then he should, too.

I move my mouth faster, rolling my tongue over his sensitive tip each time I am close to pulling away completely, and then his hands on my hair tighten, slowing me down, holding me still. His breath is rough, and I taste more of him spilling into my mouth.

I try to take him deeper but his fingers hold me still, the pressure on my scalp almost painful.

'This isn't going to end that quickly,' he says darkly, pulling me away completely and staring down at me before reaching beneath my arms and lifting me to stand. He stares into my eyes and there is so much triumph in my face that he must see it.

'Holy hell, Gemma,' he says again after a moment, and pulls me back towards the bed.

My heart twists achingly in my chest. He pushes me backwards, onto the middle of the mattress, and bends down, grabbing for something off the floor.

A second later I see what it is: his belt. He's naked—spectacularly so—and so hard and firm. He runs his hands over my arms, catching my wrists and pinning them over my head.

'Do you trust me?' he asks—deep, throaty, gravelled.

I shake my head but my lips are twitching. 'I trust you to make me come. I don't know if I trust you with anything else right now.'

His laugh is soft as he loops the belt in and out of the bedposts, and then grabs my wrists and incorporates them into it, pinning my arms behind me and above my head. It's not particularly comfortable.

'Then let me make you come again and again and again, Gemma.'

Gemma. The way he says my name like that—rich with passion and want—makes my body catch fire. Like it's not already an inferno!

He pushes at my dress, his hands on my thighs intimate. I still have no underwear on and he smiles to see my nakedness.

'You are beautiful,' he grunts, almost as though he's never noticed me before.

He brings his mouth down against me and I jerk my arms, wanting to touch him.

He laughs. 'And you're mine.'

Butterflies ravage me angrily. I *am* his. For this moment...for this night. Is this how it always is with him? When he makes love to those other women does it feel to them as though they are the only woman in the world?

The idea of being one of *them* is anathema to me.

'Remember what I told you in the boardroom?'

He pushes the dress higher, over my breasts, then leaves it bunched under my arms while he turns his attention to the scrap of lace that covers me. He doesn't bother to unclasp it—just lifts my breasts out of the delicate cups, bringing his mouth close to one of them and breathing warm air over the sensitive, erect nipple.

I arch my back instinctively and he laughs. 'Do you want this?' he murmurs, flicking it with his tongue, then circling the darker flesh slowly, teasing me, taunting me.

I nod, incoherent with need. 'I want *everything*,' I say seriously.

'Everything?'

'All of this,' I agree, pulling at my hands again, not caring that I am conceding all that I am to him. 'Please,' I add.

'Do you remember what I said?'

He is insistent. What *did* he say? 'Not to wear underpants again?'

He laughs, and then his teeth clamp down on my nipple and I cry out. The pleasure radiates through my body, slick in my abdomen.

'That, too.'

He rubs his stubble over my nipple and it's so sensitive from his mouth that I make a soft sound of surprise.

'I said I am going to fuck you until you can't remember your own name. Okay?'

I nod. I am lost, and I need him to see that. 'What's happening to us?'

His smile is haunted as he slides a condom over himself once more. 'What's happening? I think I've finally found my cure—that's what's happening.'

And he thrusts into me, so deep and hard and fast that the peculiar statement is lost. *I* am lost. I jerk my wrists so that the belt pulls against my skin, and I cry out in frustration that I can't touch him like I want to.

He is so big, and his dick reaches places inside me that I didn't know existed. He moves his mouth to my other breast and lashes his tongue against me as he pounds me hard. My hands jerk above my head. I am his prisoner, but even without the belt at my wrists I would be.

'Are you on the pill?' he demands, and I nod.

I am incoherent with pleasure, saying his name over and over again. My body is on fire. He is its master. His hands are rough on my smooth skin. He touches me everywhere as he moves inside me, thrusting deep, and still I want more.

'Please!' I cry out, not even sure what I'm begging for now.

But he knows what I need. Somehow he has mastered my body already, even though we are so new to one another. He pushes inside me and rolls his hips. I lift mine to meet him and I'm exploding, falling apart and flying at the same time, dropping through the earth's core as my body tries to cope with these sensations.

I groan loudly, wrapping my legs around his waist,

holding him right where he is. But before the waves of my pleasure have begun to subside he guides my legs over his shoulders, so that I am bent over myself and he is so deep I see stars. Pleasure is tingling through me and he blows through it, rocking me in rhythm with his needs, kissing the sensitive flesh behind my knees before running his fingers lower to cup my arse.

I am shuddering with the strength of what he's doing to me. Then he pulls out, and I almost sob with the emptiness that threatens to cut me in half.

His laugh is dark. An acknowledgement that he understands.

His hands on my hips are strong; he flips me easily onto my stomach and my arms are crisscrossed, my dress tangled around my breasts and my neck.

I don't have time to tell him this, or to shift and adjust myself. He spreads my legs wide, puts an arm under my belly and lifts me higher. And then he drives into me from behind. He brushes against new nerves, makes me feel new things, and I gather from the muttered string of dark curses that fill the room that this is different for him, too.

His fingers dig into my hips as he holds me steady, thrusting into me and making me *different*, somehow. He drops forward, kissing my shoulder, dragging his mouth down my back before biting me on the arse— gently, but enough to make me groan. And then he's sucking the flesh at the small of my back, and I wonder if I'm going to have a mark there afterwards.

His finger between my arse cheeks surprises me. It is not somewhere I've been touched before, but it's only the lightest suggestion of a touch. A finger lightly pressing against my butt. A curious flash of wonder flies through me. But instinctively I shy away from it and he understands, laughing and moving his hand to my clit.

He strums me as though I am a guitar, and it's so intense that I almost cannot bear the pleasure. But I don't dare ask him to stop because perhaps he would and I couldn't bear that. It is like being prodded by a hot iron, though: I am burning up.

I explode angrily, loudly, my body shaking from head to toe, glistening with sweat.

He holds me tight, waiting for the waves to slow, to recede a little, and then runs his hands over my flat stomach to my neat breasts. He rolls my nipples between his finger and thumb, plucking them in time with his dick as he takes me again and again.

'It's not fair…' I moan, resting my head on the pillow, trying to catch my breath. 'I want *you* to feel this.'

He makes a noise. It could be agreement or amusement; I'm not sure. 'Do you think I'm not enjoying myself?'

No. I know he's having a good time. But that's not enough. I don't want to think I'm like all those other women, just being 'had' by him. I want to rock his goddamned world.

'Do I get to tie *you* up?' My words are as fevered as my sex-stormed soul.

He laughs and shakes his head, his chin gravelly against my back. 'No.'

'Why not? What's good for the goose isn't good for the gander?'

'Not in this case.'

'Isn't that a bit sexist?'

'You don't like it?'

My cheeks flame and I'm glad I'm facing away from him.

He brings the flat of his hand down on my arse, just lightly, but enough to spark the fire back into me, to make me forget what I want to do to him momentarily and enjoy what he's doing to me instead.

I push my arse higher and he massages me with his fingers, digging hard into the muscles there. I moan, low in my throat, and then he pushes inside me. I'm so wet. I drop my head lower and now he reaches up, unclipping the belt and freeing my wrists.

He pulls out of me. 'Turn around.'

A command. I obey, even though a part of me wants to tell him to stuff it purely as a point of pride.

Flat on my back, I stare up at him, my breath rushed, my lower lip sucked between my teeth.

'I want you to see what you do to me.' The admission is hoarse; as though drawn from deep in his throat.

He pushes my legs up again, lifting them over his shoulders as he drops into me, and I welcome him as though he's been absent for months, not moments. He laces his fingers through mine, pinning my arms either side of me, and he stares down at me as he takes me once more.

I sweep my eyes closed as another wave begins to build, but he drops his mouth to mine and pulls my lower lip between his teeth, pressing into it just enough to startle me into looking at him.

'I want to see you. And I want *you* to see me.'

Mesmerised, I can't look away. I watch as his face contorts with pleasure and he rocks inside me, and my own pleasure rides high with his until we are climaxing together, my body flaming to his, leaping with his, burning like his. It is him and me, and no one else in the world exists or matters.

He explodes inside me—a powerful release that makes him cry out loudly…a guttural sound that rips through the room. And I echo it deep within my soul. I am as overwhelmed as he.

He stays above me, his breath uneven, his eyes almost accusing as my own climax recedes, and I am left weak and confused by what the hell just happened to us.

I stare up at my boss, at the man who's just given me—I don't know…four orgasms? Five orgasms? I've lost count. It's still the afternoon and my body is covered in goose bumps.

Holy shit. Is this what it's like with his other women?

They are like ghosts, immediately hovering on my subconscious. I hate it that they're there, but my brain clearly needs me to remember them. To remember what Jack's like.

'So I suppose you don't get complaints after all,' I murmur, running my fingertips down his back. Like mine, it is wet with perspiration.

'Not so much.'

He pushes up, with a smile on his face that somehow doesn't fill his eyes. He presses a light kiss to my forehead and then stands.

'I'll get Hughes to take you home.'

The words seem to be spoken in a foreign language for all the sense they make to me. He'll get Hughes to take me home? Is he fucking *serious*? Am I being *dismissed*?

I smile, even as my mind is reeling from the sheer rudeness of that statement. 'I need to finish something at the office.'

I am amazed by myself. How do I sound so unbothered? So casual? It's a bald-faced lie, but it's the best I can come up with while my body is numbed by shock and fulfilled desire.

He nods. 'Fine. He can take you there.' Another tight smile. 'You're okay to let yourself out? I'm going to grab a shower.'

Jesus fucking Christ. *Is* he indeed?

'I think I can find a door without a map,' I drawl sarcastically, reaching for my phone without so much as a smile.

I flick it to life and load my emails, but the words swim before me like one big puddle of grey matter.

Which is what his brain is going to be against the crisp white wall if I don't get the hell out of there.

He walks towards a door across the room and I continue staring at my phone. Yet I know he's paused and is watching me. So I smile at an imagined joke on my phone, then pretend I'm typing a reply.

If you'd asked me an hour ago what could go wrong I would have said exactly this. Pushing past the boundaries we've always wisely obeyed, only to have Jack reinstating them just as fast as he's able—brick by brick, blocking me out.

My fingers move over my phone but I'm play-acting, doing what I can to distract him from the fissures running through my heart, my hopes and my confidence.

Eventually Jack moves into the bathroom and I hear the shower running.

Arsehole.

It might have been the best sex I've ever had, but I'm pretty sure it was also the biggest mistake of my life.

CHAPTER FIVE

'AMBER.' I SMILE, meeting the redhead's eyes with genuine interest.

Lucy's sister is ten years older than Lucy was, and she has the same pale skin and dainty features—at least going from the photographs I've seen. Her eyes are enormous and brown, her smile slow but genuine. She is naturally plump and attractive.

I like her instantly.

'The angelic Gemma,' she responds, her Scottish accent thick. 'I've been looking forward to meeting the woman who's tamed my brother-in-law.'

Tamed him? Not bloody likely.

Flashbacks of the previous afternoon flood my brain and I push them away. I cannot think about how it felt to be made love to by Jack Grant. No—*fucked* by him. Fucked hard. So hard, so hot... Oh, my God. My insides clench with remembered need. It's a visceral awareness, and actual biological need throbs through me on a cellular level. It's every bit as compelling and real as thirst, starvation and fear. It is a need strong enough to fell me at the knees.

I swallow, hoping to calm my raging, insatiable desire. 'I'm pretty sure he's untameable,' I say, with only a hint of desperation, gesturing that she should take a seat.

I've moved us to the small conference room on-site at The Mansion. Thankfully it's nothing like the office in the City, with its modern decor and imposing outlook. This is a room far more fitted to an ancient home on the edge of Hampstead. Still expensive, with luxurious leather recliners, but homely, somehow.

'Put up with him, then. You must have the patience of a saint.'

'I must,' I agree.

'Gemma is actually very impatient.'

His voice enters the room before he does, and I straighten in the chair.

'If I don't give her what she wants straightaway she begs me until I give in.'

My cheeks flame and I'm grateful that Amber is standing and moving across the room towards Jack—arsehole that he is. How *dare* he say something so bloody obvious? I know we're both thinking of how I begged him to make love to me the day before.

My eyes cling to Jack and Amber, morbidly fascinated, as they embrace. It's a hug of true affection and, yes, grief is there, too. He's wearing navy blue pants and a pale blue shirt which he's rolled up to just below the elbows. It's a linen material, and it's crinkled a little around the chest, showing he's been sitting in it for quite some time.

He keeps an arm around Amber's waist as they walk

deeper into the room. She takes an armchair opposite
me and he sits beside her, facing me, aligning himself with her.

They are family. I'm the outsider.

It hurts. Possibly even more than the showering-
straight-after-sex thing.

Did he need to drink copious measures of Scotch
to forget me last night?

My eyes drift to his face to find him watching me.
Intensely watchful, I would have to say, peeling away
my skin and analysing each beat of my heart.

I blink, careful not to react, and then turn back to
Amber. 'How's everything going with the launch preparation?'

'Aye, good. We're getting there. I've staffed the main
headquarters and we're just getting the international
charitable recognition worked out to allow foreign do-
nations.'

'Advertising?' Jack chimes in.

'We're meeting with two agencies next week to se-
lect a final campaign. It's looking like it will be print
and digital-heavy, with the possibility of sponsoring a
major sporting event over the summer—possibly the
cricket.'

Jack pulls a face. 'Bloody hell. The *cricket*?'

'Oh, come *on*. Lucy would have wanted it.' Amber
grins, pushing a finger into his shoulder in a further
sign of their casual camaraderie.

It's strange that I don't often think of Jack like
this—as a member of other spheres.

Here, it is him and me and the work we do together.

It consumes so much of my life that I must admit I'm surprised to realise he has other people, things, memories and hobbies. Jokes and history.

Did Lucy watch cricket while Jack groaned about it? Did they laugh about his aversion to any sport other than rugby?

I blank the thoughts—or try to. But they're gnawing at my mind, unfolding like a concertinaing piano accordion that's ever so slightly out of key.

'It'll be a good show,' Amber says loudly, her smile encouraging as she winks in my direction.

Despite the fact that she's forced me to walk through a door that shows me the ghosts of Jack's Happy Past, I like her immensely, and the more she speaks about the foundation the more I know we've absolutely made the right decision. She's intimately informed on all the matters I need to consult with her about. She's thorough and quick and funny. And she's uniquely motivated to make the fundraiser a success.

She's Lucy's sister, and Lucy is dead, but I am jealous of Amber suddenly. It's ridiculous. An emotion entirely unworthy. But watching her talk, with her big red lips and her animated face, I feel wan and boring in comparison.

I would have been bland compared to Lucy, too.

I look downwards as Amber launches into a description of the view from her office. I'm wearing one of my favourite dresses—a shift in olive-green with bell sleeves and a boat neck. Oh, but it's so conservative and drab! Just the kind of dress my mother would adore. I chose it for the length of the sleeves, which

fall to partway down my hands, because my wrists—
which I see I've now accidentally left uncovered—have
a dark band of bruising around them.

Belt-burn. *Thanks, arsehole.*

I nod at something Amber's said, my eyes moving
of their own accord to Jack's face.

He's looking at my wrists, too, and the colour has
drained from his face. I shift self-consciously, uncross-
ing and crossing my legs and drawing my sleeves lower
in the process.

'Amber, we can discuss the rest over lunch. I know
Gemma's got a desk full of crap to deal with.'

'*Your* crap!' Amber laughs good-naturedly, totally
relaxed.

'That's her job,' he says pointedly.

Amber rolls her eyes. 'How you put up with him is
beyond me.'

But she stands, straightening the crinkles out of the
front of her skirt as she moves towards me. I hold out
a hand to shake but she ignores it and pulls me into a
hug instead.

'We've spoken so many times I feel like I already
know you. But it's been lovely to finally meet you.'

'Likewise,' I murmur, stepping away from her with
cringe-inducing coldness. Something else my mother
would approve of! Standoffishness is a bland green
dress. *Great.* I'm everything I swore I'd never be.

'Gemma? I need a moment with you, please.' He
turns to Amber. 'Why don't you wait for me in the car?
This won't take long.'

'I have a few calls to make,' she says, and nods, clipping out of the room.

He walks behind her, but only so far as the door, which he pushes shut emphatically and slips the lock across with equal force. And then he is prowling towards me. Yes, *prowling*. That's absolutely the word.

I have about four seconds to pull myself together. Four seconds to ignore the hammering of my heart and the throbbing of my libido. Four seconds to remind myself that he's my boss, and a total ass to boot. To remember how I felt when he rolled off me and all but asked me to leave his bed not two minutes after deserting my body.

No one has the right to make me feel like that. *No one*. And certainly not twice.

'That went well,' I say efficiently, leaving no room for the personal. 'I'm thrilled she's going to be at the helm of the foundation.'

A muscle jerks in his cheek—as though he's grinding his teeth or something. He catches my wrists and lifts them, pushing my sleeves up my arms to reveal the full extent of my bruising. He closes his eyes as he runs his finger over them, as though fortifying himself to look properly.

'You're hurt.'

I swallow, not liking this side of him any more than I do the bastard side that showered as soon as he'd pulled out of me. This is scarier, because it's doing really odd things to my heart and my tummy, seeing him show this kind of humanity and compassion.

I jerk my wrists away. 'Yeah... Can't you tell? I'm

in agony.' I roll my eyes for good measure. 'It's just a couple of bruises.'

He nods, but there's a look in his face that I don't know if I ever want to see again. 'Listen, Gemma...' The way he says it rolls my stomach. 'About yesterday...'

'It's fine.' My smile is a flicker across my face and then it's gone. 'I *know* you.'

He shakes his head. 'No, you don't understand.' His frown is one of frustration. 'Let me explain.'

I swallow. *Be strong. Remember Shower Gate.* 'You don't need to explain,' I say firmly.

Please don't let him explain. Without an explanation there's ambivalence. But if I have to listen to his regrets, worse, his apology...?

'It was good. I had fun. Let's leave it at that.'

I walk towards the door, needing an escape. My legs are unsteady and my throat is parched and sore—like it's been flamed with a blowtorch. I walk away from him because my sanity depends on distance.

But this time he follows. He puts a hand on either side of me as I reach the darkly panelled door, so that I'm trapped by him. I freeze, staring straight ahead while my body goes into overdrive, his nearness impossible to ignore.

'You want to leave it at that?' he asks, his hand dropping to my hip.

I close my eyes, waiting for the hammering of my pulse to slow. As if it's going to.

'You want to forget what that felt like? Never do it again?' His fingers run lower, down my leg to the hem of my dress. 'Say the word and I'll step backwards. I'll stop touching you. For good.'

I nod, but 'the word' clogs my throat.

'Spread your legs apart.'

You do that and I am outta here. Love from your brain.

'Jack…' I say, his name thick and hoarse.

'I've been wondering all morning,' he says quietly. 'Did you listen to me?'

And his hand creeps under my dress, up my leg towards my bottom, where he finds the fabric of my knickers and flicks at it, hard enough to make me jerk.

'No, you didn't. Shame… Because if you weren't wearing underwear I could take you right now. Here against the door. Would you like that, Gemma?'

I groan, completely frozen by the imagery of his words.

'I'm going to fuck you now unless you tell me not to.'

Not only can I not find the words, I nod my head in total surrender. I hear his exhalation of breath and smile weakly. I move to turn around, but he keeps his hands on my hip—firm.

'No. Like this.' And he pulls me backwards, bending me at a ninety-degree angle.

He doesn't remove my underpants. He links both hands around them and pulls until they tear, dropping them to the ground.

I stare at them with surprise and impatience. 'They were really expensive,' I say darkly.

'They were in my way.'

I hear him unzip his trousers, then the familiar

sound of foil being torn, rubber being snapped onto his length, and then he's inside me. No preamble, but— let's face it—the whole morning's been a total exercise in tantric delay. He runs his hands over my back as he thrusts into me and I splay my fingers wide against the door, my body taking his possession as though it's what I need to stay alive.

I am hot and cold all over, and about to come when he pulls out. It is so like the torment of the day before—the utter outrageous shock of desolation—that I cry out hoarsely into the room.

'You'd better not fucking stop,' I say angrily.

He straightens me and turns me around, pushing me hard against the door and kissing me until my knees are about to give way.

'Think of that as an IOU.' He pulls away, his eyes meshing with mine. 'One I intend to collect.' He scoops down and grabs my underwear, dangling the scrap of fabric by one finger. 'And no more of this.'

I gape at him. 'Is that an order, *sir*?'

'You'd better damned well believe it.'

'Okay, I'll call HR and have it added to my contract.'

He kisses me again and my body sways towards his; I give up the sass immediately.

'Fuck me more,' I say into his mouth.

'Wild horses won't stop me.' It's a growl. 'Later.'

Five minutes later, I'm staring at my desk, a frown on my face.

What just happened?

It's like some kind of cyclone came into the room

and settled down on top of us. All that's needed is for us to be close to one another and *bam!* The world loses its usual governance and we are wild, unshackled animals.

I tilt my head forward, catching it in my hands.

I've never felt like this.

I've always been able to control the men in my life, and I've always, *always* known what I want from them. Relationship decisions have, historically, been made by the same part of my brain that runs my career and all other aspects of my life.

I know some people talk about 'love at first sight', but that's always been a good clue to me that those people are batshit crazy.

Oh, I'm not saying I think I'm in love with Jack! I'm sexually tormented, not a sadist, and loving Jack would be stupid. But I don't have any brainpower or willpower around him.

He has all the power. *Sex* power. It makes me uneasy to acknowledge that and to accept that I would walk headfirst into whatever it is we're doing just to be with him some more. He's that good.

My body is a livewire, arcing through space, waiting to be grounded by him. But he doesn't ground me—he flares me into a violent electrical storm.

I drive him crazy, too. I remember, in a drowning attempt to have faith in my own abilities, that when I went down on him he was mine. Completely.

I don't think Jack welcomes this development any more than I do. I think his brain is probably giving him as hard a time as my own... What we had before *worked*. Sure, I pretty much had to pull up my big girl pants in the form of Maid Marian's chastity belt to make sure I didn't give in to the sexy man-pull of Jack Grant. But professionally we're a great team.

And losing that is far riskier for him. I'll get another job when I want one—I'm forever being head-hunted, in fact.

My frown deepens as I open my second drawer and rifle through it, my fingers curling around the card of the most persistent caller. Andrew Long from Saatchi & Long. He's offered me some seriously awesome job opportunities in the last year, and every time I demur he tells me I must be on an incredible package.

Little does he know! I *am* very well-paid; Jack knows he can't afford to lose me. But, more than that, I get to stare at Jack-fucking-Grant all day.

Oh, God.

This is hopeless. I scrape my chair back, dropping Andrew's card back into the drawer and pushing it closed, scooping my bag up and pulling the strap over my shoulder.

'I'm going out,' I call as I pass Sophia and Rose. 'Back soon.'

Sophia waves in acknowledgement. I keep walking, my bare ass making me feel both turned on and self-conscious as I step out into the weather. It's cold, but I forgot my coat and I don't really care.

'Ma'am?' Hughes straightens from where he's been leaning beside the limo.

'Do you just lounge about out here all day, waiting for me to walk past?' I ask teasingly. I know how busy he is.

'Better than watching paint dry. You can actually *walk* in those things?'

He nods down at my Louboutins with a smile on his lips. They're two-inch spike heels and, yes, I'm very, very good in heels.

'I could run a marathon in them,' I say, and wink. My hair is in a ponytail today and the wind blows past, flicking it against my cheek.

'Well, save yourself the effort today.' He reaches for the door handle. 'Where to?'

I look at him blankly. It's a fair question; one to which I have no answer. 'I'm just going to go for a walk,' I explain. 'I need a coffee.'

'A coffee?' His look is one of sardonic amusement. 'You mean that spaceship's stopped working?'

I shake my head. The high-end pod machine Jack's had installed makes great coffee and we both know it. 'Okay, you caught me. I want a *pain au chocolat*.'

'Really?' He grins, arching a brow. 'A weakness for patisserie goods…interesting.'

I shrug. 'Certain days,' I say in explanation.

'Say no more.'

'See you soon,' I say in farewell. Then, as an after-thought, 'Need anything?'

'No, ma'am.'

So, I've banged her against a door in the conference room of my home office *and* against a window of my boardroom in the City. And while my sister-in-law was waiting in the car for me, too.

Jesus.

The Gemma Conundrum is getting out of hand. I woke up this morning knowing I had to apologise for yesterday, to tell her I'd regretted having sex with her the second we were done. That it had been a colossal, asshole mistake.

And then she walked away from me and I panicked.

Apparently Gemma only listens when I'm inside her.

So? What? I'm going to have sex with her any time we disagree? Any time she gets annoyed?

Amber laughs at something and I smile, but my mind is on Gemma and the promise I made her—that I'd collect on my IOU later today. The thought of not doing so makes some part of me want to shrivel up. So I accept the inevitable. We're going to fuck again.

My cock tightens instantly, straining against the fabric of my pants. Is she still naked beneath her dress, waiting for me? Wanting me?

I sip my wine, and say something in response to Amber's question—I'm amazed that any part of my brain is ticking on as normal, absorbing what's being said and answering in kind, even while most of me is absorbed by the question of my assistant.

I *love* sex. I love it because it lets me forget about Lucy and what I no longer have. But Gemma is different—because I can't just fuck her and walk away for good. I have to see her every morning—and what if she starts to want more from me than I can possibly give?

'Hey, Grandma.' I can't help but smile as she answers the phone in her sunny little room.

I hear her sip her tea and imagine her lips smiling against the bone china rim. 'What's up, lovey?'

'Nothing's up. How are you?'

'It's the middle of the day on Friday and you're calling me. What's up?'

I shake my head, but those damned tears that have been dogging me for days are threatening to fall. I blink my eyes angrily, staring at a family as they walk past me. Mum and Dad holding hands and three small children of varying degrees of growth and ruggedupness run past, looking as though they're being pulled back by a magnetic force when all they want is to sprint along.

'And is that birdsong in the background?'

I bite into the *pain au chocolat*; crumbs flake down my front. Absent-mindedly I brush them aside. 'I'm on the Heath.'

'You mean you've unshackled yourself from that desk?'

I laugh. 'Yes, Grandma. From time to time I *do* get out.'

'Have you spoken to your mother recently?'

I furrow my brow. Grandma is the only person on earth who understands my relationship with my parents. She understands that I love them, but in a dutiful way—they did give me life, after all. They also gave me self-doubt and insecurity and a sense that I'd never be good enough for anything other than the life they envisaged for me. Grandma tunnelled me right out of that existence, though.

'Not for a week or so.' Actually, it's closer to a month. 'You?'

'They called yesterday. They're in Cambodia.'

I arch a brow, imagining my perfectly manicured, elegant mother in Cambodia, of all places. 'I trust the Shangri-La's penthouse is sufficient?'

Grandma laughs. 'Well, you know—they're doing volunteer work.'

I burst out laughing at this ongoing joke between us. My parents are incredibly wealthy, incredibly entitled aristocrats and they have apparently reached a point in their life where they're bored with that and are looking to 'make the world a better place'. So far this has involved paying a lot of money to buy shoes for children in Africa, travelling to Lithuania to learn about child smuggling and now a trip of Southern Asia to 'help provide vaccinations' to the poor.

I wonder how helpful my mother—who faints at the sight of blood—and my dad—who can't stand heat, mosquitos or poverty—are actually capable of being.

'I think they're going to cut their trip short,' Grandma says, almost managing to keep the droll amusement out of her voice.

'Oh, I'm *so* surprised by that.' I fail miserably. 'I daresay the philanthropic community of Cambodia will breathe a sigh of relief when they board their flight home.'

'Yes, well… Their hearts are in the right places,' she murmurs, and I nod.

Perhaps.

'They'd do better to donate to a foundation,' I say.

'Money is what these people need. And then trained staff can do their jobs without westerners assuaging their guilt over the quality of our lives getting in the way.'

'Phew, that's been building up for a while, has it?'

'Sorry. I just can't stand volunteer tourism. If I see one more photo of a schoolfriend posing with emaciated children in Africa I'm going to punch something.'

'Darling, it all brings attention to good causes.'

'Yeah—and it makes rich people feel better about their rarefied existence in the process.'

'Mmm...'

Grandma is nodding. I just know it.

'So nothing's going on, then?' she asks.

The children on the Heath are running now, and the mother and father are watching, holding hands, laughing as the littlest one tumbles down and lands in the middle of some wet grass. One of the older siblings scoops him up, cradling him and spinning in circles until the little one's laughter peals across the grass towards me, hitting me like a slap in the face.

I'm not clucky. I don't want children. The agony of my own childhood is one I would never inflict on another. Oh, it's not like I was abused or anything. My parents loved me. Loved me enough to hire only the best nannies and tutors and horse-riding coaches. To send me to the very best schools... Clue: the best schools for meeting handsome, eligible husbands-to-be.

And they loved me enough to question my sanity when I enrolled in joint honours at Oxford and then post-grad at the LSE. But there was Grandma in the front row when I accepted my Master's degree.

'I'm just flat out,' I say quietly. 'Work's crazy at the moment.'

Grandma is quiet, taking this in. Then, 'You're coming for lunch tomorrow?'

Tomorrow? *Shit*. It's almost the weekend. But the idea of seeing Grandma makes my heart soar. 'Lunch? Yeah, sure.'

'And you'll bust me out of this hellhole again? Take me out for so much champagne I get woozy and disgraceful?'

I laugh, because the 'hellhole' nursing home Grandma is in costs more per year than most people earn in a lifetime and is the last word in luxury. She has a *personal butler*, for crying out loud. But the staff there don't entirely approve of her love of bubbles, whereas I am more than happy to serve as her occasional enabler.

'Yep. You betcha.'

I stand up, giving one last look at the family as they move over the crest of a hill and disappear out of sight, then I walk across the grass, making my way to the gate nearest the lane that leads to Jack's mansion.

I try not to think about whether Jack will be in the office when I get back.

CHAPTER SIX

It's just as well I'm busy. Between running one last glance over the Wyndham contracts, checking the files I'll need and locking down the details for Australia, responding to some urgent emails and looking at some high-level staff CVs for the foundation, the day passes quickly.

It is evening before I know it and I am still at my desk. My phone bleeps just as I'm packing up.

I'm in the City. Hughes will bring you here when you're done.

I read the text three times, my bemusement growing with each moment. True, I'd basically begged him to fuck me earlier that day, but this is hardly a masterpiece in flirtation and seduction.

Do you need me for something?

I fire the message back, lifting my bag over my shoulder and switching the lights off at the door.

You know what I need you for.

I don't reply. I don't know why. But I make my way outside and smile at Hughes—possibly the only guy in the company who works hours as long as Jack and mine. He doesn't have a family. He was in the army and returned from three tours of Iraq ready for a change. He's smart, safe and we trust him implicitly.

We.

I do that a lot, but I don't mean 'we' in a romantic sense. It's just that we've almost become partners over the years without either of us realising it.

'I'm meeting Jack at his place in the City,' I murmur.

When I was sixteen my dad caught Roger Cranston and me fooling around in the kitchen. I was so mortified with embarrassment that I spent the next week making up elaborate stories that would explain exactly why Roger had been kneeling in front of me, my skirt pushed up my legs.

He dropped a pen and...um...I was reaching for another...

I feel that now. That same sense of embarrassment—like I've been caught doing completely the wrong thing and need to explain. To *Hughes*, of all people.

My cheeks flush pink and I don't meet his eye. 'I need some documents signed.'

He pulls the door open and smiles. 'Long day?'

'Yeah, you could say that.' I sit down, careful not to flash my naked self to him, then sink back into the leather seat.

I read the news on my phone as we drive, catching

up on what I've missed while I've had my head down the Jack Grant wormhole all day, and discover that a police manhunt has ended with the suspect being shot, and that a chain of supermarkets is at risk of bankruptcy.

We're at his apartment block quickly, though, and the door opens to the familiar bank of lifts. Hughes presses a button, then swipes a keycard so that I'm granted access to the floor Jack's penthouse is on.

'Thanks. Goodnight, Hughes.'

'Goodnight, ma'am.'

I laugh. 'You know I hate it when you call me that.'

The doors swish closed on his wink.

I'm still smiling when the lift opens—but it's transformed into a frown of curiosity as I step into Jack's place. A couple of lights are on, casting an ambient glow, but otherwise it's dark. There are lights coming from beyond the glass and, curious, I walk towards it.

'Hey.'

Jack's voice comes from down the hallway and I turn to see him emerging from one of the rooms, a towel knotted loosely around his waist.

'I didn't know you were on your way.'

My eyes have dropped to his bare chest. To its rhythmic rise and fall as he breathes, to the smooth tan that covers him and the hint of ink I can see above the towel.

I swallow, my throat dry, and force myself to meet his eyes. 'How was your day?' Crisp, professional. Safe, good.

'Fine.'

He unwraps the towel, uncaring of his spectacular nudity, and brings it to his hair, towelling it dry. He's semi-hard, and God knows I want to jump him then and there.

But I don't. I'm not sure why, but something holds me immobile.

'Good meeting with Amber?'

'Yeah. You were right about her. She's a good pick for the job.'

'I think she's got the perfect combination of experience and passion.'

His nod is droll. 'She sure has, Miss Picton. Cocktail first?'

Damn it. I like the way he says that. It's such a formal name, but when he says it I sound like a courtesan or something.

'First?' I can't help teasing.

He drops the towel, hooking it around his body once more, and I'm glad even though it means I can't perve at him so easily. It stops my blood from simmering itself into a fever state.

'First. As in first, before I fuck you senseless.' He grins, pulling me to him.

Something about this feels so right, and it should feel wrong. And awkward. I shake my head, my eyes dropping to the floor before I remember that I've known Jack for two years and that whatever happens we work together and I won't be cowered by him and what we are.

'Cocktails sound perfect.'

His smile is a flicker and then, his eyes holding

mine, his smile just a smudge across his handsome face, he lifts my dress with the same reverence a groom might lift his bride's veil and finds my nakedness.

He groans approvingly. 'You've been waiting for me all day?' His hands curve around my butt, pulling me tight to him.

'Well, you did tear my underpants,' I point out.

'Sorry about that.' His voice shows that he is anything but.

He releases me and I have to stifle a noise of impatience, watching as he saunters into the kitchen and pulls something from the freezer. It's a bottle, but I don't recognise it—nor the label. He shakes it, then opens the top. As he pours it into two glasses I realise that it has a thickened consistency, like a Frozen Coke.

I taste it tentatively, my eyes latched to his. 'Cherry?' I raise my brows, taking another sip.

'It's my new favourite flavour.'

My cheeks glow pink to rival the drink. 'Mine, too.'

'Good to see we're both re-evaluating our opinions,' he says with a wink. Then, almost as an afterthought, 'How was your day?'

'Busy.' I don't want to talk about work. We do enough of that. 'I spoke to my grandma and sat on the Heath, though.'

He laughs. 'Am I not giving you enough to do?'

I shoot him a look of dismissal. 'It was a short break.'

'I'm kidding.' His eyes are thoughtful. 'You never talk about your family.'

'Yes, I do,' I retort, perhaps too quickly. 'Just not with *you*.'

'I see. Why not?'

I'm pretty sure I'm scowling at him. 'Well, for starters, because up until recently our relationship has never remotely veered away from the professional...'

'That's not true. You've seen me naked. You wake me up most days.'

'Yes, I know.' Thoughts of his body sprawled over his bed make my blood simmer. 'You're my boss...'

'Then take it as a command.'

The thought of Jack commanding me is instantly memorable. My lungs are filled with thick, hot air.

'A *command*? You're my boss—not royalty.'

He shrugs. 'Is there a difference? Tell me about your grandmother.'

I laugh. A soft sound of disbelief. 'My grandmother? That's *really* what you want to talk about right now?'

'Why not?'

He sips his drink, his eyes locked to mine. It's a challenge! Just like always, he's finding my boundaries and pushing at them with a persistence I find hard to ignore. And I do like to rise to his challenges.

'Grandma is one of a kind,' I say after the smallest of pauses. 'Revolutionary. She worked until well into her seventies and has always been my biggest ally. She encourages me to push myself as hard as I can in everything I do.'

'What did she do?'

'For work? She was a nurse. Still is, actually.' My lips twitch. 'Just last month she saved a man in her nursing home after he had a heart attack. She threw off her cardigan and performed CPR until the staff got there.'

'Sounds like you're just as proud of her as she is of you.'

'Mmm…' I make a smooth noise of agreement, absent-mindedly running my fingers over the bones of my wrist.

His eyes catch the gesture and he steps around the bench towards me. Before I can guess what he's planning he dribbles some cherry daiquiri from his glass onto the skin I've just rubbed, then brings his lips to it, sucking it and kissing me gently.

'I'm sorry about this.'

Jack? Sorry? That's a novelty.

My heart squeezes at his gentle admission. My voice is soft when I speak. 'I told you, it doesn't hurt.'

'The bruising would say otherwise.'

I shrug, but the way his mouth is moving over me is making thought difficult. 'I'm fine. I would have told you if I didn't like it, believe me.'

'I do.'

He brings my thumb to his mouth and sucks on it. I shudder; the pleasure rips through me.

'So? What *do* you like? Usually?'

'With other men?' I clarify, and there is a strange darkening of his features before he wipes them clear and nods.

'Yes.'

I tilt my head to the side. 'Oh, you know—kinky shit.'

'Such as…?'

It's a calm, measured response beyond what I expect. 'I'll show you soon.'

He clears his throat. 'You bet your sweet arse, you will.' He grins and sips his drink once more.

'Anyway,' I ask throatily, 'what do *you* like? With other women? Or is the only prerequisite that they submit to your *wham-bam, thank you, ma'am* form of sex?'

He shakes his head. 'Not the *only* prerequisite, but it's an important one.'

'Why?' I push, taking another sip.

He presses his finger under my chin, tilting my face towards his. 'Because that's what I want.'

'One-night stands.'

'Two-night stands, in your case,' he says, pulling me forward.

At the same time I reach for his towel and push it down his body. He lifts me easily, settling me on a bar stool, his eyes holding mine as he slides on a condom, and then he takes me totally, driving deep inside me and winding my legs around his waist. Even as the bliss of his possession moves through me I feel a strange distaste for his statement.

A two-night stand on its second night means it's the end.

But don't I want that?

Aren't boundaries a *good* thing?

I bite down on my lip, unable to process it any more. He holds me tight, gripping me against him.

'I like being able to be inside you like this. Whenever I want.'

His fingers grab my dress and lift it up my body,

over my head, so that I'm wearing only my heels and a lace bra. He disposes of the latter easily and then, true to his word, grabs his daiquiri glass and trickles ice-cold liquid across my breasts.

His mouth on my nipple is warm and I arch my back, giving him greater access. He chases it down my body as he thrusts into me again, his ownership of me both thrilling and frightening at the same time. His chin is stubbled and rough against my neck. He takes an earlobe into his mouth, wobbling it between his teeth, and I groan, desperate for him to move faster, deeper.

'What do you want?' he asks softly.

'More!' I call the word out loudly, an incantation or an invocation, scoring my nails across his back, marking him as mine even when I know he isn't.

'Like this?'

He moves a little deeper, so that I nod, but it's not enough.

'More…'

He laughs, pulling out of me and guiding me off the stool at the same time.

'Turn around.'

'Has anyone ever told you you're a bossy son of a bitch in bed?'

'We're not in bed,' he reminds me frankly, and there's a sexy, sardonic smile at the corner of his lips.

'You're a bossy son of a bitch to fuck,' I correct dutifully, and he laughs.

'You're complaining?'

I shoot him a look over my shoulder and do as he says, turning around.

'Those fucking heels…' he says, bending me at my waist and spreading my legs before taking me from behind, his fingers digging into my naked arse. 'You have no idea how hot this is.'

But I do, because he's driving me to the point of distraction with every single move. Fire spirals inside me, coiling, spinning, taking me and making me fall apart in his arms.

The kitchen bench is marble and cold beneath my fevered palms. And then he brings the palm of his hand down on my arse and I jerk, crying out as both pleasure and pain radiate through me.

'Did you know you have a mark here from me?' He presses into what I presume must be a hickey from the last time we were together.

I shake my head and he catches my ponytail in his hand, pulling it with just enough pressure to hold me still as he thrusts inside me. His other hand trails down my spine, chasing each knot, each groove, until he reaches my arse. Once again he presses a single finger against me, and there is something so illicit and forbidden about it that I come—out of nowhere.

The orgasm is intense. He's only touching my skin, there is nothing invasive about his finger, but just the idea of what I'd let him do to me makes me fall apart.

'Shit…' I swear under my breath, sweat across my brow.

His finger pushes in a little way and I buck hard.

His dick thrusts into me and his hand around my hair pulls. It's too much. The pleasure is making me weak.

'I can't…' I say, my breath coming in pants, my eyes fevered, my body wet.

'You can do whatever you want,' he contradicts, and brings his mouth to my back.

But he moves his hand away, bringing it to cup my breasts and torment my nipples. I have never known sex like this. I have never been an instrument of pleasure. I always call the shots and yet now I am his to control, to command, and there is something so hedonistic about that I know I will never be the same again.

'You are so much more perfect than I imagined,' he groans, and now he thrusts deeper and harder and faster, and I rock my hips with him until we fall apart together, him exploding inside me while I tremble and squeeze him tight.

I bring my weight forward, pressing my head onto the marble kitchen bench, not wanting to lose him.

He belongs inside me.

It's an erroneous thought. No one person can belong to another—inside or out.

'I needed that.'

He steps away from me as though he's sated, when I'm satisfied and still needy all at once.

'You and me both.'

I walk around the kitchen bench on legs that are wobbly as all hell. I sip some of my drink, my eyes linked to his. But he's staring at my breasts. Bemused, I look down and see that they're red from his stubble.

His jaw is clenched and he looks away.

Something jars in my mind. A memory I can't quite grab, like finding soap in the bath.

'What is it?'

His smile is tight. 'I ordered Japanese.'

'Great. No karaoke, though,' I tease, referring to my last drunken night with Jack.

He nods. But something is wrong.

'What is it?' I insist.

'I've marked your entire body,' he says after a beat has passed. 'You're literally covered in marks from me.'

I frown, running my hands over my breasts, and then I shrug. 'So?'

His eyes, when they meet mine, are haunted. 'It doesn't bother you that I *like* fucking marking you? That I'm turned on by seeing proof of me on you?'

I tilt my head to one side, pretending bemusement, but my heart is accelerating and again I wonder at the risk of broken ribs in the face of a particularly aggressive heartbeat.

I shake my head slowly.

'Jesus…' He drags a hand through his hair unsteadily. 'All this time I thought you were Miss Moneypenny and you're actually Air Force Amy.'

'Who?'

He doesn't answer, just reaches down and picks up his towel, wrapping it around his waist, then walks into the kitchen to stand behind me. He runs his finger down my spine.

'There is a line here.' He drops his finger lower and presses it against my butt. 'And here, where I sucked you until you bruised.' Then he cups my arse. 'And here, where I slapped you hard enough to redden your skin.'

I swallow. This description of his touch is erotic and dangerous.

I suck my lip between my teeth. 'Don't you get it?' I don't look at him as I speak. 'When I'm here, I'm yours. I trust you. And I want this. This—what you do to me—is what turns me on. More than anything I've ever known.'

He drops his forehead to my shoulder, and then he grabs me and turns me around to face him. 'It doesn't bother you that I'm just using you?'

It's not what I expect him to say. I look at him with an obvious expression of confusion because he shakes his head.

'Not *you*, per se. Sex with you.'

I try to play the lighter side. 'Do I seem like I mind?'

He exhales, frustration and anger communicating themselves in the weighted breath. 'I don't want you to be another one of *them*.'

His eyes are hollow. No matter how I stare at him, I can't intuit his meaning.

'Another one of whom?'

'Them. The women I fuck to forget about her.'

I know instantly that he's referring to Lucy. Sadness wells inside me. Sadness for Jack, for Lucy and the whole sordid mess.

'But that's all this can be.'

There's a determination in his statement that fills me with ice.

I nod, but his words are exploding in my mind like tiny little bombs.

'I know,' I say. Because I do.

That's the worst thing. I have known this about him for a long time and yet here I am, fucking him and letting him drive me crazy when I should be running a mile in the opposite direction.

'So what are you doing here? How can you be okay with that?'

A great fucking question! One I wish I'd asked myself sooner.

'Hasn't that horse already bolted? We've had sex together. Does it really matter why?'

'I don't know.' His laugh is uncertain, his eyes cagey. 'I'm not usually this...*barbaric*.'

He drops his mouth to my shoulder and bites me gently.

'But with you...I don't know...it's like some animal instinct kicks in. I feel like I want to carry you over my shoulder and tie you to my bed.'

'You've already done that. Check and check.'

A flicker of his lips acknowledges the truth of my reply. 'I mean for days. I mean I want to feed you when it suits me. Let you drink the champagne that I tip into your mouth. But otherwise you'd exist for my pleasure alone.'

'Maybe you just want that because you know I'd never go for it,' I say hoarsely, hiding the fact that his words have evoked a powerful emotional need in me.

'Maybe.'

Suddenly, his need gives me an idea. No, it gives me a bartering chip. 'What if I let you go all Neanderthal?'

'You think I haven't already?' he asks, the words full of hoarse self-condemnation.

I shake my head. 'I think you've just scratched the surface.' I cup his face, rubbing my thumb over his stubble. 'So give me what I want and I'll give you what you want.'

'And what *is* it you want, Gemma Picton?'

I swallow my anxiety. What's the worst that can happen? He'll say no?

'I want you to answer my questions. I want to understand you better.'

The shower is warm against my skin. I rub my body all over, letting the soap bubble and froth before turning the heat off and stepping out into an enormous soft towel. I dry myself and then reach for one of the luxurious robes hanging behind the door.

I'm nervous, as though I'm on a first date. But that's stupid.

Because Jack doesn't date. Come to think of it, I don't really date either.

What we're doing is fucking—sure, the best sex of my life. But still just sex. Two nights? Maybe more? But definitely not any form of happily-ever-after.

It's sex. And it's discovery.

I'm getting my curiosity answered—and I have been curious about Jack for as long as I've worked with him. I've wondered about the demons that drive him.

The ghosts, real and imagined, that play on the edges of his mind.

Besides, it's kind of win-win for me. I love the animal passion in him. So much so I'm terrified of myself. This way I get to find out more about the beautiful darkness of Jack Grant, and I get the beast in bed.

Perfect.

When I step out of the bathroom he's arranging containers on an enormous dining table. It could easily seat twelve people, but he's placed us at one end and, in a gesture that makes my heart thump, he's even lit a candle.

'Expecting company?' I murmur with forced sarcasm, desperate to cover the trembling emotion in my chest.

'That's not what I'd call you,' he responds in kind, but he winks at me and my heart pounds harder.

'We've covered that already with—who was it? Amy someone?'

He grins. 'I called you Miss Moneypenny first.'

'Yes, and that's equally wrong. I'm not some wallflower assistant.'

'You assist me,' he says with a shrug, but he comes to a chair and pulls it out, his eyes meeting mine, silently inviting me to sit.

Electricity sparks between us like a current neither of us can control.

I'm nervous, and that makes me angry! I don't want to be nervous around Jack, like this is a date or something. I've agreed to let him ravage me so that he'll tell me stuff. It's not a date. If it were he'd tell me all that stuff without the promise of animalistic sex.

It's only when I sit that I pay attention to the kind of food he's ordered. There's sushi, sashimi, a Katsu curry, edamame and a couple of miso soups. I try not to think he's remembered that Katsu curry is my favourite thing in the world.

He takes the seat opposite mine and lifts a glass. I tilt mine towards his and then rest it back on the table.

'It's bad luck not to drink after clinking glasses.'

'I haven't heard that.'

I lift the drink to my lips and taste it. Of course it's delicious.

He rests back in the chair, his hands linked beneath his chin. 'Well, Miss Picton. We have a deal. What is it you'd like to know?'

'You'll tell me anything?'

'And you'll let me *do* anything.'

I nod, my throat dry as I wonder just what his idea of 'anything' encompasses.

'How do you know I won't chicken out, out of interest?'

His laugh makes my gut vibrate. 'Because you're you. I can't imagine you backing away from anything in your life. You're fearless.'

'Not entirely,' I say under my breath.

'No? What are you afraid of?'

I sip my wine again, and then snap my chopsticks in half reaching for a piece of salmon *nigiri*. 'I'm afraid of lightning,' I say softly. 'Terrified of it.'

'As in thunder and lightning?'

I nod. 'Yep. That one.'

'But why? It's just atmospheric discharge.'

'Yeah. It's just a weather phenomenon. But I will still hide under my covers during a storm, waiting for it to pass, without fail.'

'Why? Since when?'

My smile is lopsided. 'Since I was a girl.'

'What happened?'

'How do you know *anything* happened?'

'I just do,' he says with a shrug of his broad shoulders, lifting his own chopsticks and taking a piece of chicken *karaage*.

He's right, of course.

'I was seven years old and locked out of our home. I'd gone to pick apples and my parents presumed I was in bed. They were out to dinner with friends and Nanny Winters thought I'd gone with them. The house was locked up and I couldn't get in.'

I shiver. It was one of the most horrifying nights I can recall.

'I climbed into my tree house and waited it out there. But a flash of lightning came down so close and so loud it smoked on the ground at my feet.'

He nods thoughtfully, but I can tell he's unravelling the story.

'When did you get back into your home?'

'Not until morning. I fell asleep eventually, and it wasn't until Nanny discovered me missing and the alarm was raised that I heard the staff looking for me. I woke up and all was well. Except that I can't stand storms now. Even the smell of rain in the air makes me afraid.'

He strokes his chin thoughtfully.

'So I'm not entirely fearless,' I finish lamely.

'Lots of people are afraid of thunderstorms.'

'Are *you*?'

'No.' His smile is perfunctory. 'There isn't much I'm afraid of.'

'But…?' I ask, sipping my wine, curious to the point of distraction.

'Yes, I have fears,' he admits grudgingly.

'Like…?'

He makes a deep, guttural noise. 'This was a crappy idea.'

I laugh softly. 'Ghosts? Spiders?'

'No.' He's quiet for so long I wonder if he's not going to answer, and then he continues, his voice hoarse. 'I'm afraid of powerlessness. Of watching someone I love die.'

His grief hits me like a web and I am caught in it.

'You've watched someone you love die and you've survived.'

'Barely.' He shakes his head. 'Try the chicken. It's great.'

I don't move. The ghosts of his admission linger between us, haunting our table.

'Were you with her when she died?'

He recoils as though he's been slapped and I briefly regret the agreement we've made. But I want to *know* this stuff. It's so important to me to understand. I feel like I've got only half of the picture and bit by bit I want to piece him together.

'Yes.'

'I'm sorry.'

'I wanted to be with her.'

'Of course.' I nod. 'How long were you married?'

'A year.' He clears his throat. 'Can we talk about something else?'

Sympathy is thick inside of me but instinctively I know talking about this will help him so I don't back down. 'You told me I could ask what I want.'

'And this is what you want to know?'

'You told me you're fucking me because of her—so, yes, I want to know.'

His face pales. 'Fine.' His teeth are gritted. 'What else?'

I drink some wine and eat another piece of sushi, chewing on it thoughtfully. 'She died of cancer?'

He nods.

'And…?' I prompt.

'And *what*, Gemma?'

'Well, what kind?'

He expels an angry breath. 'Chronic Lymphocytic Leukaemia. Stage Four. It was a terminal diagnosis.'

I wince. 'I'm so sorry.'

'Why? It's not your fault.'

I understand his anger and aggression.

'Nothing could be done?'

His eyes meet mine and he shakes his head. I feel like he's holding something back, but I don't want to push him anymore. Not about this.

Sympathy trumps curiosity. So I let it go.

'This is delicious,' I say instead, reaching for another piece.

And he visibly relaxes, as though he's been in hell and I'm unlocking the gate.

'Yeah.'

'Do you spend much time here?' I look around the palatial apartment, seeing it almost as if for the first time.

'I used to.' His smile is tight. 'So…Nanny Winters, huh?'

'No, no—*you* don't get to change the subject.'

He laughs. 'I can do what I want.'

'That's not our deal.'

'Your parents worked full-time?'

It's so like Jack to push on with his line of questioning just because it suits him.

I stare at him. 'Not really.'

'Yet you were raised by a nanny?'

'I had three nannies,' I say, grabbing a piece of avocado sushi and eating it, then sipping my wine. 'Nanny Winters oversaw the other two.'

'*Three* nannies?' His voice is bordering on a scoff. 'So you were a handful even as a child?'

I roll my eyes. 'Did you not hear my thunderstorm story?'

'A runaway and a handful?' He nods with mock seriousness.

'Yep.'

'Your parents were rich?'

'*Are* rich,' I agree.

'Funny... I didn't have you picked as the daughter of some loaded guy.'

I arch a brow teasingly. 'Technically I'm the daughter of a loaded guy *and* a loaded lady. Duchess Arabella Picton, in fact.'

'No shit? *That* I did not see coming.'

He laughs then—a sound that relaxes me because it's so like us to laugh together that I am reminded of the years we've spent working together, getting to know one another. Not like this, admittedly, but in a different way.

'Why not?' I ask.

He laughs again and my gut clenches.

'So you slaving away for me is like a vanity job?'

I frown. 'No!'

'But you're going to inherit a fortune?'

I shrug, deciding it's better not to talk about my trust fund with Jack. I figure he won't really appreciate the amount that's sitting in my name in a Swiss bank account.

'One day.'

'Fascinating.'

'Not really.'

He nods, but I can see the wheels of his brain turning. 'You studied law, right?'

I roll my eyes. 'I'm your in-house counsel, what do you think?'

He grins and my tummy tilts off-balance. 'I don't pay too much attention to what my assistants do at university.'

I shoot him a look of disapproval but bite my tongue.

He's goading me, and I won't give him the satisfaction of knowing he's been successful. 'I studied law and economics at Oxford, thank you very much.'

'Let me guess…you did well?'

My gaze doesn't falter. 'Double first.'

He tilts his head back, his laugh a soft caress. 'Not at all surprising.'

'How do you not know this about me? You hired me to work for you.'

'Yeah… Expecting you to last about three seconds.'

'Really? Why?'

'Because that's how long all my other assistants lasted.'

I grit my teeth. 'Counsels.'

'Your job is pretty much unfillable.'

'Because you're such a charm to work with,' I point out.

'Whatever the reason, no one stays around. So why have you?'

'Because I like a challenge,' I say honestly, my chin jutting out, my eyes holding to his. And he is still. Watchful. The air between us thickens.

'I'm a challenge?'

I laugh. 'You're kidding, right?'

He reaches for a piece of sushi. I watch him eat it and my stomach squeezes. How can I want him again already? I am fire and flame, bursting with need.

'Were you always like this? Or is it just since… Lucy?'

He frowns and doesn't answer right away. I can

practically see the cogs turning in his brain. 'I don't know.'

'Well, before she…she died, did you have a constantly changing stream of staff?'

He shrugs. 'No.'

I nod, slowly. So this *is* a hangover of Lucy's death. My job, my being here, it all comes back to her. To Lucy.

The emotional strangulation of that is not something I think I'll easily comprehend, and so I stand up slowly.

'I've had enough for now.' My eyes meet his and now I am the one issuing a challenge. 'So show me.'

'Show you what?' he asks with a purposeful glint in his eye.

'Show me what *you* want.'

CHAPTER SEVEN

I'M IN LIMBO.

Not asleep…not awake. I lie in his bed, my body throbbing with pleasures untold, my mind exhausted.

It is late. Somewhere between midnight and dawn. And I am his.

I lift up on one elbow, my eyes hazy as I look down at him. He is beautiful and he is sexy. He is groggy. Almost asleep. But his eyes flick to mine and I see blank speculation in them.

Confusion.

Wariness.

'How are you?'

I smile—I hope it's as reassuring as I intend and not maniacal as I suspect. 'Good.'

He nods tersely, pushing up out of bed, dragging a hand through his hair as he stalks across to his wardrobe. He emerges after a moment, boxer shorts on. At least he's not showering me away immediately.

But he will soon enough. I know Jack too well to misunderstand his mood now, and it pisses me off as much as it worries me. I don't want a relationship, but I don't know how we can go from white-hot sex to awkward silence in the space of minutes.

'Do you need anything?' His voice is husky. 'Drink? Coffee? Shower?'

A flicker of annoyance draws my lips into a frown. 'No, thanks.'

I stand up, feeling as though I've run ten marathons. My body is sore and stiff, but still throbbing with pleasures previously unknown. My dress is—where? Out in the living area?

I walk towards him slowly, and pause just in front of him. What *he* wants is crystal-clear; my own needs are far more difficult to interpret but I *do* want to interpret them.

Self-preservation draws me inwards, away from Jack before he can push me away. 'I'm going to go.'

I see the emotions that flicker on his face and I recognise only one—relief.

'Are you sure?'

I laugh—a soft sound that covers whatever that heavy pain is in my chest. 'Come on, Jack. We both know how this works.'

I press a kiss against his cheek and move into the lounge. Our sushi feast is still on the table—a relic of our attempt at a date. Like normal people date. But we're *not* normal. Not on our own and definitely not together. We're misfits, both of us, operating outside the normal realms of this kind of relationship thing.

I scoop up my dress and bra and pull the dress on over my naked body, stuffing the bra into my handbag as I step into my shoes.

My hair I pull over one shoulder, brushing my fingers through its tangled length to neaten it somewhat.

'Martins will be on roster now,' he says, looking at the clock over the oven and referring to one of the junior staff drivers.

I shake my head. The last thing I want is for a company driver to see me like this, post-Jack-Grant-ravaging. 'I'll get a cab.' I walk towards him again and press a single kiss to his cheek.

'I'll see you Monday.'

'Monday…' He nods and there are more emotions in his face, these harder to comprehend. 'Right. It's the weekend.'

I swallow past a lump in my throat. 'And then Australia,' I remind him—probably unnecessarily.

'Yeah.'

His eyes probe mine. I feel like I'm escaping prison and one of those enormous floodlights has landed on me, full beam.

'You're okay?'

'I'm fine,' I reassure him.

We've just had pretty much the best sex in the world—I doubt it has ever been better for anyone than it is for us. But I know I need to go. It's important. My self-preservation instincts are blaring loudly, demanding I put some space between us.

He nods, and it's only then that I realise he's got a glass of Scotch in his hand.

It hurts. There's something about seeing him with a drink that reminds me of what he does—how often he does it and how he reacts afterwards. And I don't want that to be the case with us.

Those self-preservation instincts join forces with my brain and they pull the strings to make me smile brightly.

'Thanks for tonight. I had fun. See you soon.'

And I turn and walk slowly towards the door, my heart thudding, my mind foggy.

I watch her leave with a certainty that I'm messing up my life in a monumental way. What the *hell* am I doing? Sleeping with Gemma *once* was a disastrous cock-up. But again and again? Showing her all my dark spaces and hauntings?

No one needs to know the demons that lash me.

I am in control. That's me. It's the persona I've built and I don't like the idea of someone knowing that it's not completely true. Lucy knew, of course. And I guess Amber does; she's seen me in a pretty fucked-up state, right after Lucy died. But Gemma? Now?

Her eyes, big and intelligent, are assessing, always understanding. And the way her face scrunches when she's about to come… The way her body trembles beneath mine… Jesus. I want her now—again—more.

I turn to the door. If I chased her what would she say? God, would she think it means I want more than sex? Ironic, given that I *just* want sex. With Gemma.

An obsession is building inside me. Bit by bit it is closing me in. But Gemma Picton is hardly going to let me turn her into my own personal sex slave. Although I think she's about as caught up in all of this as I am…

All the more reason for me to fight harder, to control it.

I grip the crystal tumbler in my hands, feeling my anger and determination surge, and I pitch the glass hard against the wall. It breaks with satisfying immediacy, shattering into thousands of tiny pieces that mix with the slosh of amber liquid running fast down the wall before landing with a thud against the tiles. I drag my hand through my hair and stare at the destruction with a sense of satisfaction.

I'm good at ruining things. At breaking them.

That's what I need to stick to.

I don't think I'll ever eat again. Grandma has no such qualms. She reaches for another oyster—it must be her tenth—and swirls it inside lips she's painted bright red for the occasion.

'What's in Australia?'

I stare out at the little street, watching a small black car reverse—badly—into a narrow parking space. 'Work.'

'Always work…' She sighs.

I nod absently.

Jack will be there, too. After not going to Tokyo, I don't suppose there's the smallest hope I can get out of it.

'I promise I'll do something fun. Just for you.'

My insides quiver as I imagine what that could be. *Jack.* Doing Jack would be fun.

But even as my pulse is stirring and my heart is beginning to race my brain is demonstratively reminding me of Jack's particular brand of cold fishery. His ability to walk away from me right after we've shared mind-blowing, simultaneous orgasms is as offensive as it is unique.

Am I crazy to be letting this happen?

Yes, hisses my brain. *He's told you he's using you. He still loves his dead wife. Jesus. You're a fool.*

'Grandma...' I pause, my lips tight as I dismiss whatever the heck I'd been about to say.

She swallows the oyster—Grandma is the only person I know who actually chews the slimy little devils first...*shudder*...like phlegmatic explosions...*ugh*. Her gaze is cool and direct.

At eighty, Grandma is every bit as beautiful as she was in her youth. Lined, ephemeral and pale now, but with a glimmer in her eyes, a wave to her silver shoulder-length hair and a smile that is punctuated by straight white teeth—all her own. Her nose is straight, her eyes wide-set, her figure as svelte as ever. And she dresses in a fashion which somehow straddles the latest in trends without coming across as an attempt to be youthful.

'Something's on your mind.'

I shake my head and reach for my bread roll. Only I've already fingered it anxiously, reducing it to a pile of wheaten crumbs and ash.

'When Grandpa died, did you think about finding someone else?'

She snorts. 'There is no one else.'

The words make me smile, yet they are also sounding the death knell for the hope I hadn't realised I've been carrying.

'No one?' I tease.

'No one.' She expels a sigh. 'Your grandfather was… What we shared is impossible to explain.' She sips her champagne, her eyes growing even more intensely watchful, if that's possible. 'Have I ever told you about how we met?'

I shake my head, even though I know the story backwards.

'Liar!' She chuckles.

We're interrupted by a waiter, but Grandma dispenses with him quickly, placing an order for another bottle of champagne and then fixing me with that steady grey gaze of hers.

'He was sitting on the lawns at Huntington, his knees bent, his chin resting on them. His face was resolutely turned away from me, but as I approached his eyes shifted, locking to my face. It was as if he was telling me all his secrets and begging me to help him in that one single second. He looked at me as if he knew that I was the only person on earth who would be able to dig through his shit and find the kernel of the boy he'd once been.'

Grandma is looking over my shoulder now. The story is one she's told so many times that it comes out word for word as I remember it. Still, I lean forward, the invisible threads of magic and history curling around me.

'That enormous oak tree was just to his side—far enough away to prevent shade from darkening him, but close enough to dwarf him. He was a big man, your grandfather. Tall and strong—built for battle.' Her lips twist with undisguised disgust. 'But not strong in spirit. His spirit had been broken and the tree made that obvious to me.'

Her eyes flick back to mine and I feel it, too. Just like she did. The weight of silent communication and understanding.

'I loved him instantly.'

My heart does a weird little palpitation in my chest. 'I can't imagine that.'

'Why?'

'It's just unfathomable to me.'

'That's because you haven't met someone worth loving yet,' she says with a shrug of her elegant shoulders. 'One day you'll know just what I mean.'

I quirk my lips, hoping my smile seems dismissive. My pulse has speeded up. I try to quell it.

'I don't think it always works like that.'

'Perhaps not. Your grandfather *was* special.'

'What you shared was special,' I murmur, reaching across and squeezing her hand.

Grandma's eyes flicker, her lips tighten and she nods, as if to dismiss the conversation. The waiter appears, brandishing a bottle of champagne, and begins to unfurl the foil top. Grandma stares resolutely at the view as the waiter performs his ministrations, and doesn't smile when he pours two fresh glasses.

She is very much the Duchess in instances like this: a woman who has become so used to service and being served that it isn't even an act she needs to be grateful for.

I smile my thanks as he leaves.

Grandma waits until we are alone again. 'You will never meet anyone—no lover, no special friend, no one—if you are behind your desk all day.'

Out of nowhere I picture Jack. I picture the way he drapes himself against the doorframe, the way his body is so languid and sensual, and my stomach flops.

'Have I told you the foundation is almost ready to launch?'

Grandma tilts her head to one side. 'I admire your commitment to that...' she says, clearly trying to frame whatever she's thinking carefully. 'But you have money. If philanthropy is your aim, why not set up your own charity?'

'Perhaps I will—one day. But my job is more than just one thing... You know that.' I expel a sigh, frustration gnawing at me. 'You've always championed my work.'

'You're very clever. And I know you're brilliant at what you do. But you're sacrificing too much now. I championed your work because I hoped you would find a way to pursue your career and still live your life. You, more than anyone I've ever known, have the ability to keep multiple balls in the air at once. So why aren't you doing it?'

I drop my head, my eyes not meeting hers. There is so much truth in what she's saying, but the criticism hurts.

'I…I am.' It's a lie. We both know that. But reality is not something I want to face.

'*All* of you is focussed on that job. On that man. I'm worried you're going to wake up one day and realise what you've sacrificed. And all for *him*.'

My heart bumps against my ribs, banging them with its frantic racing. 'He's brilliant.'

'And a bastard, by all reports.'

Yes. A beautiful, arrogant, brilliant, sex-obsessed bastard.

Was it only yesterday he was inside me? It feels like forever ago. I am at a fever pitch of want—want only he can answer. My insides clench instantly, remembering him, needing him, craving his touch, smell and taste…

'He's not that bad.' The words are hoarse, punctured by breath and memory.

'With him and that job in your life you're never going to be truly happy.'

Her pronouncement is spoken in a way that is almost prophetic. A shiver dances down my spine, spiralling coldness across my flesh like a breath from the North Pole.

'Travelling and living off the family trust would be better?' I arch a brow. 'You know me better than that. I *live* for what I do. I *love* it. Maybe *that's* the love of my life.'

Silence prickles between us. Silence that is suffocating and unwelcome.

'Very well,' she clips, dismissing this conversation, as well. 'I don't like the way they've trimmed those hedges. It's so severe.'

I breathe again, but my heart is still twisting and thumping. The truth sits heavily in my mind but I step away from it.

There is no ulterior motive to my working so hard for Jack. There's no mystery as to why I don't feel like I've sacrificed a damn thing for him. It doesn't mean anything that I am fulfilled and alive, energised every time I speak to him, see him, do his bidding. But my stomach drops. Because actually I think there probably *is* a meaning—just one I don't want to appreciate.

Fuck.

His jet is the last word in space-age luxury. Cream leather armchairs on either side of the aisle, thick carpet a pale beige and lamps that would look at home in a five-star hotel make the perfect night-flight reading environment. USB docks are in every armrest to charge phones and iPads, and there are several bedrooms, a boardroom and a small cinema.

There is also a brooding billionaire sitting at the back of the plane, his head bent over a stack of files, apparently engrossed.

I ignore him. Or pretend to.

We've hardly spoken since I left his apartment on Friday night.

That was easy enough over the weekend. After sharing two bottles of champagne and being drilled in life's lessons, Grandma and I shopped in the high street, selecting a new clutch purse for Grandma to take to the anniversary dinner and pretending we weren't both dreading the damned thing.

I didn't hear from Jack, and it wasn't until I got back to my own place on Sunday evening that I realised I'd been expecting to. That I'd thought he'd text or call or email or something.

Those two days away from him, without seeing him, stretched interminably.

The knowledge prickled down my spine so that on Monday morning I steeled myself to be as standoff-ish and unaffected as possible. To fight coldness with cool unconcern, with no care.

But I didn't see him then either. He arrived late, left early and didn't speak to me.

And I didn't speak to him, despite the fact I needed his signature on some papers.

I chickened out and actually hid from him when he walked past my office, ducking beneath my desk.

Crazy, right?

Not so much.

We've moved into dangerous territory. I don't know if he realises it, but there are warnings blaring in my head. I don't want to need Jack Grant like I do. I don't mean sexually. I mean in every way.

Only I can't imagine my life without him.

We've been flying for the better part of a day now, and hardly spoken beyond a perfunctory, polite 'Hiya' as he boarded the flight, ten minutes late and looking like sex and seduction in a ten-thousand-pound suit.

I have been telling myself I don't care with vary-ing measures of success. Did I expect he'd storm up to me and kiss me? Take me passionately in his arms and hold me close? Tell me he never wants to go three days without seeing me again?

He's made it abundantly clear what he wants.

It should be what I want, too.

I shut my eyes for a moment, crossing my legs in the armchair, and am surprised when I'm woken a moment later.

'We're landing.' Jack's hands are at my hips and I bat them away instinctively.

He grabs the seatbelt and clips it across me—tight—his eyes flicking to mine. The hint of a smile on his face makes my heart flip-flop.

'Have I ever told you that you snore?'

Warmth invades my face. 'I know. I have mild asthma.'

He grins and takes the seat beside mine. My body is instantly aware of him and my brain is pretty pissed off at the rapid response.

I shift a little, looking down at my watch. I must have slept for over an hour. I blink, opening the world clock function on my phone. It's six o'clock in Sydney, which means I want to be tired—not refreshed after a quick nap on the flight.

Silence stretches between us. Debbie, one of his flight attendants, clips out efficiently, 'We'll be touching down on schedule. Can I get you anything before we land?'

'Water, thanks.' I smile at her, turning my attention back to the papers I'd been reading.

Well, half my attention. A quarter of it. A sliver. The tiny part that's not completely drawn to Jack and his nearness and his hypermasculine fragrance. The part of me that isn't all wrapped up in the way he's sitting, legs spread, arms relaxed, body warm and large and so close I could push out of my seat and sit on his lap. Unzip his pants and take him.

God. I want that.

'Dr Pepper.'

His response to Debbie's question shakes the desire from my mind, but he looks at me and my toes curl. Does he guess what I'm thinking?

I tap my pen against the side of the page I'm reading in an attempt to focus my thoughts in a more appropriate direction.

But Jack reaches across, his hand curling over mine. My pulse goes into overdrive.

'Did you have a good weekend?' he asks.

I laugh. I can't help it. A short, sharp sound of weary frustration. 'Yeah.'

He nods, and a frown pulls at his lips. 'I don't know how to speak to you now.'

And I feel sorry for him. Sorry for me. Because we're both in the middle of a patch of uncertainty too wide to navigate.

'I'm still me.'

'But it's different.'

'Yeah… I don't know if you ever asked me about my weekend before we had sex together.'

I lower my voice as Debbie walks back into the cabin. She places a glass of water on my side table and a can of soda on Jack's.

As Debbie disappears once more he winks at me. 'It's cherry flavour.'

Damn him. He knows what he's doing to me.

My pulse fires and I give him a tight half-smile before returning my attention to the document I'm partway through reading.

'You've got a breakfast meeting at seven o'clock with the mayor. While you're with him I'm going to be going over the premises. Then I'll meet with your Australian CEO, Clint Sheridan, to touch base on recruitment matters. The broker for the New Zealand deal is meeting us for lunch at Aria, and Clint's asked you to his place for dinner, with a few of the other executives.'

'Asked *us*, you mean,' he corrects, his eyes hooked to mine.

I frown. 'It's just social. You don't need me—'

'I want you there,' he says firmly, and I remember that he *is* actually my boss.

Plus, if it weren't for the fact that we've had sex I wouldn't have ever thought of *not* going. It's my own way of not blurring the lines, but he sees right through it.

'You've done most of this deal. You *should* be there.'

I pull my lips to the side thoughtfully. 'Sure.'

It's not worth arguing about. We've gone to hundreds of this kind of thing in our time. I'm sure this won't be any different.

He nods, but he's distracted. 'Do we need to talk?'

His suggestion sets off a kaleidoscope of possibilities. Talk? About what? About us? What would I say? And him?

I swallow to hide my confusion and return his question with one of my own. 'Do we?'

He reaches across and wipes his thumb over my lip. Butterflies bounce around my gut.

'I guess not. It doesn't matter.'

I stare straight ahead, moving out of his reach. Because maybe this *doesn't* matter. Maybe this is just one of those things and in a few weeks I'll wonder what the heck I got so worked up about. Why I let him get under my skin like this.

I hope it's true even as I know how unlikely that is.

CHAPTER EIGHT

I LOVE AUSTRALIA. We don't get here often—though with Jack opening this office that will probably change.

The heat and humidity hit me as soon as the doors open. Even in the air-conditioned airport there's a sultry oppressiveness that makes me ache to find the nearest swimming pool and dive straight in.

A limo is waiting for us, and a couple of reporters from the broadsheet newspapers. I forget sometimes that Jack is a 'Person of Interest', especially in the business world. Working with him for over two years has made him just 'Jack' to me, but to the world he's an enigmatic tycoon and philanthropist.

I remember feeling awestruck before I knew him. The prospect of working for him was one I pinned all my hopes to.

Now it's just my life.

Jack and I have been pretty much inseparable this whole time. I'm his right hand. Despite having been hired as his in-house counsel, my job has morphed and varied and now incorporates a wide variety of duties. I'm across his workload and can step in at any point, finishing negotiations, speaking on his behalf. When we travel together we either stay in adjoining rooms or in one of his apartments. It depends on how long we're in town and what's required of us.

This unfettered access has been helpful when we needed to proof things late at night or discuss early morning meetings. It's never been an issue. But the thought of sharing his penthouse at Woolloomooloo is filling me with a sense of apprehension. Not because I'm afraid of him. I'm afraid of what I want from him—what I need. Of what living in close confines, even temporarily, will force us to confront.

My sense of foreboding doesn't improve once we arrive and I remember how stunning the place is. How glamorous and romantic.

The thought is errant and I quash it immediately. Romance be damned. We're colleagues who happen to be sleeping together. That's all.

The penthouse is in a big converted wharf building. He bought the whole top floor from some Hollywood celebrity about five years ago, converting several luxurious flats into one enormous sky home. It has panoramic views of Sydney Harbour. From where I'm standing I can see the bridge and a beautiful little island. There's a balcony that wraps all the way around and a lap pool in a glass room to one side.

I look at the water, my temptation obvious.

'Plans for tonight?'

Jack's right behind me. I don't turn around but I can feel his nearness. My body quivers; I want to jump him.

'None. Getting into the time zone.'

'I'm *in* the time zone, baby.' He grins, and strolls towards the enormous glass windows that overlook the harbour. 'I'm also hungry enough to eat a horse.' He turns to face me, his eyes dragging from my head to my toes and then back up, slowing down over my cleavage. 'Shall we go out?'

My body is sticky from the humidity and I am weary. Wary, too. Instinctively I understand that we need to keep some boundaries in place. Going out, just the two of us, is an unacceptable boundary erosion.

I smile—hopefully politely. 'I'm going to have a swim before I do another thing. Don't feel you have to wait for me to eat.'

I walk back towards the door, to where our suitcases are, and wheel mine along beside me down the corridor.

I find the room I used last time I was here and step into it, shutting the door behind me with an emphatic click. I lean against it and suck in a deep breath, then open the case and pull out my swimsuit. A simple black one-piece. I slip it on, pausing to check my reflection before wrapping a towel around my middle and walking back into the apartment.

I hear him before I see him and my stomach twists. His powerful arms are pulling him through the water, and if you told me he had trained as an Olympic swimmer I would believe you. His tan glistens like gold beneath the Australian sun.

Trying valiantly to ignore the heat between my legs, I drop my towel onto a lounger and dive in, long and low, holding my breath for as long as I can before kicking to the surface and swimming all the way to the end.

I rest my arms on the sun-warmed coping and stare out at the harbour beneath us.

It looks like someone has shattered a thousand diamonds and thrown them over the water's top. The way it glistens is almost impossible to believe.

He swims up beside me. 'You're angry at me.'

He doesn't touch me, but the words feel like fingerprints on my chest.

I turn to him slowly, my hair wet, my eyes surrounded by clumps of black lashes. 'No.'

His expression is one of impatience. 'I'm no good at this. Tell me what I've done so I know.'

'What you've *done*?' It's so ludicrous that I almost laugh, but an equal urge to cry rises in my chest. 'You haven't "done" anything, Jack. I thought we'd agreed that this is our deal? Sex—fine. Work—fine. Nothing in between.'

But out of nowhere I remember the way my grandma talks about meeting Grandpa. I look at Jack and my heart hammers. *Damn it.*

He stares back at me. I can practically see the cogs turning. 'You're in your late twenties?'

'Twenty-six,' I clarify, and the distinction is a small but important one, for some absurd reason I can't comprehend. Am I vain about my age? *Really?*

'And you've never been in a relationship?'

'Why do you say that?' I ask, though he's right.

'I just don't see you as someone's girlfriend.'

'Gee, thanks,' I mutter, turning my attention back to the view.

His fingertip on my shoulder is so light that I almost wonder if I've imagined his touch. But then he runs it down my wet arm, all the way to my elbow, and cups me there, squeezing gently. I turn towards him once more and he pushes out from the wall of the pool, bringing me with him, deeper into the water.

I'm a good swimmer, and I tread water without his help. But he stays close, his handsome face mesmerising me with ocean-green eyes and darkly tanned skin.

'Am I wrong?'

I shake my head. 'Not necessarily.' A smile flicks across my lips without my permission. 'I've dated. And been with men when it's suited me. But I've always had demanding jobs, and not a lot of time to do the whole dinner-and-a-movie thing.'

He laughs. 'That sounds boring as shit.'

My thoughts exactly. 'How did you meet her?'

I don't need to say his wife's name. We both know who I mean. He expels a breath and looks away, his jaw clenched.

'It's fine if you don't want to talk about it,' I say, making to swim away, but he grabs my wrist and pulls me towards him. And I'm glad. I need him to need me, and it's a sign that he does. My heart smiles.

'You keep running away from me when you don't get your own way—did you know that?'

Do I? 'I'm not running away. I'm swimming away,' I say, in a very lame attempt at humour. 'And it's not because I don't get my own way—it's because talking to you is like talking to a brick wall. It's easy to...to run away when you're being pushed.'

His eyes widen in non-verbal acknowledgement of

the point I've made. 'She was working at a restaurant in Edinburgh.' His eyes flash with remembered pain. 'I'd just wrapped up a meeting and was heading to the hotel. Thought I'd stop for a late dinner.' He clears his throat, but his voice is still gravelly. 'And I saw her.'

Jealousy fires inside me at the look of total wonderment that briefly crosses his eyes.

'She was finishing up and I made her nervous as hell.'

'Nervous? Why?'

Though, I remember belatedly my first meeting with Jack and the trepidation that lived in me. I hid it beneath a layer of finely honed bravado but, yes, I was nervous, too. He has a machismo and dynamism that is at once overpowering. I have truly never met anyone like him.

'She hadn't had a lot of good experience with men,' he says tightly, a muscle jerking in his square jaw.

'I'm sorry for that,' I say quietly.

'Yeah. I was, too.' His smile was haunted. 'The guy she'd left just before meeting me seemed to have thought of her as his own personal punch bag.'

I nod slowly, imagining what that must be like. I have nothing to reference it to. It's beyond my remit even to comprehend that kind of fear and pain.

'I'm sorry,' I say again.

'Yeah.' He nods, too. 'Anyway…'

'So you guys started seeing each other?'

He winced. 'I proposed to her a week after we met. I'm not good at the whole dating thing. I don't have the patience for it.' His smile is shaded with self-deprecation. 'I steamrollered her rather than dated her.'

I can't help the soft laugh that escapes me. 'Why does that not surprise me?'

It's further proof that when Jack wants something he goes after it—immediately and unequivocally. But it's taken him two years to realise he wants my body, and there's no sign he wants more than that. He felt the same love for Lucy that my grandma describes having for Grandpa. So perhaps it is normal and common and I just don't realise that because I've never felt anything like it.

It's pretty obvious Jack doesn't feel it for me. Jealousy bubbles in my gut.

'I wanted to make her life better. I wanted to fix it all. To take away her pain and make her smile and laugh.'

'I'm sure you did,' I say, with truth.

I've only seen a few photos of Lucy around the mansion and, yes, on the internet, when I've allowed myself the morbid indulgence of looking her up. And in all of these pictures she is smiling.

'I killed her, Gemma.' His eyes meet mine for a second and then he looks away. 'If she'd never met me she'd probably still be alive.'

I freeze, ill-equipped to deal with this kind of confession. Nothing about it makes sense. And yet the way he drinks after he's slept with someone... Is it possible there's a darker truth at play? No. I know Jack. I know him through and through. He's being dramatic, not literal.

'What are you talking about?'

He swallows, then closes his eyes. 'She was pregnant. We'd just found out and then the tests showed that she had cancer. I wanted her to start treatment immediately, but it would have meant her having an abortion.'

Sadness for Jack, for Lucy and for the baby they would have had fills me all the way to the top of my soul. I don't consider myself maternal, but I know instantly what decision she made and why.

'She didn't want to do that.'

'No.' His face is grim. 'Even with treatment she had pretty much no hope.' He clears his throat. 'But still... There would have been a chance. If she hadn't fallen pregnant.' He shakes his head angrily.

'Then she wouldn't have found out about the cancer until it was too late,' I say softly.

Sympathy makes me crumble. How can I be strong in the face of his loss? I cup his face and draw him to me, kissing him gently, tenderly, hoping to reassure him and wipe away this baseless and yet unending guilt.

He is still. Not kissing me back. His guilt is still cloaked about us, but then something clicks into gear and he groans into my mouth, cupping my butt and lifting my legs to wrap them around his waist, holding me against his arousal and letting me obliterate his sadness. For one more moment. One more night.

I see now that this is how he's getting through.

A night here and there to stop feeling this weight of responsibility.

A different woman to bury himself in and forget that

he got Lucy pregnant and that because of her pregnancy she refused treatment.

His words swirl through my head. *'I wanted to make her life better. I wanted to fix it all. To take away her pain and make her smile and laugh.'*

It's exactly how I feel about Jack.

And I know one sure-fire way to bring him back from the haunted brink of the misery he's inhabiting. I kiss him hard, moving my mouth over his as I press against his cock. My hands tuck into the elastic of his swim shorts, curving around his arse, holding him tight against me.

He knows. He knows which way salvation lies and he powers through the water, walking easily to the edge and lifting me so that I'm sitting on the coping. He barely breaks our kiss as he climbs out, pressing his body over mine, his weight and wetness making me writhe against the tiles as need explodes in me.

It's the need to remove this burden from his mind, sure. But it's my own need, too. My need to *feel* him. This is what makes sense right now.

'You are like an angel,' he mutters, stripping my swimsuit from my body. The fabric is wet and stubborn, but his hands are strong and determined and dispose of it easily, rolling it down my flesh, my legs, until I can kick it off my feet. He brings his mouth back to mine and I kiss him once more, my hands grabbing his cock and guiding him towards me.

He pauses, though, his eyes seeking mine as though he's asking me something, needing something else.

I smile at him—a slow-spreading smile—and I whisper, 'Please...'

He moves inside me and something is shifting around us—changing—as tangible as the pleasure that rolls through me.

We want this to be clear-cut, yet it no longer feels that way. It's not just sex this time... It's a slow exploration that curls my toes and, I'm afraid, shakes my heart to life.

CHAPTER NINE

'I LOVE THIS CITY.'

His eyes meet mine, his smile disarming, and my body responds. I swear my breasts grin at him. Happiness settles around my shoulders.

'It's beautiful.'

A pizza box sits between us, the contents half-eaten. He reaches for another piece and I watch his fingers curl over the crust.

Making love by the pool broke something inside me and I'm glad—because it's rebuilt me in a different way. *I'm* different. *He's* different. Nothing is the same now.

'It's clean. New.' He smiles. 'Nothing like where I grew up.'

I have to shake myself into the conversation. I'm genuinely interested in where this is going, but the cobwebs of lust are hard to ignore.

'Dublin?'

'Yeah. Just outside it, anyway. A grimy little town to the east.' He wrinkles his nose.

'Do you ever get back?'

'Nah.' He throws the crust back into the box and stands up, holding his hands out to me.

I stand and put my hands in his. When did I stop questioning him and just become a part of him? And why doesn't it bother me more?

'My parents moved to Kerry—a little house over-looking the ocean, as far as you can see. It's beauti-ful there.'

'But you like cities?' I say as he pulls me towards him and holds me close.

He begins to sway, dancing with me on the balcony of his apartment as the moon casts a silver light over the Sydney Opera House.

'I like the pace,' he agrees. 'I'm not one for small towns.'

I tilt my head to the side. 'I don't know...' I say thoughtfully. 'I think cities can be almost slower than towns. It just depends on how you spend your time. There's certainly a lot of anonymity in a city. Haven't you ever just wanted to get lost? You can walk down Oxford Street on Boxing Day and not be seen by any-one.'

He presses his cheek against mine. There it is again. That clicking inside me as I acknowledge how right this feels. I know it's a very dangerous thought—one that will certainly lead me to pain.

'I can honestly tell you I have *never* contemplated walking down Oxford Street—let alone on Boxing Day. Are you fucking mad?'

I smile against his chest. 'Yes, well, I suppose you'd send someone to get whatever the hell you need, right?'

His smile indicates agreement.

'Anyway, you live in Hampstead. That's basically as small town as it's possible to get inside London.'

'But so close to everything. And might I point out that you live there, too?'

'I moved to Hampstead because *you* live there,' I say sensibly, and then stop moving, looking up at him with obvious embarrassment. 'Because my *job* is there,' I correct, but my cheeks are pink and my eyes can't quite meet his. 'You know…with the long hours it just made sense.'

'I know what you meant,' he says, his smile sending fire through my body. 'Where did you live before that?'

I let my breath out slowly, glad he's giving me a pass. 'Elephant and Castle.'

He laughs—a gravelled sound. 'Your parents must have *loved* that!'

They hated it. His insight shakes me. 'Why do you say that?'

'You had three nannies growing up, and a tree house big enough to sleep in. My guess would be they felt it was a bit of a fall from grace for you.'

I hide my smile by dipping my head forward. He lifts my hand and twirls me in his arms, as though we are dancing to a song that only he can hear.

'It wasn't their idea of sensible, no. But it was easy to get into work from there, and I had good friends in the area. Plus, I loved spending my Saturday mornings at Borough Market and it was an easy walk.'

'A closet foodie?' he prompts.

'No. I'm too busy to cook. But I'm a sucker for fresh

flowers.' I exhale. 'And cheese. I would go from stall to stall buying whichever cheese took my fancy, savouring it that afternoon with a matched glass of wine.'

'Sounds pretty damned good.' He grins.

'Yep.'

'And you gave all that up to work for *me*, huh?'

'Not all of it,' I say with a wink. 'There's a pretty amazing cheese shop on the high street, you know.'

'And flowers?'

'Always.' I tilt my head up to his and then immediately look past him, to the glittering view of Sydney by night. There is something in his face that calls to me, and I know it would be foolish to answer it.

'Let me guess. You like white Oriental lilies?'

I'm surprised that he even knows a variety of flower, let alone is hazarding a guess as to which would be my favourite.

'No.' I shake my head. 'I love peonies and ranunculus. There's something so wildly chaotic about them that it makes my heart sing.'

'So poetic!' he teases, curling me against him and holding me tight.

I can feel his hard edges and planes, so familiar to me, but my heart is racing as though it's the first time we've touched.

'I think they're naughty,' I say with a grin. 'As though someone has said to them, *"We're going to make you the most beautiful, chubby little flowers in the world, but only if you grow straight up towards the sky."* And then they looked at each other and said, *"Nah."* Have you ever really paid attention to their stems? The way they wind round and round as though they're dancing in a thunderstorm?'

His smile is mysterious. Enigmatic. He is, at times, impossible to read.

'No.'

'No? You don't agree?'

'No, I've never looked at their stems to the degree you have. Nor have I anthropomorphised them.'

'Then you've led a very deprived life, sir.'

I feel his laugh rather than hear it: a rumble from deep in his body. 'Apparently. Do you want some dessert?'

'I can think of other things I want more.'

He laughs and shakes his head, stepping away from me and disappearing.

Thwarted desire flames at the soles of my feet.

He returns a moment later, two coffee cups in his hands. Except there's no coffee in them. They're filled with a single scoop of vanilla ice cream each.

It's sweet, but truly dessert is the last thing on my mind. Before I can tell him that he pulls a hand from behind his back and holds out two perfect fresh cherries.

I grin as he places one in each cup.

'The cherry on top,' he explains unnecessarily, and my heart turns over in my chest at this gesture that is at once both sexy and sweet. Sexy, because how can I *ever* see a cherry as just a cherry again? And sweet because it is *our* thing.

We have *a thing*.

He digs a spoon into the ice cream and brings it to

my lips. I taste it, but as on that first night, with our first kiss, his mouth is on mine immediately, his tongue tasting me even as I taste the ice cream.

Dessert is forgotten.

His kiss is unlike anything I've felt with him. It's soft. Tender. Gentle.

He breathes in as though he's inhaling me and I do the same, smiling against his lips.

Despite everything we've shared, it feels like the most intimate we've ever been. As if we're connected on every level.

But then our desperate hunger takes over and his hands are pushing at my robe, connecting with my naked flesh with the same intensity that marked our first coming together. It's as though he's punishing himself now—punishing himself for wanting me in any way other than animalistic and wild.

He presses me back, his kiss hard against my face, his body firm against mine, until I connect with the glass balustrade that runs along the edge of the terrace. He drops his kiss lower, to my neck, and lower still, his stubble grazing along my front until he brushes a nipple, taking it into his mouth and sucking it, spinning whirls of pleasure through me.

He drops lower, and finally falls to his knees. His mouth against my clit is a welcome invasion, his tongue what I have been needing. I grip the railing, my hands tight around its edge, as he glides his tongue down and I moan, pressing deeper against him. He knows exactly what I like now, and it takes him only moments to stir me to a fever pitch of awareness.

I make a small sound in the night air, tilting my head back and staring up at the stars above Sydney as I fall apart against his mouth, my orgasm spellbinding in its intensity and strength. I sway, and almost fall forward, but his strong hands are gripping my hips, pulling me to him as he stands.

'You are beautiful,' he murmurs, pressing a kiss to my forehead.

My breath is burning hard in my lungs, supercharging my body. Everything about this moment is just that: beautiful.

I meet his eyes and—ridiculously—feel a stinging in the back of mine. *Don't let me cry!* How embarrassing. But there's something in his look that's spinning my gut, shifting through me with a sense of unreality. As though he's thinking something and doesn't know how to say it.

I watch him, waiting for my breath to settle and my pulse to slow. He opens his mouth. My heart is still. Then, with one of those rakish smiles I've come to love, he says, 'Let's go to bed.'

'So you're his other half? Professionally speaking.'

I smile at Clint Sheridan but my eyes are glued to Jack. Across the room he holds court easily, and a group of men and two women stand hanging on his every word.

'Technically, I'm his in-house counsel,' I say, with a sideways smile.

'But word has it that you pretty much oversee his entire workload.'

'Really?' I arch a brow and sip my champagne. 'His workload is pretty immense.'

'I can imagine.'

I like Clint. Given that he's going to be running the Australian operation, I'll have to work closely with him—certainly in the start-up phase. He's a bit nervous, but I think once he settles down into the role he'll be funny and fast. He's definitely relaxed a little, even over the course of the few hours we've been at his expansive apartment on Sydney's North Shore.

The view is spectacular—different to that from Jack's penthouse—and by night the city shimmers before us. The famed Harbour Bridge has been lit red, for some reason, and there's something almost eerie about the way it seems to glide over the water, an angry sentinel or a protective beacon. In the far distance there's a flash of lightning, and that only adds to the spectacle.

'Night show!'

Clint grins, as if following my gaze. Or perhaps he's seen the involuntary shudder—a response to the suggestion of thunder. I don't give in to temptation and ask if a storm is forecast. I'm not a little girl any more. I can recognise my phobia as just that—an illogical pattern of fear.

'Have you lived here long?' I ask.

'A few years.' He rests his hand on the back of a dark timber chair and sips his beer. 'Bought it off the plan. Thought I'd use it as a renter, but then—divorce.' He grimaces, as if the single word should communicate his entire backstory.

'I'm sorry. I didn't know.'

'Why would you?'

His smile is disarming. He's handsome, I realise. Strange that I didn't notice sooner. *Oh, yeah?* My brain is rolling its eyes again. It has a point. Finding another man attractive when I'm sleeping with Jack Grant is like taking a shower in the middle of the Niagara Falls. But there's no denying it. Clint has got eyes that are almost as dark as night, a thick crop of black hair, a swarthy tanned complexion—and he's built like a tank. Thick neck, muscled arms—like he'd be as at home on a rugby field as he would the boardroom.

Mmm.

'True. It's not really our concern if you're married or not.'

'Are you?'

My eyes lift to his, my smile hinting at a laugh. 'Definitely not.'

'That's funny?'

His eyes scan my face and there's curiosity there. I suppose I am of an age where women are generally on that path somewhere. Either dating, engaged, planning the wedding, married, just married, sick of marriage... I'm none of those things. In fact, marriage really hasn't entered my head as a desirable state into which to enter.

Out of nowhere, the wedding anniversary party fizzes into my mind. I could definitely attribute my lack of faith in the whole institution of marriage to my parents. The silence of my childhood sits like a dull weight on my periphery.

'Only in that I barely have time to plan a holiday, let alone something as monumental as—' I wave my hand in the air and the gold bangles I'm wearing jangle '—that.'

'Smart move. The whole thing's overrated.'

I arch a brow, sipping my champagne. My eyes travel across the room distractedly. They're just skimming faces and people, travelling out of habit rather than on any specific quest. But they glance across at Jack and meet his eyes and everything inside me lurches almost painfully. A primal ache of possession unfurls in my gut.

With effort, I turn my attention back to Clint. 'I suppose it's easy to feel that when you've just come out of a divorce.'

'Should never have got married,' he says with a shrug of his shoulders. 'Taught me a valuable lesson, though.'

'And what's that?'

'Gemma?'

I tilt my head, my eyes locking with Jack's once more. He's right beside me, his face unreadable.

'Am I interrupting?'

'I've never understood why people ask that. You obviously *are* interrupting.' I soften the words with a smile, but Clint tenses beside me.

'Then by all means continue,' Jack invites, his eyes challenging me silently.

'Clint was just telling me why marriage is a huge mistake.'

I turn my body away from Jack, giving Clint my full attention. Only I've made a crucial error. Jack's right behind me, and my back is completely hidden from the room. His hand curls around my arse and I have to bite my tongue to stop myself drawing in a sharp breath.

His fingers stroke my flesh, and even I can feel his warmth through the dress.

My knees are shaking suddenly.

'For me it was,' Clint backpedals, his smile dismissive.

'Sorry to hear that,' Jack says, pressing his fingers in a little deeper, shooting arrows of desire through my flesh. 'I need Gemma for a conference call I'm expecting. Is there somewhere private we can go?'

My heart is racing, beating so hard I'm surprised it can stay lodged in my chest.

'Yeah, of course—my office.' Clint nods, turning on his heel and moving through the lounge area.

Jack runs his hand higher up my back and then drops it to his side as he moves to follow Clint through the luxurious apartment. Three doors down a long, well-lit corridor, Clint pauses, his smile professional. It's clear he has no clue how Jack's been touching me, nor what Jack and I want.

'Make yourselves at home,' he invites. 'Need water? Coffee? Anything?'

Jack shakes his head and Clint leaves, pulling the door shut behind him. The office is large, and offers another view of the harbour. There's a desk in the middle, a sofa pushed hard to the wall and a bookshelf that holds a coffee machine and a bar fridge.

My inspection is cut short by Jack.

His lips find mine and his arms curl around my back, lifting me up and bringing me closer to him.

'What are you doing to me?' he groans into my mouth, the words both a plea and a hope.

'I don't know what you mean,' I manage to say. But his tongue is fighting mine and no further conversation is possible.

His hands find the hem of my dress, lifting it just enough for Jack to be able to cup my bare arse. He groans as his fingers connect with naked skin and he pushes his arousal towards me, his cock hard and firm. My body is desperate to feel more of him. But he grinds against me and I grip his shoulders, my body weakening at this contact that is so good I can barely think straight.

He lifts one hand to my hair. It's loose around my face and he tangles his fingers in its ends then pulls up from my scalp, his fingers holding me against his mouth. His other hand slips between my legs and finds my warm heat. He runs a finger along my seam and I whimper into his mouth, so wet and hot for him.

He pushes into me—just a finger, and just enough to make my body throb. I need something. Space. Breath. But his tongue lashes my mouth as his finger teases my insides, and pleasure is a spiral I cannot escape, cannot control. It spins in my gut, my chest, my heart, my blood.

I whimper again—a tiny noise locked in the back of my throat—and his fingers tighten in my hair. I am trapped by him, by this, our need for each other. His finger swirls, finding my most sensitive cluster of nerves, and I am shaking all over, from head to toe, my body his to please and command.

'Come for me,' he instructs into my mouth, as though he has heard my thoughts and knows I will do anything he asks of me.

My knees can barely hold me. Without Jack's support I would be a puddle of bones and haute couture on the elegant carpeted floor of Clint Sheridan's office.

Jack kisses me in a rhythm matched by his finger's invasion and I am falling apart in his arms, with no chance of reprieve or pause. No break in the assault of pleasure he is inflicting on me. He kisses me as I moan, my breath snatched, my blood fevered. And even as my muscles clamp around him, squeezing the pleasure from my body, his finger continues to tease me, so that the pleasure and awareness is almost unbearable.

The first orgasm is crashing around me even as a second, bigger one builds, and I grip his lapels, holding him as my world shatters in a mind-blowing moment of sexual awakening. I am fevered and limp, broken and whole.

But he's not done with me. Even as wave after wave of pleasure crashes across my brow his hands reach down, finding his zip and freeing his arousal. I know I have only seconds to regain my senses. To exercise my control in this situation that is eating me alive.

'No,' I say, and the word is thick with desire, fevered by need.

He stops, his eyes locked to mine, anguish clear in his expression. But he stops. Waits.

'Sit down,' I say, nodding towards the sofa.

Something like relief spreads over his face as he nods and moves to the sofa.

'Do you have a…'

He's reaching for his wallet before I can finish, fishing out a foil square. I groan as I slide it down his cock and then I am on top of him, straddling him, taking his length deep inside me, revelling in his possession and in his look of wonderment. Seeing that he is as lost to this pleasure as I am.

I move up and down his length, rocking on my haunches. His fingers dig into my sides, moving with me, but I am in control. When I feel him pump, so close to coming, I sit higher, so that only his tip is inside me, and he groans, tilting his head back as waves of pleasure engulf his being. I laugh softly, lowering myself back onto him and leaning forward, kissing his neck, his throat, tasting the desire that has overheated us both.

He holds my hips, keeping me low against him, and thrusts into me. My body is already on fire. It takes nothing for further flames to take hold, spreading like wildfire through my blood. My cry is muffled by his kiss, and he kisses me as together we explode.

Lightning flashes in the sky—closer now—but I barely notice. Even as rain begins to lash the windows I am aware only of *this*. Our own little storm, raging through our souls.

CHAPTER TEN

HE'S WATCHING ME, so I try to subdue my reaction. But as lightning and thunder burst almost simultaneously, and rain hammers the enormous windows and the roof of the pool room, I am quivering.

'You're actually terrified,' he murmurs with bemusement, his fingers brushing my shoulder as he removes the lightweight jacket I wore to Clint's.

'I'm not,' I lie, stepping away from him before he can detect the fine tremble in my body.

I dig my fingernails into my palms, staring out at the raging storm. It's furious and I can't stand it. If I was alone I would put earphones in and dig myself under my duvet to wait it out. But I can't, and he's still watching me.

My voice is scratchy when I speak. 'It was such a nice day. Where did this come from?'

'It's the tropics,' he points out, stepping out of his shoes and shrugging free of his jacket at the same time.

His jacket is slightly crumpled at the front, from where I curled my fingers into it as he drove me to multiple orgasms.

'Heat builds up, then it breaks in a storm.'

'Why does *that* sound familiar?'

His half-smile shows he agrees. We are our own tropical weather system. Sultry heat, storm clouds and flash floods without warning. And plenty of lightning and thunder, too.

A spike of lightning floods the lounge with an eerie glow and I jump. 'God!'

'It's only a storm,' he murmurs, closing the distance between us, his eyes locked to mine as his thumb presses beneath my chin, lifting my face to his, exposing me to his curiosity and inspection. 'It will pass.'

My stomach twists painfully now as the metaphor takes on new resonance. Is he trying to be cryptic? Is he talking about the surge of awareness that thunders between us? About us? Of course this will pass. What else do I expect?

'Sit with me.'

He squeezes my hand and draws me to him, holding me to his side as we cross the lounge to the white leather sofa that offers the most spectacular view of the harbour. The opera house is ghoulishly lit in white, and the rain lashing against it creates the impression of fog and apocalypse.

'Even the air smells different.' I inhale the acrid, electrical thickness of the atmosphere.

'Yeah…' The word is hoarse.

He sits, and I go to take the seat next to him, but he pulls me closer, landing me softly on his lap. And now his kiss is gentle. Soft. A kiss of reassurance that scares me all the more because of the way it shakes my heart to life.

I panic. This is too much. *Everything* is too much. I'm in the eye of two storms and I don't know if I'll survive either one of them.

'Tonight went well,' he says, his hand stroking my bare arm, comforting and confounding all at once.

'What do you think of the team?' I ask, finding what I hope will be common ground in our established business dynamic. Some reassurance from the familiarity of that life.

'Competent,' he says thoughtfully. 'I'm not sold on Ryan being a good fit.'

'What makes you say that?'

I feel him shrug, the movement brushing the crispness of his shirt against my skin.

'Instinct.'

'He comes highly recommended.'

'I know.'

He runs his hand over his chin and I hold my breath as I'm seared by the memory of him pressing his finger inside me, holding me as I fell apart. My gut clenches and my insides are slick with a swirling tempest of knowledge of what we've done.

'There's just something about him that seems wrong. I can't explain.'

I think back to the evening, trying to capture the same sense Jack has, and shake my head. 'We'll see, I suppose.'

'His contract has a three-month probation period?'

'Yes. I'll make a note to come over and review him at two months, though, if you're concerned.'

'Great.'

Lightning bursts again and I jump automatically.

He presses his forehead against my shoulder, the strangeness of the gesture not taking anything away from how reassuring I find it.

'Were your parents cross with you?'

'My parents? When?'

They'll be back in England now. I should probably go and see them. The thought cools the warmth in my body.

'The night you slept in the tree house.'

'Oh.' I shift a little, angling my body closer to his. 'Furious.' Then I shake my head. 'Actually, that's not true. They were disappointed.'

'Disappointed?'

'Disappointed that I'd not been cared for to their standards. Embarrassed that people might think they'd hired substandard domestic staff.' I grimace. 'Perhaps ashamed they hadn't thought to check on me when they got home—most parents would, after all.'

'You're not close to them?'

'Why do you say that?'

'Just the way you speak of them.'

'No. I'm *not* close to them. They're not that thrilled with my life choices.'

'Really? Graduating with a double first from Oxford isn't what they had in mind?'

'Hell, no. I was supposed to marry someone fancy and respectable, with a country estate to match but not better our own. And to appear in *Harper's Bazaar* articles…have tea at Kensington Palace.' I can't help rolling my eyes. 'I'm exhausted just *thinking* about what they wanted for me.'

'You don't strike me as someone who's into the society scene at all.'

'I'm not.' I shake my head. 'Their wedding anniversary is in a week, and it'll be a who's who of the British aristocracy. And, yes, *Harper's Bazaar* will be there.'

'You don't want to go?'

'I *have* to go,' I say. 'It's just—'

Thunder rolls around the apartment and I swear the windows shake in their frames. *We're going to die.*

He holds me tighter. 'It's just…?'

I don't know if he's trying to distract me from the storm or if he's really interested in my dysfunctional family, but talking *is* distracting me and distractions are good. Besides which, having opened up to him, I'm not finding it easy to curtail my thoughts.

'I'm always trotted out as proof of their happiness. Their marriage is a success. They've had a child. An heiress. I swear they actually *call* me their heiress during their toasts every year—like that's my soul function in life. To inherit.' I shake my head. 'I *hate* that. I've hated it for as long as I have understood their expectations. Or lack thereof. My existing is sufficient for their needs. My ambitions are irrelevant and slightly offensive to them. And my working for *you* is definitely tantamount to slashing the family tapestries.'

'You make them sound like selfish bastards.'

I laugh. 'Do I?'

'*Are* they?'

His fingers are glancing over my skin, stirring warmth and desire inside my chest.

'They're products of their upbringings,' I say, and then shake my head, for it's disloyal to Grandma to implicate her in my father's cold-fishery. He's really a grump of his own creation. 'Or perhaps of society's expectations. I don't know. They're very…stiff upper lip. Cold. Emotionless.'

His lips twist. 'Funny. That's just how I would have described *you* a few weeks ago.'

My eyes widen and I look at him. 'There's a huge difference between maintaining a professional distance and being cold.'

'Yes, there is.' His finger lifts higher, running a line over my cheek. 'You were doing both.'

'I was *not*,' I deny, offended by his description.

'You made ice look warm.'

I move to stand, but his hands still me. 'Why?' he asks. 'Why did you act like that around me?'

'It wasn't an *act*.' I sniff, staring out at the storm-ravaged harbour.

But Jack's insistent. 'You're not like it with anybody else. I never really noticed that until I saw you talking with Wolf DuChamp. And now I've paid better attention I see you weren't like it with anyone but me.'

'I…I was. That's just how I am.'

'No.' He's adamant. 'The guys from the Tokyo transition team all call you "Gem", like you're some long-lost buddy of theirs. You're friendly with Rose and Sophia. Amber raves about you. It's just me.'

I open my mouth to deny it, but how can I? He's totally right. I met Jack Grant and every single one of my defences was raised because I *knew*. I knew there was trouble on our doorstep: a chemistry we would need to work our butts off to deny.

'So what *is* it about me, Gemma Picton, that had you acting as though I were the plague incarnate?'

My heart hammers hard in my chest. There is danger in this conversation. Danger of truth and honesty and far too much insight.

'Maybe I thought you'd see friendliness as encouragement,' I murmur, my tone light, going for a joke.

'But not with Wolf or Barry or Clint?'

My expression is calm, but inside I'm shivering. 'No.' It's a whisper.

God. What is he doing to me? He seems to have become 'just Jack', but my brain reminds me forcefully that the man made a billion-pound fortune virtually from scratch. He's brilliant, ruthless and incisive. And determined.

'When did you realise this was going to happen?' He runs his finger higher, teasing my nipple through the flimsiness of my dress.

I arch a brow, my breath trapped in my throat. 'Um…around the night you kissed me and…touched me…'

It's a lie. I knew it from the moment I accepted the job. Proximity would feed inevitability. On reflection, I can't believe I stalled it for two years.

'I think you've wanted me longer than that.'

'Do you?' I clear my throat, and this time when I stand, he doesn't stop me.

I feel his eyes on my back as I walk into the kitchen and pour a glass of mineral water. The bubbles are frantic—hypnotic, even.

'Yeah.'

He stands, and I look at him helplessly.

'What do you want me to say?' I lift my shoulders. 'I knew you, Jack. I *know* you. I know that you're in love with your wife. I know that you sleep with women to forget her. Do you blame me for wanting to keep this insanity at bay?'

'No.' He drags a hand through his hair and his smile is ghostly on his face. 'I blame myself for not letting you.'

His shoulders are broad, and an invisible, enormous weight is upon them.

'I blame myself for not being strong, like you were. You wanted me, but you were never going to do a damned thing about it—were you?'

'Of course not. Apart from anything else, you're my boss. And that's *before* I think about the steady stream of women filing through your bedroom. This is probably the dumbest thing I've ever done.'

'Yes.' He nods, his eyes locked to mine. 'But you don't want it to end.'

I shake my head, seeking refuge in honesty at last. 'Do *you*?'

'No.' And now his smile is broader. 'Turns out I'm scared of something else.'

'What's that?'

'How much I want you. Need you. And I'm scared of hurting you, Gemma.'

'You won't.'

He nods, but I know he's not convinced. Nor am I. In fact, I would say Jack hurting me is as inevitable as the morning that will break over the harbour in the next few hours. But I don't care. Having given in to this, I am just a tree in the middle of a storm, trying my hardest to hold on, to stand tall even as it threatens to uproot me for good.

The mood is oppressive. Suddenly I want to lighten it. To make him smile. To feel his warmth and contentment.

'I bet you were a real little shit growing up.'

The ghost of our conversation lingers, but he makes a visible effort to push it away. 'Why do you say that?'

'Hmm...remember who you're talking to? You're stubborn and selfish...'

'Selfish, huh? I always look after *you*...'

My face burns hot and I'm sure it's flame-red. 'I didn't mean in bed,' I mumble.

His laugh is my reward. Sweet and husky, it makes my nerves quiver.

'I see...'

Perhaps he takes pity on me. He strides across the kitchen and props his arse against the kitchen counter. I imagine his tattoo through the tailored cut of his trousers and absent-mindedly slide my hand out and curve it over his hip.

'I was a good kid, actually,' he says, not reacting to my touch visibly.

I like the intimacy of this, though. Perhaps more than I should. Of being able to reach out and feel him, to sense his nearness.

'So your recalcitrance came later in life?'

He laughs. 'I guess so.'

His hand lifts and wraps around my cheek. I inhale. This moment, his fragrance—everything. I fold the memory away and store it for later delight. It is a perfect slice of time.

'I went away to school.'

'A boarding school?'

His nod is a small movement—just a jerk of his head. 'I won a full scholarship.'

'And you call *me* an overachiever?' I tease.

His smile is indulgent. 'I had no choice. There was only one way out of the backwater I grew up in. I succeeded because the prospect of failure was too depressing to contemplate. You, on the other hand, m'lady, are motivated by something I don't understand. You had everything… You were born with a fortune and a family lineage that dates back to the Magna Carta… It would have been so easy for you to stay within the boundaries of that life. And it would have been a *good* life.'

'It depends on how you define "good",' I say simply. 'I've never fitted in.'

'I find that impossible to believe.'

'Why?'

'You could fit in anywhere.'

'Trust me—I didn't want to feel at home in *that* crowd.'

His frown is just a very slight twist of his lips. 'So your parents are stuffy. What about your friends?'

'Most of my closest friends I met later. At university. Then at Goldman. Deloitte.'

'And here? With me?'

For a second my heart skids to a stop, because I think he's talking about himself and there is something so delightfully needy about the question that I ache for him.

But then he continues. 'Wolf. Barry. You seem to know everyone who works for me.'

'Oh, right…' Emptiness is a gulf in the pit of my stomach. 'That happens. *Your* parents must be proud of *you*.' I shift the conversation to him, hating the vulnerabilities he's able to expose in me so easily.

'Yes.'

He moves a little, bringing his body closer to mine, and then, before I know what he's doing, he lifts me onto the bench, spreading my legs and standing between them.

He's so close I'm sure he must be able to hear the thundering of my heart; it is surpassed only by the storm outside.

'My parents thought I would—at most—become an accountant. Like my father and his father before him. I was always good at numbers. It fair skittled them when I told them I'd bought my first company.'

'Yeah, I can see how that would bowl them over.'

His laugh is husky. He brushes his lips against the soft skin at the base of my throat, chasing the wildly beating pulse-point with his tongue. I moan, deep in my mouth, the sound strangled by my own hot, thick breath.

'You make it sound easy. Like you didn't want to be an accountant so you did this instead.'

'This?' He laughs, flicking the strap of my dress so it falls haphazardly down my arm, revealing my shoulder to him.

His kiss is sweet, like nectar. He finds the exposed skin and possesses it as only Jack Grant can, gliding his mouth over it, making me feel I have never before been kissed. It is at once intimate and simple and my back arches forward. Or backwards. Who can tell? The normal rules of gravity and physics seem not to apply.

'How do you know my family dates back to the Magna Carta?' I ask, though the words are squeezed tight from my chest, not quite coming out clearly.

But he hears. He understands. 'I looked you up,' he says unapologetically.

'You…?'

His mouth drops lower and at the same time he lifts my hand, drags the kiss to my inner wrist. I squeeze my eyes shut as he finds another pulse-point, tracing it with his tongue.

'I searched you on the internet,' he confirms, dropping my hand gently and cupping my arse, pulling me closer to him.

I wrap my legs around his waist. 'Why?'

'Because you surprised me the other night. I realised I should have known this stuff.'

'What stuff?'

'All of it. Your dynastic birthright.'

I laugh.

'What's funny?'

'Just… Only *you* would want to know more and decide to look it up rather than ask.'

'Asking would have taken time,' he says with an unapologetic lift of his broad strong shoulders.

'And we don't have time?'

'I'm impatient.' He grins.

'I had no idea.' Sarcasm is rich in my murmured tone.

His hands are on my knees and then they're tracing higher, his fingertips barely brushing my flesh as he searches for the softness of my inner thighs.

'Is that weird?'

I pause, concentration almost impossible. 'Is *what* weird?'

His lips are buzzing mine, just the smallest hint of contact making every nerve ending in my body sing. 'That I ran an internet search on you.'

'Oh.' I frown. 'It should be. But, no. For you it makes sense.'

His laugh is breathed across my skin, sending it into a break-out of goose bumps.

'Because I'm weird?'

'Because you're *you*,' I correct. 'Domineering, determined, somewhat wonderful you.'

He's still for a moment. Frozen by the compliment he didn't expect. Then he relaxes again, his lips are on my skin and my heart is flying out of my body, soaring above me. This is so *right*. So *perfect*. Out of nowhere I am in heaven.

'Are you saying you haven't done a search on me?' he teases, his hands lifting to the zip at the back of my dress and catching it lower, snagging it over my spine. My body is hypersensitive; I feel every single kink of his touch.

I have. I've looked him up *and* his wife. Something I am naturally hesitant to confess.

'I applied to work for you,' I say with a shrug. 'Of course I did.'

His laugh shows he knows me to be lying. Or at least being liberal with the truth.

'Why did you move your office from the City?' The question is blurted out of me before I even realise I've been wondering.

He pauses, the zip halfway down my back, his mouth so close to mine I want to push up and find him. But he's still, and the question hangs between us, and I realise I do want to hear the answer.

'Sorry?'

'I just... Speaking of questions...' My throat thumps as I swallow. 'Is it because of Lucy?'

His expression flashes with something. Anguish?

I shake my head quickly. 'Forget it. I shouldn't have asked.'

'No.' It's a gravelled denial. 'It's fine.'

But I might as well have lashed him with a stick dipped in lava.

'It *was* because of Lucy. She was sick at the end. I set my home up so I could be near her all the time. The room...the bedroom near my office... That was her room.'

Oh, God. How did I not know that? His little 'den of sin' held his dying wife's sickbed.

A shudder rips through me as the macabre sadness of it all washes over me.

'After she died I just… I didn't want life to go back to normal. I resented the implication that it would.'

He expels an angry sigh and now his fingers are pushing my zip down almost dispassionately.

'There's no textbook on grief.'

'Of course there's not.'

'But I expected to cope better than I did.'

His eyes sweep shut. He's shielding himself from me, but at least he keeps talking. That's enough. It *has* to be enough.

'We had months to prepare. To brace ourselves. She was ready. Her life at the end was…' He changes direction, as though he's somehow betraying Lucy. 'She was ready to go. My therapist tells me I spent so long being strong for Lucy that I had nothing left to give myself.'

'You have a therapist?'

'I did. Until he spouted *that* piece of pretty bullshit. As if there's a finite amount of support to give. As if I should have ignored Lucy's needs in favour of my own.'

'I don't think he meant that. Lucy's sickness must have been draining on you. I can imagine that you spent so much of your energy focussing on what she needed that you had no idea what to do with yourself once she passed.'

'It shook my world,' he said simply.

I'm so sorry for him. But I don't say that because I've said it before. My dress is loose around my waist.

I'm not wearing a bra and his hands run up my sides and cup my breasts as though holding them is his only form of salvation.

'It still does,' I say softly.

'It's different now.'

He runs his thumb over my nipple, his eyes drawn downwards, his attention focussed on the physicality of my body, rather than me.

'Different how?' I need to know. I want to understand.

'I grieve for her, but I can function. The hardest days aren't the ones that fill me with sadness.'

'No?'

'No, Gemma.'

He lifts me up, off the bench, wrapping me around him as he walks through the apartment, towards his bedroom. But I don't want him to close this conversation down.

'What are the hardest days?' I push as he shoulders the door inwards.

He lays me down on the bed and I scramble into a sitting position, not caring that my dress is simply a belt at my hips and my body is exposed to him completely.

'Days like this. Days when I am happy and distracted. Days when I forget to remember her. The worst days now are the days when I realise I haven't thought of her at all. Days like today, when all I've had room for on my mind is *you*.'

My heart turns over and, God, I am the worst kind of human because I delight in his admittance even as I realise I am triumphing over a dead woman.

Telling myself Lucy would want him to be happy, I stand up onto the tips of my toes so I can kiss him, and then pull him backwards onto the bed.

'Being happy doesn't mean you loved her any less,' I promise him softly as I flick his buttons open and run my fingertips over his chest. 'It just means you're human and that time is moving on. It's normal. It's natural.'

He doesn't answer, but his kiss is all the response I need. It is sweet and it is gentle and it is a promise from his body that I know he's not yet ready to make with his words.

The first week Gemma came to work for me I pushed her like a demon. I was so sick of the string of quitters before her that I'd developed a foolproof way to flush them out. I started them at six o'clock each morning, demanding different sets of information in advance and then what I actually required. This was to see how they thought on their feet.

She was amazing.

When she didn't have a ready answer she would procure it easily and without fuss. She was honest about what she didn't know and she stared me down when I tried to imply that her inefficiencies were a result of a flaw in her preparation.

She worked late, travelled to Paris with me on a minute's notice and never once complained.

And then one day I went into her office and found her asleep, just like she is now. Her head dropped on the desk, her hair like golden silk across her keyboard.

That was the first time I told myself she was off-limits. I wanted her even then. My body responded instantly, and in my mind I fantasised about acting on my desire. Making her mine. But it would have been a transient pleasure. And even then, when I hardly knew her, I knew she was a rare, fascinating object—someone I could never touch. Never hurt.

Yet here I am.

Here *she* is.

At some point during the night, after I'd fallen asleep, Gemma must have stirred and taken herself back to her room, respecting those unspoken boundaries we've erected even after I told her more about myself than I ever have another soul.

And that angers me. It angers me that she accepts those limitations even now.

It is not yet dawn, but the sky is glistening with the promise of morning and a hint of golden light steals through the blinds, marking her cheek and her arm. I wonder what it would be like to lift the cover and lie beside her. To wrap her to my chest and kiss her awake softly. To stir her body with mine.

But the day is breaking, and she is just as off-limits to me now as she was two years ago.

CHAPTER ELEVEN

My plane lands at seven. How soon can you be at my place?

I SMILE AT the text but my heart sinks. A week after I returned from Australia and Jack is almost home. A problem with the winery in New Zealand required his urgent personal attention, and as a result I have been in sexual purgatory for seven days and nights.

I am aching for him physically and, yes, I miss him. I miss him so much I can no longer doubt just what form my feelings take.

I love him.

I am in love with him.

And, just like Grandma described, it has hit me out of nowhere. It is a realisation and it is also an incontrovertible law of nature now, as unquestionable and rock-solid as gravity, helium, oxygen and rain.

I run a hand down my pale green sheath dress, feeling its silkiness and wishing like hell it was his hands, not mine, on my body.

Tomorrow morning…?

I wait for a moment, but he doesn't reply. Jack has Wi-Fi enabled on his jet, and he's always in contact, so I don't doubt he's got the message. I imagine his lips drawing down at the corners as he contemplates the fact that I'm not simply fitting in with what he's suggested.

By 'tomorrow morning' do you mean 7.05 p.m.?

I laugh and shake my head, reaching for my bronzer and giving my face one last flush of colour. My make-up is exquisite—I didn't do it, so I can say that. My hair has been styled into a rather vintage crimp, and a diamond clip is tethered just above one ear, adding to the *Great Gatsby* look.

I grab a stole and slip into my shoes, then scoop up my phone.

I wish. It's my parents' anniversary party, remember?

I thrust the phone into my bag and press it beneath my arm.

My driver is waiting. Not Hughes. *My* driver. The one I use when I have family stuff on and Mum and Dad like to know I'm observing the little rituals that matter to them. Like being chauffeured.

'Hey…' I smile distractedly, sliding into the back seat. I look at my phone.

Shit. I forgot. Skip it?

I laugh.

I wish.

What are you wearing?

I grin, lift the phone up and take a shot of myself.
I examine it quickly—one chin, eyes open, passably
attractive—and then send it to him.
His response is almost immediate.

Smoking hot, Lady Gemma.

My heart turns over in my chest and for a mini-
second I contemplate blowing the party off—to hell
with the consequences—and going to Jack instead.
My parents would be furious, but I suspect it would
be worth it…
I text him back.

What are YOU wearing?

A few seconds later I am rewarded with a photo of
him. I stare at the screen and my heart thumps hard
in my chest. He is gorgeous. So beautiful. So dangerously, darkly, distractingly beautiful.
I stare at his eyes and feel as though I really am
looking at him.

You're flying in a SUIT? What happened to comfort?

He doesn't respond immediately and I put my phone into my bag, letting my eyes catch up with the passing scenery. The anniversary celebration is to be at The Ritz—where else?—and the car eats up the distance from Hampstead into the West End, skirting Kensington Gardens on one side.

I check my phone again as we pull to a stop—nothing.

Disappointment fills me, but I will see him soon. Tomorrow. And we'll make up for lost time.

Just looking at that photo is enough to get me off. But I need more than that. I need to be held by him. To feel his arms wrapping around me, to look up at him and know that his heart is beating for mine...

'Madam.' The driver opens the door and I smile at him, stepping out into the cool night air.

Flashes go off in my face. I'm unprepared. Foolishly, really, given the high-profile nature of the party and the venue that's designed to draw attention. I just haven't been focussing on it at all. I plaster a smile on my face as I dip my head forward and clip towards the large glass doors.

The party is in The Music Room. I've been there once before, for my grandfather's birthday, I remember as I step over the threshold. The room is the very definition of elegance, with gold and pink highlights, enormous floral arrangements and curtains that look like they weigh a tonne.

I'm late. Only ten minutes or so, but the room is full.

The music is a perfectly refined string quartet, and my parents are at the end of a receiving line, like a scene from a Jane Austen book.

I pause, wondering if I can sneak away before they see me, go and find Grandma. I'd put money on her being near the bar...

But my mother's eyes meet mine and her hand lifts, waving me over.

I swear under my breath, plastering a smile on my face. 'Mum.' I kiss her cheek. 'You look lovely.'

She does. Mum is always stunning. And now, after her jaunting about—rather, her international philanthropy—she's acquired a caramel tan. Her outfit is almost bridal—a cream lace prom dress that falls to just below her knees. Dad is in a tux.

'Welcome home,' I say.

'Oh, yes. That's right. We haven't seen you since we got back.' Her lips pucker in disapproval.

'I've been in Australia,' I explain awkwardly, then wish I hadn't. Why the heck am I apologising? It's not like they've been tripping over themselves to organise a reunion. 'Was it a good trip?'

My father grumbles something I don't quite catch.

'Quite.' Mother nods. 'We're thinking of going again next year—aren't we, darling?'

His look is one of long-suffering tolerance. 'We'll see.'

'Is Grandma here?'

My mother nods, her eyes flitting across the room. 'In that direction.'

'I'll go and check on her,' I say, as though it's a service I can offer when in fact I am serving only myself.

'Is your speech ready, darling?' Mother calls to me as I leave.

I wince. *Shit*. Why didn't I remember I'd have to do a speech?

I cut through the crowd until my eyes land on Grandma. Her wiry figure is perfectly framed by a jet-black dress and a bolero that has a fine silver thread to it. She's wearing dark silk flowers at the collar and she manages to look rather funereal.

I laugh as I approach. 'Hey!'

'Oh, thank fuck. Someone I actually *like*.'

Several people hear her curse and move away disapprovingly. I grin, kissing her papery cheek.

'Tell me about it… I think this is an even duller crowd than usual.' I tap the bar, my eyes catching the bartender's. 'Champagne.'

He pours a glass of Bollinger and hands it to me. Grandma signals for a top-up and I wonder, with a disguised smile, how many glasses she's already knocked back. She can hold her liquor like a sailor, and age isn't slowing that down.

'Where's my koala?'

'Your…huh?'

'You went to Australia, didn't you?' she asks impatiently.

'Oh. Yeah, right. Guess what? Turns out you *do* have to go bush to see one.'

'And let me guess? You were working too hard for that?'

'Mmm...'

It wasn't all work. My body flushes with remembered pleasure. Jack's touch was worth travelling to the other side of the world for.

'I did see dolphins from Jack's balcony, though. They were amazing. A whole pod of them, just gliding and...frolicking.'

'They were on the balcony?'

'No, Grandma, they were in the harbour.' I laugh.

'Obviously, dear.' She takes another sip of champagne. 'Remember your grandfather's birthday?'

I nod. 'I was thinking of it when I came in.'

'He was so happy that night. To be surrounded by his loved ones.' She sighs, her eyes a little watery as she looks around the room. 'The mayor's here.'

I follow her gaze. 'Yes. Dad and he have been doing some work together, I think.'

Grandma's brows lift skyward, as if imbuing even that with a response of disapproval. I sip my champagne.

'You had a good time, then?'

'Yeah. Australia's beautiful. I like Sydney.'

'So why did you come back?'

I laugh. 'You're turning into a one-track record.'

'Darling, life's too short for pleasantries, and I love you too much to lie.'

'I live *here*. I'd miss *you*, apart from anything.'

'I'd come and visit.'

We're interrupted by an old friend of my father's, and for the next twenty minutes Grandma and I make polite conversation, all the while subtly—and, I fear, not so subtly—nudging one another's ankles and trying not to roll our eyes.

There is someone else after that, and then my grandma's goddaughter Laurena—another story altogether... *ugh!* And then, before I know it, it's half past seven.

Jack will have landed by now. In his suit. So handsome; such a waste.

I sigh and refocus my attention on the conversation I'm half involved in, nodding as required, and then I'm actually grateful when my father asks me to dance with him. There's only a small makeshift dance floor—a concession to the fact that there are so many guests and most of them are not interested in dancing.

But Dad and I have always danced. He wraps his arms around me and it reminds me of when I was a little girl, standing on his feet, moving in time to the music. And it's a hell of a lot better than shooting the breeze with my parents' friends.

I feel a wave of sympathy for Grandma, whom I have deserted and left to the well-heeled wolves. I look over my shoulder to see her holding court and wonder, with a distracted smile, what she's talking about.

'How's work, pumpkin?'

I blink back to my father. 'Great.'

'Really? That's a shame.'

'It is?'

'Sidney was just saying he could use a consultant with your skill set.'

'Mayor Black?' I prompt, my smile wry.

'He's admired your career for a long time. Asked if I'd set up a meeting.'

'I've got a job, Daddy. A job I love.'

And then, as if I have somehow conjured him from my longing and imagination, Jack is beside us, his eyes intense as they lock solely to mine, his expression inscrutable. It is him and me—*us*. Just us.

'Jack?' I stop dancing altogether and take a small step away from my dad. I can hardly catch my breath. 'What are you doing here?'

'You invited me. Remember?'

I did no such thing, and we both know it, but I'm not going to point that out in front of my father.

'Right, of course.' I nod. Blood is roaring through my veins. 'I forgot. Dad, this is Jack Grant. My…er… boss.'

Jack extends his hand and shakes my father's with his natural confidence. 'My Lord.'

My father is in awe—like most people who first meet Jack. It pleases me. For all he hates the hours I work, and the commitment I have to my job, he obviously understands the unique thrill that comes from working with someone like Jack.

'Mind if I cut in?'

'Oh, I… Of course not.'

My father steps back, but I don't see him move away because Jack wraps his arms around me and consumes all my senses.

He overpowers me with his nearness and his uniqueness. He moves in time to the music but I feel his body, tight and hard, and my gut clenches.

'What are you really doing here?'

There is something I don't understand in his features. A haunted expression. Anger?

'You seem kind of uptight about this. I've never seen you like that about anything.'

I nod slowly. Does he think that explains anything? 'So…?'

'I was at a loose end.'

'Oh.' My heart thumps painfully. 'Right.'

What was I expecting? Flowery declarations of love?

'You were my plan,' he says gently, his fingers running over my back. 'I wanted to see you. And you were here.'

'So you came here?' I murmur, crossing over into unnecessary repetition and not caring.

Because my heart is floating away from my body, thumping high in the sky over us.

'Pretty much.'

His smile makes my stomach flip and flop and twist and turn.

'Well, I'm not so sure I want to be here now.'

His laugh undoes the last stitch of my sanity. I want to strip my clothes off and cry out, *Take me now!*

'My evil plan.' He grins. 'How's your week been?'

Is this really happening? Is Jack Grant at my parents' wedding anniversary party, dancing with me, stroking my back, asking me about my week, telling me he's missed me? Or am I somehow dreaming this up? It doesn't make sense.

'Busy. Yours?'

Wow. I sound normal. Good job, me!

'Perfect.' He winks—so sexy. 'New Zealand is stunning; the winery is incredible.'

My sigh is wistful. 'I'll bet.'

He chuckles. 'You'll see it for yourself next time you're over.'

'Yeah…'

I try not to get too swept up in fantasies that involve Jack and me skipping down the rows of grapes, holding hands, laughing into the sunset. Fantasies are nice, but they're not real life.

'Jack Grant?'

I feel his sigh but he hides it well, turning to look at the man who's come to address us. I recognise him, but can't think of his name in that moment.

'Adam.' Jack nods, not relinquishing his grip around my waist. 'How's it going?'

'Jesus, I haven't seen you in *years*. I've kept up with you, of course. Amazing career. Got a moment? I'd love to talk to you about a project I'm in the middle of.'

'Actually…' Jack says, and my heart leaps.

But we're attracting attention, and I'm not sure either of us is ready to deal with that yet.

I clear my throat and step backwards. 'It's fine.' I wince inwardly when I hear the ice-cold tone that bleats from my lips. I soften it with effort, stretching my lips into a smile. 'I want to go check on my grandma, anyway.'

'Ah, she's here?' Jack's eyes glint with shared knowledge. My gut somersaults. 'I look forward to meeting her.'

His gaze holds mine for a moment too long and the universe vibrates differently—just for us.

I smile as I walk away, swinging my butt, knowing that not only is he here with me tonight because he cares for me, but that soon we're going to be making love and I cannot wait.

'Things are making a little more sense now,' Grandma murmurs, her eyes trained on Jack's profile.

He's locked in conversation with the man—Adam—his expression instantly businesslike. My heart thumps.

'What do you mean?' I reach down and sip her champagne, taking the seat beside her.

Grandma taps my knee. 'It isn't just a job.'

I contemplate denial, but it's Grandma. She'll see through it.

'Meaning?' I say instead, cautious. Waiting.

'You're seeing him?'

Trust Grandma. I bite down on my lip. 'Not really. Kind of.'

'You love him?'

My heart throbs. I look at her and shake my head, but my smile tells a different story.

'I see.' She tilts her head, her eyes pinned to Jack as though she's pulling him apart, piece by piece. 'Interesting…'

'Not really.' I shake my head. 'And it's very…early. New.'

'Secret?' she supplies, her eyes flitting to mine and sparkling with the hint of mystery I've evoked. I sigh. There'll be no stopping her now.

'Yes, secret,' I say after a beat.

'Fine. I can do secret.' She winks at me and taps my knee once more.

It's more than an hour before I get near Jack again, and by then I am *desperate* to touch him. To kiss him. To be alone with him. I'm almost there—just a few people to navigate—when my parents take to the stage and the music goes silent. The guests follow suit.

My mother is a natural-born performer. She speaks easily to the crowd, playing the part of happy wife perfectly. My father toasts her and then they introduce me. Their heir.

Ugh.

I paste a smile on my face, sashaying close enough to Jack on my way to the stage that his hands brush my hip and my body charges with electricity.

I'll do the damned tribute speech and then we'll go. Him and me. Alone time with him is the talisman on the periphery of my mind.

There are a heap of people looking back at me, but I see only Jack. His eyes seem to caress me, even from this distance. A pulse throbs between my legs. Desire is a tangible force, wrapping me in its determined grip.

'I've been thinking about love and marriage a lot lately. About the leap of faith required to take that step. We can enter into a relationship with the best of intentions and find that it doesn't work out. That our love alone isn't enough—that it doesn't go the distance. Or perhaps we lose the person we love most on earth, and feel robbed of our soul mate. Our love.'

My eyes hold Jack's and I blink, my heart twisting.

'Or perhaps we fall in love and marry and everything is perfect. A true happily-ever-after.'

I turn and smile at my parents, hoping that these vague descriptions of love will somehow mean something to them. It's hard to tell. Botox has rendered my mother's range of visible reactions down to single digits. There's disapproval, impatience, wry amusement and boredom. I don't know which of these she's feeling, so I turn back to the assembled guests.

'My grandma talks about meeting my grandpa almost as if the moment was divined by fate. There was an inevitability to their life and love—one she couldn't have fought even if she'd wanted to.'

I smile at Grandma and the tears in her eyes make me proud, because she understands that I *know*. I know what she felt.

'I think marriage is a remarkable thing, and I congratulate my parents on thirty years of it. To Mum and Dad.'

I lift the glass in my hand and smile at them.

My mother nods her thanks. Dad blows me a kiss. The crowd repeats my toast and I walk off stage.

I set my champagne flute down on the edge of a table and don't look at another soul. Instead I walk towards the doors, my stride meaningful, my attention unwavering.

I don't say goodbye to Grandma, and nor do I acknowledge any of the guests looking to congratulate me on my toast. I stare straight ahead until I am out. Free.

I continue to walk—down the stairs to the foyer

and then, my heels clipping noisily, across it. I am conscious only of my own breath, my own footsteps, until I reach the glass doors and wait. And wait.

Not for long. Not even a full minute in reality.

He doesn't speak. His hand on the small of my back is warm and intimate and my stomach dips. My knees almost buckle.

He guides me out of The Ritz and I smile at Hughes. I am prepared to step apart from Jack, to put some distance between us. But he doesn't let me. His hand stays glued to the base of my spine, and the moment I step into the limousine he catches my shoulder and spins me.

His eyes are charged with emotion, but I cannot fathom what he's feeling. I know only that he wants me with the same burning desperation that rips through me.

'We're going?' I prompt, my eyebrows raised.

'You'd better fucking believe it.'

And then, as if he has no choice, no free will, no say in the matter, he drops his head and presses a bone-meltingly lovely kiss against the tip of my nose.

As if I didn't love him enough already.

CHAPTER TWELVE

'CARRIE?'

My voice is croaky and my eyes sting as I answer my phone. I'm tired. What bloody time is it?

I peer into the darkness of Jack's room and panic sets in.

I've slept in his bed. With him. All night.

Or have I? He's not in the space beside me and his pillow is cool to the touch.

I look beyond it to the clock on his bedside. It's not as early as I feared—just gone eight. But it *is* Sunday, and I probably only got an hour's sleep the night before.

My cheeks flush pink as I remember the way our bodies rediscovered one another. Desperate at first, we came together as soon as we walked in the door of his apartment. Then slower, more sensually. An exploration. A reacquaintance. And finally dominatingly, Jack using my needs to control me and me letting him, loving it.

Still, I realise I haven't spoken to my friend in weeks, since our rescheduled catch-up. 'Is everything okay?' I ask.

'Um, shouldn't I be asking *you* that?'

'Why?'

I frown, running a finger over the crisp white duvet. *Where's Jack?*

'What's up?'

'I take it you haven't seen the papers yet?'

I shake my head, scrambling to remember which of Jack's business deals was at a crucial stage. What could have gone wrong?

Cursing under my breath, I find my feet are half-way to the ground when Carrie reads aloud: *'"Beauty and the Billionaire..."'*

Oh, shit.

'What is it?'

'Want me to read it?'

'Give me the gist,' I murmur urgently, dipping my head forward.

'"Renowned billionaire philanthropist and widower Jack Grant may be ready to get back into the swing of things. Spotted out and about with Lady Gemma Pic-ton at The Ritz last night, blah-blah-blah..."' Carrie says under her breath, and then resumes reading. '"The pair have worked together for some years, but it appears their relationship has moved to the next level. Is it possible Britain's favourite billionaire is about to be taken off the market?"' She pauses, letting the words sink in. 'There's some photos, too.'

'I'll bet there is.'

I stand, reaching for Jack's robe, which hangs on the back of his door. It's dark blue towelling and falls

all the way to the floor on me. It smells like him; my
senses respond predictably.

'Which paper?' I cinch the robe tightly around my
waist, my hand on the doorknob.

'The *Daily Gazette*.'

'Oh, well,' I say with relief. 'That's okay. What the
hell are you doing reading *that*?'

'My cousin emailed it to me. She knows we're
friends.'

'Great. But no one else I know will read it.'

'Sorry, mate. It's in the *Telegraph*, too.'

My eyes sweep shut. 'Shit.'

'Is it true?'

There's earnest concern in Carrie's voice.

My denial is as swift as it is untrue. 'No.'

'You guys look pretty cosy in the picture…' she
says softly.

'Pictures lie. Look, I'll… Let me get back to you,
okay?'

I disconnect the call before she answers, wrenching the door open.

Jack is fully dressed, a cup of coffee cradled in his
hands, his attention focussed on the view of London
revealed by the windows of his apartment.

Several newspapers sit on the table. I move towards
them, instead of him, and cringe when I see that one of
them has given us a whole page spread. Photos of us
separately and photos of us working together make it
look as though this has been going on for a long time.

And, yes, there's the obligatory photo of Jack and
Lucy, taken on their wedding day. I'm drawn to her

eyes, her smile, her kindness that shines through the picture.

There we all are—the three of us, together in print media for posterity, for anyone who cares to look us up in the future.

'I'm sorry,' I say softly, though I don't know what I'm apologising for, exactly.

'Why?' He turns around, a muscle throbbing in his jaw.

He looks both incredibly handsome and utterly awful at the same time. His skin is ashen beneath his tan.

'This—' he jerks his head towards the papers '—isn't your fault.'

'I know…' I shake my head slowly from side to side. 'But still…it's not ideal.'

His nod is curt agreement. 'I've left a message for Amber,' he murmurs, dragging the palm of his hand over his stubble. 'To explain.'

I nod. It makes sense that he'd want to give Lucy's sister the courtesy of a heads-up.

'Fucking paparazzi *scum*!' he says loudly, and he makes me jump when he slams his hand against the chair nearest to him. 'I wish they'd fuck off!'

'You're kind of famous,' I point out gently, and despite the palpable stress in the room my lips twist into an awkward smile.

But he's not in a joking mood. I sober.

'I guess my parents' thing…'

'I shouldn't have bloody come.'

The intensity of his reaction surprises me. I understand that he's upset; I am, too. This is invasive and unwelcome. And the timing couldn't be worse—just as we're finally morphing into something else, something perfect, we've been put in a position of needing to define what we are. But still…

'Jack.' I command his attention with a clear voice. 'This isn't the end of the world, is it?'

He stares at me, and I don't know if he's trying to work out why I don't get it or trying to calm himself down. But he doesn't speak.

I cannot make sense of this without caffeine—that much is certain. I move to the kitchen and fish a pod out of the canister, slip it in place. The whir of the coffee machine is the only noise in the cavernous apartment. I let it run through and then sip it, strangely pleased when it scalds my tongue.

'Jack?' I say again.

He's looking at me like he doesn't recognise me. A month ago this would have cowered me, but not now. Not after what we've shared.

'Damn it, Jack. You're freaking out for no reason. This is just a stupid gossip story. We can ignore it.'

'No reason?' he repeats, the words quiet but infused with angry disbelief. 'No *reason*?'

'Yes—no reason. So what? So what if you and I are seeing one another? Who cares? What's the big deal?'

'Jesus…' He spins away, his back to me, rigid as hell.

'I mean it.'

I take another sip of coffee, but when he continues to stare out of the window I slam the cup onto the marble benchtop, cross to him and grab his arm. I yank on it, drawing him around to face me. He's holding on—being CEO, cold, professional, unfeeling. But he's feeling *everything*. I know that now.

'We've been sleeping together for over a month. We had sex in Clint-bloody-Sheridan's home office. Did it never occur to you that some time, somehow, it would come out?'

'I never thought about it,' he dismisses. 'Or I sure as hell would have been more careful.'

I change tack, folding his admission into a part of my brain that will later want to analyse all that is being said and done.

'*Why* is this a big deal?'

My eyes stare into his even as he looks away. I see every flicker of emotion on his face, and it's a little like watching a ship sink all the way from shore. I can't reach him. He's being devoured by an ocean that I cannot cross.

'Apart from the gross invasion of my privacy?'

I dismiss that immediately. 'You're a big boy and you're used to that. What else?'

'It's too much.' He shakes his head with weariness, running a hand over his stubbled jaw. 'Gemma, look... I have a thing this morning. I'm already running late.'

His sentence sits between us like a little row of tiny bombs. I can't help the look of disgust that crosses my face. 'A *thing*?' I ask, scorn deep in my tone.

'Yes, a thing. A breakfast.'

'You're *kidding* me?'

I lift a hand to his chest. He stands there for a mo-

ment, a tight smile stretched on his face, and then he
steps back, dislodging my touch, breaking our contact.

His voice is coldly authoritative. 'Don't feel you
need to rush off. You can let yourself out when you're
ready. Hughes will…'

'*Fuck* Hughes!' I shout, moving behind him. 'You
aren't getting rid of me like that. *God*, Jack! I have put
up with this for long enough. You blowing hot and cold.
You want me one second—then we fuck and you're
nowhere to be seen.'

That same muscle twists in his face, and it might
as well be a bullseye for how badly I want to slap it.

'So we were photographed leaving a party? So people think we're an item? Well, guess what? We *are*.'

He steps back as though I've given in to temptation
and cracked my palm across his cheek.

'We're sleeping together. Working together. We
know each other inside out. What's the big fucking
deal?'

'I can't do this right now.'

The louder and more screechy I become, the calmer
he seems. And that just makes me even angrier! It's
like a horrible hamster wheel and I don't know how
to get off.

'We have to talk,' I snap, my voice quivering like
an arrow striking a tree.

'Yes, we do.'

It's a softly spoken confession that fills me with
more fear than it does relief.

'But not now. I really do have a thing this morning, Gemma.'

But I know his diary, his movements, and I can't for the life of me remember a single entry for today.

'What? *What* thing?'

He looks away from me, guilty, and, *God*, I am fuming. Is he lying to me? To get rid of me? Is he so desperate to avoid having an adult conversation about what our relationship's become that he's inventing reasons to get rid of me?

Fine. I'd rather go than beg him to love me—which is what I feel like doing.

But just when I'm about to flounce off like a teenager in a strop, at the very last minute, he says, 'It's Lucy's birthday.'

Boom! The bombs explode and, predictably, I reel.

'I always have breakfast with Amber on Lucy's birthday. Given this—' he gestures with outrage towards the papers '—I think it would be in poor taste to be late.'

'It's Lucy's birthday...' I say with a nod, but inside my stomach is turning and my heart is shrivelling.

Had I noticed the glass before? My eyes find it easily now. A single Scotch glass on the edge of the table.

My eyes sweep shut.

He sleeps with women to forget Lucy. And that's what last night was.

Oh, God. *Oh, God.* Panic is like bile in my mouth.

'That's why you needed to see me last night,' I say thickly. 'It wasn't about me at all, was it?'

And I was so sure we were moving to another level—that he sought me out because he needed *me*. Because he missed me.

But it hadn't been that at all, had it? It was about Lucy. Always Lucy.

His eyes are swirling with anguish and emotion. But I don't care. I grab the belt of the robe and loosen it, pushing it off as I walk back into his bedroom. My clothes are strewn all over the place, where we flung them the night before, and they've landed haphazardly—the roadkill of our passion; the pathway to his penance.

I pull my dress on without bothering with underpants; my fingers tremble. He's standing in the doorway. I hear him before I see him, but I don't pause. I slide my shoes on.

'God! I'm such an idiot! You needed to *forget*. You needed to obliterate all your grief and whatever and *that's* why it had to be last night. Right?'

He doesn't answer my question, but mutters, 'Can this wait until tomorrow?'

Obviously it's just about the worst thing he can say.

I clench my teeth together and nod—because while I'm fuming I know better than to make any rash decisions.

'You're an asshole,' I mutter, pushing past him, taking satisfaction from the way my shoulder jams against his chest as I pass.

I stalk towards the front door but then change my mind and spin around, moving back towards him. My hand pushes at his chest and tears sparkle in my eyes. I push him and then I lift up on my tiptoes and I kiss him. *Hard*.

My mouth punishes him and I sob into the kiss, hating him, hating Lucy, hating it all so much but needing him to understand.

I rip myself away, my breath dragging ferociously from my lungs, my eyes whispering warm droplets from their corners.

'That is about *you* and *me*. Nothing else. No one else. It's *us*, Jack. Got it?'

He is infuriatingly immovable. His hands on his hips, his breathing even.

'Tomorrow,' he says softly, like a plea, and I nod.

But I know what tomorrow will bring.

Tomorrow is the dawning of a new day; tomorrow will be our end.

She is everywhere I look, despite the fact no visible sign remains. She's in the rumpled sheets of my bed, the towel I dry myself with after the shower, the toothbrush next to mine in the bathroom vanity unit. She's in the half-drunk coffee on the bench and the pool of coffee beside it, from where she presumably slammed it down.

I didn't noticed at the time but she must have been angry to do that. Gemma doesn't waste coffee.

My expression ghosts with a smile but I blank it.

I find myself standing in front of the newspapers once more and I look at Lucy. It's like I've been stabbed through my heart, a pain familiar to me. She was so happy on our wedding day; we both were. How could we have known what darkness was in store?

I press a finger into the page, as though I can touch

Lucy's hair in real life if I press hard enough. But she's just a collection of black dots on cheap grey paper.

Fuck.

My finger moves to Gemma's face and lingers there, just beneath her chin. It's a larger photograph—almost half the page. The way she's looking at me... My gut twists and my throat aches.

Fuck.

The way *I'm* looking at *her*! How did I let it go this far? What madness has overtaken me?

I curl my fingers around the newspaper's edges and fold it back together, then collect them all into a stack that I carry to the wastepaper bin.

I get rid of them, and wish I could do the same to this mess.

I have to end it.

Gemma deserves better than this—to be jerked around by a man who can never give her what she wants. She wants my heart and it's no longer a part of me. I gave it to Lucy... She took it away with her.

The stars are not wanted now: put out every one;
Pack up the moon and dismantle the sun;
Pour away the ocean and sweep up the wood.

He's at my desk when I arrive the next day, looking immaculate in that blue shirt that makes me throb with the desire I partly want to cave in to. But I'm too angry, too sad, too hurt.

Grandma called me earlier, to enquire about my 'friend'. I didn't have the heart to tell her that the first 'friend' I'd had in years was about to put an end to things. Or that I was. That things had run their course.

'Coffee?' He nods to the mug in front of him.

I shake my head. I'm pretty sure I'll be ill if I eat or drink a thing.

'How was breakfast yesterday?' I ask, not meaning it to sound bitchy but suspecting it does.

'Fine.'

I'm pretty sure it *wasn't* fine, but Jack doesn't want to talk about it. And if Jack doesn't want to talk about it, then that's that.

I drop my handbag onto the floor with more force than is necessary and reach down, pulling out my Mac-Book case.

'I was blindsided by the press.'

'You and me both.' I move back to the door and click the lock in place.

'I've been careless. I shouldn't have let things go this far.'

'Bullshit,' I snap, a frown pulling at my whole face. 'Neither of us could stop this. It is what it is. We've worked together for two years—I *know* you. I'm not one of those women you bring home for a quick fuck.'

'You're not that,' he agrees, his eyes holding mine with an intensity that supercharges my blood. 'But there's no future for us.'

The words are spoken clinically, almost as though he's rehearsed them.

'Why not?' I'm not going to give in to my breaking heart and let him end this. Not just because he's afraid.

'This was never meant to be serious.' It's a short declaration.

'So? That doesn't change what we are.'

'Lucy—'

But I cut him off, shaking my head abruptly from side to side. 'Lucy and you... I don't want to infringe on that. I'm not asking you to renounce your love for her. I think you can love me, too. I think you can stay true to what she means to you and still make room for me.'

He clenches his jaw. 'I married Lucy for life.'

I nod slowly, my heart whimpering somewhere near my toes now. 'Even though she passed away?'

'Yes.'

He is so certain, so intractable.

I try a different approach. 'What would Lucy have wanted?'

He clears his throat and turns away from me. 'It doesn't matter.'

'I think it does,' I say with quiet determination. 'If you're going to invoke this woman as your reason for shutting this down, then I think you should at least pretend to consider what she would have wanted.'

'Lucy had only months to come to terms with her condition,' he says. 'She didn't grapple with how I'd live after she died.'

'Bullshit,' I dismiss angrily.

He's resigned. Frustrated. Tired. 'You didn't know her, Gemma.'

I move closer towards him, my voice a whisper. 'I know that anyone who has been in love would want their partner to be happy. Not to live out their life in a hollow, empty wasteland as some kind of sick tribute.'

He squares his shoulders as I speak, as though he can make my words bounce off. 'It doesn't matter.'

It's so arrogantly defeatist that I almost laugh. But I'm weary. So weary now. Deflation has set in and is sucking my energy.

'What are we *doing*, Jack?'

He turns to face me slowly. 'I've been asking myself that same question.'

'What do I mean to you?'

I look at him as he sweeps his eyes shut, the truth apparently not something he's ready to communicate to me.

'You're my in-house,' he says, with so much gentle concern that I feel tears sting the back of my throat. The use of my actual job title makes everything worse, somehow. 'And my lover.'

I am very still while his words sink in. 'You can't compartmentalise me. I can't be your employee at work, your lover after hours and nothing in between. It doesn't work like that.'

'Why not?' he demands with husky urgency. 'This is *good*. Those things are good.'

'But I want more.'

'That's all I have,' he says honestly. 'It's all I can give you.'

A muscle jerks in his jaw and I lift my finger to touch it lightly. 'You've already given me so much more. Don't you see that?' I say gently.

'It's not possible.'

His eyes are dead ahead, his jaw locked. I know Jack Grant—I understand him. I know when he's made his mind up and when it's useless to argue. I see his determination and in it is the answer I have been waiting for.

It is the end.

And yet knowing that and truly accepting it are two different things.

'How can you think this is just sex?'

He shakes his head. 'I should have been more careful. I'll never be what you want.'

'And what's that?' I push, approaching the precipice of what we are.

He meets my eyes; there is bleak reality in them. It breaks my heart.

He reaches for my hand and squeezes it. 'I'm not your boyfriend. I don't want to be. And I don't want us to get more serious. I just want to fuck you.'

Oh, God. The pain is like ten thousand blades running over my spine. It's unbearable and yet I revel in it, because somehow I feel I deserve it. It makes it easier to accept the truth.

My head jerks upwards. My eyes are clouded by grief. 'So that's it?'

His expression shows that he too understands the inevitability before us. 'Yes.'

His voice is pleasingly roughened by emotion so I know he's not unaffected.

I don't trust myself to speak. Not for a moment. I wait, counting to twenty in English, French and Russian, and then I reach into the neoprene case for my laptop and pull out the crisp white piece of paper I printed that morning.

'This is Carrie Johnson's CV. She'll be in at lunch-time to meet with you.'

He frowns, as if the sudden change in conversation has surprised him. As though he expected me to argue for longer, to fight for what we were.

'What for?' He doesn't look at the CV.

'For my job.'

A second passes while we both absorb the reality of that.

'She's excellent. Highly qualified. You'll like her.'

His face drains of all colour. 'What the *hell* are you talking about?'

'Obviously I can't continue to work for you,' I say with quiet determination, zipping my laptop case. My fingers are shaking, making a mockery of my calm delivery.

'Stop. That's bullshit, Gemma. Utter nonsense.'

'That you think so underscores why I need to leave.'

Fuck it. Tears are rolling down my cheeks now but I don't bother to check them. What does it matter?

I stuff the laptop into my handbag with relief.

'You've worked for me for two years. You can't just…because we…you *can't* quit this job. You can't quit on *me*.'

Quit on *him*? The nerve! *He's* the one who's quitting. I bite my tongue. More tears are stinging my throat and I don't want to indulge them.

'I can't work for you, Jack. Not for another minute.'

He's truly aghast. 'Why the fuck not? We're a team, aren't we?'

'Yeah. In bed. In the boardroom. But not in real life. No, thanks.'

He waves the résumé in the air. 'I don't want this… Carrie Whoever.'

'You'll need someone, and she's got what it takes to put up with you. She's got killer legs and a great rack. You'll probably get her into bed in a week or so.'

Jealousy rings in the statement. I don't care about that either.

'*Christ*, Gemma.' He drags a hand through his hair and it spikes in a way that makes my stomach roll. 'Don't *do* that. You're making it seem like that's all we were…'

'No. That's what *you* did,' I say angrily. 'You just said it. We're lovers. We work together.'

He tilts his head back, a growl escaping his lips. 'At least stay for the week. Let's just let the dust settle on all this…'

'I can't.'

I'm emphatic; my life depends on his acceptance of this.

'Why not? It's just a week. Seven days.'

'It's so much more than that. It's all of me. It's my heart. Don't you *get* it? This might have been just convenient sex for you, but to me… It's *everything*. I've fallen in love with you, Jack. I love you completely.'

I wait. And a part of me waits in hope. In the desperate, unfounded hope that he will say it back. That he feels it, too.

But he says nothing. He stares at me, and I stare at him, and finally—well beyond the time I should have given him—I lift my bag onto my shoulder and walk out of my office. I keep my head bent and I don't even acknowledge Hughes when I pass.

I'm so fucking *done*.

CHAPTER THIRTEEN

We need to talk.

THE MESSAGE BUZZES into my phone at three the next morning. I stare at it, my heart pounding, tears leaking out of my eyes. They make me angry.

I delete the message and turn my phone off.

When I wake up I've almost forgotten about it. I make my coffee, switch my phone on and it buzzes immediately.

Four messages from Jack.

You can't just ignore me.

I was surprised yesterday. I didn't handle it well.

Meet me for lunch today.

Please.

I turn my phone off again and leave it at home when I head out. After being tied to Jack—tied to my phone, my emails, my laptop—for the last two years, I'm look-ing up. Finally. And seeing.

I walk from Hampstead through Regent's Park to the British Museum. I don't think I've been in since I was a teenager, and strolling amongst the exhibits now gives me the perfect dose of perspective. Seeing the ancient Egyptian tombs, the mummies so perfectly preserved, the sarcophagi all shining and morbidly beautiful, I am reminded that I am just one person.

That Jack is just another.

That life is long and its adventures many.

I am philosophical enough to smile as I leave, but my heart is broken again when I walk past a man who is wearing something a little bit like Jack's aftershave.

Dejected, I head to my favourite restaurant in Dean Street and grab a counter spot, eating a roast lunch with a bucket of wine and staring out at the street as people pass.

A matinee show after that, and a slow walk home.

I'm exhausted when I finally get to my front door, and in no mood to see a huge bunch of ranunculus waiting on my step. I know they're from Jack without even looking at them, so I step over the arrangement, careful not to touch it with even the toe of my shoe.

I'll deal with them in the morning. When I have more energy. Hell, maybe I'll get lucky and someone will steal them to save me the hassle.

I stare at my phone as if it's a lit fuse. I'm torn be-tween switching it on and throwing it in the bin.

It's cowardly, I know, but I leave it off. I send a quick email to my mother and grandmother, telling them I've lost my mobile and that they can contact me on email if there's an emergency and then I go to bed without eating dinner.

I'm too wrecked.

The next morning, I am woken by his knocking at the door.

I know it's him because who else knocks with their whole palm? As though they have a God-given right to disturb you whenever the hell it suits them?

I ignore him, but my throat is thick with more damned tears and my heart is spinning in my chest.

His voice is muffled but it speaks directly to my soul. Deep and dark. He's calling my name.

I burrow deeper under the duvet, pulling the pillow over my head.

I can still hear him swear loudly.

Finally, though, he's gone.

I stay in bed all day. I doze, and I stare at the wall, and then I doze some more. I have never been in love before, and I've certainly never had my heart broken. I have no concept if this is normal.

I feel as though I've been torn into a dozen pieces, ripped apart piece by piece, and as if my brain is too sluggish to remember how to rebuild me. Some time after dark my tummy groans. I'm hungry. That's a good sign, surely?

I shove my feet out of bed, grabbing a pashmina as I pass my wardrobe and wrapping it around my shoulders. I catch a glimpse of my reflection in the hallway mirror and grimace.

Pale face. Bed hair. Red-rimmed eyes. Puckered lips

Ugh.

I haven't grocery-shopped in days, but there's a pack of soup sachets in my pantry. I check the date on them warily. Only two months past, and surely there's enough sodium in these things to outlast a zombie apocalypse?

I tip the contents of one into a mug and stare at it while waiting for the kettle to boil.

It's a proverb, I know, so it shouldn't surprise me that it feels like I am waiting for ever, staring at the kettle, waiting for it to click off and signal that the water is hot enough. After several minutes I realise I haven't turned it on at the wall.

I curse under my breath and rectify the oversight. The kettle immediately spurts to life. I drum my fingers as I wait some more and finally, when I can hear it's near enough to boiling, I slosh a little water into the cup and whisk it noisily with a fork.

Halfway through the surprisingly *not* awful soup, I remember I told my mother I'd be available on email. I doubt she's tried to contact me, but I feel honour-bound at least to take a peek. I open my laptop and wait for the emails to come in.

Jack's I delete without reading.

Curiosity is burning in me, but I know he has nothing to say that will change what has happened. However he wants to make himself feel better, I won't allow it. He *did* hurt me. He *should* be sorry. It's not my job to assuage his guilt.

I force myself to concentrate on the other emails, to put Jack from my mind. There is one from Grandma

and I smile weakly, imagining her typing it on the iPad
I gave her for Christmas. It probably took her an hour.

Darling.
I'm worried. I can't explain it in any way that makes
sense—I've had the heaviest feeling in my heart for
days.
    I'm sure it's connected with you.
    Can you call me tomorrow?
Gma Xx

My heart squeezes with affection for her. And the
sense that she and I are connected in some way floods
through me.

Trust Grandma to just 'know' when things aren't
right in my world.

Everything's fine. But I'll call you tomorrow. Love.

I switch my computer off and finish the soup. I'm
exhausted, but not sleepy. I've dozed all day, so I suppose that makes sense. I turn on the TV and stare at it
for a few hours before going back to my nest.

I wake up with the sun, and only the thought of Jack
coming again spurs me on to get out of bed. I doubt
he'll be content to bang on my door a second time, and
I don't particularly want to press charges for trespass.

I dress in running gear—for a quick getaway rather
than any genuine interest in exercise—and pull the
door open. The breeze slaps me in the face. I take care
to step over the flowers, resolving to deal with them

when I get back—really this time. I lock the door and begin to jog around the corner and up the narrow laneway that leads to several cafés.

Only I don't plan to stay in Hampstead. It's too close to Jack.

I catch a cab into Soho and lose myself in the throng of people and busyness. But as I kick out of Tottenham Court Road and get pulled into the riptide of shoppers on Oxford Street I have to stop walking and grip the brick wall beside me for support.

The pain is visceral and sharp.

The realisation that it's over—whatever we were, whatever it was—is deep and sudden. It ruptures my chest like barbed wire pulled at high speed.

I no longer want to be around people.

I move towards the road, lifting my hand and flagging down a cab. It pulls over on a double yellow, blocking a bus that lets us know its displeasure by sounding its horn loudly. I wave in acknowledgement and hurl myself into the back, giving my address and collapsing against the seat.

I must doze off because the cab driver speaks loudly as we arrive home and I'm startled as if from a deep sleep.

'Thank you.'

I tap my credit card and step out. It's early afternoon and my tummy groans with hunger. The breakfast I planned on didn't happen and I have only just realised. I step over the flowers once more, promising myself I'll throw them out soon, and push the door shut behind myself.

I've been home ten minutes when a knock sounds.
My heart thuds heavily.

I know it is Jack.

My eyes fly to the mirror opposite. I am still pale,
but I brushed my hair this morning, and at least I'm
dressed in something other than ill-fitting pyjamas.

'Open the door, Gemma.'

My heart twists. I have never doubted my strength
in all my life, but now…I don't know if I can do this.
Can I look at Jack, knowing I can't touch him? That it
is over? That we are over?

'Gemma? I will stay here all goddamned day if I
have to.'

I don't doubt the sincerity of his statement.

Sympathy for my neighbours has me wrenching the
door inwards.

And the sight of him causes me to suck in a huge
breath. Because he looks so much like *himself*—so
strong and powerful, so confident, so *unaffected*—
that any lingering hopes I've nurtured of his being as
destroyed by this as me die an immediate, suffocating death.

He's staring at me. His dark eyes are haunting my
face, dragging over my cheekbones, my lips, down to
my throat and then back up again. He blinks as if to
clear his thoughts.

'You're home.'

I frown, keeping my hand firmly tethered to the
door, holding it in place as if my life depends on it.
'Yes.'

He bends down and lifts the flowers. A pool of dark

brown has formed on one side of the waxed paper, where the overnight dew has set in. I look at the once-cheery blooms and am sorry for them. Sorry I gave them such a cold reception.

None of this is their fault.

I narrow my eyes, my heart pounding and breaking at the same time, like one enormous wrenching storm inside my chest. 'What do you want, Jack?'

I see his throat bob as he swallows, and I resist the urge to make this easier for him.

'May I come in?'

Just the question alone sets fire to my veins. It's so unlike Jack that I am surprised enough to consider relenting. But I don't.

I have seen his dark places. All of them. And he has birthed new ones in me.

'No.'

Exasperation flickers on his face. 'I reacted badly the other day. I'm sorry.'

He did. But it doesn't change the facts. Perhaps at another time he might have found a softer way to let me down, but nothing will alter the truth. I love him completely, and when I told him he made it obvious he just wanted me to go.

The memories strengthen my spine and fire my determination.

'It's fine,' I say, even managing to dredge up a smile. 'Let's just chalk it up to life's experience and move on.'

He groans and shakes his head. 'I don't *want* to move on.'

'And yet you ended it.' I swallow, afraid I'm going to cry yet again.

'I didn't fucking *end* it.' His eyes are earnest as they meet mine. 'I didn't *mean* to end it.'

My heart screws down inside me. 'You freaked out when our story went into the papers.'

'It was Lucy's birthday,' he says softly. 'I think it's fair to say I wasn't in a good headspace.'

'That night...' I look over his shoulder, my throat thick and tasting acrid. 'You used me to forget her.' My eyes sweep shut. I can't bear this anymore. 'I thought you were there to see *me*.'

He takes advantage of my temporary weakness to push the door inwards, to catch my face with his hands and hold me steady, and then he kisses me as though his whole life has come down to this moment.

As though it is the most important thing he's ever done.

He kisses me with hot, fiery need and I sob in my throat as I kiss him back—but only for a second. And then my hands are on his chest, pushing him, and my back is against the wall, holding me upright as my breath is dragged out of me. He stares at me for a moment and pushes the door shut. The flowers are discarded once more, but inside now, nestling against my shoes.

'You said you love me.'

He says it like a challenge. A cold line of truth that I can't take back.

'Yeah. I remember. I was there.'

His eyes narrow at my sarcastic retort. 'And? Is it true?'

I screw my face up and drop my head into my hands. 'Fuck you, Jack.'

He grabs me by the wrists, pulling my hands away so he can see my face, and he's so close that I take comfort from his body even when I know I shouldn't. When I know I should be demanding he get out of my house.

'Because I've been thinking about love, and how it's not something you can just walk out on.' He pauses, perhaps waiting for his words to sink in. 'You think you love me? Prove it.'

I suck in a breath and lift my eyes to his face. He's stroking my wrists, his strong legs straddling me. Without him and the wall I think I'd slide to the floor.

'Don't walk away from me.'

'Why should I stay?' I whisper, the words coloured by a thousand shades of sadness. 'You told me in black-and-white terms there's no future. I can't be with you. I sure as hell can't *work* for you.'

He nods, but his hand lifts and strokes my cheek. 'When I met Lucy I fell in love with her straightaway.'

I spin my head away, twisting it to the side, hurting as though he's punched me in the gut. The pain is no less intense. I want to shove him away from me, but there's such earnestness in his voice, and I am obviously such a glutton for punishment that I stay, my mind absorbing the fact that the man I am hopelessly in love with is now telling me about his wife.

'But it was partly a selfish love. I loved her because

she needed me. She made me feel like I was her entire world and I was addicted to that.'

His eyes hold mine, staring deep into my soul. I am exposed and self-conscious, because I find it hard to feel anything but resentment for his poor late wife.

'I wanted to save her. She needed me and I thought that was what love *was*. I didn't know it could be so different.'

The words form a crack. In my certainty and in my heart. 'What are you saying?'

'I feel like someone has cut inside me and excavated the very middle of my chest.' He grabs my hand and holds it against him. 'I'm empty *here*. I wake up and I can't believe I have to get through another day without you.'

His eyes probe mine deeper, deeper, watching and waiting.

'It's been three days. I can't do another one without you. I don't know when you became my reason for being, Gemma, but you *are*.'

Tears are burning my throat. I look away again, swallowing, hurting, *hoping*. But my brain won't let me be such a fool. Not again.

'It's just good sex,' I say stonily.

'I've *had* good sex,' he dismisses with deep-voiced urgency. 'I know the difference between that and what *we* are.'

My cheeks flush pink and I shake my head. 'You think that now because you didn't expect me to leave you. I *believe* you miss me. I believe you miss *fuck-*

ing me. I believe you miss me at work. But none of that is love.'

I force myself to meet his eyes and am instantly burned by the lie I've just told. Because I love him enough for both of us.

'How can you *say* that?'

It is a groan that perfectly echoes my own frustrations.

'How can *I* say it? *You're* the one who said it! And I think you spoke the truth. I think that's how you feel.'

'I was wrong. An idiot. I hadn't expected to love anyone ever again, and after two years you blew up my whole world. Everything I thought I knew and wanted exploded in front of me. I fucked up. *I fucked up.* I should *never* have let you walk away from me. I should never have let you quit.'

I swallow, my mind rushing to comprehend what he is saying, my brain working overtime trying to pick faults with his rationale.

'I don't believe you. You had so many chances to make this work. I think you can't stand that I've left you, but that's not the same as wanting this—us.'

'I wanted to convince myself that I could contain our relationship. That we could be lovers and work together without any emotional fallout.'

I nod, and then I shiver. I realise belatedly that I haven't turned the heating on and the house is frozen.

'I know that. You did a great job. You were able to flick a switch and turn yourself off when it suited you. That's not love either.'

'No,' he groans. 'I couldn't. That's the problem.

From the first time we kissed you have been all I can think about. That whole trip to Tokyo I was counting down the minutes till I could see you again. God, when you walked into the boardroom and you were so fucking *cold*—as though you could barely remember my name, let alone the fact I'd made you come against the wall of my office… Gemma…you've had me since then. I have been yours completely.'

A sob is silenced by my throat.

His voice is gravelly and I hear his sincerity, but my brain doesn't buy it.

'I'm messed up. I *know* that. What happened with Lucy was a shitstorm I never braced myself for. There are going to be days when I don't cope as well as others. Days when I am reminded of the tragedy of her loss.'

'I know that,' I whisper. 'That's natural.'

'Lucy's birthday—it's hard. It's a day that should be spent celebrating her chalking up another year and instead I just… I really feel her absence on those days.'

His eyes are bleak when they meet mine.

'The hardest part about realising I love you is accepting that I'll always feel like this. Like I'm betraying her by being with you.'

'No.' I shake my head, sadness for him filling me up. 'I don't want that. I don't need you to choose between Lucy and me. We're different, and how you love us is different. You never have to hide that sadness from me. Don't you get it? I love *all* of you, Jack, and that means loving your grief and your sadness. Loving you even when you are lost and alone. Loving Lucy, too, and honouring your relationship.'

His eyes are wide, as though he has never imagined I could say that.

'She'd have been as pissed off as all hell at the way I've jerked you around,' he mutters. 'She'd have been glad I've fallen in love with you. She would have liked you.'

He strokes my cheek, his lips close to mine. So close. I breathe in deeply and can almost taste him.

'*I* like you,' he whispers against my mouth. 'I like the way you drink almost as much coffee as I do. I like the way you can't hold a tune to save your life. I like the way you don't put up with my bullshit. I like the way you use that magnificent brain of yours and make me exhausted just trying to keep up with you. I like the way you see me and know that beneath all the fucked-upness there's something about me that you actually like. That I'm worth loving.'

He is. He *is* worth loving, and I do completely. But it is all so complicated.

I bite down on my lip, staring at him through new eyes. 'I just don't… I braced myself for this to end. But for me it was never just sex.'

'No.' He cups my cheek, his smile a secret communication from his heart to mine. 'It was definitely never that.'

He kisses the tip of my nose, like he did after my parents' party, and as then my heart soars.

'I know there are no guarantees in life or love, Gemma. I know that better than anyone. But I'm not going to waste another second when we can be together. You mean too much to me. So? What do you say?'

'About what?' I ask, my lips twitching into a smile.

'Let's *do* this.'

'Do *what*?' I prompt, shaking my head slightly, feeling a sense of bemusement wrapping around me.

'Life. Together. You—me. For as long as we have. Never wasting a day or taking it for granted.' He pulls me into a bear hug. 'I want this. I want *you*—so much.'

I expel the breath I've probably been holding, in part, since I stormed out of my office three days earlier.

'Let's do this,' I agree, my smile stretching my face.

I have known happiness and sadness, but I have never known such perfect, utter rightness before. It settles into my heart and brings me peace and pleasure.

I am Gemma, he is Jack, and we have found each other at last.

EPILOGUE

'GEMMA? ARE YOU in here?'

Strange that in all the time I worked for Jack I never came to this side of his home. The mysterious 'Private Wing' of his mansion. And now I am here almost all the time—in his bedroom, his kitchen, his living room. We have barely been apart since that afternoon three weeks ago, when he came to my home and broke down all my defences.

'Yeah?'

I set down my laptop and stand, butterflies bouncing about in my stomach as though it is a forest and they its sole occupants.

He sweeps in and I hold my breath—as always, bowled over by his physical perfection. In dark jeans and a simple white T-shirt he is hypermasculine and edibly delicious. The idea fans my stomach and I'm walking towards him before I realise it, itching to touch him, to taste him.

He sees the intent in my eyes and chuckles. 'Wait until you've heard me out!'

But he pulls me to him, his hands seeking the hem

of my shirt and lifting it so that he can hold my bare hips. He makes a small sound of relief at the contact and I echo it in my heart.

I understand.

This—being naked, touching—this is how we need to be.

'Remember my hunch about Ryan?'

It takes me a few seconds to remember the guy in Australia he didn't think would work out. 'Yes?'

His eyes are sparkling with something I don't understand. 'Well, it occurs to me that you would be an *excellent* candidate for his job.'

I blink, confusion and excitement at war within me. 'He's left?'

'Yeah. Just wasn't up to it. The job is difficult. I need someone I can trust.'

Of course the idea is instantly appealing. Building the Australian office from scratch would be a challenge to relish. And yet...

'It's a long way away,' I point out, as though perhaps my sexy, brilliant lover doesn't comprehend the logistics of geography.

'From London, yes. But we'd come back whenever you wanted.'

I freeze, my eyes flying to his face. 'We?'

A smile cracks over his face and I hold my breath.

'Why not?' He pulls at my top, lifting it over my head so that his hands can roam my bare back. 'Do you *really* think I'd let you move to Sydney without me?'

I stare at him and wonder if perhaps he's lost his mind a little bit. 'Jack...your business is *here*.'

'*I* am my business,' he says with a shrug. 'I can fly here whenever I need to. Fly people out to us. But I have it on good authority, my beautiful, distracting, brilliant Gemma, that you need to spread your wings before you settle down.'

'What?' I blink my eyes, realisation settling. 'Grandma?'

'Mmm…'

He drops his mouth, dragging his lips along my collarbone. I dig my fingers into his shirt front, a feeling of bliss spreading through me.

'She called me when she heard about our "developments".'

I laugh. 'That sounds about right.'

'She's given me a list of her requirements for when she comes to visit.'

'Oh, God.' I groan and laugh at the same time.

'I've told her she's welcome to come for as long as she wants. I think she's fancying a year or two in our guest room.'

I laugh and shake my head, but Jack leans closer, whispering, 'I've got an apartment downstairs. I think we'll set her up there so we can continue to enjoy our… *privacy.*'

I nod, grateful for his understanding. 'But, Jack, it's such a big move. Are you sure…?'

'Life's too short, Gem. You want to travel? To see the world? Let's do it. If we don't like it we'll come back.'

He lifts me up around the waist, carrying me easily to his bedroom.

His *real* bedroom. *Our* bedroom, I suppose, seeing as I have been with him here nonstop since the day he came to my house.

'Of course, if you need some extra convincing...'

I don't, but his lips around my nipple make speech impossible. I nod and murmur something incoherent, and as he kisses me until my body is vibrating and my insides are heated with need I see our future.

I see our home in Sydney, our love, and I fall apart in his arms, knowing that wherever we live happiness will surround us.

For as long as we both shall live.

* * * * *

RULED

ANNE MARSH

MILLS & BOON

For Aunt Monica.

For the Monday morning Skype calls, squirrel and
slug advice, and the best pictures of a California
anemone ever…

Our time together means so much! Thank you.

CHAPTER ONE

Eve

You see that big pink RV parked next to Lake Mead? That vehicle screams *look at me*. I painted sparkly rainbows and unicorns on both sides, along with my business name. Perfectly Princess Parties. The bling is great advertising, like driving a moving billboard around Las Vegas.

I put the *princess* in *party*—there isn't a five-year-old girl (or boy, frankly) in Vegas who doesn't believe I'm made of awesome. I specialize in birthday parties—we're the precake entertainment. We've got the dresses, the sparkle and the attitude to keep our audience riveted and wanting to be us when they grow up. Eventually, at some point between five and twenty-five, those same girls will realize it takes more than a dress and a crown to rule the universe, but the fantasy's fun while it lasts. And yes, I'm cynical. You meet more frogs than princes in my business. Ever notice how there's an overabundance of amphibians in every fairy tale—and a corresponding drought of royal suitors?

It's a numbers game.

Since it's about a million degrees in Vegas today, we're holding our monthly company meeting lakeside. Despite being as manmade as most Vegas attractions, the lake's gorgeous. After running through our bookings for the next month and brainstorming new party ideas, we've vacated our temporary boardroom (the picnic table underneath a particularly gnarly Joshua tree) for a well-earned swim.

I float in the lake, trying to pretend I'm not still thinking about our financial bottom line and how to drum up more business. Income-wise, we haven't hit survival levels yet. I tilt my head back, and everything's better in my relaxed, upside-down world. My three part-time princesses may moonlight as showgirls on the Strip, but they're paying their bills. Our singing dragon doubles as an Elvis impersonator. He's crooning the King's finest to my accountant. Everybody's taking a moment to let loose just a little and enjoy. We're going to get there eventually—*there* being financial security, fat 401Ks and permanent employment.

In fact, the only person *not* here? Rocker. My business partner and baby brother swore he'd meet us here, but he's once again failed to make an appearance. He's busy at an auto body shop where he does custom paint jobs. Plus, he rides with the Black Dogs MC. He swears the motorcycle club is completely on the up-and-up. According to him, the stuff you see in the TV shows or read about on the internet is 98 percent crap and untrue.

It's the other 2 percent that worries me.

My baby brother now stands a whopping six feet two

inches tall. I practically raised Rocker after our parents flaked out on us, and I did the best I could. Money and education—those two things keep you safe, get you out of the lousy neighborhood and into the good places. The princess party business is our first-class ticket out of East Las Vegas to somewhere else. Somewhere safe. I may not know much about clubs or colors, but I do know that bikers are the opposite of safe—and Rocker's been acting secretive.

A splash sounds somewhere south of my feet and someone tugs on my toes. "Cavalry's here."

I sit up fast, butt bumping on the bottom of the lake. Carlie laughs, but she's already staring up the road, longing painted all over her face. My brother turned out to be hot and the bad-boy-biker thing is just the cherry on the sundae as far as some of my employees are concerned. Carlie starts finger-combing her hair and plumping her boobs up in her teeny-tiny bikini top—a definite Rocker alert.

Sure enough, a big, shiny, way-too-loud Harley approaches our temporary campsite at Mach Seven speed. Rocker drives too fast. He also brakes too late and too hard, his tires sending up a cloud of dust as he stops next to the RV. I wade out of the lake, grab my towel and brace myself for the excuses. He's endlessly creative when it comes to explaining his absences.

"Looks like I'm late to the party." A charmingly rueful grin curves Rocker's mouth. Objectively, I see exactly what makes Carlie daydream about my brother. Dark blond scruff shadows killer high cheekbones and his hair falls around his face in wicked disarray. His legs straddle the bike, encased in worn denim and ending in a pair of impressive black motorcycle boots.

He hops off the bike and sweeps me into a bear hug, grinning down at me. This is why I can't stay mad at him—no matter what we've done or how infrequently we see each other now, he's always glad to see me. He loves me, and he's not afraid to let other people know it. Carlie practically swoons behind me as he plants a gentle kiss on my forehead. A guy who's not afraid to admit his feelings is a prince and is just as rare.

"Fashionably late, Rocker?"

He flicks my nose lightly. "I got held up. Club business."

It's always club business with him. "I needed you here."

He makes a show of looking around the site. "Looks like you've got everything covered."

Uh-huh. We've had this conversation before, and it does not improve with age. "We're supposed to be partners."

"I'm the silent partner who provided the start-up cash. You provided the brains."

He gives me another easy smile, but I can tell he's done discussing this. He's got a point, too. I need a squeaky-clean image to appeal to the mom crowd—so by hanging back, he's actually doing me a favor. Plus, if I push him too hard, he'll just get back on his bike and leave. So I cave.

"You look tired." This isn't a polite lie on my part—there are purple shadows beneath his eyes and his pretty face is slightly worn.

"Club's keeping me busy." His tone makes it clear that this is another conversational no-fly zone.

"You know you have a job with me anytime you want it." We've had this conversation only about a million times, but it bears repeating. I will always be here for Rocker.

He tilts his head at the RV. "You really see me driving around in that thing?"

"What's wrong with the Princess Mobile?" Admittedly, the gas mileage sucks, but she gets us where we need to go, she's great advertising and she has honest-to-God turrets. Pop that sucker up and I can play Rapunzel on demand. It holds my costumes and props, and it gets my princesses from one party to the next.

Rocker's just starting to list all the reasons a pink ride isn't his thing when his phone goes off. He looks down and then disappears briefly to take the call.

"I have to go," he says, sauntering toward me.

Yeah. Color me shocked.

He pulls me into a one-armed hug. "Be extra careful for me, Evie girl?"

"I'm always careful," I tell him, and sadly, it's the truth. I'm a color-between-the-lines girl—he doesn't need to worry about me.

"Promise me," he insists and I think he's actually serious.

"You want to be more specific?"

He curses. "Evie—"

"Does it have anything to do with your club?" I point to the patch on his vest. I'd like to rip the thing off his chest, but it wouldn't solve the problem.

"Might do. Trouble's brewing," he says slowly. "Trust me. You don't want the details, Evie. I've got it handled, though. You don't need to worry."

Some things never change—Rocker swears he's got a situation under control, I worry, and then I conceive a half dozen plans for salvaging said situation. I love my baby brother, but I don't approve of his life-style choices. His biker buddies are bad news. Today, though, he really doesn't want to talk about whatever's bothering him, so I nod and promise to be extra careful. He gets back on his bike and tears out of the campsite faster than I've ever seen him go. Whatever trouble he's facing down must be really bad.

It's one hell of an exit—even more dramatic than the Princess Mobile. It makes it impossible to ignore his departure, which Samantha makes clear when she wanders over, fanning herself.

"God, your brother's hot."

I force a smile, although the last thing I want to discuss with my fellow princess is the degree of my brother's attractiveness. I've got bigger things to worry about. "In the category of things I don't need to know…"

"Who's hot? And are we sharing secrets?" Carlie wades out of the lake to join us.

"Rocker's in trouble."

Samantha wraps an arm around my shoulders and squeezes gently. "You need to stop worrying about that man. He's an adult, doing adult things."

"Funny. That's *exactly* what I'm worried about. Life

was way easier when he was just afraid of the monsters in the closet."

"You should be thinking about dating or at least getting laid," Samantha counters. "Ask Rocker to introduce you to some hot biker."

"No bikers," I say firmly.

"Really?" Carlie sounds doubtful.

Bikers are fascinating, but they're the polar bears of the dating world—a look-don't-touch breed of man you're better off spotting in a zoo than in the wild. So freaking touchable on the outside, but completely wild on the inside. I love bad boys, but I prefer to do my loving from a nice, safe distance.

"*Biker* is a synonym for *bad boy*. I don't need that."

"What if I find you a bad boy with a heart of gold?" Samantha is the eternal optimist.

Reality check. "I'll be ninety before you find one of those. Give me someone who's nice."

"Imagine the sex. Booooring." Samantha makes a face and wades back into the lake. As she executes a spectacular belly flop into the cool water, I check my phone. We need to be on the road in twenty minutes or we'll hit traffic. Still, I can afford five more minutes.

I wade back in and rejoin my girls. "It's been so long since I had sex that I'm not sure I remember how to do it."

Obviously, that's an exaggeration, but both Carlie and Samantha look like I've just announced that there will never, ever be another episode of *Game of Thrones*. Possibly combined with a nationwide shortage of chocolate. And wine. Maybe I could kick a puppy and complete my elevation to total loserdom.

"Who doesn't get laid?" Carlie floats over to me. It feels like high school, except the margaritas are no longer illegal. "Do you have a disease? Or did you take a religious vow when I wasn't around to stop you?"

"Not everyone has to have sex. Not everyone *wants* to." Most days I'm too tired to even think about taking my clothes off, let alone doing so in a sexy fashion and then making sure my man comes. I've been working twelve-hour days for the last eighteen months to get my princess party business off the ground, and my efforts are finally paying off.

"Intervention?" Carlie gives Samantha a look I have no problem interpreting. Neither one of them has a filter and they both have frequent, fantastic sex (at least to hear them tell it—and believe me, they certain don't hesitate to tell).

Samantha nods and heads for her purse. She trots back into the water a few seconds later, phone in her hand, and thumbs like a mad woman. Water-based internet surfing seems like an obvious recipe for disaster—while I wish the good folks at Apple would come up with a waterproof number, so far they've dropped the ball on that particular winner.

"We're finding you a booty call," Samantha announces.

"How about this one?" Carlie taps a picture on the phone, but Samantha's already shaking her head vigorously enough to spray me (and the phone—she really is living dangerously) with water.

"He's a taxi and not a long-haul trucker, if you take my meaning. Eve needs someone with stamina. She has a drought to work off."

I mentally run time trials on my previous two boy-friends for the next few minutes (they'd both qualify for gold in any track-and-field sprinting contest) while Carlie and Samantha review and reject various single men. Eventually they linger on a dark-haired hottie with a nice face and a strong jaw. He's wearing a suit and a tie, although there's always the possibility that's an aberration. Maybe Samantha snapped him at a funeral or a wedding.

"Jack Turner." Samantha taps the screen and Jack zooms into focus. "He runs numbers for a casino. He's twenty-eight, currently single, never married and he has his own place. Rumor has it that he's really, really good at putting his partner first. I like a man with manners."

Nice to know the man has been sexually pre-approved. I examine his face. He looks normal. Of course, Samantha and I have also been up since six, preparing for and then throwing a purple-themed princess celebration for the four-year-old daughter of a blackjack dealer who'd received the tip of a lifetime two weeks ago and decided to invest part of it in his daughter's dream party. It's possible I'm not thinking straight.

"Is he nice?"

Carlie pokes me in the stomach. "Trust me. You want fun, not nice."

Says she. "Why can't he be both? You guys said you could find me a bad boy with a heart of gold."

"We lied for a good cause. It would be like winning the lottery. Don't raise the bar impossibly high for Jack."

"I know nice guys," Samantha announces. Since she's been married and divorced twice and she's not even thirty, I'm skeptical. Her first impressions don't seem to be borne out in the long run.

Carlie reaches for the phone. "Name one who can still make your panties wet just by walking into the room. Evie needs chemistry. Not a nap."

See? She agrees with me. Nice guys are more endangered than the rhino these days.

Samantha looks blank. The way she stares down into the water, you'd think she's expecting a name to float to the top.

Shit. Surely one of us knows a guy who's both dating material *and* nice. Or…maybe not. Maybe finding Mr. Nice is like going to the zoo and hoping to spot a unicorn. Fuck the polar bears—we want mythical creatures.

Samantha waves her phone at me. "I'm texting Jack right now. We can go out next weekend."

If today is Saturday, that gives me at least six nights to find my libido. It has to be here somewhere.

Samantha doesn't look up from her phone. "And don't tell me that you're not free. Our clientele are three to eight years of age. They do not host birthday parties after 10:00 p.m. Ergo, you're free and clear for drinks.

There's no excuse to not go out and have fun. Let loose and forget about your responsibilities for a few hours."

Fun.

A simple, three-letter word.

I'd like to pretend I can't remember the last time I had fun because I work so hard and am such an astute businesswoman.

It wouldn't be true. I know *exactly* when I last cut loose, went out and had a few, did some dancing and kissed a boy. I was seventeen and in high school.

Unfortunately, I was also supposed to be at home, watching Rocker while our dad was out taking care of some "business" for his MC. Sucks to be a teenager stuck with babysitting duty when everyone else is out partying. My sneak exit through the window had been awesome up until the moment I returned and discovered our house surrounded by the blue-and-whites. Dear old dad got busted running arms, and I got busted as a deadbeat who'd put having a good time ahead of looking out for her little brother.

That was on me.

And yeah, I know that the ten years that have passed since that night should count for something. That Rocker doesn't blame me for the six months of foster homes he'd survived before I'd turned eighteen and convinced the judge to let him live with me. Six months in which I'd turned my life around, found a job and done everything right.

Rocker and I don't talk about our dad or that night everything changed. Once a month, we send a check to the state prison where dear old dad is serving a twenty-five-to-fifty-year sentence, and he sends back a postcard with a scrawled *thanks*. He also sends the occasional Christmas and birthday card. Mostly, Rocker and I pretend our childhood is a big happy blank. Nothing to write home or talk about—just something we got through on our way to being reasonably happy, productive adults.

At least, that's what I do. I'm a business owner and halfway to a degree in finance at the University of Nevada, Las Vegas. I have a mortgage, a minuscule retirement account and enough shit that I had to rent a medium-sized U-Haul when I moved into my new house. It's wonderful and scary at the same time—I'm so close to finally getting us out of the series of bad neighborhoods and loser streets we've lived on all our life and I should be celebrating. I *should* be able to go out on a Friday night and cut loose for the space of a song or two. And yet I'm so tired that I just want to crawl into bed and sleep instead.

"Jack says he'd love to meet you," Samantha announces triumphantly.

"Okay," I tell her. "I'll do it."

While Samantha texts an opus to Jack and Carlie cackles gleefully next to her, I pack us up. I need to double-check the site, too, and make sure no one's leaving anything behind. I'm busy tying up our loose ends when I hear the small plop from the lake followed by Carlie's giggle and Samantha's curse. Yeah. Guess we'll be stopping by the Apple store, too.

CHAPTER TWO

Rev

I'M NO SUPERHERO. Definitely no Prince Charming. Your first clue is my ride. I'm all about the Harley Davidson—not a fucking white horse in sight. The Hard Riders club president must have ignored that memo when he put me in charge of today's mission, because the woman in front of 837 Second Street is dressed exactly like a princess, right down to the tiara. Although the diamonds have to be fake, like so many things in Vegas, the crown still sparkles in the setting sun. A disorganized mob of small girls in rainbow-colored dresses surrounds her, talking and shrieking in an ungodly racket. Fucking looks like a rainbow exploded everywhere and rained glitter.

"Goddamn," Vik announces loud enough to be heard over the pipe's roar as he pulls his bike into the curb. I kill my engine and follow, both of us focused on the commotion happening on the lawn of the run-down rental. The lawn isn't much to look at—the Nevada sun has cooked the grass to a crispy brown and the place hasn't had a paint job in decades. Two bedrooms, one bath, based on the visible square footage, but gone to seed like a hooker working the nearby Strip, still open for business even though she won't command top dollar. The neighborhood hosts mostly working class, the usual mix of single moms and family units where cheap rentals are always in demand. The place squats on the edge of Hard Rider MC territory, and it might be time to expand our holdings. Claim this block, make it ours, put it back to rights.

I fucking love that idea.

Princess sticks out. The neighbors hanging over the chain link watching the show have dressed down for the heat because East Las Vegas in August is hotter than any armpit of hell I've visited as a US Navy SEAL. Today's audience wears mainly shorts and tank tops. Princess, on the other hand, sports a puffy yellow dress made out of some kind of fluffy shit. The fabric bells out revealing a really nice pair of legs as she gets into it with…a dragon? The thing's about ten feet tall, bright purple, and has a tail with floppy cloth spikes on it. Princess retrieves a ginormous plastic sword from somewhere and proceeds to attack. While I applaud the enthusiasm that makes her tits bounce, she doesn't know the first thing about fighting.

Vik groans. Brother's a fucking drama queen. "I could have taken that dragon in the first twenty seconds."

As the dragon collapses in mock death on the crap lawn, Princess whirls, declaiming something that wins applause from her host of mini-me's. I can't see her face, which is a pity, because her back's damn spectacular. Soft, honey-colored curls are piled up on top of her head, kinda pinned in place by the tiara, and the dress dips all the way to her ass, the straight line of her spine a lick-me-here-big-boy invitation I'd like to take her up on. As I watch, some of those curls go AWOL, bouncing around her face and down her neck. I want to take her apart, undoing first her hair and then her dress. Wouldn't stop either until I had her screaming my name as she came undone in my arms.

"Showgirl?" Vik's mutter interrupts the unwelcome fantasy. Daydreaming on the job is a rookie mistake. We've seen some crazy shit in our day, but this is unfamiliar territory. Since Princess doesn't show so much as an inch of tit and the dress drags on the dead grass rather than stopping two inches short of her ass, I'm certain she isn't working a Vegas show on the Strip. Her audience is our second clue. Third clue? The enormous pink-and-purple inflatable castle poking up over the roof of the house from the backyard and the equally outsized sheet cake with a number 5 candle poking out of the center. We've crashed a birthday party.

"You sure we got the right address?" GPS isn't a magic bullet and maybe we aren't parked in front of Eve Kent's workplace.

Vik leans back on his bike, folding his arms across his chest as he surveys the front lawn. A happy grin lights up his face, because he's definitely enjoying the show and most of the audience is female because hello...birthday party for kids. Vik likes women. Women like him. It all works out, usually with Vik naked, in bed, and banging his newest acquaintance. He may be the vice president of the Hard Rider motorcycle club, but you can bet every one of us gives him shit about the mileage on his dick. "Let's go introduce ourselves."

Vik also subscribes to the *act first, think later* school of thought. Probably explains why our prez put me in charge of this particular mission. If it involves pussy, Vik's gonna want to make a detour before he gets down to business. While he checks out the women on the lawn, I check my phone and confirm we're hitting the right party.

"We can't just go in there and make demands." I do a quick headcount and arrive at fifteen possible adult witnesses in addition to the dragon and the screaming, frosting-smeared horde. Never mind that we're not doing anything illegal—yet.

We're assholes, but we're not criminals. Being a biker isn't a crime, even if the boys in blue sometimes act as if it is. There's no free pass—you earn your place in the Hard Riders MC. To ride with the Hard Riders, you have to be ex-military. Most of us are SEALs or Spec Ops, but we got a few exceptions. We ride in East Las Vegas, but the Vegas area is home to multiple MCs and tensions run high. The steady flow of drugs controlled by Los Angeles–based gangs like the Hells Angels, Mongols, Crips and the Vagos add to the tension. Too many fighters, too little turf. That's a bad fucking recipe right there, and the Black Dogs MC recently made it their personal mission to be a pain in our ass.

Sin City is the country's playground, but almost

two million people also live and work here, just trying to make a decent life for their kids and that's a
goddamned right, to my mind. Forty thousand decent, hardworking people in East Las Vegas and almost seven square miles of streets of working-class
apartment complexes, bars, liquor stores, check-cash-
ing businesses and single-story adobe ranches with
palm trees in the front yards and fucking geraniums
in pots. You don't get much more American than that.

We get plenty of people from Nellis Air Force Base,
too, people who have either come to serve or to support
a loved one who was serving. The Hard Riders MC is
behind that shit. Makes our neighbors honorary brothers and so we watch their backs since we've served,
too. We're more sinner than saint, but our territory is
as free as we can make it from the drugs and violence
that plague the rest of Las Vegas.

You prospect and then you patch in and get your colors. Get club ink, too. Our club president likes to call
that our bar code—Vik jokes it's our expiration date.
You remain in the club until the day you die, and if you
screw up, the club cleans up the mess. Locals respect
our vests and the club patch. When they see that MC
cut, they know we mean business, and they usually get
the hell out of our way. You don't disrespect us.

Unless you're Rocker Kent, Eve Kent's baby brother,
who rides with the Black Dogs and who's recently decided he and his crew should run illegal street guns
through Hard Riders territory. He's the reason we are
here. Idiot compounded that brilliant plan by networking with the Colombian drug cartels (he's had a busy

fucking month), and that's trouble the Hard Riders plan
to shut down if we can run him to ground long enough
to talk. We're mature like that—gonna start with words
and then work up to fists. Practically deserve the key to
the city for that restraint, but we may have to make do
with Eve. Word on the street is that her brother checks
up on her regularly.

She'd make one hell of a hostage.

"You really think she knows where Rocker's at?"

Vik swings off his bike and leans against it. "Give
it a minute and we'll ask. The show's winding down."

While the knee-high crowd stampedes into the
house after the lady carrying the cake, I keep my eyes
peeled for Rocker. He's shown up at three of his sister's last four gigs according to a girl who works for
her. Usually slinks in quietly because apparently Eve
has a no-bikes rule—something about us big, bad biker
types scares her mom crowd. If I can catch him now,
it will solve all sorts of problems. Of course, since the
girl in question provided this information after Vik
banged her silly, she may have been just babbling shit.
All that mileage on his dick? Plenty of it is repeat business from happy customers.

My phone buzzes, distracting me from the rapidly
emptying front yard.

How's the party?

Fucker.
"Sachs is checking in."

Vik nods, his eyes are glued to a mom in a pair of

pink sweats, a white tank and flip-flops. She looks curvy and sweeter than the cake her kid is mainlining as they disappear into the house—and Vik has always had a sweet tooth. Momma better watch out, or he'll take a bite out of her.

What's up?

Shrieks sound from the backyard, the purple castle rocketing back and forth like it's about to take off. Princess and the dragon disappear inside. I'm getting impatient when Sachs finally texts back.

Had another drive-by. Heading over to check it out. Save me a cupcake.

Ever since the Black Dogs MC hopped into bed with the Colombians, our streets have been heating up. This is the second drive-by in as many weeks, and it's two too many. This shit ends now, and the best way to accomplish that is through Rocker. I don't care if he tenders his resignation to his drug-dealing buddies, or if they take it out of his ass in trade, but he runs no more drugs or guns in Hard Rider territory. It's gonna take the entire club to bring him down without escalating shit to a full-blown war, though—and Sachs has a hair-trigger temper. He's more likely to Rambo his way inside the other clubhouse and do his discussing with his fists.

I text him back.

Wait for backup.

Sachs's only response is a kissy-face emoticon. Someday, his lack of caution is going to bite him on the ass.

"Time to get serious." I throw a leg over my bike. "Take one for the club."

Vik grunts and motions me forward. I may be joking about the kiddo's party, but we both know I'd lay everything on the line for the club. So would Vik. That's how we roll—the club and our brothers come first.

When I stride up the walk, what's left of the peanut gallery hanging over the fence turns to stare, because six feet of former SEAL in motorcycle boots and a club vest makes an impression. Fuck them. I don't try to hide what I am. I'm the MC's muscle. I make some stuff happen—and I make other stuff go away. Whatever my club prez needs, I do—and right now he needs Rocker's buy-in on getting the hell out of our territory and the drug trade.

Since staking out a birthday party for kiddies isn't getting me any closer to this goal, I need to find another way to get to Rocker. I do another quick survey of the house, but there's still no sign of that asshole, and I don't have his number. But I bet Evie knows how to call her brother—and I bet I can motivate her to share. I'm fucking awesome at motivating.

And today's my lucky day because turns out that I don't even have to go in after her. She pops out of the house alone and heads for the pink monstrosity parked by the curb, juggling a plate of cake in flapping plas-

tic wrap. She looks like Christmas and the fucking
Tooth Fairy rolled into one, with a dash of Tinkerbell
and porn star. Okay. That last bit may be pure fantasy
on my part, because she looks as sweet as Vik's MILF
in that fluffy-ass get-up. Unless my luck has changed,
she's not hiding a dirty girl underneath all that sparkle. I change course and wait on the other side of the
pink RV for her.

CHAPTER THREE

Eve

"GOING SOMEWHERE, SUNSHINE?" The deep voice comes out of nowhere and I whirl. Off balance, I promptly trip on my dress and head for the pavement.

An arm fastens around my waist, rescuing me from my imminent face-plant. The plate of cake is plucked from my hands and set down by my feet. Huh. The arm tightens briefly as we dip and it's a big, hard, tattooed, scary-as-shit arm, although the tattoo actually isn't bad. Bold black ink covers the skin between his sleeve and his wrist... Is that a dragon? The animal looks almost Viking. Or as if the beast is seriously contemplating eating anyone who gets too close. If I need to file a police report, I have plenty to say when they ask about distinguishing marks.

The arm's owner is sun-bronzed, and when I inhale, I breathe in leather, oil and something else. That *something else* spells trouble because the scent is hot and male. What my head can't describe, my body recognizes, my libido perking up and demanding we revert

to our former bad girl ways. Immediately. My princess costume works better than a chastity belt thanks
to all that material, so it's difficult to fully appreciate
the hard male body pressed up against my butt, but I
make an effort.

Maybe I'm hallucinating because men like this don't
exist.

I pinch his arm hard.

"The fuck?" Those two offended words rumble in
my ear. I guess he's real after all. He sets me carefully back on my feet and backs up, giving me twelve
inches of space. Maybe a whole eighteen. And I mean
the distance between us, not anything else, because...

This man is a whole lot of wow. I brace myself
against the side of the RV. *Knees don't fail me now.*

His face is way better than his arm. He's a big guy,
tall and broad-shouldered, traits that tick all the best
boxes on my sexual wish list. He's also more rough
than good-looking, with short, dark hair and a cold,
watchful expression that never leaves his face as he
takes in the happenings on the lawn. Almost military,
except that the local air force base would never let
this bad boy in. He wears a leather vest covered with
patches, a dark T-shirt and jeans that are white around
the seams. Despite the full-sleeve tattoo on both arms,
I spot no visible piercings, but trust me—he doesn't
need the metal to shout trouble.

He braces an arm on either side of my head. Despite his not actually touching me, it suddenly feels
like we're naked and he's got his dick inside me. Under
other circumstances, I might not mind. Since keeping

up appearances in front of my paying public matters, I reach out and give his chest a discreet shove. We have an entire RV between us and any party guests, but I shouldn't take chances.

He doesn't budge. "I need to reach your brother, princess."

There are so many different ways to define *reach*. Still, however you define it, he's not here for me. I know I shouldn't be disappointed about that, but I am.

"You're a friend of Rocker's?"

His face gives nothing away. "We've got business."

I treat myself to a second glance at his leathers, the faded T-shirt that hugs a muscled chest and the boots. God. The *boots*. You know how some boots are made for dancing? These boots are made for pain, for kicking ass and for getting a point across one steel-toed tip at a time. And just in case there's any question at all about where this man falls on the naughty or nice side of things, he rocks a leather vest with a club patch on it. Whatever Rocker's done this time, he's in deep. Pulling him out is going to be a bitch.

Ergo, despite my pressing need to get him away from Perfectly Princess Parties's current place of business, I stall. Big-time. "I don't even know your name."

"Rev. You tell him Rev is looking for him."

I'm pretty sure my mouth hangs open for a minute, because *Rev* looks amused. What kind of a name is that?

Since that's not the kind of thing you ask a man, I go for the obvious. "Why?"

"Club business," he says tightly.

In other words? Penis business. Also known as *none of my business.* I love my brother, but he has his head up his ass about things like sticking on the right side of the law and boy things versus girl things. When I try to duck under Rev's arm, the man moves effortlessly with me. Shit. Pretty soon, we'll start attracting attention.

"If I let him know you're looking, you'll leave?" Giving Rocker a heads-up that trouble is knocking on his door seems like my best two-for-one solution at the moment, so when Rev nods, I fish inside the bodice of my dress. I also do my best to ignore the slow grin spreading across Rev's face as I retrieve my phone from its hiding place. What is it about men and boobs? He doesn't back off and give me any space either, which makes dialing awkward.

"What's up?" Miracle of miracles, Rocker actually answers his phone on the second ring.

"I have a friend of yours here who wants your number," I say carefully. Pretty sure this is the *trouble* he mentioned back at the lake.

"Sure." There's enough background noise for me to be almost certain Rocker's parked at a bar somewhere.

"He says his name is Rev."

As my brother silently digests that revelation, Rev moves closer still and traces a finger over my ear. He smells good, although I wish I didn't have a secret thing for leather and man. Plus, he has no business touching me. I shake my head as if he's some kind of annoying gnat, but he just drops his fingers to my jaw and then plays with my hair as if I'm his own personal toy. Big fingers carefully untangle a snarl and smooth the strands down. I slap at his fingers with my free hand and he grins.

Rocker promptly proves that his brotherly radar still works fine. "He right there?"

"Couldn't get much closer," I tell him.

"Rev's not a nice guy," he says slowly. "And I don't want him around you."

News flash—I've already determined the *not nice* part for myself. In fact, it's probably twelve inches long and located directly behind the zipper of his jeans. I look him up and down, or as much as I can since the man still has me pinned up against the RV. Somehow, I can't work up any indignation. Later, I'll regret letting him walk all over me in public view, but right now I'm enjoying the feel of his big, muscled body touching mine. It's been way too long since I had someone just hold me.

I focus on breathing in, hold for a count of three, and then out, because maybe then I won't say something I shouldn't. "Good to know, but I think he still wants to talk to you."

"*He* absolutely does, princess." Rev plucks the phone out of my hand. While I'm trying to figure out how I feel about that, he and Rocker go back and forth on a possible get together. Rev doesn't stop staring at me, either, one hand braced by my face and the other wrapped around my phone. The man's a talented multi-tasker, because his fingers keep grazing my cheek, sending little skitters down my spine.

Why am I standing here letting him take charge? *Because you like it,* my bad voice whispers (or shrieks

gleefully in my head). *Damn. It.* I reach for his wrist as
he signs off the call. I still can't tell if he and Rocker
are friends, if Rocker owes him money (which would
be a bad idea), or if there's something else entirely between them (which would be even worse). But there's
something. There's definitely something.

"Return my phone."

His face doesn't reveal a flicker of emotion. Bet he
could make a killing playing poker on the Strip. "This
isn't a democracy. You got a pen hiding in that dress,
sunshine?"

His gaze flicks over me. Maybe he's looking for
said pen—or maybe he just likes looking…at me. Shit.
The hard-eyed steely-stare thing he's got going on is
not supposed to be a turn-on. My inner bad girl, however, won't be shut down without a fight. *She* thinks
we should jump him. Right here on the sunburned,
stabby lawn works for that hussy. I opt for going on
the defensive.

"Don't call me sunshine."

He shrugs. "You're the one in the big yellow dress."

"Occupational hazard." I yank a business card out
of my cleavage and slap it in his empty palm. The
move may not be the classiest, but the look on his face
is worth it. Naturally, birthday parties for the two- to
five-year-old crowd are not his territory. He's undoubtedly more into murder and mayhem.

"You want a princess to grace your next party? I
make it happen. Forty dresses that drip sparkles, fairy
wings, tiaras and enough faux glass slippers to shoe

an entire beauty pageant—we'll have a real good time. I promise."

He makes a rough sound. Can't tell if he's laughing at me or if I've actually managed to shock the big, bad biker. "Since when do princesses have wings?"

Clearly, he has limited knowledge of five-year-old girls.

"All the best princesses can fly," I inform him. Unlike him, I have extensive knowledge of five-year-old girls, and their preference for fairy princesses have been made abundantly clear to me. Ergo, I've responded to my market demands (and hey, I like wings and sparkles, too).

This time, he definitely snorts. "Why don't you fly your ass on inside that RV and grab a pen?"

I don't have to think about that "request" too hard. The man needs to work on his manners.

I don't budge. "Rocker's not your number-one fan."

He grunts and returns his gaze to my phone. "He wants you safe. You should listen to him."

"You should know something about me," I tell him.

"What's that, Evie?"

"I'm not big on orders."

He actually winks at me. "Bet you'd feel differently in bed."

I really shouldn't hit him, not when there's a birthday party happening in the backyard behind us, but the urge is almost overwhelming. This man has no filter. "Do you have any idea how insulting you are?"

He shrugs and texts something from my phone, before looking me in the eye. God, the man might be filterless, but he does have gorgeous eyes. "Put my number in your contacts."

Um. Okay. And perhaps hell will freeze over despite the record hundred-and-something-degrees Vegas weather. I reach for my phone, but he holds it just out of reach. "If I change my position on order-taking, I'll be sure to give you a call."

"Thought maybe we could get together sometime," he says.

Didn't see that one coming.

"You want to go out on a date with me?"

"It's a free country—you don't have to say yes. Thought you might like a ride on my bike or a drink."

He wants to give. Me. A ride. My brain stutters. The bike parked by the curb is a big, death-defying, powerful menace. Black leather saddlebags hang off the side that I'd bet my sheet cake he doesn't use to transport groceries or crap from a Target run. Riding anywhere with a strange man would be crazy.

He has a friend with him, too, another man I've never met before. When I peer over Rev's shoulders a little myopically (the best princesses don't pair glasses with fairy wings and this particular princess has run out of disposable contacts), the guy offers me a slow grin and a little waggle of his fingers. He certainly makes pretty eye candy, but I prefer Mr. Tall, Dark and Grumpy.

I narrow my eyes at him. "It's the dress, isn't it?"

He doesn't bother to hide his amusement. "You think I've got a thing for sparkly shit?"

There isn't a man alive who looks rougher and

fiercer than Rev. I'm trying to figure out a polite way
to tell him so when he tucks the phone back inside my
dress before I can so much as squeak out a protest. The
backs of his fingers brush against the top of my boobs,
issuing an invitation of their own.

I have to be more cautious. From the rising volume
of the squeals emanating from the backyard, cake con-
sumption has concluded and the party will be wrapping
up as the sugar highs hit, the early departers fleeing
past my RV parked out front. Spotting the princess in
an R-rated embrace with a biker would be bad for my
business. You can't be a dirty girl and host children's
birthday parties for a living. The moms will kill you.
Fortunately, the moms aren't mind readers. I'm only a
party-perfect princess on the outside. Riding anywhere
with Rev would be career suicide.

My bad voice promptly weighs in. *But only if you
get caught.*

"I don't do bikers."

Something flashes across Rev's face. "You don't get
hurt on my watch. I promise."

"You're not an ax murderer?"

He reaches into his pocket and pulls out the wallet attached to his belt by a silver chain. Silently, he
flips it open and holds it out so I can read his driver's
license. There's a military ID underneath it, too, the
kind of card that gets you into Nellis Air Force Base.

"Your name isn't Rev." According to the State of
Nevada's laminated plastic, he's one Jaxon Brady.

"Road name," he says tersely.

I examine the license again. He's also turning thirty-three in four weeks. I bet he won't be booking a celebratory princess party.

"Wow." I hand back his wallet. "Former navy?"

He nods, as if it's no big deal. "SEAL. You'd be safe with me."

He's not big on talking. Or negotiating, asking, or sweet-talking. I've always trusted my instincts, though, and right now they're on board with Rev Brady. Completely, totally, 100 percent in favor of getting on this man's bike and riding off with him. Somewhere. Wherever he wants to go. He's big and strong and tempting. He's fought for our country and kept everyone safe.

How bad can he be?

The little voice in my head pipes right up. *How bad do you want him to be?*

That voice needs a gag.

"Think about it," he says and then he turns and saunters toward his bike. I stand there, watching his ass the whole way, and wondering why I don't mind his attitude. He's scary as shit. He's not Mr. White Picket Fence and he's not promising happily ever after, but the man has a fantastic butt and I'm lonely. That's all it is. I need to get out more, need to make a point of seeing someone.

Someone else.

Anyone else.

There are absolutely, positively no bikers anywhere in my future.

CHAPTER FOUR

Eve

THE CARNIVAL MUSIC vibrates through every inch of my body, and I lose myself in the beat. I love everything about hitting the Strip, from getting dolled up to the pulse-pounding, searing rhythm of the clubs. Everybody's equal on the dance floor, all part of the same moving, gyrating body. On the Strip, you end up packed too close to even tell who can dance and who's merely enthusiastic. It's exactly what I need, my happy place where I can let go and all that matters is finding my next breath and the rhythm.

Unlike my day-job wear, my dress tonight barely skims my butt. Sequins cover the short pink tank dress and whenever the lights hit me, I light the place up. Over the top? Check. Girly as hell? Check, check. The first stop on tonight's girls' night out is Circus Circus and Samantha and I have already hit the Midway and gone two rounds on the roller coaster. I'm barefoot because I kicked off my shoes as soon as we scored a table, and right now it's officially fun time. And while

I usually keep busy, busy, busy, it feels good to have some time off. Tonight I can let go and enjoy life. Tomorrow is soon enough to worry about the bills, the taxes and the fourteen hundred other items on my to-do list.

I could start with that man headed toward our table. He's good-looking, he's definitely friendly and he's managed to hunt down a cocktail waitress with a tray of drinks.

Jack. His name is Jack. I'm too old or too tired—too *something*—because I have to fight the urge to write his name on my hand lest I forget it. I'd been hoping he'd rate higher on the droolworthy factor.

"I told you he was even cuter in person," Samantha crows as she catches me watching Jack. Unlike so many dating app pictures, he actually looks like the picture I picked out on my phone at the lake. Turns out, the six intervening days have not been enough time to rediscover my libido. I've done some solo workouts in bed, but a few self-induced orgasms haven't made me hungrier for one-on-one action. Guess it was like hoping running a mile would prepare me for the marathon—so I shouldn't feel so disappointed.

Jack is a good-looking guy and he has lovely manners as promised. He looks really nice in his jeans and a blue button-up shirt, too. He's a vice president of something at one of the casinos, which means that not only is he pretty on the outside, but he's gainfully employed and scores frequent free drinks. The man is total keeper material, which is exactly what I told Samantha I wanted.

This is torture.

I don't care if Jack never finds our table again, and that's just not right. He's so perfect on paper, and yet there's not a single spark of chemistry between us. There's nothing horribly, wonderfully electric, no sparks. I should try harder. Hell, the *sparks* between that biker and me were enough to start a forest fire or some other kind of world-ending conflagration and my libido needs a good talking-to. *No bikers.*

"Wasn't sure what you'd like," Mr. I'm Perfect On Paper says, tipping the waitress generously after she sets the drinks down on the table. "So I got a bunch of stuff. You can try it all or go for the fallback beer."

God. Could he be more thoughtful?

He gestures toward the row of drinks and I grab the first drink I touch. The crap in the glass is frozen and sweet, some kind of adult slushie. *Okay.* That's a departure from my usual beer, but I definitely want to try new things. I want to dance, to grind against Jack and to discover he's my Mr. Right. I'm so ready to get right on that happily ever after. Get married, start a family, do things right. Jack ticks all the boxes. He's absolutely perfect. I knock back the first inch of my drink, trying to ignore the way it suddenly tastes too sweet.

Jack slides an arm around my shoulders, tucking me against his side. He goes for the beer, and we stand there all couple-like for a long moment, watching Samantha bob and weave across the casino floor to greet someone she knows. It feels as if we've been married for ten years already and not in a good way.

Run away, my bad voice whispers.

Not listening.

"Let's dance." I slip out of his hold. The bar and burger joint has live music tonight, and a group of people are already dancing. I grab his hand, threading my fingers through his. He lets me tug him out into the heart of the dance floor, following my lead effortlessly. Maybe it's a sign that I've found a man who can take direction? Jack even turns out to be a decent dancer. We dance a few faster songs, and then sway slowly in place when the band drops a romantic number on us. This is perfect. Still, when the band segues into a faster song, I pop out of his hold.

"Little girls' room," I tell him and he nods.

I make a pit stop at our table for my shoes, which turns out to be the best decision I've made all night. The bathrooms are at the end of a narrow, dirty, dark hallway. Every time I pick my feet up, a sticky, crunching sound assaults my ears and I make a mental note to Lysol the bottom of my shoes when I get home. I do my business as quickly as I can, wash my hands and exit. Clearly, the casino wants its ladies out on the main floor or knocking back drinks at the bar, because absolutely nothing about the grimy, dark facilities encourages you to linger. This place has a pee-and-get-the-hell-out vibe.

When I come out, turns out the night has at least one surprise in store for me. Rev is leaning against the wall opposite the door, beer bottle held loosely in his hand. He raises the bottle in a silent salute when he sees me. *He* doesn't look surprised to see me, although I hadn't pegged him for the club scene. When he takes a swallow from the longneck, the muscles in his throat working, I start wondering what he'd taste like.

"Hey," he says, and my feet immediately cease their forward momentum. I have no idea how he does that to me.

"Hey yourself." I gesture toward him. "You waiting for someone or do you regularly stake out the women's room?"

We've only met once before, but somehow I already know he's not the kind of guy who holds his girl's purse while she pees. Plus, I was the only gal in the restroom, so I've kind of already answered my question.

A slow smile touches his face. "Saw you out there on the dance floor. Bought you a beer." He starts to hand me the second beer bottle and then pauses. "You like that lime crap?"

I make a face before I can stop myself. "Not really."

"Good call." He flicks the offending lime toward a nearby trash can and then swipes his thumb over the mouth of the bottle before passing it to me. "Gotcha covered."

Free beer is always good, right? We drink in strangely companionable silence for a moment.

"You come here often?" I joke lamely when the whole not-speaking thing starts to feel uncomfortable.

He bumps my shoulder companionably with his, gesturing toward the dance floor with his bottle. "Worse places to hang out."

"True," I agree. "But I hadn't pegged you for a clubber."

He takes another swallow of his beer. "I like watching."

He'd said he'd spotted me on the dance floor earlier—did he watch me? Did he like what he saw? Is that what this beer is about, or is he still trying to track down Rocker and he figures buttering me up is a shortcut? Since there's no way to know for certain, I decide to just enjoy the scenery for now because looking at Rev is pretty darn awesome. I let my gaze trail the length of his body, taking him all in—and there's lots to admire. His faded jeans hug powerful thighs and the T-shirt beneath his leather vest outlines a chest that promises to be downright perfect. Whatever the man does with his free time, he doesn't sit around on his ass all day. His big body radiates power, deadly but relaxed enough for now that I don't sprint for the dance floor or the safety in numbers it offers—which makes me as stupid as the slowest gazelle in the pack, because Rev is a predator and we both know it.

About three inches from the bottom of my beer, the band starts in on one of my favorite songs, making my feet itch to be out there on the dance floor. A lazy smile tugs at the corner of Rev's mouth. Whatever he is tonight, he's in no rush and somehow I'm in no hurry to return to Jack, either. When my buzz dies down, this will probably worry me.

His shoulder bumps mine gently. "You in a dancing mood tonight, princess?"

"You dance?" Shoot. I sound breathless.

He takes another swig from his bottle. "Do I look like I dance?"

"Uh—no?" I inspect him again, looking for any reason to say yes. "But you've got two feet, right? It's not hard."

He looks down at me, reaching out to circle my wrist with his fingers. Heat shoots through me. Jack and Samantha probably think I've fallen in or gotten lost, and yet I don't want to move away from Rev. Of course, he's hot and I'm buzzing, but even so I know that standing here with him is a bad idea.

"Come on." He tugs me out of the hallway, then heads for one of the booths lining the side of the bar. Stupidly, I follow along. I do manage to fish in my purse and find my phone so that I can shoot off a quick text to Samantha.

Met friend. BRB.

Friend is a misnomer, but since Samantha didn't spot Rev at the birthday party, she wouldn't know who he is anyhow.

Rev slides my purse down my arm and tosses it toward the back of the booth. The little pink square at the end of a silver chain doesn't hold much. I slide in after it and then wonder if I've made a mistake. Now the only way out is through Rev. Not that I really think he'd hurt me, but I barely know him.

"You look nice," he says, snagging my phone and sliding in after me. Somehow, I'm not surprised when he looks down and reads the message I just sent.

"Thanks. Maybe we should talk about boundaries."

He looks up and winks at me. "If you've got hard limits, you tell me."

Did that sound sexual to anyone else?

"We what you said?" He gestures toward the phone in his hand and then tucks it into my purse.

"Friends?"

"Yeah," he says. My beer is mysteriously empty, so I snag his and help myself to a drink. "Never had a girl friend before."

"I'll go easy on you," I tell him and finish off his beer.

His fingers graze the bare skin above my knee. "You here with someone?"

My pulse rockets into overdrive.

"Kind of." I blurt the words out. Think them over. "Not really. Yes. No."

He gives me a slow smile. "Hard to be all of those things."

"I'm here with friends," I say firmly.

He nods thoughtfully. "You should know that if you stay here, I'm gonna want a taste of you."

I stiffen before I can stop myself. This is not the kind of thing you discuss with an almost total stranger. "You did not just say that."

His fingers move a little higher. I slap them and only end up smacking myself. Real smooth. "That's disgusting."

His grin gets broader. "You not a fan of oral, Evie?"

Great. Now my face *and* my pussy are on fire.

"Not really my thing." I blurt the words out before I can think them through.

"Why not?" He sounds thoughtful, rather than pissed off or offended, so I tell him the truth.

"I've tried it, but it wasn't all that." I give my previous boyfriends full points for enthusiasm, but oral sex just isn't the fireworks-inducing pleasure that my *Cosmo* assures me it is. I can and have lived without it for years. There's just something about the enthusiastic licking and the slurping that put me off. Reminds me of puppy dogs or something, and that's not sexy at all.

Rev gives me a look. He's totally still, but somehow I get the feeling he's about to pounce. "We really friends?"

"I think so." I nod cautiously. Probably shouldn't have finished his beer because now the room whirls gently around me and a pillow sounds like nirvana. Bet Rev would let me put my head on his chest. Bet he'd let me do a lot of things.

"Then I gotta tell you something, as a friend." He pulls me onto his lap, settling my back against his chest as he rests his chin on my shoulder. "Fucking waste, your not liking oral."

He doesn't sound mad that I've shot down his *friendly* offer, but this is undoubtedly my cue to go back to my own table. Still, when he pulls me tighter, the closeness doesn't feel scary or like a threat. More like he's putting himself between me and the rest of the world, just in case shit starts happening. Which it probably does in his world, now that I come to think of it.

"So show me how you like it," he rumbles in my ear.

"What?" Pretty sure I sound as dazed as I feel.

He tugs the empty beer bottle away from me and sets it on the table.

"Kiss me the way you'd like to have your pussy kissed," he offers. "Promise you one thing, Evie—I'm a fast learner."

"But I don't like it," I point out with the careful logic of the slightly inebriated. "And we're just friends. Friends don't go down on friends."

Or have conversations about oral techniques in the middle of a bar—but, details.

He sounds sincere when he says, "Nothing wrong with one friend making another feel good."

I think about that while he runs his hands down my back, cupping my butt and lifting me until I'm sitting on his dick. The only things between us are my panties and his jeans. Or wait—maybe he's pro-underwear and not naked underneath his denim? The beer must be talking, because I skim my fingers under the edge of his jeans on an exploratory mission. Not commando. Okay. That's one question settled.

"This is a bad idea," I inform him even as I turn and straddle him. I can't be that drunk, because I manage it without sticking my knees in any unfortunate places. Or maybe that's because his hands guide me and it's so easy to let him take control.

"Never a bad idea to tell me what you want." The words sound like a promise. I lose the thought as I slide my hands up his chest and over his shoulders to cup his neck. God, his skin's warm. I wonder how he feels about licking, because right now his dick is aligned with my pussy and it feels absolutely perfect. "Plus, sweetheart? I've got one rule. The game stops the minute you tell me you're not having fun."

That's a good rule and I tell him so.

He nudges my chin up until I meet his eyes. "You've got my promise on that."

"And you always keep your promises."

"Damn straight."

He's smiling when he says it, but the words are like a safety line. Nothing too bad can happen now. He's said so.

"First thing? I don't like to rush," I whisper, leaning up.

"Got all the time in the world," he tells me.

No.

He's so wrong.

All I have is right now, this one stolen moment.

I cup his head with my hands, one thumb tracing the soft line of his ear. Must be the only place the man isn't hard, because I'm definitely sitting on an impressive erection and his chest isn't any softer. I tug his head down toward my mouth before I can think too much. He helps me by cupping my butt and boosting me up his chest, his fingers skimming the curve of my butt just below my panties.

"I don't like to go for gold right away." I brush my mouth over his throat. He's inked in so many places. In addition to the dark bands on his wrists and forearms, he's got more ink on his throat.

"This is pretty." I trace the black swirl nearest his ear with my tongue.

"Got nothing on you," he growls. "Girls are pretty."

"Mmmm." I eat him, kissing my way toward his ear. I lick him and he groans.

"Pretend you're a girl," I whisper. "And let me call you pretty."

"Fuck," he says hoarsely. "Asking the impossible, princess. I've definitely got a dick."

The tip of that dick bumps against my clit in a bull's-eye. Nothing subtle about the move, but somehow the very bluntness of it makes me hotter. Plus, he grabs my hips when I buck, holding me rock-steady in his hands. My internal temperature rockets up to *on fire* and it's all I can do to not grind down on him and come right now.

"Are we still playing show-and-tell?" he asks with a hoarse groan. "Because you're giving me ideas."

"Shut up." I lick his ear lightly, teasing him. "This is my show."

"For now," he agrees, making it clear I'm only in control because he's letting me be. That apparently turns me on, too, because my pussy clenches, reaching for the dick I've decided it can't have. Still, since he asked for a lesson in how to lick my pussy, I need to be thorough, right? Just in case we ever end up putting this plan into action, I'd hate to be the one to give him bad advice. So I go back to work on his ear, sucking hard on the lobe until he's the one bucking up. Imagine that. What works for the princess works for the big, bad biker.

"I think we're gonna be real close friends." His hands trace the top of my thong through my dress, and when he tugs gently on the tiny strip, I feel it right in my clit. My panties are his own personal leash to my libido. God, I should get up. Should go. Should—

"You like it slow," he whispers roughly, and my thoughts grind to a happy halt. Right now, I'd like it however he wanted to give it to me.

"My fantasy," I whisper back. "My rules."

"You want to hear about mine?" He wraps my hair around his hand, pulling my head back until I meet his gaze.

"I have friends waiting for me." I sound the opposite of decisive.

"Had a real shitty day, princess," he growls. "Don't make it worse by leaving now."

"Funny," I gasp. "Because mine is getting better by the second."

"Tease," he whispers softly, but he doesn't sound mad any longer. "Didn't think you'd play these kinds of games."

I press down on him. "What kind?"

"The dirty kind."

His fingers tighten in my hair and my heartbeat jacks up, announcing the imminent arrival of my first heart attack. We're in public. Sure, the booth gives us some privacy, but it's nowhere near enough for him to be all but fingering my pussy. Why don't I mind? Why am I still sitting here on his lap, my legs hugging his hips like he's my life raft in the Sea of Orgasm? His legs shift beneath me, the muscles bunching and pressing, and a new heartbeat explodes between my legs. Rev is dirty. Wicked. Biker. Outlaw. All the words drain right out of my head when his hand disappears between us. Oh my God, he's going to touch me.

"Didn't think you'd let me do this."

His fingers stroke beneath the edge of my panties.

"Why not?"

"You usually date bikers?" His fingers move higher. My breath catches.

"I don't usually date," I admit. "Tonight's the first time in a long time for me, and I'm kind of sucking at it."

I should care. I should feel bad that I've left people waiting for me at our table while I climb all over Rev like he's the only orgasm left in town. Instead, all I can feel is the pleasure. He strokes along the crotch of my panties and my world stills and then explodes in a new beat. He works his finger beneath the edge and my pussy rolls out the welcome mat. Like he knows all I can do is wait, holding my breath and trying not to beg, he works the damp cotton against me, rubbing and pressing. They're not even *good* panties, date night panties I wouldn't mind flashing the world, but they're my lifeline in the storm that is Rev. Just an everyday Hanes cotton thong that's practical, sturdy and out of this world in Rev's hands.

"You like these?" He tugs the side of my panties.

"They get the job done," I say drily and he laughs.

"Guess that means you won't miss them."

He rips my panties apart with two sharp tugs and I don't have a problem with that, either. Apparently, I'm up for whatever he wants to do tonight.

"Tell me about your day," I gasp, desperate for distraction. I so need to put the brakes on this crazy attraction.

His knuckle finds my bare clit and presses. It's too much, too fast, his fingers sliding over my slick, wet flesh. I feel my orgasm coming, and I want to stretch this moment out. Make it last as long as possible, because the best sex of my life shouldn't be this short.

"Got some unresolved club business." He circles my clit with his thumb and I reward him with a moan. "Some guys trying to run drugs on our turf. Not good for the neighborhood—civvies keep getting shot."

"You're worried about your neighbors?" It's a minor miracle I can get the words out, because he makes another slow pass around my clit.

He gives me a hard look. "You don't think I should love my neighbor as myself, sunshine?"

Right now, the only *loving* I'm worried about is what's happening between us. He presses. I moan.

"I don't worry, princess. I fix shit."

From the expression on his face, those drug dealers will be out of business shortly. Rev clearly has a plan and a goal for shutting them down and part of me wants to stand up and applaud him. I mean, I probably don't want to know exactly *how* he intends to eliminate the drug trade from the streets he's claimed, but the idea's solid. Instead of saying anything, however, I slide down, more than meeting him halfway. God. I need him in me, and not just his fingers.

A throat clears behind us. "Eve?"

Oh shit. I turn around at light speed, ignoring the way Rev groans when my knee rams into his thigh.

Jack takes an involuntary step backward, looking un-comfortable.

"Hi," I bleat, sounding like the idiot I am.

"I'm headed out." From the way Jack's looking at us, he knows exactly what we were doing—and he won't be calling me. "Play some blackjack and then head home. You okay?"

"Fine. You go on." My face is probably tomato-red. Jack is the perfect recipe for a forever man, and he's just busted me humping another guy. It's not like meeting him here at the casino was my idea (thank you, Samantha), but I still feel bad. I picked him out of the phone lineup, and now I officially suck. He won't give me a second chance—and worse? I don't want one.

What I *want* is to come, to demand Rev finish what he started. We haven't exchanged much small talk, and we haven't done any of the get-to-know-you stuff that you're supposed to do *before* you hook up. But I know some important things about him already. He's a member of the Hard Riders MC, which means that he lives for the club and he plays by a code I can't al-ways agree with. He's loyal. He's protective as fuck. He'll never bring me roses or stop by Hallmark, but it's not as if I'm planning on doing that for him, either. I'm an equal opportunity kind of girl and I might be up for borrowing his penis, but there's no long-term in dating a biker.

Which is why I scoot off his lap as Jack turns and walks away. I'll bet he's thinking he had a near miss. That if I'd hook up with a different guy when we'd just met that I'd do worse down the road. Rev's phone buzzes and naturally he checks it. Those fingers moving over the screen were just—

He makes a rough sound. "Got a meeting or we'd be discussing this further."

This is a first. My dating life hasn't been a flaming success, but the guys I've met have been interested in pussy first, fun second and nothing else third. Sometimes, they've mixed it up and put the fun first, but they've never left a sure thing for a meeting.

That's okay.

"Go." I slide out of the booth. Rev is more than a little out of my league. I like playing games, but I'm not even sure this man knows how to play.

"We're good?" He gives me another one of those intent, scary looks. He's big and not particularly happy-looking, and I'm an idiot for grinding on him.

He sighs, as if he can see right inside my head. "You worry too much."

Worrying is part of the natural order of things. I have a long list of shit to deal with, topped by growing my business, dealing with handsy dads and uncles at my princess parties, whether or not my girls will show up for a gig and where my baby brother has taken himself.

"I *plan*," I tell him. "There's a difference."

Some days it doesn't feel like a big one, but it's who I am.

He follows me out of the booth, setting his hands on my hips and drawing me back against him. His dick makes itself at home in the crack of my butt. The man's built like a small mountain.

"You gotta stop thinking about it all."

And then he bends his head toward mine and brushes his lips over my mouth. He's there so fast, I almost think I dreamed it. Just like that, he's taking up all the space and all of my air. My stupid heart races and all I can think about is what kissing Rev will feel like. His lips brush over mine, once, twice. A third time. He sucks my lower lip in, and then he pulls away.

"'Night, sweetheart," he says and heads for the door.

Goddamned biker.

He's gone before I realize he still has my panties.

CHAPTER FIVE

Rev

I LEAVE NOTHING to chance. This is a recipe for fucking disaster, and I don't bake. I also don't cook, and I definitely don't screw up. Must be the finger bang at the club, because I've decided Evie's safety comes first and I've got my eyes and ears in place since Rocker was a no-show at the meeting *he'd* fucking set up to discuss our mutual problem. He needs to understand the Hard Riders aren't backing down. And me? I need to know no one gets close to Evie. If the Colombians come knocking, I'm ready. I followed Evie to her next birthday party gig and stationed myself outside. Don't think the Colombians are gonna smuggle themselves inside in a gift bag, but eyes on the street are a safer bet. Came in a cage, too, so I wouldn't scare Evie's customers off.

Bet most of her mommies wouldn't mind a biker, though. Bet we'd be their favorite flavor of bad.

Evie's been doing her princess thing for a good hour when Rocker pulls up and parks down the street at a discreet distance. I'm leaning against the garage door, watching the house. The prospect on the south end of the street texted me when Rocker turned into the cul-de-sac. The street's full of cars thanks to the birthday party happening in the backyard, which makes it easier for Rocker to hide his bike.

Rocker and I don't have much of an acquaintance, but I've seen him around and I recognize the colors. Plus, he looks like Evie. Got the same color eyes and hair, although after that the resemblance stops. The sunglasses don't hide the hard-eyed gaze he directs as me, but fuck him. I get that he's not happy about my presence here. I feel like shooting his ass, too, but that's not how this game gets played. He nudges the glasses up and tips his head to me in greeting, taking in the balloons bobbing over the mailbox as the screams coming from the backyard assault us both. It's like being locked in the seventh circle of hell.

The smile that curls up the corner of Rocker's mouth doesn't reach his eyes as he braces a boot against the edge of the sidewalk. "Heard you met my sister the other night at the club."

"She's real nice." I shrug casually. We could be two guys exchanging small talk over a couple of beers. "Might be seeing her."

I'll respect his colors up to a point, but not gonna lie—I enjoy needling him. Plus, taking one for the club and spending time with Evie is a win-win situation for me. She's hot as hell. Gotta hand it to Rocker, though—he keeps his cool and nods as if he isn't imagining ripping me apart with his bare hands. Probably running me over with his bike in that fantasy, too.

"Evie's not big on club life. She's not part of this."

"She is now," I tell him. Wish it wasn't true, but I don't believe in denial. "When you got in bed with the Colombians, she stopped being a bystander. If you can tell me straight up that no one's gonna come gunning for her, I'll consider backing the hell off."

"Shit's complicated," Rocker says slowly. "Not saying I don't understand where you're coming from, but it's not as simple as just saying I'm out of the trade."

I need an angle I can work. "Call it what you want, but you're running shit in our territory and the cartel's got their nose in our business. Step one is for you to back the hell off and stay away from what the Hard Riders claim. Step two? Pick a new career, because drug dealing isn't a long-term proposition. If I don't shoot you first, there's gonna be a long line behind me."

Rocker rolls his shoulders. Must have a knot there the size of a fucking tree, because he does it again.

"Shit's complicated," he repeats. "But I don't want anything happening to Evie. That point's nonnegotiable."

"I'm making her my girl." I usually take my time and think shit over, but claiming Evie feels right. "Not saying she's my old lady just yet, but she's with me. I'll look out for her. You don't come round her until you've got the cartel off your back. You don't talk to her, don't hang with her, don't come near her."

"She's my sister." Rocker crosses his arms over his chest. Evie's a small woman, but her brother's built like a fucking mountain man. Not that I'm intimidated, but knocking him on his ass will take time and Evie's bound to notice. Plus, I'm pretty sure the princess party people would frown on violence. Could probably start a line of parties for boys, though—maybe I should mention it to Evie. Do some MMA fighting demonstrations. Help her branch out and shit.

"Evie's a big girl—old enough to make her own dating choices."

Rocker studies me. Got no idea what he sees and I wouldn't care except Evie seems to have some inconveniently fond feelings for the fuck, which means I can't just kill him. Pretty sure she's gonna get pissed if I even ding him.

"True," he says finally. "So she talks to who she wants to talk to—you don't get to be the bouncer at the door and run me off. There's no chance she's gonna agree to be your old lady, and you need her okay for any other kind of relationship, you feel me?"

The unspoken *or I'll shoot you* hangs in the air between us. Guess we have something in common after all.

"And you don't get to sell your bullshit on my streets." I'll see his threat with one of my own.

"I'd like to say I don't give a shit about what my sister gets up to with you," he says slowly. "But that wouldn't be true. She's a good woman and she deserves nothing but the best. If that's what you are, I'd be happy to slap a bow on your ass."

I flip him the bird. "I look best in blue."

"You hurt her, and that blue will be a coffin lining, you feel me?"

"Right back at you."

"In fact, keep your hands off her entirely. Keep a couple of feet between you and I won't come back and kill you."

We're still staring at each other, and I'm calculating the chances we go at each other, when the first kids and moms flood out of the house waving plastic bags full of sparkly shit and paper plates of cupcakes. Princess Number One rocks a purple number, while her princess companion sports yellow. The rainbow effect is blinding. The mom stops dead when she spots Rocker and me, sweeping her girls behind her. Bet she's reaching for her phone.

Rocker must come to the same conclusion that I do, because he flicks me a salute and saunters back down the street. Seconds later, he's off on his hog and the princesses are staring after him open-mouthed. Bet Evie kicks his ass for bringing a bike anywhere near her party.

"Does he work with you?" Momma Princess isn't ready to let go of either her suspicions or her cell phone. Ten dollars says she's got 9 and 1 pushed, with that last digit cranked up and ready to go.

"Boy parties," I tell her.

"We could do that for my party," the purple princess stage whispers, tugging on her momma. "Because girls can do whatever boys do."

Momma Princess blinks, but it's not like she can deny logic like that. Kids see the bikes and think *fun ride*—the parents are the ones who jump straight to felonies and jailbait.

"Let me find a card," I say with a straight face.

"I've got a cupcake," the mini-me announces and holds her plate up for my inspection. "You can have it as a down payment."

Kid's gonna be a master negotiator someday. I take the cupcake while it's still on offer and before she starts laying down terms. Chocolate with chocolate frosting—fucking awesome.

"Can you come to my party next week?" Mini-me proves she's smart, going on the attack as soon as my mouth is full of her cupcake. Momma Princess shoots me a nervous look and beats a hasty retreat. Naturally, this is when Evie comes flouncing out of the party looking ready to bust my balls. Bet she heard the bike—which means I'm blaming Rocker. *Fucker.*

CHAPTER SIX

Eve

"WAS THAT *ROCKER?*" I clutch my phone so tight that the case bites into my fingers. I'm surprised it doesn't fly out of my hand with the force of my grip—and frankly, I suspect I should be aiming it at the biker lounging against the Princess Mobile.

Rev actually finishes his cupcake before he bothers responding. "He came by," he growls, jerking his thumb up the street.

"And then he just left?" Although Rocker is the silent partner in our party business and his job description is limited to behind-the-scenes stuff like moving heavy objects and paperwork, my baby brother is super protective of me. He's never quite gotten the memo that it's my job to look after him—so he likes to show up occasionally and poke his nose in my business. For him to light out without so much as talking to me is highly unusual and I know exactly who to blame. The mom and the baby princess hovering near Rev must register the tension between the two of us, because they skedaddle for a battered minivan parked curbside.

"No shit." I blame this entirely on Rev. It's not difficult to imagine how his meet-up with my brother went—both of them act like dogs and I'm a hotly contested tree.

"He came by to see me."

I'm trying to give Rev the benefit of the doubt. I'm not under any illusions that he's a good guy, but maybe this isn't as bad as it seems. Perhaps Rocker got a call and will be back in a few minutes. Perhaps he went to pick up something. Okay. I'm stretching and I can admit it.

"You ready to roll?" Rev ignores my last comment.

"That wasn't a question," I grit out. "That was my *brother* who stopped by to see *me*. Why did you run him off?"

We're starting to attract attention. I'm not kidding myself—the dress helps, as does the bright pink RV, but the star attraction here is Rev. More than one of the departing mothers glances sidewise at him as they shepherd their little darlings down the driveway. The man is undeniably hot. Maybe it's the casual power in the way he stands or the stubble that roughens his jaw. There's nothing soft about Rev and absolutely everything about him screams dirty sex. I squeeze my thighs together, grateful for the dress that hides the betraying motion. God, I want this man. We don't have much of a history together and he won't remember my name in a year, but right now none of that matters and that's a problem.

"It's not safe for you to hang around him," he says. At least Rev has the decency to not lie to me about having run Rocker off. Or maybe he knows he's busted and not getting out of this one.

"The lack of detail is not helping your case," I tell him, trying really hard not to stare at his thighs. Or his hands. There's a whole lot of sexy real estate to choose from.

"I'm going to find out what's going on," I continue. "You might as well tell me."

He makes a rough sound that absolutely, totally does not make my panties wet. Much. "Ask Rocker."

"You ran him off—that makes this your problem."

He nods slowly. "You know that your brother rides with the Black Dogs, right? He patched in with them a couple of years ago."

"Unfortunately, yes." I've done some asking around—wouldn't you?—and so far I haven't discovered any magic escape clause. It sure seems like membership in an MC is pretty much a lifetime commitment until death do you part.

"Your brother's been a busy boy. He cut a deal with a Colombian cartel to move their product, but then he tried to cut them *out* of the picture."

I try and fail to imagine my baby brother as a drug dealer. I mean, he doesn't even smoke—how can he be committing felonies on that kind of level? *You know he's up to something.* He was worried out at the lake, sure, but would he really do *this*?

"My brother wouldn't have anything to do with drugs."

Rev looks pained. "Loyalty's good, princess, but you need to keep your eyes open, too. Ask him what's up."

Rev doesn't sound like he's bluffing. In fact, he sounds way too confident. This is *Rocker* we're talking about. I mean, he colors out of the lines a little, but this would be the equivalent of taking a black Sharpie to the whole goddamned coloring book. If I knew for certain he was selling drugs, I'd have to do something. Drugs hurt innocent people. Drugs mean money, violence and turf wars. I've lived in East Las Vegas long enough to know that.

"Come for a ride with me." Rev changes tactics. "I'll drop you at your place afterward. It'll be fun."

"Does the caveman approach usually work for you?"

He shrugs. "It's just a ride."

Uh-huh. "You have a bridge you want to sell me, too?"

As much as I'd like to continue living in the land of denial—the weather's awesome and orgasms for all—I'm a realist. This man wants something. I just don't know if it has something to do with Rocker, my panties, or both. Maybe he wants to pick up where we left off the other night, or maybe there's something else going on here.

"Ride with me," he says, sounding a little impatient. "I promise you'll enjoy the fuck out of it, Evie."

So sexy.

So wrong.

This has to explain my answer. "Pick me up at six."

CHAPTER SEVEN

Eve

NO ONE WARNED me that straddling a Harley with a hot guy is like using a gigantic vibrator as your pony ride. As a kid, I used to shove a broomstick between my legs and gallop up and down the yard in pursuit of runaway cattle, ponies, and bad guys. Riding with Rev is the grown-up version of that game and different from any other bike ride I've ever taken. As soon as I slide my arms around his waist, locking my fingers just above his belt buckle, he takes off.

Slow isn't part of the man's vocabulary. His speedometer never drops below sixty. He takes us out into the desert, the big bike eating up the asphalt with blinding speed. Even through the helmet, the wind whips at my face, tears my hair, chokes my voice in my throat. It's terrifying. It's the best feeling ever. My heart pounds in my ears and an answering pulse springs to life between my legs. My pussy clenches with each turn Rev takes, a hot, heavy beat anticipating the way his body leans into the road's curves, the muscles in his body flexing as he guides us faster, harder, tighter.

When finally we pull over I'm not sure if my throat is hoarse from screaming—or from holding back my moans. Damn, I'm horny.

My partner in crime, however, is oblivious. He waves a big hand toward the open air in front of us. "Lookout."

Since that appears to be a noun and not a verb, I follow his fingers pointing off into space. I don't want to admire canyons or vistas or (frankly) anything other than his dick. I don't even need him to come for me—I just want those big, rough, banged-up fingers shoved inside me and I can do the rest. Apparently, *all* of me wants to live dangerously, not just the part that thought it was a great idea to get on a Harley with this man.

"Thanks." *For nothing.*

I hop off his bike, not sure my legs will hold me. I should be glad he's hands-off. That his definition of *ride* is textbook nice and not a dirty, filthy, orgasm-filled euphemism. Should be. Am not.

I'm such a liar.

I stroll over to the railing and look out. The view is pretty. I even whip out my phone and snap a picture. See? I'm absolutely enjoying my ride. This fun companionship is what I need.

Not sex.

And definitely not sex with Rev.

"Like what you see?" His rough voice rolls out of the silence behind me. It sounds lower, deeper, *darker* than before. I'm not sure he's actually talking about the canyons and the desert at all. Or maybe that's wishful thinking combined with the heat.

Because it's hot out here. I lift a hand to fan myself, tilting my face into the weak draft of cooler air as I tug open the leather jacket Rev insisted I wear. Jeans and boots in Nevada in the summer? I'm definitely overheated.

I don't hear him move. One moment he's still straddling that big, too-hot bike of his and the next he's right up behind me, his thighs pressed against mine, his arms caging me against the railing.

"I like what I see." He growls the words, his mouth trailing over the damp skin of my throat. He does? Heat flashes through my body as I spontaneously combust.

His mouth moves down. "I want you, princess."

My mouth opens and I'm sure there are a dozen witty, sexy, fabulous responses to his statement—but I draw a blank. Suck in air and stare down at his hands wrapped around the railing.

Those hands could be wrapped around me.

Say *yes.*

"It's a bad idea," I say instead. See? I'm being responsible. Mature. Putting my job first. My pussy all but whimpers in protest.

"No one has to know," he counters. The man must be the devil. Or omniscient. A mind reader. It would make for awesome sex but is the risk worth the reward?

"I'll make it good for you," he promises. "I'll be your dirty little secret. Don't you want to come right now?"

Hell *yes* I do.

"Just once?" Because tonight I'm feeling greedy. If you're going off the diet, diving face-first into the three-layer chocolate cake that's been teasing you all day, you don't want just one slice. You want the whole thing. You want to eat until you can't swallow one more bite, until just the smell of all that sweet makes you sick, until you're over it. Done. Kaput.

Rev's my cake.

I've been so good and now, just this once, I'm breaking all my rules and I get to taste him. Lick him. Devour him whole. By tomorrow, I'll be cured of this obsessive need to eat him up, to find out if his skin can possibly taste as good as it looks. Tomorrow, I'll see him and be all ho-hum, been there, done that, couldn't possibly have another bite. We'll be over.

Tonight... I want it all.

All of him.

Once can't possibly be enough, not with Rev.

His slow grin makes my panties wetter. As if I wasn't soaked already from the ride. "How many orgasms you want?"

Maybe I don't need to give him a number. Maybe he isn't cake, but is instead an all-you-can-eat buffet and I can go back for more, more, more whenever I want. That so works for me.

I lean up and nip his bottom lip. "Surprise me."

His eyes darken. "You got any hard limits I should know about?"

I lick where I bit because why play safe now? "Stay the hell away from my ass. Otherwise, I'll give you a play-by-play update."

Some stuff I'm just not into—and something tells me this man has no limits whatsoever. Adventurous is good, but I still have to ride his bike back to my house. Of course, I could take him there, too. Have sex in an actual bed with sheets and pillows and something cushier than the ground but…he's not a keeper man. This is a onetime thing and I don't want him there in my space. I need an orgasm, not memories.

"Gotcha." He gives me a quick, hard kiss, his lips pressing against mine with erotic intensity before they release me. Nope. I don't want him to let go. Not yet.

I reach for his shoulders and he laughs, scooping me up in his arms. He stops to grab his saddlebag—maybe it's the biker equivalent of a toy box because a girl can hope, right?—and then he's effortlessly striding down a small ravine just out of sight of the highway. I probably should worry. Hello, this is bad movie material right here. I've just given him a free pass to have his wicked way with me and bikers aren't particularly known for their upstanding moral values. And yet… I feel free. Free and somehow safe at the same time because whatever Rev does to me, I trust him not to hurt me.

Rev

I should kiss her.

Trot out all the tricks I've learned from fucking too many women on too many different nights. Give her the orgasms she's all but begging for and mark her as mine. Somehow, though, the smooth, practiced moves disappear from my head and all I can do is enjoy being here with her, right now, right this moment. I've driven out to the lookout before, although I've never tapped ass here. Doesn't take a genius to know, however, that we need to get off the road for this. Don't know why she's suddenly so impatient, but I roll with it, carrying her down a small ravine. As soon as we're out of sight of the road, I drop my saddlebag and shift her in my arms so I can peel my jacket off to use as a blanket. She's working out of hers, too, so maybe we don't end up with dirt where dirt has no business going.

Her hands start on my shirt next, trying to get the hem up, but that's not how I want this to go. So when she starts snapping out commands to go faster, get naked, do this, do that, I kiss her hard. My mouth covers her mouth, my lips parting hers, as I pour myself into the kiss. She tastes good, like mint and sweet tea. Fuck, maybe she tastes like sunshine or whiskey or any one of a dozen things, but I know one thing for certain. Evie's my Kryptonite. I lay her down without breaking our kiss, planting myself between her legs, cupping her head between my hands as I bury my fingers in her pretty hair. I devour her, pressing my dick against her pussy as her legs wrap around my hips. Fuck, she's greedy.

Love that about her, even though the L-word isn't one I trot out about sex or women.

She swallows a moan when I finally tear my mouth away, leaning back. She's wearing too many clothes and I need her naked. If I start tearing shit, however, we're gonna have a problem with the drive back to

Vegas. I'd enjoy the shit out of her riding naked behind
me but we'd definitely attract attention. Plus, I bet that's
one of those hard limit things she mentioned. No Lady
Godiva on my bike.

"Don't stop," she orders, eyes half-closed. Her hands
go to the waist of her jeans, unbuttoning and shoving
the denim down. If I don't hurry, she won't wait for
me. "You owe me an orgasm."

"Never broke a promise yet," I tell her. She toes her
jeans off, but her panties are mine. I tear them off her
because they're the cutest little thing—and my sou-
venir. Perfect spank bank material for later. Gonna
wrap that silky blue-and-white scrap around my dick
and rub one out—dessert to go, for later. I shove them
in my jacket. My next step in this erotic battle we're
fighting has to be her tits.

Fun fact of the day—Evie's tits drive me crazy.

I've jerked off to the fantasy of ripping off her shirt,
tearing open her bra, and then ramming myself between her breasts, shoving my dick up the tight, sweat-
slicked valley until my head hits her lips and she opens
up for me. She swallows a moan as I make the first
part of my multistep plan reality rather than fiction. I
drag her shirt up, and then fuck it, I leave the cotton
tangled around her arms, her wrists stretched over her
head, braceleted in one hand of mine. Don't need ropes
when I've got her like this.

Hot.

Eager.

And all for me.

I unbuckle, unzip and shove my jeans down just enough to get my dick out.

"Hurry," she whispers as if she's got a schedule, a plan, a time table in her head. Fuck doing this on Fast-forward when I could hit Pause and enjoy her for hours. I want her screaming my name, desperate for me, knowing exactly who has his hands, his tongue, his dick all over her sweet, needy body. If she has an itch to scratch, I'm in no position to judge—but I'll make damn certain she knows who's making her fantasies come to life.

I drag the fingers of my free hand down her chest, between her tits, until I'm cupping her, my thumb teasing her nipples. She rewards me with a whimper.

Not good enough.

Her tits are fucking gorgeous, big enough to fill my palms but small enough that I can cup them. Lying on her back pushes her tits up and out, putting those sweet curves on display for me and I'm gonna need both hands to appreciate her right. I give her wrists a gentle squeeze. "Don't move."

Her eyes narrow as her fingers tangle with mine. "Orders?"

Woman's a total back seat driver. We'll work on that.

"Yeah." I lean down and give her another quick, hard kiss. "You got one job here and that's to take what I've got to give you."

She shifts beneath me, stretching, making space for herself. "And what if I don't like it?"

"You've got words. Fucking use them." Not as if she's held back in the mouthy department before, so she can tell me if something I do fails to get her off. If I don't make this good for her, I deserve everything she can dish out.

Her fingers fall away from mine. "Okay."

"You want me dirty?"

Guess she hears the challenge in my words because her eyes darken and flick down my body. No way she misses the bulge in the front of my jeans.

"Yes. Touch me," she demands. Doesn't move her hands, though, so she definitely deserves a reward.

"Hold your tits for me."

She shakes off her shirt, lowers her hands and squeezes her tits together around my dick. Love how she takes instruction. Since I first saw her, I've been fantasizing about getting her naked. Opening her up, putting myself inside her.

I straddle her, bracing my hands on either side of her head. Spread out on my jacket, strands of her hair tease my fingers, wrapping themselves around me. There's a lesson there. She's the one who's really in charge here.

I wish I could draw this moment out forever, wish I could whip out my phone and snap a picture of her body welcoming mine. Fuck. She feels amazing. I drive forward, her tits hold me tight, and my eyes all but roll back in my head. Gotta get it together. Gotta do her right, make this good for her.

And then she licks the tip of my dick.

I give it to her harder, faster, pistoning my dick in and out of the snug channel she's made for me. Fuck if I can hold back—or want to. I find a rhythm that makes my dick happy, the slick, tight grasp of her skin on mine pushing me higher, tighter, closer.

"This work for you?" I whisper.

She flashes me a grin. "Who wants his happy ending?"

That's all the warning she gives me before she sucks the tip of my dick into her mouth, the head disappearing beneath the perfect O of her lips. Fuck. Me. I'm hard as nails, rough as shit, and she opens wider, swallowing me down. I must look like some monster beast, crouched over her, fucking her mouth, and I don't care. She lets me and I'm far too close to coming.

Fuck happy endings—this is heaven.

I bump against the back of her throat and she doesn't tell me no—just groans and sucks harder like she loves the taste of me. I'm going to blow all over her face, mark her with my come. Her lashes drift down, hiding her eyes from me. Not sure what I expect to see to be honest, but looking at her is sexy as hell.

Fuck this.

I'm not coming until I'm balls-deep inside her, which makes it her turn.

I drop and roll, pulling her over me. Her legs hug my face, her pussy planted above my mouth. She squeals, bracing herself on her arms. Guess she didn't see that coming, but then she whimpers, her thighs trembling, and I cup her sweet little ass with my hands.

"I've got you."

Let go.

Let me.

She asked for it dirty and I'm just giving her what

she wants. Making sure she's ready before I tap her. And because the taste of her is addictive and I'm not ready to be done. She relaxes in my grip and I part her with my fingers. Another whimper. A sexy-as-hell moan. Her pussy's the prettiest shade of pink, her bush neatly trimmed into a dark arrow of soft hair. Not bare, not quite, just a fucking tease to look at.

"Look at you." I blow lightly, trailing my fingertips over her folds.

"Rev—" She shudders.

Yeah, she likes this.

Bet she likes this even more. Bet I do, too. I lean in and get my first taste of her. I pull her wide and lick her slowly over and over. When she's squirming, I suck her clit, alternating between the two until she's gasping, her breath catching as I push her closer and closer to the edge. Her tits heave up and down, still wet from my kisses.

I pull away before she comes, grabbing a condom and ripping the package open. Fuck finesse. I need to be inside her *now*. Playing dirty games doesn't mean putting her at risk. I get the condom out, roll it down my dick and yank her down my body. Seconds later I'm pushing my way inside her body.

Eve

Rev's monster dick opens me up.

He's big.

It's not like his proportions are a revelation. Deep-throating him wasn't an option, so it's no surprise it takes him long, fabulous, thank-you-Jesus minutes to work himself inside me. He's not holding back, he's giving it to me good, but he's not in any rush, either. He doesn't slam deep, doesn't force my body to yield.

He just waits me out.

I soften around him—he moves deeper. Cause and effect.

My legs open wider, hugging his hips, bumping into the ground, and he grunts, catching my knees with his palms. Putting himself between me and the dirt. I use my new leverage to ride him hard. I don't want slow, I don't want sweet and gentle. Fortunately, he's in the mood to give me exactly what I want.

He slams up and I meet his thrust, coming down hard. A shriek forces itself from my throat, but to hell with it. The sensation is so good. I feel him everywhere, inside, outside, in my head and right goddamned there between my legs. I brace my hands on his shoulders, and yes I dig in with my nails. We're both going to bear marks tomorrow.

"Eyes open," he grunts when my lashes drift down. Not sure what he thinks I'm really looking at because right now all I can do is feel. And feel and feel.

His eyes watch me, dark and intense with need and emotions I can't interpret. He's so different from anyone else I've done this with. He's more in control of this, of *us*, than I like but it's too late to stop, to step back, to hold off the orgasm building deep within me. He so wins this battle we're fighting between us.

"Come," he orders, sliding a hand free to find and press my clit as he drives inside me. God. He fills me

up. There's no room left, so I do the only thing I can
and come apart. I let everything go and scream with the
pleasure, the desire, the feeling of fucking flying and
flying, knowing he's here to catch me. It's too much,
too everything—too fast and definitely too close.

He grunts something, moving faster and harder, his
hands grasping my hips and holding me tight. My head
hits his chest, my face pressed against his sweat-slicked
skin and I breathe him in as he pounds deeper, finding his own release. I lie there and let him do what he
wants with me.

God, he's dangerous.

And then I can't think anymore because his fingers find my clit again and press and just like that I'm
soaring, flying and fighting with him toward another
release.

Rev

Christ. What just happened here?

I wrap my arms around Evie, holding her tight, and
try to figure out when dirty sex took a dangerous right-
hand turn into something…else. Not sure what to fucking call it, but all I know is that I'm not done with her.
She sags against my chest, her face buried against my
skin, her hair tickling my nose.

"Rev?" Her voice floats up at me.

"Yeah?" I can feel a smile tugging at the corners
of my mouth. I'll tell her whatever she wants to hear.
Fucking gospel truth right there. She's amazing. I run
my hands over her bare skin. We need to find a bed

stat because the shit I want to do to her, with her deserves that much.

"You give good dirty sex," she whispers, rolling off me and standing up. The. Fuck?

I'm not done with her.

Not even close.

But she's already pulling on her jeans, wiggling and tugging, zipping and buttoning. She's not thinking about what else I could do for her. Now I'm just her ride back to Vegas, and maybe, if I did this right, a happy memory. I'm her been there, done that boy. Her past.

She asked for dirty sex, so I'm not sure why *I* suddenly feel dirty. Yes, I'm her not-so-fucking-little secret and that part's okay because it's what I agreed to after all, but I'd also like to do her in a bed, and not some forty-buck-a-night motel, either. Satin sheets, fucking candles—the whole nine yards before I give her the twelve inches that has her name written all over it.

Except she really doesn't want that. Has to be a first in my life, that a woman doesn't want a repeat from me.

"Thanks," she says and heads for my bike. Feels like she slapped me on the ass and sent me on my way.

What the fuck just happened?

CHAPTER EIGHT

Rev

SOME CLUB BROTHERS have permanent women in their lives, old ladies they love and protect. It's a hell of a choice to make and not the kind of shit you can end in divorce court. The day your woman puts on your patch, you take 100 percent responsibility for her actions. She screws up—you pay. That takes more trust than there's gold in Fort Knox. There's nothing easy about being a woman in an MC. We're ornery, protective, and don't just demand respect—we fucking earn it. Play in our world and play by our rules. Not too many women can or will do it.

My future holds no old lady.

No keeper girl.

Evie Kent is a blip on the radar, a pothole in the highway of life. We have no future together. She's untouchable, off-limits, property-of-someone-else material. She made that perfectly clear when she banged my brains out and proceeded on her way as if taking my dick deep inside her meant absolutely nothing at all.

She's right.

Abso-fucking-lutely correct.

What went down on our ride was just sex—and *not* the reason my bike is parked across the street from her house when I could just order a prospect to watch her. Worse, I'm phone in hand, thumb poised to tap her name in my contacts.

Rocker's not on board with ditching the cartel. It will take weeks or months to straighten his shit out. On the other hand, sticking close to Evie will make it easier to discover Rocker's plans. If the Colombian cartel makes a move on her, I'll be in place. And what's the easiest way to stay close?

Make her believe I'm dating material not a quick bang.

We all see the problem here, right?

I don't date.

Ever.

I am, for all intents and purposes, a dating virgin. Dating has the learning curve of nuclear physics—not the kind of shit you casually pick up over the weekend. Sure, fucking Evie Kent would rock, but I hadn't been planning on date nights—or sexting, flirty looks and too-casual questions about the gals hanging at the clubhouse. Phone chats, shared plans and sleepovers? Also not on my to-do list.

Yet here I am.

Waiting on the curb.

Her place looks real cute. No kids, no cats or dogs, but bright red flowers march up the walkway next to a stupid-ass have-a-nice-day flag. She grows roses and

owns wicker furniture with matching goddamned pillows. My throat actually itches and starts to close up
at all this happy Suzy Homemaker shit.

Before I can text, she pops out, hauling a trash bag
half her size. Her tiny cotton shorts don't quite cover
an ass that's even sexier than I remember. The shorts
are either way too small or they shrank in the wash. Or
fuck me, maybe she chose them on purpose to drive
me crazy.

Her evil plan is definitely working.

She flips open the trash can, going on tiptoe. The
shorts get shorter—my view gets hotter. And yeah, I
debate taking a picture since I have my phone handy.
Decide against going all paparazzi on her ass because
stalking isn't wooing. She tosses the bag, slams the lid
shut and starts back to the house.

Stops.

I am pretty hard to miss.

Just in case she's short-sighted, I waggle my fingers
at her. She flips me the bird and marches into the house
while my head replays every ass fantasy I've ever had.

My phone buzzes.

EVIE: You're a stalker now too?

ME: Just in the neighborhood.

I tap the smiley face button in my message app.
Turns out there's a million little pictures you can add
to your message, most of which make absolutely no

sense. Who the fuck needs pictures of bananas or broccoli? I pick one and hit Send.

And wait.

Maybe she's writing *War and Peace*. Or maybe she's taking a nap. On her bed in those sexy little shorts. I imagine a half dozen ways to peel those shorts down her legs. As the minutes tick closer to a half hour, however, I run out of patience.

ME: Should I apologize?

I'm not sorry at all for fucking her when she gave me the green light, but if she needs to hear the words, I'll give them to her.

EVIE: You move fast

If that's a complaint, I can happily spend longer eating her pussy. I'm still typing my text message when UPS pulls up and Mr. Brown bounds out carrying an enormous pink box. He rings the bell, drops his load on the doormat and leaves. While my inner caveman rejoices he's gone, the rest of me wants more service. This is my grand gesture, after all. I need delivery with a fucking mariachi band and a big bouquet of overdone from the florist. Fireworks and a rocket launcher. Your standard dating shit.

ME: It's safe

EVIE: Not scared

And because my Evie's a doer and not just a talker, she yanks opens the door and stares down at the box. My dick promptly gets hard imagining what's in the box. Her gaze finds me as the delivery truck pulls away.

Yes, I ordered her stuff. I tore her panties off her. I owe her new ones. Plus, shopping's hard to stop. I got started. Each picture I clicked on the website became my new favorite fantasy. If Victoria's Secret let you drag your girl's face over the model's, they'd sell a shit-ton more underwear.

ME: Open it and send me some pictures?

I make it a request. I may be stuck across the street, but I'm getting a handle on this dating stuff. I cross my legs and lean back against my bike. A few seconds later, my phone buzzes with an incoming text.

She's sent me a picture.

Of her middle finger.

I so like this girl.

Her door reopens and her ass appears first. No matter how fast she stripped, I don't think she's had time to put my stuff on. We'll have to work on that. If we're dating, she needs to appreciate what I do for her.

She's carrying a tray with two glasses of something brown with ice cubes. She sets it down, drops onto one of the chairs, and then looks at me and pats the cushions of the seat next to her. Apparently, my dick *can* get harder. Walking across the street is downright painful.

She crosses her legs when I get close. My gaze follows. *Big mistake.* Her left thigh brushes the top of her right, where I've had my fingers, run my tongue up her silky-smooth skin and hit the jackpot. No way she misses my reaction to that memory, because she's sitting in the chair closest to the door and an escape route—so I have to brush past her to sit down. God bless the total lack of space because my erection rubs against her shoulder.

She sighs. "You're impossible."

Complaint or not—you be the judge. I sit, knees brushing hers as I angle the seat closer to hers. Be happy to pull her into my lap if that was what she wanted.

She hands me a glass of tea and launches her opening salvo. "You can't send me underwear."

"Already did." I knock back half my tea. It's actually not bad. Hanging around on the curb is hot work.

"Return it." She launches into a stream of blah blah blah about not accepting presents from me and it's totally inappropriate and how did I know her size because that's creepy (I've had my hands all over her ass and her pussy—I can do the math from there) and who do I think she is? The words wash over me because I'm stuck on a visual of her in those pretty new panties that's way better than the words she throws at me.

I've spent five years earning the respect of my club. Before that, I earned the respect of the men in my SEAL team. I don't expect her to give me anything, but I do demand a chance. I set my glass down and interrupt the flow of talk.

"What's a guy got to do to have a chance with you?"

She blinks and fidgets with her glass. "You really want to date me?"

She actually looks surprised. Maybe we're both new to the dating game? Because that would actually be fucking awesome. We could make up our own rules.

"Yeah," I say gruffly. "I sure do."

She waves a hand and I'm goddamned lucky it's the empty one. "We're completely incompatible."

I give her a slow smile because I sure as hell remember what went on between us. "Not everywhere. You like some things about me."

"That's just sex." The cutest pink blush paints her cheeks.

"You fucking love dirty sex." *Truth.*

She volleys right back.

"Which doesn't mean I love *you*."

"I don't need that." Love is on my personal no-fly list, remember? Evie developing feelings for me—other than the jump-my-bones kind—would be downright inconvenient. "Let's date. Have some fun."

"Have sex." Now she sounds completely disgruntled.

Fuck, yeah.

I cup her bare knee with my hand. Her skin is warm and soft, and she jumps ever so slightly when I skim my thumb over the vulnerable curve. "Sex works for me."

"There are rules for dating," she says firmly. "You don't like rules."

"What if I played by your rules?"

She stares at me like that's the craziest idea ever. "You can't play by the rules."

"Why not?" I settle back in my seat, stretching my legs out. My legs bump hers, and so far, this is pretty freaking awesome. "Tell me the rules."

She makes a face. "So you can break them?"

"Hit me." I've so got this. Doesn't matter if I'm a dating virgin—she's gonna spell it all out.

She leans forward and picks up my hand. "Five rules."

I can work with that number. Club bylaws are larger.

"First rule?" She folds down my thumb. "I won't cry about you. You don't get to make me feel bad. If you piss me off, I tell you."

No fucking way I *want* to make her cry. "You've been dating the wrong guys, princess. I can work with that, as long as you show me some respect in front of the club. You want to tear into my ass, you do it when we're alone."

Her fingers skim up the length of my index finger as if it's my dick, pinching the tip lightly. "I do 40 percent of the dating work. You do the other 60. This is not a partnership, nor is it a dictatorship."

I curl my finger around hers. "I chase you. Got it."

She tucks my index finger into my palm and tugs on my middle finger. "Three? You pick me up and we go out. If we do this, I'm not your booty call. You don't come over to my place and I don't go to yours until we have a relationship."

I can work with that, too, although celibacy is definitely not my first choice. Don't think it's hers, either. But it's up to me to earn a repeat in her bed, and I'm good with that. Anything I've put my mind to, it's come to me.

"Four. You plan ahead if you want to see me. You don't just text or show up."

"You're gonna have to forgive me for today." I lift her hand to my mouth and press a kiss against her fingertips. "Since I didn't have the rulebook."

She goes for the kill. "And we're not having sex on the first date. Maybe not the second. If it happens again, it's because I feel close to you."

She wants the whole enchilada. Dating, a relationship, emotional intimacy. And *then* maybe she tosses me the sexual cherry and we get around to having hot, dirty sex. Sex is the epilogue in her book, when in mine it's all of the chapters except for the afterword where we say our goodbyes and head in opposite directions. Still, the only hard and fast *rule* I'm hearing is the not-on-the-first-date thing. After that? Everything is fucking negotiable.

"And then what?"

She shrugs. "And then we see what happens. Maybe we have sex. Or a relationship. Maybe we head in different directions and it's over."

"Then we've got a deal. I'm playing by your rules and you're giving me a chance."

CHAPTER NINE

Rev

MY PRINCESS MAY be unavailable for sexcapades—which is fucking a-okay with me because I'm all for the slow build if that gets her hot—but I have one of the old ladies from the MC book a birthday party for the coming weekend. I figure this falls under the plan-in-advance rule in the Evie Rulebook and since Mary Jane's two girls are four and six, she's perfectly happy to have me spring for some Saturday entertainment.

Tío, her old man and my club brother, has ten years on me. His last tour of duty screwed with his head—I like to think Mary Jane's his goddamned reward because finding an old lady like her is like hitting the rolling jackpot at the casino. Boom—you're richer than fucking Midas himself because you plugged your lucky quarter into the right slot at the right moment. Tío deserves every second of his good fortune.

I'd hung around while Mary Jane made the call, in case she needed an assist, but she handled the party details like a pro. Evie sounded way too perky. It's not like I want her *un*happy, but I wouldn't have minded her sounding lonely or like she needed something. Then I could have headed on over to her place and offered to help her. Rub her back. Fix some shit. Be the fucking boyfriend of her dreams.

That was such a strange thought that I'd done my best to forget about it the entire four days until the party. I ensured a prospect kept watch over her from a nice, discreet distance and I took my turn. Not gonna ask them to do what I won't do. The Colombians were no-shows, and let me tell you, Evie leads a really boring life. The woman does nothing but work. Not like I want to see her partying and getting it on with some random stranger (because then I'd have to fucking kill him), but it can't be good for her.

Mary Jane and Tío have a two-story house with a pool about a mile from the clubhouse. One of those home security system signs is stuck in the front yard, but the real deterrent are the bikes. One look and anyone with eyes in his head knows not to mess with their house. Since Mary Jane had promised her girlfriends would pony up enough kids for a bona fide party, I'd sent over a prospect with a big-ass cake and balloons. I figured that covered all the party bases.

When the Princess Mobile pulls up, I can practically feel Evie taking in the bikes crowding the driveway. The engine keeps right on running as she peeks left, then right. Fucking looks up, too, as if she expects someone big, bad and dangerous to land on the roof of the monstrosity she drives. I whip out my phone and send her a quick text.

ME: Didn't think you were chicken.

The pause is long enough that I start to worry she might actually bail, leaving me alone with a dozen tutu-sporting, tiara-wearing little girls, when she finally responds.

EVIE: You got kids? Bcz...dating no no

If I had a kid, I'd never fuck around on the side.

ME: Kids belong to Tío's old lady

EVIE: Tío's a busy man

ME: Got some loaner kids along for the ride

EVIE: How come you're here?

ME: Cake and a beautiful woman? Come on out and make my day

I can imagine her rolling her eyes at that one. Still, she and a couple of princess chicks emerge. Mary Jane bustles out before things get too awkward, so I owe the woman. She sends Princesses Two and Three into the backyard where, she warns, *the hordes are getting restless.* No clue why we don't let women patch into the MC—they're bloodthirsty enough.

Evie kind of flutters on the walk like she's not sure

what to do—bet that pisses her off. Since I'm working on my boyfriend skills, I help her out.

"Good to see you." I brush a kiss over her cheek, same as I would for Mary Jane except for the way my dick waves a greeting of its own. "See? I planned ahead."

CHAPTER TEN

Eve

LITTLE KIDS DON'T bottle their feelings up. When the five-year-old girl spots me from the doorway, tiara twinkling in the scorching sunlight, her eyes go wide and a grin splits her face. I'm pink, I sparkle and I'm there for *her*. That's all it takes.

Princesses rock. Yes, I read all those magazines by the supermarket checkout counter. I got up early to watch Kate and Will tie the knot and once upon a time I knew precisely how many unmarried princes were running around Europe in expensive sports cars and designer wear. I watched brides emerge from medieval churches, all big smiles because they'd landed their princes and were about to get on with the happily-ever-after part of the fairy tale.

I don't really want a prince. I don't need to be a princess either, although pretending's fun. The last ten years taught me how to take care of myself, and more importantly, Rocker. Independence is worth more than any crown of diamonds. Still, the way Mary Jane looks at her husband makes me think of princes and endless, public, fairy-tale kisses shared with princesses.

Sort of.

Because Tío is no prince.

He's a biker.

He's also big, his ratty T-shirt promoting a second-rate rock band that will still be playing Vegas lounges when his daughter's friends are old enough to drink legally. But he listens when his wife talks. He brings her a cupcake and a beer. He runs his hand down her hair, her arms, her back, and yes, her butt. He can't get enough of her and he's clearly anticipating the moment we all get the hell out of his yard and he can take her inside and show her how much he cares.

Exhibit A? He calls her *pumpkin* and plants a big, smacking kiss on her cheek before stepping out to take a call.

"Wow." Samantha watches him go. "You think he's for real?"

Yes. Yes, I do. Mary Jane has that look in her eye. It's part satisfaction, part happiness, and part keep-your-hands-and-your-eyes-off-my-man. She knows she's got a keeper and no one's making a move on him. Between the diamond bands on Mary Jane's ring finger and Tío's leather vest with its Hard Riders patch, her Tío is safe. I need no more bikers in my life, thank you very much.

Instead, I focus on making today's party the best party ever. It's the secret to my success. I treat each birthday like it's my first and best party ever, and whichever little girl (or boy) is birthday queen receives my undivided attention. I perform. I sing, I dance and I kill the dragon.

Afterward, while party guests scream and mainline cake, I pack up my props. The house is gorgeous, the kind of place I've secretly dreamed of owning years in the future. Mary Jane's kid is cute and her husband hot. I'm just not sure where or how the MC factors in. I didn't even know bikers bought real estate that wasn't a dive bar, pawnshop, or some other seedy enterprise. The bikers I've known had addresses like Lovelock Correctional Center and Ely State Prison.

Mary Jane hums off-key as she saunters up to me to hand me an envelope of cash. "Thanks for making my daughter's day."

"You're welcome." If I had my way, every kid who wanted a princess party would get one, too. I'd spend my waking hours in tiaras and tulle.

Mary Jane's silent for a moment and I try playing it cool—but we're both staring at Tío and Rev. Sprawled in lawn chairs on the opposite side of the stamped concrete patio, they hold longnecks and watch the kids' antics like there's nowhere they'd rather be. I've always assumed bikerly debauches involve adult women, kegs and salacious X-rated activities, but they seem to be having a good time.

"They're great guys," Mary Jane says with a little sigh.

"Uh-huh." I pack my shit faster. Rev's a gorgeous guy, and I'd have to be blind not to notice. My libido wakes up when he's around and it's easy to forget he's a biker and a badass watching him listen intently to a five-year-girl explaining why purple is her favorite color. And another part of my anatomy stirs when he announces that *his* favorite color is blue. I'm sure he's just being polite (although Rev is one of the *least* polite people I've met), but the girl nods and runs off happily. I like that he listened. That it didn't matter to him that she wasn't discussing the fate of the nation or the tanking economy or supersecret biker stuff. He listened. He volunteered a few words of his own.

Hell, I like blue, too.

He stands up, so I stare some more. The man has legs that deserve to be looked at. The faded denim of his jeans tightens with each step he takes—and I'd like to start at the bottom and work my way up. When he stops in front of me, I'm still staring. He plucks the plastic box of props out of my arms and aims a crooked grin at me that should be illegal. Hell, the entire man is a walking felony.

He tips his head at the box. "Where to?"

The question would be easier to answer if I stopped staring. His eyes are warm and heated, a dark brown reminding me of my favorite things. Chocolate. This great faux-fur blanket I bought for my house. Puppy dogs and cowboy boots. I bet he'd taste as good, too. Bet he'd feel—

"Evie?" He sounds amused.

"Yeah?"

"You wanna tell me where to put this?" He hefts the container higher in his arms, in case I need the visual. Which I totally do. I'm staring at the man like I've been on a no-carbs diet for a week and he's the world's biggest, sweetest, tastiest doughnut ever. I'm pretty sure I'm drooling.

It's not my fault his package is so appealing.

"The RV," I blurt out.

"Uh-huh." He shoots me that crooked half grin again, as if he can see the X-rated party taking place in my head. He brushes past me, his arm rubbing some very non-PG areas. I follow because he's got my stuff and I have questions.

"Why are you really here?"

Behind us come the sounds of Mary Jane wrapping up the party. He opens the door to the RV and steps inside. This is the point where I'd like to pretend I stop following him and do something strong and independent. It's not like I want or need to knee him in the balls to assert my ability to stand on my own two feet, but he's just so effortlessly in control that it grates. I hesitate, but he disappears inside my RV and I'm not done talking with him. To him. Fuck if I know what I'm really doing here, other than going in after him.

I step inside.

"Where does this go?" He hefts the box. There's not much space inside the RV. In addition to the built-in table and benches, there's a bed, a tiny bathroom and a galley kitchen consisting of a Mr. Coffee, a toaster oven and a mini-fridge whose capacity maxes out at a six-pack.

"On the bed. Why are you really here today?"

He deposits the box and turns around, reminding me the RV's short on space. Without even trying, the man consumes every inch and then some. He's even bigger

than Mary Jane's Tío and the way his shoulders brush
the wall just calls attention (my attention) to his body.

He shrugs. "You made the rules."

Words blah blah words. I fight the urge to step forward and run my hands up that big, broad chest.

"About?"

He looks at me like he's never been more serious in
his life. "Dating."

"And you're playing by my rules?" Hello. It's hard
to imagine Rev putting the brakes on anything at my
say-so.

"I'm giving it a shot, princess. The way I see it, if I
hang out here with you, I can keep an eye out for the
Colombians. They're not gonna give a shit that you're
a civvie in this war."

"So you're here entirely as my bodyguard? To protect me?" I take a moment to imagine Rev as my bodyguard, pressing me beneath or behind his big body at
the first hint of danger. Taking the Colombian business
seriously is hard because I'm not sure I've ever met
somebody from Colombia, let alone a somebody who
engages in illegal drug-running and wants to maim
or kill me. The only danger right now is to my panties
and that's all Rev's fault.

"Entirely?" He looks amused. "Let's give it 30 percent, okay?"

"I only merit a 30 percent effort?"

"No." The man *moves*. God, he has great moves.
He closes the space between us in two steps that are
part swagger, part prowl, and that's not even the best
part. Nope. The RV is so small that now he's pressed

against me. He threads his fingers through mine (I'm in no mood to resist) and draws my hands over my head with one of his. Pretty sure he notices the shiver that rocks me with *that* move.

"Ask me about the other 70 percent," he whispers, mouth against my ear. "Ask *nicely*."

Holy. *Shit*.

True confession time. "I'm not sure I'm capable of conversation right now."

His free hand finds my hip and his mouth moves over my ear—is he tasting me? Whatever he's doing, I'm melting. "Thirty percent for the fucking Colombians because I promised to keep you safe and I never break a promise. The other 70 percent is my favorite part, though. You said I was supposed to chase you. You made it a fucking rule, babe."

"Those were dating rules," I protest. Not hard, mind you, because who wouldn't enjoy this?

"This was a party. You're dressed up. There's beer and good times. Sounds date-worthy to me."

The party's over but—details. I thread my fingers through his. We fit together, our fingers meshing like we've done this a million times before.

Like we really do belong together.

"Do you want it to count?"

"If we were on a date, I'd want to kiss you good-night."

"Are you asking me if I kiss on the first date?"

We've had dirty sex, but we haven't had a date. Rev's crooked grin reaches his eyes and makes me want to smile back. To nod my head and agree whole-

heartedly with whatever he proposes. I can't think
when I'm around him—all I do is feel.

Feel wonderful.

Alive.

On fire for him.

He runs a finger over my bottom lip and I feel his
touch everywhere, from my mouth to my pussy to parts
in between that feel suspiciously like my heart.

He's the best kind of trouble, his fingers exploring
my mouth, leaving shivers and heat where he touches.
He doesn't push, doesn't hurry. Just takes his time as
if we have hours, days, just plain forever to kiss.

He sucks my finger into his mouth, his tongue exploring my skin. Licking, teasing, coaxing me into re-
laxing and letting go because the feelings fill me up
until I forget where we are and all the reasons to slow
this thing down still further.

When he nips my bottom lip, I catch his lower lip
between my own teeth and bite right back. Harder.
The sensations threaten to drown me, sweeping over
me in bright, hot waves of pleasure. He kisses me and
kisses me, like he doesn't want to lose the contact either, taking and then taking more. His hand settles on
my thighs, his palms easing upward beneath my dress.

And then he stops because, clearly, the man is a born
tease. He turns his face until his cheek rests against
mine, his face buried in my hair.

"Go out with me." I feel his question on my skin.

"Kiss me again," I counter.

"Answer first." He gives orders, but he also gives
me what I need.

He covers my mouth with his, his tongue parting my lips. The sweetest of pressures and he's in, his tongue stroking mine as he goes as deep as he can. He tastes like the vanilla from the cupcake frosting he stole, like chocolate and all the things I shouldn't crave. He's a wild, wicked flavor, a million guilty calories and midnight cravings, and I won't say no. This is just a kiss, but Rev is someone special. I can't help but recognize the truth even as he slants his mouth deeper, taking more.

When he lifts his head, my fingers are digging into his shoulders. He's not close enough.

"You got an answer for me, princess?"

"Remind me of the question."

A look of smug contentment flashes over his face. He's earned it.

"Go out with me for real." He cups my face in his hands and rests his forehead against mine. "Fucking dying here, Evie, so help me out."

He's never asked me for anything before. Told, yes. Ordered, absolutely. But asked? Never. I can't help but wonder if he knows his thumb is stroking my skin.

"One date," he says. "A dozen. You don't have to like me. Fuck, you don't have to put out again. I just want the time. With you."

The lost look in his eyes makes something inside me turn over.

"Yes," I say, because I like that look. I like *him*.

CHAPTER ELEVEN

Eve

YOU KNOW WHEN you're having a nightmare? How you try to wake yourself up and point out all the reasons to your sleeping self that the shit unfolding around you is dream rather than reality? And in the dream, you start by pinching and poking, and then you escalate to just standing there in front of the train or the psycho killer or whatever it is that's trying to kill you? That's kind of how my week goes. It's a blur of birthday parties and business meetings, of increasingly demanding phone calls to ever-louder radio silence from Rocker. That's the nightmare.

But then there are the really sweet, also-can't-be-real moments where Rev flexes his dating muscle. He's always riding past or in the neighborhood when I'm out. He's sticking to his promise to look out for me, and that's more annoying-cute than anything. But we also go for coffee and I tease him about the barista checking him out. We spend an evening playing penny lines at a casino on the Strip, me perched on his lap as we fed the coins in together. When we win five bucks, Rev calls me his good luck charm and shares the luck—and the five bucks—with a homeless veteran panhandling outside. He gives good date—and he doesn't rush me.

The moments in between our dates and work are trickier, leaving way too much time for worrying about Rocker. I tell myself Rocker probably believes he has reasons for networking with the Colombian cartel. God, I hate even thinking about him as a drug dealer. Because if he's selling drugs or in any way making it possible, he's not *just* my little brother anymore. He's a drug dealer.

Since Rev's accusations and my own suspicions aren't indisputable fact, I reach out to Rocker. And yes, this means I call and text him in every free moment. I can tell from my phone when Rocker's seen my texts, but he only answers one in ten. Tonight is apparently one of those buy-a-lottery-ticket exceptions and God's in a good mood or looking out for big sisters, because when I look down at my phone, the line of bouncing dots means Rocker is typing.

ROCKER: Where you at?

ME: Home. We need to talk.

ROCKER: You okay?

ME: Dating a friend of yours

ROCKER: ?

ME: Try reading yr messages. Seeing yr friend Rev.

I use the long pause that follows to shimmy into my pajamas. I might want to do some preemptive shopping before any sleepovers with Rev. My usual nightwear is a pair of yoga pants and an old University of Nevada T-shirt. Not precisely Sexyville and the man clearly likes his Victoria's Secret.

I try the T-shirt without the pants, but that doesn't send the right message, either. I've been hesitant to tap Rev's present, but I own no date-worthy underwear. My panties go under princess party dresses—and princesses are good girls.

Eventually my phone buzzes again.

ROCKER: Not xctly friends.

ME: Give me more words.

ROCKER: Different club, k? And your boy's trouble. Works as club enforcer. So keep your eyes open. Lemme know what you see. Inside intel on the MC good.

ME: WTF? I look like Mata Hari to you?

ROCKER: Got some serious shit going down. Need to know you're safe.

ME: You are a pain in my ass.

ROCKER: Love you. Do it for me?

ME: Love you too. Lemme know when you have time to talk?

The roar of a Harley pulling into my driveway has never been so welcome. I need answers from Rocker, but I'm not sure I really want them. If everything was fine, if he wasn't doing something he knew would worry me, he'd tease me about treating him like he's five. He'd laugh, but he'd make sure I stopped worrying. Rocker's good like that.

He's what family should be.

We have each other's back and we do it with love. No matter what's happened or going down or screwed up, we love each other. That's the ultimate rule and neither of us has ever broken it. Why would we? Love isn't something you turn on or off.

My phone buzzes again. This time, when I look down this time, I'll have answers. Everything will be okay and I'll go out front, get on Rev's bike and tell him he was wrong about Rocker. Power of positive thinking for the win. But when I look down, I've got just one word.

ROCKER: Later

CHAPTER TWELVE

Rev

WHEN I PULL UP for our date, Evie flies out the door of her house. I swing off my bike and intercept her coming down the path. Pretty sure that's in the dating rulebook, but I just want an excuse to put my hands on her. Her jeans hug her ass and legs, the faded denim disappearing into a pair of boots that are perfect spank bank material. They lace up her calves, the tall heel giving her step a sexy swing. The fitted pink T-shirt cupping her tits is even better, as is the ponytail I could fist while I drill into her. Hold her still for my kiss.

Christ.

I'm supposed to be dating her, not mentally stripping her on the sidewalk.

"Hey." I cup her elbows, drawing her close. Brush a kiss over her mouth.

"Rev." Her smile makes me feel like I just won gold in the world's biggest competition. I do a quick sanity check, and spot the brown leather jacket dangling from her fingers. Good. Don't want her getting chewed up on the road.

"Come on." I curl my fingers around hers and tug her toward my bike. Even as a preacher's kid, I got more than my share of girls growing up, but we weren't in it for the long haul. I was the king of fun and sex, but that was as far as it went. Kind of like taking the bike from one side of town to the other, when this thing with Evie is more long-distance haul, the best kind of ride on the highway where I can open it up and just ride wherever the road leads.

I pop a helmet on her head and straddle the bike. She swings on behind me like she's been doing that all her life. Her legs grip my hips, her pussy tucked against my ass. She slides her arms around my stomach, linking her fingers just above my belt buckle. Heading back inside her place sounds better and better. Instead, I take us to the Strip. Figure she's never ridden down it on the back of a bike.

First time I've ever been glad for traffic, too. The Strip's jammed with cars and those vans with the twelve-foot dirty pictures of women inviting guys to call now for the ultimate party. Surprised the T&A display doesn't cause more accidents, frankly. When the lights change, we wait for the crowds of sightseeing, gambling, drunk-ass people to cross.

She admires the view and I admire her. Figure it's a fair trade. Whenever she shifts to look at something new, her tits skim my back. You know those little brush things percussionists use on their cymbals? She plays me just like that. Each time I feel Evie against me, soft and gentle, I get harder and the urge to toss all my plans—for protecting her and the club's interests—

grows stronger. I mean, fuck—we're surrounded by hotels with rooms for rent. Not like I'm not gonna get ideas about Evie, a bed and a few hours of alone time.

But that's not what she wants. I mean, I could talk her into it. Slide my hand back between us and stroke her through her jeans until she's squirming and begging for it. Evie's hot and she's lonely. It would feel really good too until it was over. And then what? Shit would get awkward.

She makes another happy noise and does more squirming. My dick's about to bust out of my jeans, so I look around, desperate for a distraction. We're idling in traffic right in front of Paris Las Vegas. Not content with little French bistros, the developers decided to recreate the entire Eiffel Tower. It soars above us like some big French dick. At night, it's lit up and the view from the top rocks. Went up there once and watched the fountains at the Bellagio shoot off.

"You ever been to France?" That's me. King of the fucking small talk.

I feel her shake her head. "I'd like to go. And you?"

"Never." I fight the urge to head straight to the airport. Airlines never fill all of their seats. Bet we could be on a flight headed to France before tomorrow. Instead, I take us out to Red Rock. They've got a thirteen-mile scenic drive that I think she'll like. It's not the most romantic shit in the world, but riding's who I am. It's what I do.

We spend a couple of hours exploring the rock formations. The sun goes down late in the summer, so we've still got more shadows than dark when we head back. Although the road's been more or less empty the last hour or so, there's an SUV coming up fast behind us now, one of those big, black numbers you see in the movies or in the hands of the Feds. Probably just some suburban wannabe who likes driving the biggest goddamned thing in the parking lot, but I don't like its speed. I consider pulling my gun, but this is my fucking date. Reaching between us to grab my piece won't endear me to Evie. So I ride, watching our company in my mirror.

The SUV gains.

I could cut across the sand right now, but that's not a smooth ride.

"Think we might have company," I tell her.

Of course she twists, scouting for trouble. Bastards know we know they're there now. The SUV responds by accelerating until they're riding my ass. Don't think they're actually out for blood, because we're an easy target out here. Question is what they do want.

That's when the second SUV crests a small rise in the road in front of us. Fuck. That's not good. Looks like they have a plan after all. I should have kept the club's eyes on Evie, but I wanted this date with her. Didn't want to share her, but full coverage would have been good now.

"Shit may get rocky," I warn her. "Need you to hang on tight and do whatever I say, you hear me? Not the time for any independent bullshit."

God bless her, Evie threads her fingers through my belt and her grip on my legs tightens.

Thirty seconds later, the first shot rings out, kicking up gravel two feet to the right of the bike. Evie screams a curse into my ear and her hands almost cut me in half. Good girl.

In order to fire back, I'll have to slow down, reach behind me and free my piece. Not like it's rocket science, but I don't know how Evie's gonna react. I'm licensed to conceal-carry, but there's some shit we haven't talked about yet. Right now, my safest bet is to ride like hell and get her under cover. I double-check the fuel tank, but it's not a long ride—just a hard one.

The fuckers in the SUV behind us pop off another series of shots. Can't tell if they're missing on purpose or just that bad.

"Hold on," I bark and hang a hard right. We fly off the road, the bike's front end slamming down into a sand wash. I throttle back as much as I can because the desert's not a hospitality suite and a flat tire or a hidden rock now would kill us. Hell, a tip-over wouldn't be better—the shooter could pick us off from the shoulder. The scenery snaps past us in a wild rush, sand kicking up as we tear through the mesquite. Low-hanging branches slap at us as I weave through the rough, aiming for the rocky canyons. As soon as we're under cover, I kill the motor. Highway's a good mile behind us, and it's practically silent.

Evie hasn't let go once.

I reach around between us and slip my gun free.

I scoop her up and drag her into my lap. "You okay?" Since I really need to know the answer to that, seems like the right place to start.

"No." She makes a little hiccuping sound. Shit. Is she crying? I don't want to take my eyes off the road, because those SUV-driving bastards may be coming after us, but is she hurt? I didn't feel her take a hit, but anything's possible.

Fuck it.

"Where are you hurt?" I pat her down, not waiting for her answer. She looks fine. No visible entrance or exit wounds. No blood. She's just pale, those goddamned tears spilling down her cheeks and punching a hole in me.

"Somebody tried to kill us."

In her nice, safe, normal world, people don't gun for other people. They probably say please and thank you all the time, too, go to church on Sundays and feed the homeless. My world—Rocker's world—is different.

She burrows her face into my chest and I ignore the spreading damp patch. The SUV's stopped on the shoulder. Nobody gets out, however, and a couple of minutes later, it pulls back onto the highway, headed toward Vegas.

Thank fuck when she lifts her head, she's not crying anymore. "Were those Colombians?"

Since no one stopped and made introductions, there's no way to know. It's entirely possible that her fuckwit brother has pissed off multiple groups of people—or that they were gunning for me.

"Definite possibility," I bite out before I can lift her off the bike, take her to the ground and get inside her. We're in the desert, for Christ's sake, and shit's happened that she's upset about. I should not be thinking about pushing her shirt up, her jeans down, and ripping her panties off.

I'm a biker, not a fucking psychologist. Evie's face twists and she bites down on her lower lip hard enough to bleed. Hearing your shit's gone south isn't good news, so there's probably something else I'm supposed to say here, but all I can think is what the fuck was Rocker thinking? Her brother should have known this would hurt her. All I can do is pat her back like an idiot, making sure my body's between hers and anyone coming at us.

"Pretty sure that was someone making a point. I think we should head back," I say slowly. Don't want to scare her more, but we're not in a great position here. I text my president because he needs to know what's up. Hawke promises to send some brothers to check out Evie's place. Good. No point in riding into an ambush. I fire off a couple more texts while I'm at it, because you can never have too much security.

"What did Rocker get himself into?"

We've gone over this once before, but she wasn't ready to listen. Now, she is. That's the power of show-and-tell for you, ladies and gentlemen.

"Bad shit." I shrug. "Moving product isn't the safest thing, but there are better and worse ways to do it. He's definitely picked the worse way."

Too blunt? Too bad. Lying gets people killed and she deserves the truth.

"There's no way for you to get him out of this?" She stares at me as if I'm some kind of superhero, and for her, I'd like to be.

"Not sure," I admit. "Gonna find out for you, okay? Just give me a little time, Evie."

"He might die," she says way too softly.

Not much I can say, because it's the truth. Her brother has a goddamned death wish.

CHAPTER THIRTEEN

Eve

I'VE NEVER LIKED a side of danger with my sex. But by the time Rev and I reach my house, the fear has become something else. Getting shot at tops no foreplay list I've read, but I'm turned on. Or maybe it's my safety-seeking instinct, my hormones certain that hooking up with the man mountain in front of me would be wise in light of my Colombian situation. Or maybe I'm just looking for excuses.

Rev moves fast for such a big man. He has me off the bike, up the sidewalk and at the door before I can say anything. When I unlock it, he's so close that my butt brushes his front.

"I'm gonna come by and install a security system tomorrow," he tells me. "Should have done it before, but didn't want to freak you out. I've got a couple of prospects watching over you, too, and I've texted Rocker so he knows there's a problem."

"Rev?"

"Yeah?"

"Shut up." I tug him inside.

Grabbing a bottle of wine from the counter, I head for the fireplace. I don't give a shit it's summer. I turn on the gas low, letting the flames lick up the logs. When Rev turns away from the door, the gun tucked in the waistband of his jeans is a visual reminder that he's a biker and not a nice guy.

"Is being in the club always like that?"

He gives me a hard look. "Got to admit, today's not been a winner."

"Help me fix that?" Yes. I'm breaking all my rules. I take a long drink from the bottle and set it down on the floor. Lay down on my stomach watching the flames flicker on the ceramic logs in the fireplace.

"No do-overs in life, princess." I wouldn't take the option anyhow. My choices have led me straight here to him and losing him isn't something I can imagine right now. He's the best kind of all wrong. So when he drops onto the rug beside me, stretching his legs out? Screw it. Tonight, I'm all in. All about living and feeling, make-believing everything's going to be a-okay.

I roll over, straddling his legs as I reach for his belt. I pause for a brief second to appreciate the impressive bulge and then, fingers flying, I undo the buckle. His buttons pop, one after another. The dark cotton of his boxer briefs is the tissue paper inside the box of the best Christmas present ever. God, the man's built. I skim my hands up the outline of his dick to where the tip juts above the edge of his boxers. He makes me feel so much.

He grabs the bottle and steals a swallow of wine. "This really what you want, babe?"

I want him so much that I have no words.

"Less talking, more doing," I whisper and pull his jeans down his body. Seconds later his boots are off, followed by his shirt. I told Rev to take things slow because I needed to make sure sex with him was the right thing to do, but getting shot at changes everything. Rev feels good, neither of us is dead, and those are the only priorities that matter. Foreplay and patience aren't necessary because I just want him in me now. Plus, his dick's a work of art. He jerks when I run a finger up his thick erection. Time to make shit perfectly clear.

"That's mine," I tell him.

"You think?" He sounds amused.

"Possession's nine-tenths of the law." Leaning forward, I suck him into my mouth.

"Jesus Christ." He falls back on his elbows, big hands tangling in my hair. His dick goes from zero to sixty, the thick head pushing at the back of my throat. I relax and take him deeper, savoring his harsh groan.

Right now, he's all mine.

Rev

Evie sucks me like a pro, making me the luckiest fucking man alive. When she said she wasn't putting out until we had a relationship going, I agreed to respect her boundaries. Not sure how that translated into a blowjob, but when her lips close around my dick, my hips shoot off the floor.

So much for slow. I'm about to come in her mouth and that's way too fast for both of us. I've had women go down on me, but this is different. This is the best.

This is my Evie.

She sucks harder, lips moving up and down my dick like I'm her favorite flavor and my balls tighten. Fuck, she's good. The best kind of dirty bad. I'm supposed to make sure of her because she's the club's ace in the hole, but how do I turn down this? I fist her hair, guiding her deeper and lower. Makes me even more of a bastard—I know that.

I tug her face away from my dick when we get way too close to the point of no return. "You want to do this? No more waiting?"

Her face turns pink and not from the fire. She bites her lip, momentarily uncertain, then her face turns fierce. "Yes."

Green fucking light.

I roll her onto her back, desperate to get her naked. Her clothes go flying. Shirt, jeans, bra, panties. Thank Christ she lost her shoes somewhere between the front door and the fire, because otherwise I'd be slamming into her half-dressed.

Not gonna lie—eating Evie out is my all-time favorite. Who knew ten minutes could be a fucking lifetime highlight? I stretch my time, licking and teasing, plumping her tits in my hand and pinching the nipples when I stop playing and let go. I'm supposed to give it to her slow, but I always ride balls-out on the highway.

Really hope her curtains aren't for shit because her neighbors are about to get a show. Kneeing her legs apart, I make a place for myself. She bucks up against me. Nope, nothing slow about this at all. My dick is hard as a rock, and I need to be inside her. She's on the same page because she tilts her hips up.

Engraved invitation right there.

I yank her legs over my thighs and sit back. World's best view ever. The fire's heat plays over her bare skin, lighting up her eyes. Her hair goes every which way and her pussy's slick and wet.

Mine.

I find her clit, circling her with my thumb. God-damned beautiful. She's soaking wet, which will make this easier.

"You want to fuck any particular way?"

She whimpers something, eyes closing, but the sounds coming out of her mouth make no sense. Guess that means it's my turn to choose.

I stroke my fingers up and down, dipping deeper into her pussy with each pass. When my thumb rubs her clit, she breathes faster and faster. I'm trying to be sweet and slow, to check all the boxes on her list. It's not me, this nice guy, but for Evie I'll give it a shot.

"Now," she gasps. "How about now?"

Now sure works for me. I won't last long once I'm in her. I tear the condom open, rolling the rubber down in record time. I want her bare, but I won't make her feel unsafe.

As she whimpers and clenches beneath me, work-ing her way toward her own orgasm, I shove her legs farther apart. I want her to come *for* me, on me, be-cause I'm the man who does it for her and she trusts me to give her nothing but pleasure. Yeah, I know life doesn't work that way, but reality's taking a temporary vacation.

I set my dick against her and push inside. I'm big, she's small, and so it's slow going. She's tight and her pussy grips me like she's never letting go, but when I thrust harder, she rewards me with a moan.

"Relax," I grunt against her ear. She's gotta open up and let me in. When she squirms, trying to take me, I pin her in place. Makes me a fucking Neanderthal, but I thread my fingers through hers and draw her hands over her head so I'm in control.

She finally relaxes beneath me when I find her clit with my free hand.

"Fast or slow?"

"Fast," she groans. I slam into her, riding her hard, and it feels so damned good. I finger her clit, stroking her with each downward thrust, and she more than meets me. And when she clenches around me, gasping and shrieking, that's my name on her lips.

Best. Sound. Ever.

I drive into her, holding her hips and thrusting faster and faster. Giving her the words because she gets everything I've got. "You're fucking gorgeous."

She collapses beneath me as she comes, clutching me with her arms and legs, and I flip her around, drilling into her from behind. I wrap her ponytail around my wrist, pulling her head back for my kiss.

"Make me forget," she whispers, and I wonder if it's possible to come apart with all these feelings coming alive inside me. The pleasure rockets through me and

I come fast and dirty, slamming into her once, twice, three times. She whimpers and relaxes as if there's no more anything left in her.

And yeah, I'm smiling against her throat. Might not move for the next couple of hours. Might be days. Rolling onto my side, I wrap an arm around her waist and haul her against me. She wriggles, but I'm not letting go now.

"We should get up," she announces.

"Enjoy the moment, princess."

I tangle one hand in her hair, playing with the silky strands. Who fucking knew I could cuddle? It's nice, though. Kinda like the two of us just lying here together.

"We're going to make a mess on the rug." She makes another bid for freedom. "And you probably need to get going."

"You're really not one for afterglow, are you?"

"Is that a problem?" The grumpy in her voice makes me smile.

"Might want to give it a shot. See what you think," I suggest. "And let me worry about any mess. I got this."

She must agree with me because she yawns, and next thing I know, she's drifting off to sleep.

CHAPTER FOURTEEN

Eve

THE MAN SCREWED me into a coma. This must be why I wake up in bed.

Alone. And naked.

I never noticed when he picked me up and moved me in the middle of the night. Forget melatonin—Rev is a one-man testament to the superior sleeping power of a good orgasm. I grab a quick shower, pull on some clothes and stagger out to the kitchen in search of coffee. Rev's passed out on my couch. Sprawled on his back, he looks bigger than ever, which has to be impossible. Heat flushes my body as I take in his relaxed form. His legs are bent, one arm thrown over his head. *Boyfriend* is such a weird word. I try it silently, not quite ready to say it out loud. *My boyfriend, Rev.* Or maybe *this is* my *boyfriend.* So what if he rocks my world sexually? It does *not* mean I canonize him.

He certainly doesn't look saintlike. Saints absolutely do not come with broad shoulders or such powerful biceps. Tattoos are also definitely not saintly accessories. I don't own a single throw pillow—he can't possibly be comfortable. Instead of worrying about the man's comfort, however, I'm helplessly focused on the way his T-shirt rides up, exposing his stomach and six-pack abs. How does he manage to take up all the space in my house?

"Feel free to touch," he rumbles, eyes still closed. "Or you just gonna stand there?"

I reach for him, trailing my fingers over that tempting strip of skin. God. He's hard and silky, heated and so impossibly, wonderfully male. Or maybe that's thanks to the impossible-to-ignore ridge beneath the worn denim clinging to his body. Denim. My favorite kind of gift-wrapping.

"My bed had room for two," I whisper.

"I have a hard time sleeping with other people around." He opens his eyes.

Calloused fingers wrap around my wrist and tug gently. Funny how he reads both deadly and safe at the same time, as if he's ready to give the rest of the world a beat down but then he holds me with such care. Despite my awkward perch on the side of the couch, I go all in. I throw my leg over his hips and straddle him like I'm a cowgirl and he's my best saddle. He invited me down, so he can put up or shut up.

"Hell of a way to wake up." His smile is slow, sleepy and so fucking perfect.

"Tell me about it," I whisper back. Since I need to put my hands somewhere, I set them on his chest. The heat of him radiates through the thin T-shirt, and his musky scent teases me. Rev smells like oil and leather and danger. Like the open road and freedom. The sleepy smile transforms his face from fierce to sensually predatory, as if he's thinking about taking a bite out of me—or having himself a taste.

Please, please taste me.

Rev takes his time, running his thumbs over my hips, tracing the line of my bikini panties through my jeans. I fight the urge to relax into that wicked touch, leaning toward him when he doesn't move further. He just takes me in, sprawled beneath me like some great beast.

"I need to know something." The man's a mystery, but part of me feels as if I've known him for years. God. This is so bad. In the dating world, I've just cannonballed into the deep end of the pool—and the water might be way too shallow.

"Shoot," he says casually.

"What's the deal between you and my brother? Are you friends or what?"

Rocker hasn't touched base with me yet this morning and that's unusual. He usually has a sixth sense about when I'm trouble. Or bothered. Worked up about anything. For Rev, I'm all three, plus there's my SUV run-in yesterday.

"Shit's complicated." Nope. Not an answer at all.

"I'm generally not considered stupid." I don't like playing games—and I really don't want to play with Rev. Throw him down, rip his clothes off, have my way with him? Yes, yes and hell yes. Word games, however, aren't my thing.

Rev mutters an obscenity. "I'm Hard Rider. He's

Black Dog. Our clubs have some differences of opinion."

"Anything I should be concerned about?"

His eyes hold mine, hardening with resolution.
"Not one goddamned thing for you to worry about.
You know much about club life?"

I wiggle, getting comfortable—although the impressive erection pressed against my pussy doesn't lend
itself to *comfort*. "Rocker and I grew up as club rats.
Our dad rode with a local club. He never made officer, but he patched in and rode with them. Helped out
when they called and stuff, which didn't work out so
well for us."

Rev could make a killing playing poker because I
can't tell what he's thinking. His face is blank and unreadable, his eyes no longer warm and hot. Am I piss-
ing him off by talking shit about someone else's club?
I won't bullshit about this, however, because my dad's
club wasn't good for our family. It ripped us apart.

"He got twenty-five to fifty for transporting weapons," I say way too loudly. "He went away and then
Rocker and I bounced around after that. Our mom
wasn't making much and times were tough."

"Club shoulda taken care of you," Rev growls.

"If wishes were horses, I'd be able to run the Preak-
ness single-handed. That part of my life is over and
done with, but I'm not a big club fan."

He nods, hand dipping lower. "Hear you on that.
You got plans for today?"

"Work." I offer him a regretful smile.

"Be better if you stayed put today."

"For who? I have a job. Money to earn. Five-year-olds to please. No work means no cash and I've got my bills to pay."

Rev stills. It's not as if he was a sea of motion before, but something in him goes quiet as if he's working on not unleashing his inner predator. "Ask Rocker about your going into work today."

I swing off Rev's lap. Clearly, we need to work on his relationship skills before he's ready for me to make my next move, because hello? It's the twenty-first century and I don't take orders from whatever man's decorating my life at the moment. "We should be clear on one thing. Rocker's not my owner."

I look after Rocker, not the other way round.

"Fuck." Rev shoves upright, running a hand over his head. "Didn't mean to imply he was, but shit's going down."

"Rev?"

"Yeah?"

"This is where you tell me about the *shit going down* and then I make my own decision, like the big girl I am."

"If you grew up in a club, you know I can't discuss club business with you."

This isn't a battle I'm winning today, so I head for the kitchen and my BFF, Mr. Coffee. I need to leave and I'd prefer to go caffeinated. While the coffee brews, I retreat down the hall and do my princess hair and makeup. When I come back, a fully dressed Rev is by the front door, holding out a to-go mug of coffee.

"Thanks, honey," I say, rolling my eyes.

He promptly raises the cup up too high for me to reach. "Nobody's forcing you to drink it."

Since coffee is both the elixir of the gods and mandatory this early in the morning, I reach for the cup, plastering my body against his as I stretch. No point in letting him have all the fun. When my fingers close around the handle, I plant a quick, hard kiss on his gorgeous mouth. The man's lips are downright sinful, and not just because they make me think about sex. And talking dirty.

And a million other things I shouldn't do.

He grunts as I let go of his beautiful body and brush past him. My girls are waiting in my driveway.

Rev follows me outside. "Still wish you'd rethink."

"You have information to share with me?" Rocker asked me to keep my eyes and ears peeled, so I'll touch bases with him. Club business that worries Rev could touch Rocker, too. Maybe he'll benefit from the heads-up.

"Nope," he says easily, gaze moving over the pink RV.

"Bye," I say at the same moment Rev hooks a finger in the back of my jeans and tugs. I take an involuntary step backward and debate the wisdom of launching my coffee cup at his head. Bet that would piss him off and he'd do something about it. This leads to dirty thoughts about how Rev might express that displeasure, starting with his big hand on my butt. *No sexy fantasies on a workday.* Shit. I need to schedule time with my vibrator. In real life, I have zero interest in being draped

over my guy's knee for a spanking, but I sure enjoy the
hell out of the fantasy.

"Your brother lost the guy we had watching his ass,
so change of plans. Where you go, I go. Fucking bib-
lical."

"Ummm. What?" My childhood didn't exactly
feature Bible camps, but I'm certain that Jesus Christ
didn't encourage swearing, seeing as how there's a
commandment specifically forbidding it.

"I'm your bodyguard," Rev announces like it makes
perfect sense.

"Not sure I understand," I admit. "You've been following my brother?"

He gives me a small, hard smile. "I'm gonna stick by
your side today. Tomorrow. As many days as it takes.
You know that story in the Bible about Ruth?"

Uh, no. I sure don't. I'll never be one of those people
name-dropping chapters and verses. Rev wraps me up
in his big arms.

"Ruth hooks up with this guy. Marries him and
moves in with him, which is a big deal because he's
from a different country and worships different gods.
He up and dies, and then it's just Ruth and her mother-
in-law, Naomi."

"Is this a mother-in-law horror story?" I try and fail
to imagine Rev married. He's not the kind of guy you'd
spot standing at the altar in a black tux.

He shakes his head. "Ruth and Naomi are tight.
Naomi's trying to convince Ruth to pack up and move
back to her own country because shit's not going well
for Naomi and she doesn't want to suck Ruth into her

mess. They're family, they've made commitments to each other, so Ruth isn't having it."

He gives me a hard-eyed look at this. Am I supposed to be Naomi in this scenario?

"Ruth tells Naomi straight-up that Naomi's stuck with her. Where Naomi goes, Ruth goes. Where Naomi stays, Ruth stays. Ruth vows she's making Naomi's people and Naomi's gods her own."

Color me confused. He must read that truth on my face, because he sighs, and keeps talking. "When someone patches into a club, he promises the club comes first, no matter what. And I've made those promises to Hard Riders. Won't lie to you about that. But I'm making you a promise of my own—no matter how bad your situation gets, I've got your back. You count on me. I'm not free to ask you to be my old lady and wear my patch—too much shit between my club and your brother's. But if I was looking for that kind of relationship, you'd be the woman I'd be looking for."

"So I'm...Naomi?" Pretty sure my voice sounds slightly hysterical.

He nods. "And I'm sticking by you."

I think about it. Nope. I'm still confused as hell.

"Not worried about the state of my soul," he allows. "So never mind the Bible story. But I am worried about the state of your ass. It's mine and you're stuck with me. Made a promise to keep you safe, remember? Where you go, I'm going, so give me the address of today's party."

I give up trying to understand him.

"When did you read the Bible?"

He reaches around me to take the birthday party invitation Samantha silently extends from the RV. "My daddy was a pastor. Some of it stuck."

"How about we try the explanations again, but without the metaphors?"

He just looks at me. Story of my life.

"Never mind," I say. "I'm leaving. Stick or don't stick. It's your call."

CHAPTER FIFTEEN

Rev

I LIKE A GIRL who's willing. Someone who takes orders
in bed and prefers her sex dirty. Someone who understands the club comes first and that I'm out when my
prez calls. Evie should fucking be grateful I'm body-
guarding her fine ass because the Colombians make
me look like the choirboy I never was. So yeah, she
should thank me.

I know something about gratitude, too. Not a day's
gone by when I haven't acknowledged to myself that
my club saved my ass and set me on the road I'm riding on today. At seventeen, I'd been my old man's rebel
son. I'd liked sex, I'd liked sin and I'd never met a rule
I didn't want to break. Shit had hit the fan the night my
old man had been hit by a drunk driver, and the club
had been there for me.

Gratitude is not part of Princess's repertoire. After
finishing her second party, she stalks past me and into
the Princess Mobile as if I'm the invisible man. I'm de-
bating how to respond when my phone rings and caller

ID warns fun and games are over. Hawke's on the line and the Hard Riders president doesn't sound happy.

"We've got a situation. Black Dogs grabbed Sachs. Word on the street is Sachs stuck his nose into a drug deal and BD leadership took offense. Guess the Colombians also want in on the action in case Sachs overshares with the cops. BD's prez is still arguin' with the cartel leadership over what to do with Sachs, but we're not waitin' around for them to hold a vote."

"We know where he's being held?"

"Yeah," Hawke replies. "Fuckers have him in their clubhouse. Not tryin' to hide it, either—they're darin' us to come in there with guns blazin'."

"Trap?"

Hawke's mean-as-fuck smile broadcasts through the phone just fine. "'Cause they think if they shut down the Hard Riders, they get free access to East Las Vegas? They can try."

I'm pro-violence myself, but I'm also calculating the odds. I don't want to go in for Sachs and trade his life for that of another brother's.

Shit. Trade. I look at the pink RV. Fuck, I already hate myself, but it has to be done.

"We trade. We go after someone they care about and make a swap."

"You got an idea?"

"Evie Kent." We can trade Rocker—give him Evie, take back Sachs. Win-win for everyone involved.

"Not goin' to be a problem, you snatchin' Evie?" I love and respect my president, but the club comes first. Questioning my loyalty is for shit.

"Tell me to bring her in, and it's done."

"Do it," Hawke says. "The longer Sachs stays at the Black Dogs' clubhouse, the longer those Colombian fuckers have to mess with him."

Evie'll be safer at our clubhouse anyhow. I can protect her better there. It was stupid as shit to try for any kind of relationship with a woman like Evie. I'm not a repeat guy and we've had our fun.

Still, when Evie emerges from the RV, I discover the gratitude business is actually the other way around. Any thanking that gets done? It's gonna be me on my knees before her, because I'd be happy to drop and do some worshipping. Must be her version of biker chic, but she's wearing a pair of faded jeans that hug her ass. A blue-and-white T-shirt announces Happy Camper, which I certainly am because the thin cotton does nothing to disguise her red bra. Bright come-fuck-me red— my favorite color.

"Got a call." I need to tell her enough to get her to go with me willingly. "The Colombians are gunning for Rocker and there's a good chance they come after you since you matter to him. I'm seeing you back to your place. Or mine. Lady's choice."

"I'm not the one running drugs, so why target me?" Her fingers twist the edge of her shirt, and the gesture would be cute if she wasn't so naive. She's not part of the club and she runs a legitimate business for kids, for Christ's sake. Her life is as different from mine as a rabbit's is from a shark's. I'm the one swimming around all predatory and scaring the fuck out of people—she's the soft and fluffy vegetarian. But I've seen what the cartels do to make their point and now we have that road rage incident from the other day as Exhibit A. I'm not letting that kind of bad shit happen to her.

I pace her. Just keep walking, baby doll, and we don't have a problem. She looks at me as if I'm her Prince Charming and white knight extraordinaire. Which honestly makes me feel more like the horse's ass, because I'm not nice. More like I'm a founding member of Bastards Unlimited.

"Rocker's in deep." I fight the inexplicable urge to smooth the little crinkle between her eyebrows. I don't do comfort, either. All I have for Evie is a talented tongue, ten fingers and a dick I know what to do with. I shouldn't have started this with her. She's gonna hate me. Fuck. *I* hate me. "His club cut a deal and sounds like Rocker may have tried to up the ante."

She sucks in a breath. "What do you mean?"

"Rocker double-crossed the cartel, so they'll go after him any way they can—maybe put out a hit on you."

Her eyes widen and she makes a startled sound. Okay. So she really didn't know what her asshole brother has been up to. Either Rocker kept her in the dark or she refused to believe someone she loved could be that dumb. Problem is, she can't fix this for him and staying blind will only get her killed.

"Today sucks," she says softly.

"Sorry," I offer, meaning it. I'd like to fix her problems, although so far I'm coming up empty. Shooting Rocker only fixes *my* shit.

"If he's in trouble, I need to be there for him."

Appreciate her loyalty, but it's misplaced. Her brother is an asshole. When he turns up dead or worse, she'll hurt. Fuck that. Vik pulls up while I'm working through these unexpected thoughts. "You really want to get into this now? Because we both know I'm not part of your brother's fan club. Let me take you home. We'll figure something out."

She chews on her lower lip, thinking shit over. I've seen military campaigns conducted with less strategizing.

"Okay." She sighs and gestures toward the RV's passenger-side door. "Hop in."

CHAPTER SIXTEEN

Eve

REV FIXES ME with a lethal stare. It's kind of cute—the man's more bark than bite.

"You want me to ride in a cage?"

Since he's the one who volunteered…yeah. "I have to get the Princess Mobile back to my place, and since I'm pretty certain flying and boating are out, that leaves driving."

There's a brief pause and then Rev holds out his hand. "Give me your keys."

"Do I look stupid?" I ignore him and head for the driver's side. He can ride with me or not, but I'm done. When I slide inside the RV and shove the keys into the ignition, however, Rev's right there beside me. He scoops his hands beneath my butt and lifts me off the seat.

"No cavemen allowed."

He grunts and drops me onto the passenger-side seat. "Out of your hands now, princess."

A guy who must be one of his friends strolls up. He and Rev make arrangements for the other man to drive his bike back to his place and then we hit the road. Way too fast.

Rev drives the Princess Mobile the way he rides his bike. He's lightning quick, his gaze concentrated on the road as he takes each turn tight and hard. My poor vehicle hasn't exceeded twenty-five miles an hour in years, and he's pushing fifty. On city streets.

"Slow down. I can't afford a ticket."

"This thing doesn't go fast enough for a ticket." I silently point out the window at a speed limit sign and he grunts. "You think I can't afford to pay a ticket?"

"I don't want a ticket."

"Because you're such a good girl?"

"Because I have a strong personal preference for not breaking the law," I snap and roll my eyes. "I'm not unusual in that regard."

"Uh-huh." He brakes for a red light and slides me a sidelong look. "You gonna pout about my driving all the way home?"

I focus on the road. So I don't like breaking rules. I follow the law religiously. I don't even cheat the smallest bit on my taxes, which likely makes me the IRS's favorite small business owner. I've never written off so much as a single personal item. These are not character flaws.

Rev taps my knee. "Nothing to say?"

"I'm not in the mood to talk to you."

He hits the gas when the light changes. "Don't let me stop you, because I'm never gonna fucking live this down."

"You're the one who insisted on sitting in the driv-

er's seat," I point out smugly. "This isn't my fault—
and this isn't the way to my house. Do you need GPS?"

We're in an unfamiliar industrial area. Rev's sense
of direction must suck.

"You need to know something," he says slowly.

You know what? I don't need to know whatever it is
he's about to share. It's a safe bet it's designed to piss
me off, and I've already achieved that state, thank you
very much. In fact, I have a point I need to make very
clear to Rev. Immediately. Do not pass Go, do not collect two hundred dollars.

"Pull over."

I'm tired of being the good girl. Of doing what I
should, when I should. I reach over and grab Rev's
dick through his jeans.

He freezes. "The fuck?"

I have to hand it to him—he doesn't crash us. He
jerks the RV over to the side of the road.

I squeeze harder. "Now that I've got your attention, let's talk."

I'm not sure what happens next exactly, but Rev
twists, my hand loses its grip and I fly backward. My
head bounces against the seat as my back plants on the
vinyl and Rev comes down over me, pinning me with
his weight. My hands are trapped beneath me, which
is my first clue that this teach-Rev-a-lesson scenario
just derailed.

"I'm listening," he says slowly. "In fact, I'm in the
mood to be perfectly fair. Tit for tat. You want my attention, it's all yours."

Crap.

"Think you made it a rule," he adds thoughtfully. "You do 30 percent of the chasing. I do the other 70. I owe you something now."

I should say *stop*.

I should stay mad.

Instead, just one word comes out of my mouth. "Please."

It's a stupid word and one I'll regret saying tomorrow, if not sooner. But I'm horny, I'm pissed off and I think there's something special between Rev and I, even if neither one of us knows how to talk about it. We both need more practice at this relationship thing.

His hand finds the waistband of my jeans. "You want this?"

"Please," I repeat, but this time it's more order than request. Screw asking him for what I want—I'll settle for telling.

He eases the jeans down to my ankles and then I step out of them. This shouldn't turn me on.

But it does.

Oh, God, does it turn me on.

My left leg brushes the seat; my right leg smacks into the dashboard. The lack of room is absolutely the only reason I hook my traitorous leg around Rev's ass. Truly, it is. I don't like him all that much right now. He's obnoxious, arrogant and way too demanding. No matter what we've done together, he's not in the driver seat of my life. I am.

Except I'm also spread wide on the front seat.

"Rev—"

"Shut up," he says calmly. "It's my turn."

I look down, as much as I can, and that's a huge mistake because heat rushes south. His hand disappears from view and then I feel his fingers stroking over the crotch of my panties. I yelp.

"You grabbed me." He sounds like the voice of reason. Given the way he's straddling me, I can feel his dick. Rev isn't a small man anywhere, as the long, thick part of him pressing against me attests. I wriggle, trying to free my hands, and he gets bigger.

I am such a lucky girl.

"We can't do this here." I'd like to say I protest because I'm sensible of where we are (parked by the side of a road). And maybe that factors in—but the real reason is logistical. There's not enough space to have sex here, no matter how badly I want it.

The pinning-me-down part is a little iffy, too. I've never tried tying a guy up or being tied up, and I should tell him to get the fuck off me. He'd do it. Rev promised me the first time he touched me that the games ended the minute I told him stop, so while I'd love to tell him he doesn't do it for me… I'd be lying. And with his fingers pressed against the crotch of my panties, he's gonna figure the truth out for himself anyhow.

"You're wet," he whispers roughly. "Even wetter than in the club."

He just had to bring that up. Yes. I'm that turned on. My panties are soaked, and if he moves his fingers, I'll come for him. The guys I've dated in the past have been foreplay guys. They've kissed and touched and run through bedroom tricks like they're working their way through a back issue of *Cosmopolitan*. And while

I appreciated their efforts, none of them made me feel the way Rev does. It's like riding the orgasm Tilt-A-Whirl, one endless round of pleasure, when before I'd been standing all alone in line for the teacup ride.

He drags his fingers down my crotch and then tunnels beneath the lacy edge. Heat races through me as his fingers skim my slick folds, the pleasure so sharp and intense I swear I see stars. Or maybe that's just sunlight on a passing car. I don't know. I can't think, can't make my head figure out the logical thing to do. All I can do is feel.

"I could fuck you right here." His voice gets lower, rougher. Darker. I bet he gives brilliant phone sex. I buck and he pins me down.

"Tell me no, Evie, if this isn't what you want."

"Can't," I gasp out. I have no idea why he wants to talk now, when we could be doing other things. Kissing. Kissing would be good.

"Can." He gives me a dark smile and then shoves his fingers through my slick, swollen folds. Yes. I scream for him. God, I'd do anything he wanted right now. He penetrates me with two fingers, opening me up and pushing deep into my body.

"Ask me for it," he growls, twisting his fingers inside me and finding a magic spot. What should feel like an invasion feels so goddamned good. He works his fingers deeper as his thumb zeroes in on my clit. I collapse shamelessly beneath him, giving up any thought of resistance as my pussy tightens. Rev's shoulder strikes the steering wheel and he grunts.

"Let me up." We can drive to his place or mine. Find a motel. Something.

"Kinda like having you like this." He looks down, watching his hand, seeing me take his fingers and ride him. It turns me on, knowing he's so confident. He knows what he likes—and he's certain he can make me like it, too.

He penetrates me with three fingers this time, driving deep into my body. Not as if I put up any resistance. I'm swollen, wet for him, so slick that I can hear the wetness as he plays with me.

He brushes his mouth over my ear. "You still mad at me?"

This kind of discussion would guarantee world peace. Maybe our leaders should try it. I giggle at the thought and Rev nips my ear hard.

"Don't laugh at the man who's making you feel good." Warm amusement threads through his voice, though. That's something I'm figuring out about Rev. He doesn't judge in bed. Whatever works for me is his favorite thing, too. He finds my G-spot, his calloused fingers rubbing just right against a place that makes me see not just stars but an entire fucking galaxy.

My head shuts down, my body tight and focused on Rev. He's the center of the universe for me.

"Remember," he says roughly, as if he hasn't tattooed himself on every nerve ending in my body. "You started this."

"And you'd better finish it before I kill you." I finally manage to wriggle my hands free, but Rev is ready for me. He draws them over my head until my fingers close around the door handle.

"Don't let go," he orders.

I'm stretched tight, anticipation thrumming through me, as his thumb circles my clit and his fingers push slowly in and out.

"Or?"

"Or I'll stop." His laugh taunts me. "You want to end like this, Evie? Wet and tight, needing what I can give you?"

The man should have been a lawyer.

Not waiting for an answer, he moves down my body and I do my best to make room for him. He shoves my sopping panties to the side, his thumb still working my clit in lazy circles.

"You like me just fine," he announces, sounding way too fucking pleased. "This doesn't feel mad to me."

He works me with his tongue, tasting me, owning me. My panties vanish, along with all rational thought. Rev doesn't hesitate. He opens me up shamelessly, holding me in place with his hands on my hips. His mouth finds my clit, his tongue licking my slick folds as he pushes his thumb and fingers back inside me. I can't breathe, can't scream, and holding back isn't part of my plan. I hurtle toward my orgasm so fast that I yell loud enough to be heard on the street.

Pretty sure I scream his name. Might make more than a few promises, too, my thighs squeezing his head, my fingers clenched around the handle. I'm pulled tight, stretched, and when the tension breaks, I'm all his.

CHAPTER SEVENTEEN

Rev

EVIE IS FUCKING AMAZING. She moans and hollers, making rough, needy sounds that make me crazy for her. My dick wants to be inside her *now*, and never mind that we barely fit in the front seat of her ride. I want to shove myself deep inside her, so deep she'll never get rid of me. Mark her. Own her.

Fuck.

Evie demanded a relationship with her sex and I want to give her that, too. After the orgasms, the women at the club want to be paid or they want to talk. They want words, they want holding, or they plain want something I just don't have in me. As a result, I've dated my palm almost exclusively except for a few quick bangs when shit got too lonely or hard. Evie and I can't happen for real. She's my insurance plan for Rocker's good behavior. She's a marker I'm calling in.

She deserves more than a rough, quick finger bang in a car.

She deserves more than me.

Staring at the pussy I shouldn't tap, my fingers still buried in her sweet, slick body, I face the truth. I'm an asshole and I'm proud of it. She came hard, screaming my name as I rocked her world. Fuck the rules and what we should or shouldn't do.

I slide my fingers out of her pussy. For a second, she lies there, relaxed and open. Her T-shirt's pushed up above her tits and her panties are on the floor. Don't remember tearing them off, but I must have. Her pussy's the prettiest sight ever, pink and wet, the little hole begging for me to shove my dick inside her. Flip her over and get into her ass, too. No way I don't want to take her—and right now she'd let me.

I move back to the driver's seat. I'm in too deep here. "Nice show."

Kinda cute how she angry blushes. The pretty pink starts on her cheeks and it sure as shit extends everywhere I can see. She scrambles upright, shoving her shirt back down.

"You suck," she splutters, rummaging on the floor and coming up with her ruined panties. She looks at them for a minute but she's not a miracle worker. She drags her jeans on and shoves the scraps into her bag.

"And you came." I suck the taste of her from my fingers. Goddamned flavor of the month right there. Doesn't matter the expression on her face announces I'm the worst kind of pig. Doesn't matter because I know her dirty little secret.

She liked what I did.

She might not like me, but she likes my fingers and that's enough. She starts to say something, but I'm in no mood to hear it. I'm a complete fucking idiot because I can't keep my hands off her, and yet I'm handing her off to my club. What happened here will take on a whole new meaning, at least in her mind, when she understands the situation. I won't be her boyfriend, her down-low lover, her feel-good guy. I'll be the criminal who kidnapped her and made her face the unfortunate reality that her beloved baby brother is pond-sucking scum.

"You—"

I shut her up by sliding my palm over her mouth. Her teeth scrape my palm. "Bite me and I paddle your ass."

Fuck if she doesn't lick me. Christ. Heat tunnels straight to my dick, making thinking almost impossible.

"Whatever you start, I'll finish."

CHAPTER EIGHTEEN

Eve

REV DROPS HIS hand and pulls the Princess Mobile back onto the road. That hand just did unspeakable things to me—and I loved it. He touched me and ate me out and now… Yeah. Now I have no clue what to do.

Bet Emily Post wouldn't have a clue, either.

I lean against the window in a daze, trying not to squeeze my thighs together. Holy crap. The man is out-of-this-world good. Little white-hot pulses of pleasure tease me as we drive and he knows it. The smug smile on his face makes me want to hit him. Okay, and then I want to shove him onto his back and ride him until he's the one seeing stars.

Huh. We seem to be taking the scenic route to my house.

We're in industrial central—and my neighborhood is row after row of matching houses with one palm tree and a small grass square in front and a concrete patio in the back. The only difference is the paint color and make of the car in the driveway. Rocker always jokes people will hit the wrong house when they come home drunk or tired.

These are not my streets, not my neighbors.

Granted, Rev has a penis. He's genetically incapable
of asking Siri for directions or using the GPS, but he's
been to my place before. He's no stranger to East Las
Vegas. If he'd missed an exit or taken a wrong turn,
I'd expect him to curse or to slow down. Instead, his
face is cold and closed off, and the Princess Mobile is
driving down the road at exactly the speed limit.

As if Rev really doesn't want to get pulled over or
draw attention to himself right now.

Something's so wrong.

I fidget with my bag, working my phone out.

He doesn't take his eyes off the road. "Whatever
you're thinking, just sit tight."

"This is not the way home." I punch the seat belt free
and reach for the door handle. Yes, this is the stupidest
choice I could make since jumping out of a moving vehicle at thirty-five miles an hour will hurt. A lot. But
something's wrong here and I have an excellent imagination. I shove the door open and the road spools away
beneath us, a lethal ribbon of hard, unyielding surface.
I really don't want to do this—but I can't stay, either.

"Jesus." Rev curses and slams on the brakes.

I launch myself out of the RV, duck around the RV
and run like hell.

A bike pulls up in front of me hard and Vik leans
forward. "Princess doesn't get parole."

Oh. God.

I spin away from him, but Rev's out of the RV, stalking toward me.

Rev

This is what happens when I let my dick do the thinking.

Evie tasted so sweet that I forgot to remember what she is.

Insurance.

She bolted out of the RV like I'd held a gun to her head. She's pulling a runner on me and Vik's laughing his ass off. She ducks and weaves around the open car door, but Vik cuts her off easily.

"Hard way or the easy way?" I hold a hand out to her and her mouth opens. "Don't scream if you're voting easy."

There's a curse from behind her as Vik registers his opinion. He's not stupid, though. He doesn't touch what's mine. Because Evie is mine, even if she doesn't know it. Gonna make that clear real soon, along with a few other things.

"Fuck you," she breathes. That's not a scream, but then she turns and sprints away from me. Not sure where she thinks she's going because she's stuck between me and Vik. She tries to cut around the RV, feet flying. The fear radiating off her isn't unjustified because as much as I'd like to say I'm not planning on hunting her, I am.

I love hunting.

I count to three (I'm such a fucking gentleman) and then pound after her, not trying to hide my approach. Her feet scrabble for purchase as I lunge, fisting her T-shirt. Her ass hits my dick and I snake an arm around her waist, lifting her off her feet. No way she misses the hard-on poking her. Chasing her is a hell of a turn-on.

"You pig," she hisses. Pretty sure she's just mentally painted an X on my dick and plans on introducing her knee to that target.

"Sticks and stones, princess," I whisper against her ear and nip hard. I'd like to play with her until she's screaming for me, and not because she's hurting, either. "Are you still wet?"

She splutters incoherently, which will piss her off when she gets her head straight. Evie hates being out of control and not knowing what to say. I give her a few seconds to pull her shit together.

I toss her over my shoulder, immobilizing her kicking legs against my chest with one arm. Still, I take her point. She really doesn't like me right now. Fine. There's a long line of people who hate me—she can get in the fucking queue and take a number.

"Might want to be nice to me seeing as how I'm kidnapping you," I tell her.

She goes straight for the denial. "You can't do that."

I pat her ass. "Don't see how you can stop me."

Evie's learned something from our time together. She doesn't bother announcing her attentions—just opens her mouth and tries to scream. I flip her around, slap a palm over her pretty mouth, and adjust my grip so she can't bite. The neighborhood's shit, but somebody might notice.

"Stop playing," Vik says from behind me.

"Fucking love my job," I shoot back. "Don't rush me." I nudge Evie's face up so I can see her eyes.

"We've got a problem, princess. Shit's happened between the clubs and that means you and me have a date at the Hard Rider clubhouse."

Fuck, that sounds dirty.

From the choking noise Evie makes, she agrees with me 100 percent, except I'm clearly the issue from her point of view.

"We're riding out of here. You can come with us, or you can fight. Gonna end up at my clubhouse either way, but I'll be in a better mood if you don't fight me on this."

She nods carefully and I lift my palm away from her mouth and set her back on her feet.

"I think you should go to hell," she says slowly. Vik snorts.

She tries to duck under my arm, as if that shit's gonna fly. I step closer, pinning her in place against the RV with my legs. She feels sweet as always.

"What's it gonna be, sweetheart?"

She goes wild, kicking and biting. Fuck, it's a good thing I'm wearing boots. Vik's laughing his ass off, the bastard. I grab her wrists and heft her over my shoulder. Her feet drum my ass, her mouth hovering perilously close to my dick and not because she wants to deliver my fantasy blowjob.

"Knock it off." I slap her on the ass, partly because I have a point to make and partly because goddamn she feels good. Love the soft give as my fingers mark her, putting my stamp on her skin. "Bite me and you kiss it better."

That stops her, although we both know she'll rally.

Evie doesn't know how to quit for good. Hell, she probably still thinks I can be redeemed or saved or some shit. I adjust her weight so my shoulder's not digging into her stomach and open the passenger-side door. I drop her onto the seat and stare down at her.

I grip her chin in my hand and force her to look at me. "It would be a real bad idea to fight me right now. You might buy yourself a few minutes, but then I'd catch you again and I'd be pissed."

She opens her mouth, undoubtedly to argue. Her mistake is that she thinks I won't hurt her. I don't *want* to hurt her, but the MC comes first and I'll do what I have to do.

"Rocker fucked up. He took a brother and we want him back. You're gonna make sure that happens."

She licks her lips. "How do I do that?"

"Think of yourself as a bargaining chip."

"But—"

"Nuh-uh. The other option is that I shoot Rocker dearest the next time I see him."

Being Mr. Helpful, Vik pulls his gun out and thumbs the safety off. Evie stares at him, her panicked breathing coming way too quick as her gaze darts between the gun and me. If she hyperventilates, I'll have an even bigger problem on my hands.

"Come quietly and we'll save the bullets for later."

CHAPTER NINETEEN

Eve

DEATH CHANGES EVERYTHING.

No one's dead yet, but Rev and his friend have made it plenty clear that the operative word is *yet*. No matter what my brother's done or not done, I'm not letting him get shot on my watch. I'm not entirely certain what just happened, but I think it goes something like this: I let Rev eat me out, he threatened to kidnap me, I ran, he caught me, and now we're driving somewhere I'm going to be really unhappy because kidnapping never works out as well as orgasms.

Also? My taste in men totally sucks.

I don't want to think about what I've let Rev do to me (or what I've done to him), so I focus on the basics. "Promise me something?"

He grunts and eases the Princess Mobile back out onto the road. He's entirely too comfortable committing felonies. I thought he was a decent guy underneath the rough exterior, but I've made my usual mistake, confusing a really talented penis with long-term rela-

tionship material. Okay. Lesson learned. If—when—
I get out of this, no more dating for the next seventy
years.

"Promised you you'd stay safe," he volunteers. "You
want something else?"

My wish list right now is impossibly long.

Yes, yes I want something.

"Promise me Rocker doesn't get hurt."

The words sound pathetic. I don't want to think
about how Rev's going to interpret them, but I'm more
than willing to beg. This is my brother, and he's in so
much trouble that my heart bleeds for him. And *that*,
ladies and gentlemen, is still better than what happens
when actual, real-life bullets start flying.

Rev shoots me an incredulous look. "Are you fucking kidding me?"

"No." I tuck my hands between my legs. "I'd really appreciate it if you promised me that my brother
doesn't get hurt. Whatever biker beat-down you think
you have planned for him, please don't."

He shakes his head. "You're incredible."

I don't think he means this in a good way, but I have
to keep trying. "He's my brother, I love him, and shooting would be murder."

"Don't have a problem with any of that," Rev mutters.

I believe him.

"But if you promise to keep him safe, I'll be quiet. I
won't tell anyone about—" I wave a hand. There really
ought to be a way to refer to your kidnapping politely.

"You'll come quietly?" Now Rev just sounds amused.

"Silent as the grave." *Bad choice of words.*

His curse doesn't say much for Rocker's chances. "I can maybe guarantee that the Hard Riders don't kick his ass too hard—because right now, sweetheart, I'll be honest and tell you that my president has a bullet with your brother's name on it—but I can't speak for the Colombians. He double-crossed them and they make me look like an angel."

"Just try?"

"Fuck." Rev's grip on the steering wheel tightens. "I'll do what I can, but I'm not a miracle worker. You need to accept the fact that your brother has pissed off a whole lot of people."

I can't be Rev's hostage or his insurance plan for Rocker's good behavior forever, which means I need a plan. The only thing I can think of, though, is that I still have my phone. As soon as I'm alone, I can warn Rocker and dial for help.

When we slow down, however, reality is waiting. Two big, ropey young men saunter forward when we pull up in front of a warehouse. Didn't know MCs came with valet parking. When I shift, looking around and trying to get my bearings, I can just make out the Strip, off on the horizon. When the sun finally sets, the whole sky will light up, but the artificial world of the casinos is so distant it might as well be on another planet. Not that the Strip isn't about money and power—it absolutely is—but the players there are less blunt about it.

"Is this the secret clubhouse?"

Rev grunts, which I decide is an affirmative.

Vik joins us and immediately passes a very familiar bag to Rev, who takes it and heads for a door about twenty feet away. Guess he figures I have no choice but to follow him. Well, fuck him and the Harley he road in on, because I'm not feeling real submissive right now.

Ergo, I stall. "You packed for me?"

Vik smiles slowly. "Had some time to kill and didn't think I was invited to the roadside party you were hosting earlier. Let me know if you're issuing rain checks."

My brain stutters to a complete and mortifying halt. Not only does Vik know what Rev and I just did, but he'd be happy to join us for some kind of kinky three-peat?

"Some bikers like sharing, baby girl." Vik whispers his next filthy suggestion against my ear as his big shoulders and body block out the rest of the world.

Catching up with Rev suddenly seems like the smarter plan. I hotfoot it over to where he waits by an industrial-strength door with a big metal grille.

"Don't fuck with her," he growls at Vik. The other biker flicks Rev a two-fingered salute and then saunters away. Rev shoves the key in the lock, opens the door and hesitates. Makes a girl wonder if he's hiding dead bodies in there because Rev is not a guy who hits the pause button on life often.

"It's not much."

"This is a kidnapping, not a five-star getaway."

"Uh-huh," he says and heads inside.

I'm not a Four Seasons gal. My finances won't stretch to even a Motel 6, which means my vacation options are limited. Rev's place turns out to be an enormous loft. The walls are old brick and light pours in from a trio of skylights high above the floor. Rev could make a killing if he put this on the market—and if having a biker MC as your neighbor wasn't considered a drawback.

Still, it's gorgeous. The light is awesome. And…

"I thought you said this was your place."

Rev shoves his keys into his pocket. "Problem?"

Absolutely. I have a long list, rank-ordered from easiest to fix to outright impossibility. "Where's the furniture?"

He shrugs. "Got a bed and a couch—what else do I need?"

I snort and he swivels to stare at me.

"Classy," he mutters. I flash him the bird.

"Don't be fooled by the tiara." He's not kidding about the lack of stuff. All I see is empty space. Rev's place is one big room. I spot a small kitchenette at the back and another door that looks like it leads to a bathroom. A circular metal staircase leads up to a loft. The air smells like lemons and it's freakishly clean for a guy. Maybe he has a service?

He glances around. "Kitchen's there. Bathroom's on this floor—bedroom's up the stairs. Got clean towels in the bathroom. Not sure the sheets are as clean."

"I'm not staying. I have work."

"You're not going anywhere," he snaps.

"So we're having an extended slumber party, just like that?"

Because…no.

"You stay here," he repeats. "Take a break from the party gig for a few days."

"No." I can maybe miss a couple of events, but there's only so long my girls can cover for me.

"Like it better when you say yes," he says roughly. "Might want to work on that."

Rev hasn't hurt me yet, but I'd be stupid to trust him. Nothing about this situation is right. Kidnapping does not a dream date make. Sure I cut a deal with Rev that he'd let my brother leave without any bullet holes, but Rocker is free and clear for the moment and now I'm stuck here with a biker who is at best crazy and at worst homicidal. It's the story of my dating life—pretty on the outside and batshit crazy on the inside.

I need a plan, preferably a really good one. The bathroom door gives me the first inklings of an idea. Bolting won't get me far. Rev outweighs and outguns me, and I'm not desperate enough yet to hunt for a fire escape or a convenient window. Dropping from an upper-story window in a loft would kill me. My phone, however, is a lifeline.

"Permission to pee. Sir." I snap him a mock salute and gesture toward the bathroom.

Rev nods, so score one for me. Unfortunately, however, he falls into step beside me. Maybe he senses I'm up to something. Maybe he's got a thing for dirty kink, or maybe he just really doesn't have any personal boundaries. I throw out a hand at the door, slapping my palm against his chest.

"Personal space, big guy. You stay out here."

"The door stays open," he growls.

"I don't pee for an audience." Frankly, there's no way

I could unclench with that kind of pressure. There's nothing sexy about using the bathroom in my book.

He curses. Worse, he actually has to *think it over*.

"You've got two minutes," he snaps. "And then I'm coming in after you."

Two minutes is better than nothing, so I nod and hightail it inside his bathroom, slamming the door behind me. It's spotlessly clean, but missing any kind of pictures, knickknacks or hand towels. It also lacks a window, which may explain his willingness to let me pee in private, and the lock is one of those stupid flimsy things set into the doorknob.

"Wouldn't bother with that lock." Rev's voice vibrates through the door. "It's been busted for months."

Shit.

I have one chance.

I slam up the toilet seat since he's clearly listening, and then I fish down my bra where I keep my phone and an emergency twenty-dollar bill. I message Rocker with shaking fingers.

ME: At Hard Riders clubhouse? Kidnapped by bikers. Need help ASAP.

ROCKER: Fck.

ME: Not kidding here.

I bring up the maps application, grab my address, and paste it into the text window. Rocker may know where the Hard Rider clubhouse is, but I'm not taking chances.

ROCKER: Gotcha

ME: Dialing 911 now

ROCKER: Hold that thought? Cops in club biz not a good idea. Sit tight and do what you're told.

ME: That's your plan?!

ROCKER: Cops can't help. Safest for me 2 if you stay quiet.

ME: 911 seems like better plan. Cops have guns and can help. Thought I taught you about Officer Friendly?

Rev slams a palm against the door. "Thirty seconds, princess."

ROCKER: I have their boy. We'll trade. Make it up to you later.

This is not a Pokemon card swap—this is my life. I glare down at my phone, torn. And what kind of life does Rocker lead that he's entirely unsurprised to learn I've been taken hostage by a hostile biker gang? That he actually recommends I not call 911? And that he *kidnapped* a Hard Rider club member? I may not be a patch holder or own a bike, but I know a felony when

I see one. I bring up my contacts, my fingers hovering over the 911 emergency contact info.

I should dial.

The bathroom door slams open. I back up as far as the too-small space will permit, but Rev's hard gaze narrows in on the phone in my hand. He moves so fast, I don't have time to flinch. His arms come around me, his hands twisting the phone out of mine as he drops the phone on the ground and rams his boot heel down on it, disconnecting my distress call.

"Get your ass in here, Vik," he hollers as I buck and twist against his hold. He kicks what's left of my phone out into the main room and then lifts me off my feet, bouncing me over his shoulder. The impact knocks the breath out of me—the man's shoulder is as hard as the rest of him—but I'm done playing by Rev's rules. I open my mouth and scream.

The front door flies open and Vik hurtles into the loft. He palms a gun as he comes toward us. Adrenaline pumps through me in a sickening rush. This is it. And because that pisses me off almost as much as it scares me, I scream louder. I'm not going out on a whimper.

"Fuck, she's loud." Vik stoops to collect the phone.

Rev slaps a hand over my mouth. I try biting him, kicking with my feet, but he simply shifts his palm to cover my mouth and my nose, cutting off my air supply.

"Fight me now and it won't end well for you," he growls. "You don't have to get hurt if you do what you're told. Nod your head."

Since I'm seeing spots, I nod. I'll recant later. Booted feet eat up the floor that spins nauseatingly beneath me. He removes his hand from my face, but doesn't slow down as he takes the stairs two at a time. I don't think Rev is an ax murderer, even if he is stupidly loyal to his MC, but this isn't the time to be taking anything on faith.

I open my mouth and Rev bounces me again.

"Really wouldn't do that," he says quietly. Despite hauling my ass up the stairs, he's not out of breath and unwelcome excitement pings through me. My libido has a horrible sense of timing.

He follows his warning with a slap to my butt that sends another tingle through me, the kind that homes in on my clit and reminds me that Rev has a dirty side. Vik shouts something about getting rid of my phone and then a door slams.

There's only one room at the top of the stairs, a wide-open loft with skylights in the twenty-foot ceiling. Spider-Man I'm not—I'm stuck unless I can get down the stairs. Rev drops me on the bed and stands over me, hands on his hips.

"We need to discuss the value of keeping your word."

"Or maybe you should look up the definition of *felony*."

This is crazy wrong, but a delicious shiver runs through me as he frowns. He's big and pissed off and I like this? Okay. I like him—and the only feelings he has for me are the wrong kind of possessive.

"We've got trust issues, princess."

"You think?"

"Yeah." He leans down, bracing his hands on either

side of my shoulders. "See, now I don't trust you, and that means we're gonna do shit the hard way."

He drops onto the bed, swinging a leg over my hips. I squeak. It's embarrassing as hell, but the small, startled sound escapes from my mouth before I can bite it back. I blame it on the impressive bulge in his jeans now on eye level. He kneels over me, braceleting my wrists with his hands and drawing them up over my head.

Pinning me in place.

Is this another dirty game?

Why am I so stupidly conflicted?

"Rev?"

"Right here, princess." He reaches over and yanks open a drawer in the bedside table. Handcuffs. The man has handcuffs in his bedside table. Not like I was expecting him to keep the Bible there, but I'd have guessed porn. Maybe a paperback or a strip of condoms. I start wriggling in earnest because this is the opposite of safe. Those cuffs look like the real deal rather than a toy.

He tightens his grip on my hips and the bulge in his pants is definitely bigger than before. The cuffs click shut around my wrists.

Shit.

"Can we discuss this?"

"Time to do that, princess, was when we struck a deal that you'd come quietly."

For a moment I think he's done. Part of me is disappointed, but most of me is going for the gold in relieved. There's no relationship future when you end up tied to the bed without a safe word. I've coached girlfriends through shitty dates; I know how this goes. The minute Rev whipped out his shiny toys was the minute any chance we had together was over.

He stares down at me for a second, then curses.

"We're back to the trust issue," he informs me and then pulls a hunting knife out of his right boot. I shove away from him as far as the cuffs will let me go.

"Sorry, princess." He brings the knife down and I freeze. Can't even suck enough air in for a scream because no one can get here quick enough to rescue me. The blade slides between my bra and my T-shirt, the fabric parting far too easily. Cool air hits my bare skin. Shit. *Shit.*

"Don't scream," he repeats, his voice low and menacing. "No one's gonna hear—or care. You're my property now."

I squeeze my eyes shut. Okay. I'm a coward. I thought I knew Rev, but apparently I have no idea who he is or what he's capable of. He *told* me he wasn't a nice guy—and he didn't lie.

He peels my clothes from me, running his hands over the ruined fabric and coming up with my spare cash and keys.

The bed rustles as he shoves upright, then one big hand cups the side of my face. He brushes a kiss over the top of my head.

"Coulda kept your clothes on if you followed the rules. Might want to think about that, princess."

CHAPTER TWENTY

Rev

THIS IS THE problem with hostage situations—they go
FUBAR, leaving you holding the pieces. Evie's col-
lateral damage and I don't like it. Hard Riders MC
doesn't want to hurt her, but Sachs is ours and we've
got a bigger problem in the form of the Colombian cartel anyhow. Hard to justify putting one person first—
no matter how badly I want to fuck her. Nice to see the
greater good bite me in the ass.

When Rocker finally calls me, I make him wait before I answer. "You know I'm not gonna talk to you
about shit."

Guess his Colombian buddies haven't taught him
any Spanish yet, because I understand every curse he
aims my way.

"I want your word that Eve doesn't get hurt," he
says.

There's a pause I don't try to fill. Let Rocker imagine what could happen to his sister while she's our
"guest."

"You know I like her," I say finally. "She's a great girl."

"Promise me," he growls. "There's shit going on here that's out of my control. I can tell you that Sachs is safe enough for now, so make me the same guarantee about Eve."

"You don't want to demand I set her free immediately?" Have to admit, I'm kind of curious about that.

"The Colombians and I are not BFFs." He gives a grunt that might have been a laugh. "It's better she's not running around on her own."

"An eye for an eye. You know how I work." Even as I tell him this, I try to imagine hurting Evie. Epic fucking fail.

Another curse. "I hear you, but that's my sister. You hurt her, I hurt you back."

"While Sachs is with you, I keep Evie in my bed. Sooner you let him go, the sooner Evie can get on with her own life."

Eve

Being kidnapped is actually pretty fucking boring.

Turns out, I'm used to working and panicking about *not* working just doesn't fill enough time. Plus, Rev's underfurnished bachelor pad is not my idea of fun. The man could give Marie Kondo a run for her money in living minimalist because he owns no stuff. No books, no DVDs, no electronics. It's like he uses the place for sleeping, fucking and nothing else.

The one highlight? The handcuffs are back in his

bedside table. I woke up unlocked and I've stayed that way. I'd like to think if he tried tying me up again, he'd be in for a world of hurt. That I'd kick, punch and fight my way to freedom. It's hard to avoid reality, though. He's big, stronger, and he has a gun. If he wants to cuff me to the bed, he can.

When the door opens, I'm actually relieved.

Yes. I'm that bored.

Rev saunters in, carrying a plastic grocery bag. I'd like to ignore him and the delicious odors emanating from the bag. After all, I'm camped out on his couch because I'm desperate for a change of scenery. Downstairs, upstairs on the bed, or in the bathroom—those are my choices, and this is the safest one. I'm wearing a pair of yoga pants and a tiny pink tank top. Apparently when Vik packed for me, he either overlooked the bra drawer in my dresser or he couldn't be bothered, because there's not a bra in sight in my bag. I'm also barefoot because apparently shoes of any kind were also not on the packing list.

I bolt upright. "I have a job. You can't keep me here."

He walks right on past me and into the kitchen. The fridge door opens. Shuts. There's a faint clink as he twists off the top of a Budweiser. I'm not the neatest person in the world—I'm messy and I own it. But Rocker and his friends make me look like Martha fucking Stewart, as do my previous boyfriends. Rev likes things clean. And organized. I don't have to look to know that his bottle cap has gone straight into the trash.

He reemerges, bottle in hand, and sets the bag on the counter. "Dinner."

Great. I merit one word.

"How was your day, honey?" I blow him an exaggerated kiss, and score one for me, because his face darkens. "I missed work, thanks to a kidnapping asshole."

"Eating's optional," he growls.

How can he be so thoughtful and such a pig at the same time? And yes, I want to pick a fight with him. I'm missing work, Rocker's in trouble and something has to give. Surely Rev can't really keep me locked up here like some kind of medieval hostage. I'm aware that his MC is a law unto itself, but I do have friends—and that job. When you don't show up at a birthday party, the mom who was left in the lurch with her little darling sobbing her disappointed heart out will track you down and kill you. Plus, I have employees who like their paychecks. Eventually, someone's going to notice I'm gone.

"Nice to know you're not planning on starving me."

"I'm not fighting with you," he says slowly. "Fight's with Rocker."

"So explain to me what's up with *my brother*," I emphasize. "Tell me he's okay."

I've screwed up before and let Rocker down, but I've always had a choice about being there for him or not. This time, however, Rev's taken that choice away from me. Rocker needs me more than ever, and yet I'm not allowed to go to him?

"You always protect him?" Rev sounds amused, proving he's not as smart as I think he is.

"You think of your club brothers as family, right?"

He drains half his beer. "Fucking straight."

"Rocker is my brother. I protect him. I look out for him."

Rev sets his bottle down. "You can't fix this for him, princess. He took Sachs."

"But kidnapping me won't make Rocker miraculously do what you want. It's just going to get you sent to the nearest correctional center for ten long years."

Rev shakes his head. "Keep thinking that all you want, but you might want to spend your time figuring out how to get through Rocker's head that he's lost. If he wants you back, he gives Sachs back."

"What if he doesn't?" I don't believe Rev would hurt me, but I'm not so sure about the rest of the Hard Rider club.

Rev gives me a hard look. "Let's hope it doesn't come to that, princess."

After dropping that little bombshell, he strolls up the stairs. A few minutes later, I hear water running.

Fresh out of plans and workable ideas, I try the front door. There's always the chance that Rev's gotten sloppy and left the thing unlocked with a getaway car parked out front. Hope's not a strategy, but it's all I've got.

The door's not locked, but when I open it, I discover two prospects standing outside. I flip them the bird and the closest one blows me an answering kiss. "Is that a suggestion, sunshine?"

"Fuck you," I snap. The kisser has a sense of humor worthy of a ten-year-old boy. He leans against the wall, shoulders shaking with laughter.

I march up the stairs and toward the bathroom.

And…hello.

Not only did Rev not lock the door, but he's whacking off in his shower. It's pretty damned impressive, and I don't mean the ink on his arms and down his back. I stand there for a moment, but there's just so much goddamned Rev to take in. The dick he's fisting is every bit as thick and long as I remember. The water cascades over him, droplets sliding down his chest and onto powerful thighs. His ass flexes as he hits some sweet spot and groans.

He raises his head and meets my glare. I don't know why I'm surprised, because Rev doesn't back down from anything. His club, his place, his rules. He thinks he's in charge of it all—and me.

"You want to have sex with me now, princess?"

Oh, fuck him.

He did not just say that.

Never mind that it's the truth—I know a power play when I hear one, which means I absolutely have to have the upper hand.

It's the principle of the thing.

Rev

Evie steps into the shower fully dressed and drops to her knees.

Jesus.

Not sure if I should cup my balls or say a prayer for my dick.

Narrowed eyes watch me from beneath thick lashes as she leans in and licks the tip. Holy. Fuck. Maybe that should be a prayer of thanksgiving I'm sending up because she owns me right now and we both know it. My body blocks most of the spray as I lean over her, bracing my hand against the slick tile, but she still gets plenty wet. Her top's fucking transparent in seconds, and given she's on her knees, she can see firsthand the effect her show has.

She's got gorgeous tits, the perfect handful with tight little nipples. Not sure why she's in here with me, but I'm enjoying my view. She licks again, her tongue rimming the head, and I bite back a curse. When she wraps her hand around my dick, I more than meet her halfway. Practically drill myself into her palm, but she just laughs. She's got a great laugh to go with those tits. Whole damned package is spectacular, but I can't let her control this moment.

"You gonna suck me or just admire the scenery?"

"You shouldn't be in such a rush." Her tongue makes another slow pass around my tip. Gonna fucking blow right there on her lips, mark her mouth and her face. Hit her tits, too.

She's beautiful.

Then she pulls back, and for a moment I think that's the whole point of our shower time. Makes sense she'd be out for a little revenge. She's gonna get to her feet and leave me standing here with my dick out and hard. But then she licks her palms slowly and I almost blow on the spot.

"Dirty girl." Mean that as a compliment, too.

"Not sure I should agree with you," she answers and then wraps a hand around my dick and uses me as her very own slip-and-slide. Her free hand cups my tight balls, rolling and touching. Fucking show-and-tell as she sucks me into her mouth until I'm bumping the back of her throat and then somehow she takes that, too, making every wet dream I ever had come true.

And then she runs her tongue down my dick, her teeth lightly scraping sensitive skin, and there's only room for the two of us in this shower. She sucks and licks, and I'm fucking her mouth sweet and fast, watching her pretty pink lips form the dirtiest O around me. Don't know how she went from pissed off to this.

She drives me crazy, sucking harder and picking up her pace. Blow job's not a job and she knows it. Rough sounds tear from the back of my throat, filling up the space around us, and my hands fist her hair, guiding her down. I'm so close, so fucking ready to fill her mouth with my load.

"Fuck, princess." I tug her head gently. "Gotta warn you—"

She sucks me in deeper, and I lose the power of speech. She wraps her mouth around the head until her lips are bumping her fist with each hard thrust I make and I explode.

Bracing my hand against the wall, I force myself to stay upright. Holy. Fuck.

"You're goddamned amazing."

I pull her up into my arms so fast her head must swim, but when I'm with Evie I've only got the one speed. I'm balls-out and slow isn't happening. She reaches around me with a mean laugh that makes my dick twitch—fucker's already getting ready for round two—and kills the water. As if I care about that right now.

I carry her into my bedroom.

Kissing her like my life depends on it.

And maybe it fucking does, right? I head for the bed, ignoring her protests about water and the sheets. Evie worries too much. I yank the covers off the bed and set her down so quickly she bounces. Her arms and legs spread as she instinctively reacts to the free fall. Kinda like having her off balance for me, so I don't give her a chance to find her control. I fall, too.

I'd like to say I make this all about her, that it's her turn, and I've got plans to tease her for hours. Instead, I cover her body with mine. There's water everywhere, but she's slick and hot when I drag my dick between her pussy lips. So fucking ready for me.

"Rev." She moans my name, her fingers digging into my shoulder. I love the way she holds on to me, like I'm her anchor and she's about to fly apart.

Guess what happened in my shower was as good for her as it was for me, which just makes me harder. She needs me to give her this, and so I do. I always will. I roll on a condom and push myself into her. Don't stop until I'm all the way inside, her body hugging me as tight as her arms do. Her shriek almost fucking deafens me, and those sexy, happy noises she's making are definitely doing it for me, as well.

She just enjoys what I do to her. With her. In her. I pull back and then slide in faster, harder, drilling her into the bed. I know she likes her shit slow and sweet, but she drives me crazy and this is working for both of us. I love her hard and fast, arms braced on either side of her head because that way I can kiss her, touch her beautiful face, tangle myself up in her hair. She holds on tighter, her hips tilting up to meet my next downward thrust.

"Tell me you like this," I whisper into her ear.

Not like I can't tell, because her pussy clenches hard on my dick, doing some taking of its own, but I want the words. She moans something completely incoherent and so I pull back, give her just the tip. The next moan is a definite protest.

"Gotta give me the words, princess."

"I hate that name." She turns her head and fucking bites my ear. Hard.

She might not like the label, but I think she likes me. The way she comes is my first clue. And then, while she's still collapsed beneath me, I pull out and flip her over. Gonna hit her ass now. Not being a complete bastard, I lube my finger up good before I slip it inside it. She tenses up.

"Rev." My name's not a question, not a sigh, not a plea. Nope. She sounds nervous as hell.

"All of you, Evie. That's what I want." I ease my finger out, then push it back in, stretching her. Fuck, she's tight. Can't wait to get inside. "You want to tell me no, tell me now."

Evie sucks in a breath and squirms. Then she sighs. I fist her hair, pulling her head back until I meet her gaze. She doesn't say a thing, but she pushes her ass back against my hand. I give her a second finger, pushing deep as she inhales sharply, and then I scissor them open. Move slow and careful because I don't want to hurt her.

"I own this ass," I whisper against her ear. "You're mine."

"And you talk too much. Be gentle?"

"Yeah," I promise her.

I ease her up onto her knees, head braced on her arm. Goddamn, she's gorgeous like that, all trusting and open. I lube my dick because anything else would hurt her, and then I pull her cheeks apart and notch the head at the cute little pucker.

"Finger yourself," I order. When she hesitates, I cover her fingers with mine and we do it together. She's wet—I can hear it.

I thrust into her ass, slow and easy. Fuck, it feels good.

"Relax," I mutter. Reaching beneath her, I cover the fingers working her clit with my own. She deserves a reward for letting me have my way.

"Easy for you to say." Her words end on a gasp and a low moan as I seat myself inside her. God. Damn.

I fuck her ass sure and slow. Pull back until I almost pop out and then push back into her. When I go deeper, she gasps and bucks, but she takes me, her clit getting harder and fuller as we stroke together. She doesn't move from the position I put her in, either—just waits for me to move. Leaves me the illusion of control, because I can't hold back. I move faster and harder, rubbing her clit with the same rhythm until we're both gasping and reaching for the pleasure. Fucking find it, too. I come hard, filling her up, and she's right there with me.

I own her.

Mission accomplished. She's this biker's property.

CHAPTER TWENTY-ONE

Rev

WAY TOO EARLY, my phone goes off somewhere near my head. Still naked, Eve's curled up against my side, her mouth pressed against my chest. Call had better be goddamned important.

"We've got company," Hawke says when I answer. "Think it's go time."

Hawke's the kind of man you follow because, wherever he's headed, it's either the right place to be or some special kind of hell that needs to be blown sky-high. I've done both with him. He's tall and rangy, dark ink covering both arms. A scar wraps around his neck like some kind of sick necklace—the most popular rumor is that someone (ex-wife, turncoat traitor, enemy soldier) tried to garrote him with his own dog tags. You can take two things as gospel. First, Hawke's hard to kill. Second, if you try to kill him, you'd better succeed or die in the attempt. Hawke doesn't do forgiveness—or second chances.

"Thank fuck." We've spent the last couple of days

hunting for Sachs and floating plans to pull him out of the Black Dogs clubhouse without losing any other brothers. None of us would hesitate to lay down our lives for him, but as Hawke points out, two-for-one is only an upside when you're stocking up on beer and chips.

If Rocker and his club were smart, they'd have handed Sachs over. Fuck, they wouldn't have touched him because starting a war between the clubs isn't in anyone's best interests. We've had a couple of tense, go-nowhere meetings discussing possible exchanges, but nothing concrete yet. Looks like things are finally changing.

"Twenty minutes," Hawke says.

"You planning on offering them tea and cookies?"

Hawke laughs. He's never been the nicest son of a bitch. "Thought I'd leave 'em at the front door. Let 'em think things over."

"Got a corner you can put them in," I volunteer. Beside me, Evie stirs and stretches. Waking her up is one more thing I can put on the Black Dogs' tab. I spread the fingers of my free hand over her belly.

"I assume you've got Evie close to hand," my president says drily.

I look down at my hand on her ass. Couldn't get much closer than that.

"She's right here."

"Get her ready," he says. "We'll make the swap and then we're in a better position to clean house."

"Promise me she's gonna be safe. I need to hear she's not walking into anything bad."

Hawke gives a bark of laughter. "Sounds like someone got too close."

Not too much I can say, since it's true.

"Rocker's her goddamned brother. He wants her back—you think he'd go to all this trouble just so he could hurt her?"

"I'm more worried about the rest of his club," I admit. "They could decide she's a liability and all this Colombian shit gives them a good cover story if they decide to make a move."

"You think they'd screw one of their own?"

"How do I know how they run their club? Seems clear they're not thinking straight, though, what with snatching Sachs and all."

"We make the trade," Hawke says. "If it looks like shit's headed south, we can step in. You want to go after her when Sachs is free and clear, that's your business and we'll have your back. You tell me if you're serious about her and we'll make it happen."

I've never thought about making a woman my old lady. Calling it a huge step is an understatement. I think about it for a moment, but we're under the gun here and I don't have the luxury of time. "Gotcha."

Hawke hangs up and I toss the phone onto the bedside table. Evie's still cuddled up next to me. She looks relaxed and soft, like a princess just waiting for me to wake her up with a kiss. Pretty sure I read a story like that once, but the reality's even sexier. I brush a kiss over her forehead and start moving lower. Not sure how Prince Charming stays hands-off because my dick has plenty of suggestions to make.

I plant a kiss on her shoulder. "We have to get up."

"Right now?" Evie's voice is warm and sleepy, her mouth grazing my chest. Another inch and she'd be tonguing my nipple.

Twenty minutes isn't much time. I've never had a problem getting up, putting my pants on and heading out the door, but this is Evie. As soon as I get her in my arms, I start thinking about staying. And yeah, banging the hell out of her because she's so damned sexy. She's also strong, which would make her a fucking amazing old lady. Not just because she's the hottest thing ever in bed (she totally is), but because she smiles when she sees me and she won't take my shit. Doesn't matter that I'm bigger, badder and could hurt her six ways to Sunday (not that I would, but she can't fucking know that, right?). She's still fighting for her asshole brother—and I'd like her to fight for *me* that way.

"Fucking love waking up next to you," I say roughly.

She sucks in a breath. "Not much for pretty words, are you?"

If she wants poetry, she's in bed with the wrong biker. I roll her onto her side, ease her leg forward and…shit. Can't take her bareback, no matter how much I want that. I grab a condom from the bedside table, roll it on and slip my fingers between her legs. She's warm and slick, but I need to hear her screaming my name so I press my thigh between hers. Glide my fingers over her soft lips, from her ass to her clit. It's like the world's best fucking happy trail. I could play with her all day.

"Rev?"

"Give me a minute." She's so soft, I could fucking come just grinding against her ass.

When I stroke my thumb over her clit, she moans and tenses up. She's wet, and that's good, but it's not enough. I cup her, pressing in with my fingertips, drawing slow circles on her slick flesh. Squeeze carefully.

"Come for me," I whisper.

She whimpers something. Doesn't sound like a *no*, so I stroke her some more. When I pinch her clit gently, she arches back into me, demanding more.

She can fucking have whatever she wants.

I roll a condom on and thrust inside her slowly. Don't stop until I've filled her up. And then I hang onto her hips, guiding her, letting her ride me as I move faster and faster, the two of us headed straight for the same goddamned wonderful place. *Perfect*. She clenches down hard, her fingers twisting in the sheets, and I drill into her one last time. Fuck, but she owns me.

I hold her tight, breathing hard. I've never felt like this, but I'm damned sure I want to do it again. And again. I look down at her, lying relaxed and boneless against me, and I'm pretty sure she feels the same way. Can't stop touching her, either. My fingers trace the soft undercurve of her spectacular tits, smooth down her belly, head south.

She wriggles away.

"Have to pee," she whispers, sounding a little tense. I can appreciate she's not used to sharing her space like this. We'll get used to it together. Not sure how to tell her what I'm feeling, but I'll figure it out.

I roll over onto my back, letting her go. By the time

she gets back, I'll know exactly what to say to her. There's got to be a way to tell your woman that she's so perfect she's divine. And I'll find those words—in the ten minutes before our asses have to be downstairs and ready to roll—and somehow I'll get it right. Yeah. It's ridiculous, one of those long shots you see on TV when some world-class gymnast falls ass-first off the balance beam and is staring at those four inches. Knowing he has to get back up, get back on and kick ass. Somehow. With the whole goddamned world watching and armchair quarterbacking.

The bathroom door closes. I cover my face with my arm, because I'm happy living in the land of denial. Weather's awesome, scenery's great. This is absolutely all gonna work out. Evie brushes the side of the bed. Didn't hear the door open—woman moves like a ninja.

There's a soft, metallic click. Not a biker alive who doesn't know that sound of the handcuffs locking into place.

The fuck?

CHAPTER TWENTY-TWO

Rev

I JACKKNIFE UPRIGHT as Evie scrambles away from the bed. Her foot catches in the sheets we kicked off—we've made a disaster of the bedroom—and she hits the floor. The landing doesn't stop her, though, because she pops back up and keeps moving until she's put the room between us.

Smart girl.

Takes a moment for me to focus though, which I blame on her. She's still naked and still so gorgeous I could look at her all night. Probably the rest of tomorrow and—because I won't shit myself about this—the rest of my life, too. I've already had this conversation with myself. She's got curves on her that demand a man appreciate them, curves that bear red marks on her skin from where my face scraped her. Fucking love seeing her wearing my mark.

She hesitates, the look on her face torn between elation and fear. Then she edges for the closet where her stuff is. Guess she's decided to pull a runner. I love her taking the initiative, but I need to shut this down.

She can't leave me.

I won't let her.

"You're into some kinky shit, sweetheart." I reach behind my head for the cuff, exploring the hinge with my fingers. She got it closed right, though, so I'm temporarily stuck. The key's across the room and although I could break the lock, right now I've got about ten minutes to see how this plays out.

"This isn't a game," she says softly. She yanks some clothes out of the closet and jerks them on. Shame to cover up such a pretty body.

"You think you can just walk out my front door?"

She shrugs. The motion sets her tits to jiggling, which is distracting. "Did you think I'd just let you keep me here? Do you really think I'm that naive?"

"Come back to bed." I pat the mattress beside my hip. "We can talk about shit."

I liked it better when she was cuddled up to me. I'd be happy to tell her that, or I could go for the show-and-tell. Way I see it, we fucked each other last night and it felt damned good. She let me in, and not just into her body. Christ, there's no way I let her walk away from me now. She's everything I didn't know I needed, and I may act dumb sometimes, but I appreciate her.

Fucking love her.

Huh.

Imagine that.

And since she's not a mind reader, I have to tell her. That part's gonna be awkward, but I have to do it. I'm not gonna risk losing her, and I sure as fuck want the whole world to know she belongs with me, same way I belong with her. Of course, the woman's hell-bent on putting some distance between us. She'll make it down the stairs, but I have prospects on the front door.

She hesitates. Don't think it's because she's missing me, although we'll work on that. Sure enough, she heads for the dresser. My gun's sitting on top, nice and visible.

"You want to shoot me?"

She glares at me. "Don't think I'm not tempted."

"Because personally, I think the sex was pretty damned good."

She ignores me, checking the gun to see if it's loaded. As if I'd carry an empty piece. I don't make threats—I make promises.

"Can I ask you something?" Shooting me will bring the MC running and the gun doesn't hold enough bullets to handle that kind of trouble.

"Let's trade," she says tightly. "You ask your question. I'll ask mine."

"Sounds like a deal, as long as you're not asking about club business. There's some shit I can't discuss with you. Club business stays club business."

"Believe me, I'm well aware of that," she snaps. She's definitely holding a grudge. "You've got thirty seconds to ask your question and then it's my turn."

Bet she doesn't realize it turns me on when she gets all bossy. It gives me ideas about showing her just who's the boss in our bed. But this is about more than just sex, no matter how hot she is. I need an answer to my question, which means I have to get the words out there. This isn't something I can force, and it's nothing I deserve.

"I'd like you to be my old lady."

She flinches, but I keep talking.

"Know that doesn't sound like every little girl's dream, but it means everything to me. Means we're a couple and we're in it for the long haul. You're mine. I'm yours. I'd be damned proud for the whole world to see you wearing my patch and to stand for you. I respect that you're pissed off right now, but this thing between Rocker and the Hard Riders is business."

"And kidnapping me was just business?" Her scowl doesn't look like a happy acceptance of my offer.

"You know how it works between the clubs. He disrespected us and he brought the cartel into our territory. We had to shut him down, and you were the quickest way to do that."

Her fingers tighten on the gun.

"Was the whole thing a set up? Were you ever interested in me at all?"

Since my *interest* is rock-hard and sticking out for her to see, I think she knows the answer to that.

"Why track me down? Why ask me out? Why follow me around? Do you fuck everyone who's related to guys you want to shut down?"

"I do what my president asks." That answer's not winning me any prizes, and sure as shit she flips me the bird. "But we're more than that. No matter what went down between you and my club, you're my woman. I've never claimed anyone before, and my brothers will respect that. You're different."

"So different you tied me to the bed," she mocks.

"Rocker's willing to trade Sachs for your safety." No point in not being blunt. "He's on his way over here to make the swap."

"Fuck," she says.

Yeah. That pretty much sums up our situation.

"Get your cute little ass over here and untie me." Part of it is a respect thing in front of my brothers—letting my girl handcuff me to the bed is the kind of shit that earns a man a new road name. No way I want to spend the rest of my life answering to Spanky or BD. Not the kind of moniker that inspires fear and respect in anyone. But most of it's that I just put my heart on the line for her. I asked her to be my old lady, to partner with me—and she hasn't answered.

Someone bangs on the door downstairs and Evie freezes.

"Out of time, sweetheart."

It's one thing to play sex games with her in our bed, but this is club business. The door opens—never should have fucking given my brothers a key—and boots thud on the floor. Vik bellows my name.

I give Evie a hard look. "Last chance."

She raises her chin and points the gun at me. Gotta give her full points for courage. "I'm walking out of here. Rocker's walking out of here."

The bedroom door busts open. Vik shoves his head in.

"Rev, get your ass out of bed."

Evie scampers over to my side, but then follows up the wise action with another stupid one. She raises the gun to the side of my head.

I gotta hand it to Vik. He keeps a straight face. I straighten up on the bed, trying to decide how to play this.

"See you're a little tied up," he deadpans.

I grunt something he decides to take as an affirmative.

His eyes take in the whole scene. Thank fuck Evie's dressed. "Didn't know you rolled like this."

"Shut up," I tell him.

"You gonna handle this? Hawke's getting impatient."

"Hey," Evie snaps. "I'm the one with the gun."

She sort of waves the gun around, which makes Vik briefly close his eyes. We need to go over a few basic safety rules, possibly after I paddle her butt.

"Handle it now," he growls at me. "Done waiting for you."

I'm done here, too. I tackle her, yanking her back against my body and twisting the wrist holding the gun. Hate doing it, but I can't let her keep threatening my brother. Plus, Vik's not the most patient guy—sooner rather than later, he'll disarm her himself and he won't be as careful. The gun hits the floor and I kick it away. I pin her against my side with one arm while she yells curses at me and I slam the cuff against the wall. Takes two tries for me to pop the hinge, but then I'm free.

Vik smirks. "Getting slow in your old age."

"Get the hell out of my bedroom."

Vik flashes me a salute and ambles out of the room. I shift my grip on Evie, who must realize that she's in a world of trouble here, because she's actually—briefly—silent.

"I'll give you some free advice. You pick up a gun, you keep it pointed in a safe direction."

The sound that comes out of her is more squeak than affirmative, but fuck this shit. I toss her over my shoulder, drag on my pants, shove the gun into my waistband and head downstairs. She fights me every inch of the way. Naturally. This would be way more fun if we were doing it naked in bed, but that's not happening now.

I smack her ass at the top of the stairs. "Keep it up and I'll drop you."

She screeches something highly uncomplimentary.

Our audience at the bottom of the stairs takes in the show. Nice to know my brothers are enjoying my pain. During the quick journey down the steps, I do a quick inventory. In addition to Rocker and two Black Dog brothers, Hawke and Vik crowd my living room.

"Put her down," Rocker snarls, starting toward us.

"You got Sachs hiding in your back pocket?"

Rocker snatches his phone out of said pocket and punches something in. "Pulling up in a cage now."

Hawke nods. "Put her down."

It sucks, but I do it. Evie flies straight into Rocker's arms. He tries to tuck her behind him, but she keeps hugging and patting him, like he's fucking five or something. She doesn't spare me another glance.

Hawke gives me a look. "You sure about this?"

"Make the trade," I tell him.

CHAPTER TWENTY-THREE

Rev

ROCKER'S NOT THE dumb fuck I had him pegged for. After the Hard Riders trade Evie for Sachs, he moves into Evie's house. I know this because I still keep an eye on her. He also keeps a couple of prospects nearby, so either he's wised up and decided she needs a body-guard, or he knows there's a credible threat. Not sure which pisses me off more.

I pull up behind her house two weeks after the trade. It took four days to find the right guy for this job, which is two days longer than I expected. The Feds never believe that most of the MCs are on the up-and-up, so they always have their plants. I trust my brothers and the prospects are vouched for, but that leaves the hang-arounds and wannabes. There are always guys looking to join, who show up at the clubhouse and on runs, buying rounds and looking for an in. That's where the Feds like to place their boys. If one guy doesn't move up in the club hierarchy, they just send in another and another. I'd done some looking and some talking, and it turns out Benjy had joined us just three months ago. He had a big, shiny-ass bike and way too many questions for a guy looking to patch in.

Hello, plant.

Hawke and the club leadership discussed it. Doesn't sit right, bringing in the Feds, but it's the cleanest solution. Rocker is the connection between the Black Dogs and the cartel; Sachs confirmed as much.

Sachs made the call from a burner phone and wouldn't you know—Benjy's all over that intel like a dog with a stick. Couldn't drag him away from Rocker after that, which solves two problems. Gets him out of our club and sets Rocker up for the fall. Whatever happens now, it takes Rocker out of the picture. Even if he doesn't talk when they bring him in, the cartel is gonna suspect he did. They'll throttle back on their operation, too, waiting to see if the feds have made them, too. It buys the Hard Riders time to come up with a permanent solution.

We've gone over the plan a dozen times and now it's out of our hands. I wonder if Hawke's planning any side action. Now's the time to hit the Black Dogs. After Rocker goes down, they'll be reeling and looking for the sneak who sold them out. Damned glad I'm not Benjy, but I'm betting he's got an escape plan in place. We're uneasy allies in the war on drugs, but I don't want to see him get plugged. We're fighting on the same side—just with different weapons. Still, feels safer to go in myself. This outsourcing shit isn't my thing. Can't control the outcome the way I can when it's my finger on the trigger.

Rocker pulls up in a white van, Evie right behind him in her pink RV. He's been glued to her side since he brought her out of the Hard Rider clubhouse. She parks, but for a minute I think Rocker's not gonna stop. The van idles, but he doesn't kill the engine. Evie pops out of the RV, smiling and laughing. Christ, she looks good. She heads for Rocker's van, her skirts all sparkly and shit in the sunshine, and I'll bet he's cursing up a storm.

He kills the engine—and all hell breaks loose.

Local authorities bring out the SWAT team for anything involving gangs and guns. They must have a warrant to go with their suspicions and Benjy's intel. Not like they pop out of fucking nowhere, but it feels like it. One minute, the street's empty and the next it's full of SUVs and there's a BearCat driving down the center of the road. Doors fly open and there are suddenly about twenty police officers in black vests marked PO-LICE swarming all over Rocker's ride. And then the SWAT team members in full camo and Kevlar. Not like I like seeing a bunch of M-16s pointed at my girl. Nothing I can do from here but pray, and I'm damned rusty at that.

Evie screams and she's surrounded, rushed to the sidelines. The cops bark out orders and Rocker emerges from the van, hands up.

He rakes the boys in blue with a smile. "One fuck of a welcome home committee."

Those cops put him on the ground way harder than necessary and pat him down. Doesn't take them long to find his piece tucked in the small of his back. That's almost all they find, though. Rocker's got a couple of illegal semiautomatics in the back of the van, but he's drug-free.

Weed makes for a bulky cargo. It takes a hell of a lot of product to make good money, and it stinks like crazy if you don't package it right. There's not a drug dog alive that won't tear you and your ride apart to get at it and the customers who buy that shit aren't loyal. They're not addicts and most of them have lives they'd like to keep. If they get busted, they sing. Plus, if you get busted while carrying a gun, the penalties get stiffer. Rocker's Colombian connections are pushing harder stuff than that and the man's a pro. He does exactly what he's told. No resistance, no extra words. Just tells them he pleads the fifth and wants a lawyer.

They won't get him for drugs, but the weapons charge will stick. The dogs find nothing in the van, but it's merry fucking Christmas when the cops go in. Not like the back is full of coke or guns, but the fact that Rocker's transporting a pair of semiautomatics is enough in the hands of a zealous prosecutor. They know he's dealing, even if they can't prove it, and they'll use the guns as an excuse to put him away.

I watch, Vik by my side. When the cop cars pull away with Evie and Rocker, I fire off a quick message to Hawke from a burner phone. There's no point in being stupid about this.

ME: Rocker busted. Feds all over him, but no drugs. Dumbass was transporting guns, so he's not walking. Worried that they took Evie in too.

HAWKE: Got a lawyer on it. If your girl's clean, it's a bad couple of hours and then done.

ME: Gonna head down and meet the lawyer. Wanna be there when she gets out.

HAWKE: Your call. You show, she gonna suspect?

ME: Not stupid

HAWKE: So that's a yes

ME: Thinking so

HAWKE: Bring a big fucking bunch of flowers

Shoving the phone back into my pocket, I nod to Vik. "Let's ride."

He sighs dramatically. "Are we playing white knight? You about to ride to the rescue?"

I flip him the bird and peel away from the curb. He's right behind me all the way to the police station. When I get there, the club's lawyer is just pulling up in his fancy-ass Mercedes. James Brandon didn't waste any time getting here and I appreciate that. Lawyer Boy's not bad-looking, which probably helps with the jury, and he's wearing a real slick suit.

"Mr. Brady." He tips his head at me. Then he strides into the station. I follow right on his ass. He gives me a look, but doesn't say anything. When the front desk asks his business, he announces he's representing Eve Kent and they wave him through.

I'm more of a problem. We're not married. I'm not her brother, her family, or her legal representation.

James earns his goddamned paycheck. "He's Ms. Kent's fiancé."

This white lie earns me a seat in the waiting room. It's not the happiest place on the earth, so I'm ready to go when James texts me an hour later that we're good to go. I head out to meet them. Evie's gonna need a ride home.

CHAPTER TWENTY-FOUR

Eve

NO ONE PRESSES CHARGES. Even though I've done absolutely nothing illegal, this still feels downright miraculous. Better yet, my mistaken arrest didn't happen at a party, so I may be safe business-wise. I want to belt out "Miracle of Miracles" and get my inner *Fiddler on the Roof* on. Except this particular problem is just the tip of the iceberg, isn't it? Rocker's not striding down the hall next to me and the lawyer Rev provided—he's still locked up somewhere.

There has to be something I can do. "When does my brother get out?"

James hesitates so briefly that I almost don't catch it. "Mr. Kent has different legal representation."

"But surely his lawyer can get him bail?"

"I'm not sure if the judge will refuse to set bail or not. In forty-eight to seventy-two hours, the District Attorney will bring charges against him at a hearing. You'll know then."

You. Not *we*.

I'm about to press for more details when I spot Rev leaning against the wall, waiting for me. I don't know what to say or do—I'm pretty sure today is out of miracles and Rev scares the hell out of me at the same time he comforts me. Right now I don't know how to work with that.

Rev shoves his hand in my direction. "Let me take you home."

I'm too tired to protest. We head outside. There's a brief problem when I realize that riding behind him on his bike in my princess costume is a challenge. We work it out, though, bunching up the fabric between us. It looks ridiculous, but I'm beyond caring. I manage to hold out most of the ride without talking or crying, but then I fold.

"I can't do this," I tell his back.

"Why not?" he asks.

"You ride to my rescue, but maybe I wouldn't need the rescue if you weren't…"

"If I weren't what?" His voice is tense.

I wish I had an answer to that question. Rev's been good to me. I can't deny it. He ponied up a lawyer and I'll bet he had bail money ready, too. He'd promised to have my back and he did. Problem is, things happen around him. Illegal, rule-breaking, stressful-as-shit things.

He looks around at me. "Is this about Rocker getting arrested?"

Rev's plenty of things, but stupid isn't one of them.

"Are you telling me you had nothing to do with that?"

His grip on the bike tightens. "Thought you'd prefer that to the alternative. Usually, when I take care of a problem, the solution's more permanent."

That kind of problem-solving approach is why we can't be together. I use my words—he uses his gun.

He curses loud enough to be heard over the bike's engine. "Just tell me what you want."

"I don't know." Honestly, there are so many competing wants and needs in my head that by rights I should explode. Rocker walking out of that jail a free man tops the list, however. I'd like him to head off to a glorious future complete with gainful employment, a college degree and a two-story house with a swimming pool. I'd like to know that even if he doesn't achieve those things, he'll be happy with whatever he does decide to do. Given the minimum sentencing requirements in the fine state of Nevada, however, all of those plans will be on hold for at least five years.

Way too quickly, Rev pulls into my driveway. It's not a quiet entrance, thanks to the bike. Plus, the entire neighborhood seems to have a pressing need to take out their trash—and they're taking their sweet time, eyes fixed on me and Rev. And since their last sight of me was in the back seat of a cop car, getting carted downtown, I can imagine all too easily what they're thinking.

Samantha comes rushing out to wrap me in an embrace. "Are you okay?"

The short answer? No. No, I'm not. I've been arrested. Rocker's gone and it's unlikely he's coming back. I've talked to more law enforcement today than

I have in my entire life, and I now have a lawyer of my very own. The long answer is still no, but comes with a hundred-point, itemized bullet list of everything that's gone wrong with my life in the last twenty-four hours.

I pick the most obvious problem. "Rocker got arrested."

Samantha sighs. "Yeah. I heard about that."

"I think he's in trouble for real this time."

Samantha gives me a *no shit* look that urges my sorry ass to move out of the land of denial, stat. Rocker's *definitely* in trouble, the kind of trouble accompanied by a six-figure bail bond and an urgent, pressing need to find the very best of lawyers.

The neighbors' stares bore into me, and it's far too like that last time I left Rocker and came home to find him sitting on the couch with Officer Friendly making plans to take him away from me. I should have done something different, done something more. There had to have been some way to fix this before things ended with Rocker in jail and me accepting legal advice from a lawyer working on retainer for a motorcycle club.

Bottom line?

I failed Rocker.

Again.

Rev stands behind me, his hand on the small of my back. It's actually quite nice and supportive. Downright polite and civilized, except that I can feel every inch of that touch burning through my dress, making me want to drag him inside and lose myself in him. Hot sex followed by a side of orgasm-induced oblivion is tempting, but I've already tried it.

It hasn't worked out well for me.

Rev

Evie gives me a death glare. "This has been the worst summer ever." And then she fucking smacks me in the middle of my chest. Hard. "I blame you."

I'll take the blame up to a certain point. "Rocker came up with his shit drug-running plan all on his own."

Her face sort of crumbles and she chews on her lower lip, blinking her eyes like crazy. Screw the plan to stay away from her—I pull her into my arms, ignoring Samantha.

"Sorry, babe," I whisper against her hair. I am, too. I'd like to kill whoever approached Rocker and talked him into dealing. I either break shit on purpose or I fix it. That's how I'm wired. My old man was in the business of fixing people's souls, but I'm more practical.

"Promise me you'll help him," she orders.

I run my hand down her back. Avoid her ass, too, because I'm a gentleman like that. "You gotta learn to ask nicely."

"Maybe you need to learn to do what you're told."

Yeah. Not a fucking chance of that.

"I do requests," I offer.

"This is why we'd never work out." She sighs.

"Not disagreeing with you." I ignore the unfamiliar stab of something at her casual dismissal of an *us*. She's not wrong, and hooking up with my hostage is downright stupid.

We stand there for way too fucking long. The Colombians could swing by and make a house call and there we'd be. Standing in plain sight. Might as well paint a target on our chests now. Not bad here, though, holding my girl. Evie's soft and warm against my chest as she leans into me. Parts of her trust me, at least when she's not talking.

"Please," she says finally, although she says the words to my shirt and not to my face. Guess she needs some practice, too.

"It's club business."

"You guys are crazy," she announces and I can't disagree with her. When you ride with the club, you live by a different set of rules. In my world, you figure out who made shit explode and then you go after them. If the cartel came into our territory and stirred shit up, we'll hit them back hard. Otherwise, they'll keep pushing and taking until there's nothing left.

She hates my club. To be fair, I think all MCs are on her shit list at the moment, with the Black Dogs sitting at the top. She doesn't understand what makes a bunch of men decide to ride together, to band together and pledge their lives to one another and a largely unwritten set of rules. We're family the same way she and Rocker are, and I've just put my family first at the expense of hers. I rub my hand up and down her back, but there's no way to fix this now. The only way to right the wrong I've done her would be to magic her dumbass brother out of jail and back into her life.

I'd like to tell you I'd do it, too. That I'd give her whatever she wants, when she wants it. In bed, that's true. Hell, pretty much any other time it would be true But this thing with Rocker is bigger than both of us.

I'd like to give him back to her, but I can't.

He's a fucking menace who runs arms and sells drugs, and I can't let him do that anymore. And don't tell me it's not my job to stop him. I may not be an FBI agent, a cop, or a member of the goddamned SWAT team, but I have a responsibility to say something when I see shit that's not right. You ever see those signs in the airport? "See something, say something"? That applies here, too, and Evie knows it—she's just not ready to admit it yet.

And so no matter what I tell her, no matter how nicely I rub her back and promise her that everything's going to be okay and I'll do what I can to help the dumbass, we both know it's not entirely true. At some point, I'm going to let him hang himself with the noose he made. I wouldn't bring him back even if I could, because then he'd just do it all over again.

And that's not right.

Think she's got that figured out finally, because she steps away from me and grabs Samantha's hand. "Thanks for the ride."

She's dismissing me.

I grunt something as she heads inside, but fuck if my feet don't move. It's like they're permanently planted in Evie's driveway, watching her walk away from me. I get that she doesn't trust me.

Hell, I wouldn't trust me, either.

CHAPTER TWENTY-FIVE

Eve

EVERY KID DESERVES the birthday party of his or her dreams. I've brought some weird requests to life—kids ask for the strangest things and then enjoy the shit out of them. There's no point in not going for what you want—or in letting other people make you feel weird or bad for your own personal preferences.

Rev's like that in bed, although I'd rather not think about his prowess in the context of kids. That's just creepy.

After I left him standing on my driveway like the ending of a bad, sad movie, I went inside and did some thinking. Lots of thinking—it was days before I came to any conclusions. I found Rocker a lawyer. I learned that the district attorney considered him a major flight risk and bail had been denied. I visited, which was thirty minutes of awkward on my part followed by fifteen minutes with a box of tissues afterward. I hope he's going to be okay. We all make choices every day, and I still want nothing but the best for him. His recent choices, however, have been the wrong ones and they come with a price tag.

In a few years, I hope he can make new, better choices. I hope he finds a new beginning and a new life, even if the old one is now on hold. Forgiveness. Atonement. Redemption. Pick a noun. I wish all of those for Rocker. Today, however, I'm making a choice for myself.

The day's sunny, the weather perfect for BBQ and beer. The bikers aren't my usual crowd, but a few kids run around the bikes like sugar-fueled maniacs. Mary Jane brought hers and Tío gives me a head nod from across the courtyard.

When I called Vik, I thought he was going to have a stroke. You remember the offer he made me the last time I was here? About bikers sharing? Yeah. I told him I wanted to take him up on it. He almost hung up on me, which was both cute and inconvenient. Not that he's opposed to a threesome in bed, but he's decided I belonged to Rev and my pussy has a no-poaching sign on it.

I straightened him out.

I want to share Rev with the Hard Riders MC.

Which is why I'm here now. It's Rev's birthday today, according to the driver's license he flashed in my direction the day I met him.

Vik slides me a glance. "You sure about this?"

Nope. Not at all. But I want my man back. I want the guy who discusses favorite colors with a five-year-old girl, who eats cupcakes and takes me for rides in the desert and who believes oral sex is the answer to every argument. He's not a nice guy, but he's mine and I need him in a way I've never needed anyone before.

And if he's a biker who comes with a bunch of rough, loud, filterless bikers, I'll love that part of him, too, because *they* love him and they're his family.

Rev tears into the courtyard, going too fast as always, and then he brings the bike to a fast stop. Does some staring.

We redecorated when he rode out this morning. The Princess Mobile is parked on one side of the courtyard with enough balloons to float the thing into outer space. We've got cake and beer, and yes, we have fairy wings. I tried to convince the club to jump out and yell "surprise," but Vik said that would get us all shot and then he and Hawke started arguing about how many guys would get plugged if Rev was startled.

Rev straddles his bike, silently taking in the scene, but it's a good sign he doesn't point his bike toward the exit and leave. His gaze moves down my body, taking in my outfit.

What there is of it.

Since this is a biker princess party, I've made a few modifications. My dress is still pink and sparkly, but it now stops mere inches south of my butt. I'm wearing black motorcycle boots (with pink laces) and a leather vest I borrowed from Vik. It doesn't have any patches on it, but I improvised and embroidered Happy Birthday on the back. It's silly, it's fun, and…

I have no idea how Rev will react.

Maybe…

"Happy birthday." I walk up to him, still watching his face closely. Then I lean in and put my hands on his thighs as I brush a kiss over his cheek.

Oh my God. What if he lied about his birthday on his license? What if today *isn't* his day?

He looks me over. "That's one hell of an outfit."

"Dress for success, right?" I pivot slowly so he can get the full effect. He must like it because he lifts me up onto the bike in front of him. There's not a hell of a lot of room, so I end up facing him, my legs wrapped around his hips.

"Hey." He drops his forehead to mine.

"I missed you."

Please let that be enough.

He's quiet for a moment. "Is that all you have to say to me?"

"You want me to sing to you? I do a mean rendition of 'Happy Birthday.'"

"I want to know where we're at." His thumb teases the corner of my mouth.

"Truth?"

"Always."

"I want to choose you. I want you to be in my life, both when I get up in the morning and when I go to bed at night. I want to wake up with you and fuck with you and do a whole lot of loving and living together. I want us to ride and then come home and do whatever it is that couples do when they're not fighting or having makeup sex. I want us to figure it out together, and I want you to be happy."

He pulls me closer, so close that I'm straddling his dick. His dick's ready to kiss and make up, or maybe that's because I wriggle a little, just in the interest of getting comfortable.

"Makeup sex?" His mouth brushes my ear.

Please.

"I want another chance at us."

He wraps his arms around me. "That it?"

There's one thing I haven't told Rev yet, and I need to do it before I chicken out. "No. I love you. I know you don't do relationships and I'm pretty damned rusty at them. I overplan and overthink, and I've never met a rule I didn't like, while you're more of a saddle-up-and-ride guy. I have a plan and you have a mission, and we're bound to fight. But... I love you and everything else is just a detail."

Rev's hands slip beneath my short skirt and cup my butt.

"So I'd like you to tell me if you're willing to give us another shot. Tell me what you need to make this happen, and I'll figure it out."

Rev stares me. He looks a little stunned.

"You love me."

"I do."

See? That wasn't so hard to say.

And then he makes me wait. He stares, his mouth dipping to my mouth and lower. His fingers tighten on my butt, and time sort of stretches out and out and out

God, he's killing me.

"You made me a promise."

"Uh-huh. Said all sorts of things." He buries his face in my neck.

"You promised I'd be safe with you, that I'd never be hurt again. And then you made me an offer."

I'm stretching the truth a little, but it's in a good cause

He raises his head, frowning. "Who the fuck hurt you?"

"You can."

His frown gets deeper.

"Better tell me how, because I promise you I'll never fucking do it again."

"I want us to stay together and I want to be your old lady. You promised to keep me safe, and I'd like to think that means my heart, too."

I study his face anxiously, because maybe he's changed his mind, or maybe he didn't mean it at all. I've thought of a thousand different *maybe*s since I walked away from him.

"Fuck yeah," he growls. "I love you."

Rev

No fucking trumpets. No bells, no fireworks, no sign in the heavens. I pour out my heart to Evie and she stares at me, wiggling nervously on my lap. Don't think she knows what she's doing to me, but she's gonna find out soon. My dick's already skipped ahead to our happy ending.

"Gotta get a couple of things straight, though." I appreciate her coming here and the birthday party's cute, but we haven't done enough talking recently.

"Okay," she says, more slowly this time.

"We good when it comes to Rocker?" Her brother's looking at some serious time, and we both know I had a hand in it. If he gets his act together, I'll wish him the best, but he's currently out of choices.

She slides her arms around my waist. "Wish things could have gone differently, but…yeah. We're okay."

I make a note to get the club's lawyer on Rocker's case. Maybe there's some way to make things easier. Worth looking into.

"And you understand that this thing between us is long-term?"

She nods.

"Then we're straight. Didn't think I'd get a princess out of it."

She grins up at me. "No more princesses."

"Huh. I kind of liked it."

"I'm upgrading." She gives me a determined look. Probably should be getting nervous right now, but this is Evie. She gets whatever she wants. "I'm planning on being the queen of your heart—the same way you're king of mine."

"Uh-huh." I almost keep a straight face, but then I bust out laughing. She slaps at my chest, but she's giggling, too. "Fucking corniest line I've ever heard, sweetheart."

I pull her close, kissing her cheek and making for her mouth. Probably should stop there since we're sitting on my bike in full view of my club. "Love you anyhow. Can't believe you're choosing me."

"Always," she whispers. "As long as you want me."

Not gonna have a problem there.

That's one fucking promise I can make. "Forever. You and me."

* * * * *

Read on for the next book in
Anne Marsh's HARD RIDER MC *miniseries,*
INKED.

CHAPTER ONE

Vik

Before I touch even so much as an inch of sweet, creamy skin I know I want to mark her. Make her mine. Doesn't hurt that she's wearing plain white cotton panties, the kind designed to cover up rather than to showcase. But that makes a man like me think about turning good girls bad. She's tucked the waistband down to give me more room to work. Thoughtful, right? I can't stop looking at the tattoo chair where she's spread out, waiting for me to ink her. I'll be her first because nothing but virgin skin meets my greedy eye.

I grab my sketch pad from my rolling table. "You got a design in mind?"

She shrugs and her blouse rides up her spine. "Not yet."

"You trust me?"

"Absolutely not," she says, proving she's as smart as she looks. "Tell me what you're thinking."

"Firebird." I drag the Sharpie over her skin, bringing to life the image I see in my head. Maybe she won't appreciate wearing a Russian fairy tale on her skin for the rest of her life, but she's not exactly timid and the bold black, orange and red lines tracing the equally strong lines of her back feel right.

"Firebird's a thief and hard to catch. She almost gets busted stealing the king's apples when the king sets his sons to catch whoever's been trespassing on his shit. Ivan gets a hand on her, but all he's left with is a single fucking feather. She leaves and he spends fucking forever chasing after her."

"Okay."

I embrace the familiar adrenaline rush as I draw, sketching the outline of a bird, wings outstretched as she takes flight. To freedom. Her tail curls down, teasing, flirting, broadcasting a fuck you to the man she leaves behind her in the orchard of the king. This is my skin, my piece of her to ink, to own, to give back to her filled up with the story she's shared with me. Right now, I own her and she's mine. She relaxes into my touch, my calloused fingers scraping gently, carefully over her skin, preparing her. Fuck playing by the rules.

I grab my needle and brush my mouth over her ear. "This is gonna hurt so good."

* * * * *

INKED by Anne Marsh
is available April 2018,
only from Harlequin Dare!

LET'S TALK
Romance

For exclusive extracts, competitions
and special offers, find us online:

- f facebook.com/millsandboon
- ⃝ @millsandboonuk
- ⃝ @millsandboon

Or get in touch on 0844 844 1351*

For all the latest titles coming soon, visit
millsandboon.co.uk/nextmonth

Want even more
ROMANCE?

Join our bookclub today!

'Mills & Boon books, the perfect way to escape for an hour or so.'

Miss W. Dyer

'Excellent service, promptly delivered and very good subscription choices.'

Miss A. Pearson

'You get fantastic special offer and the chance to get books before they hit the shops'

Mrs V Hall

Visit millsandbook.co.uk/Bookclub
and save on brand new books.

MILLS & BOON